Imagination Theatre's
Sherlock Holmes

A Collection of Scripts From
The Further Adventures
of
Sherlock Holmes

Imagination Theatre's *Sherlock Holmes*

A Collection of Scripts From
The Further Adventures of Sherlock Holmes

Compiled for the Benefit
of the Restoration of
Undershaw

Edited by
David Marcum

With Illustrations by
Sidney Paget

MX Publishing
2017

ISBN Hardback 978-1-78705-242-0
ISBN Paperback 978-1-78705-243-7
ePub ISBN 978-1-78705-244-4
PDF ISBN 978-1-78705-245-1

Published in the UK by
MX Publishing
335 Princess Park Manor, Royal Drive,
London, N11 3GX
www.mxpublishing.co.uk

Cover design by Brian Belanger
www.belangerbooks.com and *www.redbubble.com/people/zhahadun*

Cover Illustration by Stu Roach
John Patrick Lowrie and Larry Albert as
Sherlock Holmes and Dr. Watson

CONTENTS

(Continued on the next page . . . .)

Appendix

COPYRIGHT INFORMATION

<u>NOTICE</u>

These scripts are protected by copyright.

For permission to reproduce them in any way or to perform them in any medium, please apply to the authors.

Very Fortunate: Being a Part of the Sherlock Holmes Radio Legacy
by David Marcum

Sherlock Holmes may be the first multimedia hero. Not long after his printed adventures took the world by storm in the late nineteenth century, making him one of the most recognized figures in history, he successfully made the leap to plays, comics, and advertisements, and subsequently to film, radio, and television.

The image of a deerstalker, or a Holmesian silhouette with that aquiline nose, fore-and-aft cap, and pipe, is identifiable all over the world as the symbol for *detective*. Bill Blackbeard's massive volume, *Sherlock Holmes in America* (1981), is filled with examples of how Holmes worked his way into the Cosmic Consciousness from the earliest of days.

In his extensively researched book *Sherlock Holmes – Screen and Sound Guide* (1994), Gordon Kelly simply states, *"There have been many detectives portrayed in radio programs, but the most enduring has been Sherlock Holmes."* It's said that Holmes is the most represented character in film, and while I'm not certain, I'd be willing to bet that this is true of radio as well.

Holmes was first portrayed on radio on October 20th, 1930, when – quite fittingly – William Gillette, the legendary stage actor who defined Holmes for a generation or more, starred in NBC's version of "The Adventure of the Speckled Band". This was the beginning of an amazing body of work representing that most amazing of men, Sherlock Holmes, that has continued to the present.

This is sadly not the place to completely discuss Holmes's history on radio – that would take volumes, and someone with much better knowledge about it than me. I'd like to explore the amazing contributions of Edith Meiser, who did so much to further Holmes and keep his memory green during those early years of the 20th Century when the flame might have fizzled. I'd love to write about how Basil Rathbone and Nigel Bruce portrayed Holmes and Watson on the air, initially when they filmed two 1939 Holmes movies (set in the correct Victorian period), and then continuing on radio from 1939, and on through that period until their films resumed (with a different studio and an updated 1940's setting) in 1942. While the rest of the Rathbone and Bruce films were ostensibly taking place in

1

or just after World War II, the radio shows continued to be set in the correct years of the 1880's, the 1890's, and the early 1900's. The two actors continued in these career-defining roles until 1946, when Rathbone left. Even then, Bruce remained with the show for one more season, this time with Tom Conway as the Great Detective.

There were so many actors who contributed over the years, including Carlton Hobbes and Norman Shelley on the BBC in the 1950's and 1960's. And of course, there are the giants in the field, Clive Merrison and Michael Williams, the Holmes and Watson representing the team led by Bert Coules. This group was finally were able to broadcast, with the support of the BBC, the entire Holmesian Canon with the same two actors in the title roles – an amazing feat with two amazingly perfect portrayals.

But this book, *Imagination Theatre*'s *Sherlock Holmes*, is about two other actors who have also done an amazingly perfect job, fitting their roles perfectly and bringing Holmes and Watson to a new generation. It's also to honor the man who created that *Imagination Theatre*, and the writers who gave Holmes and Watson the adventures portrayed there . . . .

Although I certainly knew who Holmes was from a much younger age, I first became a Sherlock Holmes disciple in 1975, when I was ten years old. I had one Holmes book, an abridged copy of *The Adventures*, and it was just taking up space on a shelf. Then, one rainy Saturday afternoon, I saw a piece of the film *A Study in Terror* (1965) on television, was greatly intrigued, went and pulled out my sole Holmes book to read a story, and never looked back. Now, forty-plus years later, I've collected, read, and chronologicized literally thousands of traditional Holmes stories, both the pitifully few contained in the original Canon, and so many others that have that came later, all part of The Great Holmes Tapestry.

But in my early years – heck, in my early decades – finding new Holmes stories was extremely difficult, especially in the small East Tennessee town where I grew up and still live. Back then, my Holmes shelves were quite unassuming.

From those first days, I read what Holmes adventures that I could find. Along with The Canon, I kept an eye open for additional stories, those known as *pastiches*. I read them right along with the original tales, and to me they were just as important. There were some bad or weird or offensive ones that had to be ignored, but a great many were just as good (and some, dare I say, *better*) than those brought to us by Watson's first (but not only!) Literary Agent,

Sir Arthur Conan Doyle. And as I absorbed these pastiches right along with the originals, I gave them equal weight and importance. As I've written elsewhere, The Canon is the wire core of the Holmesian Rope, but the pastiches are all the fibers around it that thicken it and give it strength. They are all part of that previously mentioned Great Holmes Tapestry, and I assert that without all of these additional pastiches to augment The Canon, and to further illustrate exactly *why* Sherlock Holmes is the greatest detective of them all, his popularity wouldn't be nearly as great as it is today.

One of the earliest sources of new (at least to me) Holmes stories that I discovered while still a boy was at my local library, which had several collections of old Basil Rathbone and Nigel Bruce radio shows from the 1940's – both dramatizations of The Canon, and original stories written by Denis Green and Anthony Boucher. I remember checking a set of them out for the first time – it was one of those old Murray Hill boxed sets of records – and bringing them home, and hearing that wonderful Rathbone voice crisply reciting the words of Mr. Sherlock Holmes. He *was* Holmes – at least, that's how I heard him in my head. (Sadly, I can't say the same for Nigel Bruce as Dr. Watson, and I'm sure most people reading this will agree.) It didn't hurt that my mother was a Rathbone, making me half-Rathbone as well, and over the years, we've always jokingly referred to the great Holmesian actor as "*Cousin Basil*".

For a number of years, those old Rathbone and Bruce radio shows, along with other sets that my dad bought for me as birthday and Christmas presents, were the only way I could *hear* Holmes. There were only a couple of occasions when I was able to *see* Holmes on screen during those long years, when one had to wait for the random chance of something being shown on one of the four (and only four) television networks, ABC, CBS, NBC, and PBS. Once, I recall getting permission to stay up late to see a re-run of Billy Wilder's *The Private Life of Sherlock Holmes* (1970) – A clever plot, but the actors as Holmes and Watson left a great deal to be desired. And Christopher Lee as a rail-thin Mycroft? Umm, no.

Another time during this period that I saw the briefest glimpse of Holmes was when a tiny clip appeared on a CBS evening newscast – a little piece from the 1939 *The Hound of the Baskervilles* that was thrown in as part of some end-of-the-broadcast comical story. Holmes and Watson are on Dartmoor, and Rathbone's Holmes says to Watson, "*Murder, my dear Watson. Refined, cold-blooded murder!*" That sharp delivery rang in my head for years. I guess that it still does.

I only saw one other Holmes movie during all that time when, in the early 1980's, one of my high school friends acquired a wonderful new device known as a *VCR*. Knowing that I liked Holmes, he and his mother rented a Holmes movie and invited me over. Sadly, even though it was a Rathbone film, it was one of the ones set in the wartime-1940's. And even worse, my hosts were the type of people that talked and chattered and bickered and laughed and argued and ate noisily and sulked and asked questions and wandered in-in-out through the entire thing. So I *saw* my first Rathbone Holmes film, mostly, but I certainly didn't *hear* it.

But through that otherwise long drought, I continued to accumulate some Rathbone radio shows, and finally some films, along with many other printed Holmes stories. In 1988, the year I got married and became employed as a U.S. Federal Investigator with an obscure three-letter agency (long since shut down), I was in a local bookstore on my lunchbreak and found a new cassette tape – Remember those? – of two previously unreleased Rathbone and Bruce shows, "The Unfortunate Tobacconist" (04-30-45) and "The Paradol Chamber" (05-21-45). Of course I snapped it up in a heartbeat, and listened to it in the car before the day was done. It was the first of a long series of newly discovered Rathbone and Bruce broadcasts from the 1940's that appeared on cassette, brought to a hungry Sherlockian public by a group known as *221A Baker Street Associates*. For the next several years, a steady stream of these shows were released, and I happily acquired all of them.

Later, after all of that Rathbone and Bruce cache was made available, they moved on to releasing the next season, when Rathbone had departed and Holmes was played by Tom Conway. Although there was some difference, I didn't care. More Holmes stories please!

As time passed, and especially as the internet became more pervasive, it became easier to track down obscure Holmes radio shows, either by downloading them, or purchasing from vendors who were now much easier to find because of their online presence. (One incredible source that I highly recommend is *www.theradiolady.com* For around thirty dollars, one can acquire hundreds of public domain Holmes broadcasts, some quite rare.)

Holmes and Watson have appeared an amazing number of times on radio, all the way back to when radio first became viable. An incomplete list of the acting duos that have portrayed them includes:

- Basil Rathbone and Nigel Bruce
- Tom Conway and Nigel Bruce
- Clive Merrison and Michael Williams
- Clive Merrison and Andrew Sachs
- John Stanley and Alfred Shirley
- Sir John Gielgud and Sir Ralph Richardson
- William Gillette and Leigh Lovell
- Richard Gordon and Leigh Lovell
- Louis Hector and Leigh Lovell
- Richard Gordon and Harry West
- Carlton Hobbs and Norman Shelley
- Roy Marsden and John Moffett
- Barry Foster and David Buck
- Graham Armitage and Kerry Jordan
- Robert Hardy and Nigel Stock
- Robert Langford and Kenneth Baker
- William Gaminara and Walter Hall
- Edward Petherbridge and David Peart
- Jim Crozier and Dave Hawkes
- Simon Callow and Nicky Henson
- John Neville and Donald MacDonald
- Christopher Newton and Leon Connell
- Tim Pigott-Smith and Andrew Hilton
- Roger Rees and Crawford Logan
- John Gilbert and Lawrence Albert, *and of course . . . .*
- John Patrick Lowrie and Lawrence Albert

There have been many, many others, some in a series, and others part of one-time broadcasts. Over the years, my own collection of Old Time Radio Holmes broadcasts grew and grew.

And into that mix came my discovery of *Imagination Theatre.*

I don't recall the date, but I suspect I discovered *Imagination Theatre* in approximately 2002, when a box set of the first sixteen episodes of their *The Further Adventures of Sherlock Holmes* was released on cassette tape. Of course, I bought it (and later replaced them on CD). Those initial episodes featured the *first* actor to play Holmes in the series, John Gilbert, and Larry Albert as Watson, a role he has portrayed wonderfully to the present. I was mightily impressed from the very beginning, both with the production values,

5

and also how Holmes and Watson were shown – particularly Watson. Larry understood that Watson was not a buffoon or a comedic figure. So often, those who have adapted Holmes and Watson's cases for broadcast in various mediums had no idea how to use Watson. He's often observing and narrating from the sidelines in the original stories, so to find a way to include him in a media presentation usually means that he's given the role of comic relief. And Watson is NOT comic relief.

Another thing I liked about *The Further Adventures* was the fact that such care was taken to get things right in terms of *chronology*. I've collected literally thousands of traditional Holmes pastiches, and since the mid-1990's, I've organized them into a chronology that arranges both Canon and pastiche by book, chapter, page, and even paragraph (or the equivalent for other formats, such as radio broadcasts) into years, days, and even hours. It's an ever-changing document, now over six-hundred dense pages stretching from 1844 (when Holmes's parents meet) to 1957 (the year of Sherlock Holmes's death), and as an initial basis of that effort, I used the chronology established by famed Sherlockian William S. Baring-Gould in his seminal biography, *Sherlock Holmes of Baker Street* (1962). I don't agree with everything Baring-Gould established, but it's a great jumping-off place. One thing that he espouses that I completely support is that Watson had a first wife named *Constance* from 1886 to late 1887, before his second (and more famous) marriage to Mary Watson *née* Morstan from 1889 to 1893. (Constance's existence helps to explain a great many chronological inconsistencies within The Canon.) I was amazed and wonderfully pleased to discover that, as I listened to those *Further Adventures* broadcasts, Constance was acknowledged as Watson's first wife, and even mentioned by name upon occasion.

I quickly found that the new *Imagination Theatre* episodes were streamed online, and I checked every week to see if it was a Holmes week, and listened with rapt attention. (And this was a true commitment in those days, I assure you, when we had dial-up internet, and the twenty-plus minute shows sometimes ran into an hour or more as I sat through endless buffering.)

By this time, John Gilbert had left the show, and Holmes was being portrayed by someone who sounds exactly like Holmes should – John Patrick Lowrie. (I was amazed, years later, to learn that Mr. Lowrie isn't British.)

I continued to enjoy each new entry, completely confident that these versions of Our Heroes wouldn't disappoint me with some behavior that would steer things off the cliff – such as what happened later with a couple of really terrible television Holmes shows that – except for the stolen character names – had absolutely nothing whatsoever to do with the TRUE Holmes, instead choosing to make him into a murderous sociopath or a tattooed drug addict.

In 2008, during a period when I was laid off from a civil engineering job, I happened to find one of Watson's notebooks, and I worked it up into a more easily readable form. After simply placing the manuscript on my collection shelves for several years, I finally decided that I wanted to see it published. The first edition of that first book, *The Papers of Sherlock Holmes*, appeared in Autumn 2011. I had several author copies, and I used some to send to both friends and also Sherlockians that I admired, simply as a way of saying thanks. And one of the books went to *Imagination Theatre*.

Of course, I also hoped that it would be a stepping stone to possibly having one of my stories turned into a broadcast. I knew that several other adventures in my ever-growing Holmes collection, written by such people as *Imagination Theatre* Script Phenom Matthew Elliott, John Hall, and others, had successfully made the transition from original prose version to script, and I hoped that mine could too. And in December 2011, I received an email from Larry "Dr. Watson" Albert indicating that he had received my book and would read it with an eye toward seeing if anything there was worthy of being a part of *Imagination Theatre*'s *Further Adventures.*

He and I emailed some through the early part of 2012, as he had identified two stories that might work as scripts. I hadn't written a script before, but he gave me some guidance and a sample from which to work, and I set about converting a story. It wasn't immediate, as I had a lot to learn. We exchanged more emails, and he read through my various drafts, acting as a wonderful and encouraging mentor, always being patient as I shaped and reshaped the manuscript. Somewhere along the way, we also had a few telephone calls, and it was really fun to actually speak with him (and also sometimes Jim French.)

An interesting and fun thing that I noticed through the process was that, as I adapted my short story for the script, I found myself hearing Larry and John in my head performing the dialogue, and it affected the way things were phrased. Finally, my first script, "The Terrible Tragedy of Lytton House", was recorded, and then broadcast on Sunday, November 24th, 2013. *Imagination Theatre* wasn't on any of my local radio stations, and I didn't want to wait to hear it on the internet stream in a week or so. Therefore, I hunted until I found a station broadcasting it that night, and my family and I listened, huddled 'round our computer in the same way that families in generations past had surrounded their radios, once again enjoying Old Time Radio as we experienced "movies for your mind". It was then that I was able to, in my own small way, contribute to the great Sherlock Holmes radio legacy.

During the following months, I got busy on my next submission. I'd learned a lot, so I avoided a lot of the dead-ends that had plagued my first effort. Larry had showed me that excessive narration was to be avoided – trust the audience. Avoid long passages recited by one character – such as Holmes's explanations at the end of the case. Break them up so that Watson gets some of the action. And sometimes, painful as that might be, the original material has to be altered. For instance, a scene in the prose version that is related after the fact to Watson (who wasn't present) works much better if it's reworked so that Watson is there and participating.

That second script, "The Singular Affair at Sissinghurst Castle", was finally finished, recorded and broadcast nearly a year after the first, November 23rd, 2014. And just like when the first was broadcast, I was thrilled to be a part of it all.

I became busy with other projects after that, but stayed in touch with Larry. In early 2015, I came up with the idea of a series of Holmes anthologies, *The MX Book of New Sherlock Holmes Stories*, which I would edit. The stories would be about the traditional Holmes, a push-back against that certain television show that maligned and tried its best to greatly damage Holmes's reputation by making him a creep and a modern-day killer and an all-around jerk. The author royalties from these anthologies would go to support the Stepping Stones School for special needs children at Undershaw, one of Sir Arthur Conan Doyle's former homes. I reached out to Larry about including one of Jim French's Holmes scripts in the collection. He happily helped me out, and that became the first of many of Jim's scripts that have since appeared as the MX anthology series continues to grow.

This, by the way, was the start of fulfilling another idea I'd suggested to both Jim and Larry way back – publishing a collection of *Imagination Theatre* scripts in book form. Matthew Elliott had already done the same thing with his book, *Sherlock Holmes On the Air* (2012), and more recently, Matthew and Steven Phillip Jones also published a different set of *Imagination Theatre* scripts (with a different publisher) in a different book, similarly called *Sherlock Holmes On the Air!* (2014). (With those books, and now this one, and also the scripts published in the MX Anthologies, a start has been made on someday having all of them in print. Ambitious? Maybe, but I'd sure love to have such a volume, or set of volumes, in my collection!)

In the meantime, I set about writing another script, which I finished and submitted. "The Stolen Relic", was based on a Christmas adventure that I wrote for one of the MX Anthologies that I edit. With kind words, Larry and Jim passed on that one – too much philosophical talk at the end, not enough action – and they gave me some good comments. So I started working on another submission called "The London Wheel", also based upon something of mine from a different MX Anthology volume. This one, a story that almost feels like an old Rathbone and Bruce episode, had promise, and Larry was interested. He and I went back and forth as I worked on various iterations and corrections and comments. I was still editing and revising it when word began to circulate, in early 2017, that *Imagination Theatre* was closing its doors. Fans were in shock – and so were the small group of Holmes writers that had been associated with the show. In February, I sent Larry a message about the rumor. He replied, "Why not give me a call on my cell." I did, and found out that the news was true.

Fortunately, another project – this book – was already in the works to help preserve some of the *Imagination Theatre* scripts, and also to honor the efforts of Jim French, who had done so much to rescue, revive, and encourage radio drama over the previous decades. Additionally, this volume would honor both Larry and John, who have given Holmes and Watson such excellent representations on radio, and also that band of writers behind the scenes.

In late 2016, I approached both Larry and publisher Steve Emecz with the idea for this book, and both were very encouraging. I set about researching, and discovered that, even though *Imagination Theatre* had produced what would end up being 128 Holmes episodes before closing its doors (and more since then), and had also recorded the entire Canon with the same two actors as Holmes and Watson, (with all scripts being adapted by one person, Matthew Elliott,) there really weren't that many of us *Imagination Theatre* Holmes writers. I began contacting them – most were easy to find, as I had worked with them on previous MX Anthology projects, while a few others were more difficult. We are a diverse group, living in both North America and Great Britain – which explains some of the spelling differences, in case you happen to notice. Like the MX Anthologies, the royalties for this book go to support the Stepping

Stones School. The earlier anthologies have raised almost $25,000, and I was sure that this would be just as popular, both with Holmes fans, and to all those supporters of *Imagination Theatre*.

Authors sent me copies of their scripts. Where those weren't easily available, Larry gathered working copies direct from the *Imagination Theatre* files – all of this taking place during that period of time in Spring 2016 when he was immensely distracted and over-worked and involved in the *Imagination Theatre* shutting-down process, which included frantic weeks of taking last-minute orders and mailing CD's to collectors while there was still time. (I was one of those people, jumping in and ordering the Holmes volumes that I hadn't purchased already. Luckily, I was already mostly caught up.)

Preparation of this book has progressed throughout 2017, and I was thrilled to be working, in many cases, from the original scripts that had been used in the studio, marked up with handwritten notes, full of changed and cut dialogue and whole rearranged sections, and even in one case a completely changed title from the original to what would became the final version.

If you're lucky enough to own tapes, CD's, or downloads of these shows, it will be quite edifying to read along and see how things were altered, even from the working scripts. The actors added in their own touches and interpretations, whether it's a pause or a snort of amusement or disgust, all bringing the written words to life in a really unique way. This book is a great representation of the writers' efforts, but that's only half of it – if you haven't heard them already, do your best to track down the broadcasts and hear these scripts performed by the wonderful actors. You won't regret it!

This project has been a labor of love for all of us who were involved. Personally, I'm so very fortunate at having been a small part of *Imagination Theatre*'s Sherlock Holmes, contributing to that incredible body of work that makes up the entirety of Sherlock Holmes on Radio. It's continuous legacy stretching back for decades – no approaching a century! – and I'm incredibly proud to have been a small part of it.

Personally I'd like to thank the following:

- My wife Rebecca and son Dan, who continually support me as I find new ways to play in this amazing Sherlockian sandbox.

- Larry Albert – From the enjoyment you've given me playing Watson the RIGHT way, to the time we started corresponding about my first Holmes book, to the incredibly helpful advice you gave as I started writing scripts, and then the monumental bend-over-backwards effort you made to gather materials for use in this book: Cheers to you, sir!
- John Patrick Lowrie – Likewise, for giving such an amazing performance as Holmes, and for the help and encouragement as this project progressed. (Also, for the fun that I had when my son realized that I was communicating with "The Sniper", and the husband of *GlaDOS*.)
- Jim French – Your work and efforts are amazing, and you truly deserve all the admiration that people have for you. Thank you.
- Matthew Elliott – I've enjoyed your Holmes stories from way back, when I first found them in various publications such as the old *Sherlock* Magazine, and later when I found *Imagination Theatre*. I always knew that I could count on you to write a story about the *Correct* Holmes. Then, when the idea for the MX Anthologies came along, you were incredibly supportive. I was very glad to get the opportunity to meet you at the MX Anthology launch part in London in 2015, and I hope to get the chance again someday.
- The Contributors – I can't ever express enough gratitude for all of you who have donated your scripts and royalties to this ongoing project. I'm so glad to have gotten to know all of you through this process. It's an undeniable fact that Sherlock Holmes authors are the best people!
- Stu Roach – Thank you very much for generously letting us use your drawing of John Patrick Lowrie and Larry Albert as Holmes on Watson on the front cover. You first presented this to Larry Albert, and when I saw it, I knew that it would be perfect for the cover of this book.
- Brian Bellanger – Thanks once again for such wonderful work. I've enjoyed working with you on many projects now, and look forward to many

11

more. And one of these days, I'll visit your part of the world and shake your hand. You have been warned!

- Steve Emecz – As always, you are incredibly supportive with these various ideas that pop into my brain, and you've helped me to explore the aforementioned Sherlockian Sandbox in ways that I would have never had otherwise. Thanks, my friend.

And last, but certainly *not* least: **Sir Arthur Conan Doyle**. Author, doctor, adventurer, and the Founder of the Sherlockian Feast. Present in spirit, and honored by all of us here.

Everyone involved in this collection did their sincerest best to show just why Holmes and Watson have been so popular for so long. These are just more tiny threads woven into the ongoing Great Holmes Tapestry, continuing to grow and grow, for there can *never* be enough stories about the man whom Watson described as *"the best and wisest . . . whom I have ever known."*

David Marcum
October 4th, 2017
The 117th Anniversary of the Beginning of
"The Problem of Thor Bridge"

Questions, comments, or story submissions
may be addressed to David Marcum at
thepapersofsherlockholmes@gmail.com

Writing for Sherlock Holmes
An Interview with Jim French

Jim *French is now eighty-eight years old, and sadly not the best of health. When it was suggested to him that he write a piece for this volume, he was ready, but ultimately unable to do so. However, you can't keep a good radio man down, and he asked if it could be done as an interview instead, and if that could be used that to fill the bill. Brilliant!*

Below is that interview – not in its entirety, as that would take too many pages. It's not a comprehensive story of his life, for that would fill a different volume. The man started in radio back in the mid-forties as a teenager, and has only retired this year, with over seventy years in the medium. He wrote his first dramas in the late nineteen-forties for Armed Forces Radio while stationed with the occupation forces in post-World War II Japan, and he really never gave up on the idea that good audio drama has a place in the lives of the people. Some say that almost single-handedly, Jim reintroduced professional quality dramatic radio back onto the American airwaves. Jim doesn't like that idea and denies it almost vehemently.

But I digress. Now it's Jim's turn to talk . . . .

Lawrence Albert

WHY DID YOU WANT WRITE A RADIO PLAY ABOUT SHERLOCK HOLMES?

Why does any serious writer want to see if they can copy the style of a master like Conan Doyle? To see if he can do it and do it well. Several people suggested the idea to me over the years, so after I left daily broadcasting, I thought I'd give it a try.

IS THAT PLAY INCLUDED IN THIS COLLECTION?

Heavens no! I never finished it. Can't recall why just now, but it sat in the files for quite a long while. As matter of fact, I'd forgotten all about it. It wasn't many years later that my friend Larry (Albert) was going through the drawers, trying to straighten out my filing system, that the thing resurfaced. Being a Holmes fan, he asked if he could read it.

HOW DID HE LIKE IT?

Well, his feelings as I recall were mixed. He liked the story, but he hated the treatment of Watson – said it was too *Nigel Bruce*. I was up front with him and said that the Rathbone and Bruce films were my main source of information when it came to writing about Holmes and Watson, and that I'd never read a real Sherlock Holmes story. He came in the next day with a complete collection of Conan Doyle's stories and told me to read some of these and then finish the script.

I did, and this time I got Watson down correctly, at least according to Larry. It was all easy after that. Another friend of mine, the late Bill Brooks, was able to direct me to the attorney who handles the rights to the characters for the Estate of Doyle's daughter, Jean. Through him, we arranged to do five or six plays and pay a royalty for each. This allowed us to use the tag *"With permission from the Estate of Dame Jean Conan Doyle"*.

TELL ME ABOUT CASTING THE SHOWS.

(Laughs) Well, that was fairly easy. Larry, who worked with me full time as my operations manager, as well an actor and director, and I went to lunch to discuss that very thing. Turns out, we were both in sync when it came to casting Holmes: John Gilbert.

WHY HIM?

John in real life was Sherlock Holmes when it came to intensity, focus, and the ability to make the most mundane seem exciting. I'd used him several times over the years in different types of roles, and he never disappointed. Plus I knew his stage work, so there was never any doubt who should be Holmes.

AND WATSON?

Well, now that wasn't so easy. When I asked Larry that question, he didn't miss a beat. He named himself. Apparently, I hesitated just long enough for him to start selling me on him as Watson. I finally said yes, and we scheduled the first session in front

14

of a live audience. People loved John and the script, but I wasn't all that sure about Larry and in the next week, I held some quiet auditions for the role. However, the night of the broadcast, I heard Watson through Larry's voice and knew I had the right guy.

HOW DID JOHN PATRICK LOWRIE JOIN THE CAST?

Well, sadly after eighteen episodes as Holmes, John Gilbert's health started to deteriorate, and he decided to give up acting. Naturally, that left me with the decision of either ending the series or finding another actor. I decided to recast, and again Larry and I were in line with each other. We both chose John Patrick Lowrie and he agreed. Unfortunately, he was touring in the East with a production of *The Diary of Anne Frank* and wouldn't be back for a few months.

Rather than go so long without a Holmes story, I wrote two shows that featured Dr. Watson as the main hero, assisted by Mycroft Holmes, as played by Ted D'Arms. Then John returned, and that's when the show really took on a life of its own. He and Larry were a perfect match as far as I'm concerned, and John's interpretation of Holmes stands with the best.

HOW DID YOU DISCOVER M. J. ELLIOTT?

Matthew told me that he'd been surfacing the Internet for Holmes audio and ran across our website. I don't recall if he managed to hear any episodes, but he was curious enough to send us one of his scripts. Now, that alone is not too unusual – folks had been sending plays to me for years – but Matthew's was from England via snail mail. I opened the envelope, read the piece, and told Larry we were going to record it without any changes. This is the first time in my career I'd ever done such a thing.

After that, M. J. Elliott became a familiar name to our listeners, and over the years he wrote for several of our series, and as well as Holmes, we even let him create his own successful show, *The Hilary Caine Mysteries.* By the time we closed our doors, the man had written and we had produced over two-hundred of his plays, including his adaptations the entire Holmes Canon.

Of even greater value, as I see it, is the fact that he opened the doors for others to join our ranks as writers and make real contributions – not only to Holmes, but also to the libraries of truly well-done mysteries. Matthew Booth, Iain McLaughlin, Claire Bartlett, J. R. Campbell, David Marcum, Daniel McGachey, Steven

Phillip Jones, John Hall, Roger Silverwood, Teresa Collard, Jeremy Holstein, Gareth Tilley, and on a couple of occasions John Patrick Lowrie and Lawrence "Larry" Albert.

NOW THAT IT'S OVER, DO YOU HAVE A SENSE OF SPECIAL ACCOMPLISHMENT?

To a small degree perhaps. I don't know. Our job was to produce and syndicate quality audio drama, and in that, yes, there is a sense of achievement. We did it for twenty-one years, one thousand-ninety-three weeks, without missing a week. As far as Sherlock Holmes – well, we aired one hundred and twenty-eight new stories and all sixty of the stories from The Canon, so you could say we added more to his body of work then just a small amount.

Oddly enough, even though *The Further Adventures* ran for nineteen years and *The Classic Adventures* ran for ten, and even though John and Larry are the longest running Holmes and Watson in the history of American radio, and Larry is the longest running audio Dr. Watson anywhere, we are quite probably the least known of the all the audio series ever done, and it really doesn't matter. We did it with seasoned professionals, with marvelous writing, with attention to detail, with dedication, and determination to get it right, and most of all with humor and heart.

Jim French
July 2017

16

Foreword
by Lawrence Albert
"Dr. John H. Watson"

There have been numberless Sherlock Holmes pastiches written over years in all media, but my particular favorites have always been the radio shows done around the English-speaking world. Well, I don't speak or understand any other languages – a shortcoming I know, but let's get past that. As a collector of radio dramas, my favorites have always been the detective mystery shows: Sam Spade, Philip Marlow, Miss Maple, and Paul Temple, to name all the ones my aged brain can recall. However, my Number One is Sherlock Holmes.

I missed the Golden Age of Radio here in the U.S., and there are times when I regret that – until I remember how much I love cable, cell phones, the internet, and Dancing With the Stars. That aside, many years ago I became an avid collector of what is now called Old Time Radio, acquiring several thousand shows from all over the planet, but my main focus was on the Holmes shows. Never in my life did I ever think that I would become the longest running Dr. Watson in the history of radio, or that John Patrick Lowrie and I would be the longest running Baker Street duo in the history of American broadcasting. We owe it all to Jim French.

Jim French's career dates back to the mid 1940's in Southern California where, as a sixteen year old, he was on the air with a small station in San Bernardino. Jim French who, in the 1970's on station KVI in Seattle, almost single-handedly wrote, directed, and produced close to two-hundred full cast audio plays, using union talent from the start, in a valiant effort to resurrect the art of *The Theater of the Mind*. Jim French who, in the 1990's, came back to create many more episodes for the CBS radio affiliate in Seattle KIRO, and who, in 1996, said yes to an offer to syndicate his shows under the umbrella title of *Imagination Theatre*. The show ran for twenty-one years, 1,093 weeks,

Jim French who, in that time, natured new writers both here and abroad: M. J. Elliott, Matthew Booth, Jeremy Holstein, J. R. Campbell, Mike Murphy etc., etc., and gave professional actors a chance to perform in a venue that might otherwise might have remained the domain of the talented amateur. Jim French who revitalized the world of Sherlock Holmes.

In 1998, I discovered an unfinished script in the files of Jim French Productions. It was a Holmes radio play that Jim had never finished. I read it and suggested he finish it – with one caveat. The Dr. Watson in the play was a Nigel Bruce-type. Why not write the character as Doyle wrote him? He agreed, and in two months we recorded "The Poet of Death", Episode One of *The Further Adventures of Sherlock Holmes*. John Gilbert was our first Holmes, and I've been Watson from the beginning. John G. stayed in the part for eighteen episodes and then retired from acting. Jim then cast John Patrick Lowrie and the series took off. We eventually recorded and aired one-hundred-and-twenty-eight in the series. Not to rest there, we decided to see if we could become the second company and the first American outfit to record and broadcast all sixty of the classic stories written by Sir Arthur Conan Doyle. It took us ten years, but we made it, and all because of Jim French's passion for full cast audio drama and the stimulation of the imagination.

In this volume, you'll find plays by Jim and many others, those who wrote of the Greatest Detective of them all for the Greatest Theater of them all, *The Theater of the Mind*. I am proud to be a small footnote in this history.

Lawrence Albert
May 2017

18

Forward

by John Patrick Lowrie
"Sherlock Holmes"

I can't even remember when I was introduced to the character of Sherlock Holmes. It seems to me that he was simply always in my life, in my imagination. I certainly remember seeing Peter Cushing, Christopher Lee, and Basil Rathbone playing the character in movies that I watched on our black-and-white television as a child. These actors played a part in my developing interest in dialects and in acting itself. The possibility that I would get my own chance to create Sherlock Holmes seemed a dream beyond pursuing, a child's fantasy that had no hope of coming true.

I started working for *Imagination Theatre* as the announcer that introduced the shows with John Gilbert, an actor whose skill I greatly admired, playing Holmes. It was in these early shows that I became acquainted with Jim French and Larry Albert and, in particular, their goal of creating new stories that never violated The Canon, either in character or history. Watson was always married to the correct wife or unmarried according to the year in which our new story took place, and Larry had the kind of encyclopedic knowledge of The Canon to make sure that was always true. Holmes always behaved like Holmes – no modern sensibilities informed his actions or his attitudes – and Watson was always recognizable as the character Doyle created.

This pleased me a great deal, for the only Holmes movies I didn't really care for were the ones that were updated: Holmes fighting the Nazis, or, more recently, Holmes with obviously 21st Century attitudes. A central part of the Holmes stories, to me, was Victorian England, with all its contradictions and hypocrisies. Fog-filled, cobblestone streets and horse-drawn four-wheelers, superstitious villagers in need of 19th century enlightenment: The trials of a distant time and place. I wanted to re-create that world, a world that only ever existed in Sir Arthur Conan Doyle's mind.

To be able to do this on the radio was an added treat, for I had always enjoyed listening to stories, and my mother and father had told me about listening to the shows: Holmes, Buck Rogers, Flash Gordon, The Shadow, and more on their radios as children. Another far-off time, removed from my own by a magical gate of imagination. And when John Gilbert retired and I was offered the role of Sherlock Holmes, that magical time became mine.

Creating the character, to me, was the task of stripping away the present, un-knowing all the history and social theory and technological advances that had taken place since the late 19th century. I approached every client and every mystery with the attitudes of an impatient genius, but one who had never seen an airplane, never seen a woman vote, who knew in his heart that Britannia would always rule the waves and the world. A world of ignorance and assumption, of conclusions jumped to without evidence, of prejudice and chauvinism. And where Sherlock Holmes endeavored to bring light to the darkness, he never escaped his own darkness: His distrust of women, of emotion, of humanity in general. And yet, it was this same humanity that he was determined to protect and save, to enlighten and educate.

Without Watson, Sherlock Holmes would be one of the most terrifying characters ever devised, a man so able to see through us, to see our flaws and weaknesses, a man unmatched in intellect and drive – who could ever protect us from such a man? But this same man befriended a fairly ordinary doctor, a doctor who liked his chops and ale, a doctor who fell in love, who married, who had a home life. If Sherlock Holmes admired and trusted Watson, then he'd probably think we were okay, too. Holmes *alone* would have been simply mystifying and uncontrollable. Holmes *with Watson* was one of us – impatient, perhaps, but never disloyal.

Getting to play this character through so many adventures, and getting to direct so many and even to help write some of the episodes, will remain one of my fondest memories.

Sometimes even the most far-fetched childhood fantasies come true.

John Patrick Lowrie
May 2017

John Patrick Lowrie and Lawrence Albert

Foreword
by M.J. Elliott

It's no exaggeration to say that, without Jim French, I wouldn't have a career in audio drama. 2003 is longer ago than I care to think about, and it keeps getting further away with each passing second (time's funny like that), but at that stage, I only had some short story credits to my name, and didn't think it likely that I'd ever move beyond that phase – In fact, part of me wanted to be the British Edward D. Hoch, a title I did not deserve and have never earned. Then I discovered *Jim French Productions*.

I dread to think how I would have conducted my business as a writer before the invention of the internet. I wouldn't have been able to do so – that's why I dread to think of it. But it has certainly made things a lot easier, and has meant that the greater part of my work has been written or published on the other side of the Atlantic. Naturally, as a Holmes enthusiast, I trawled the web for anything I could find on the Master Detective. And that was how I inevitably found the *Imagination Theatre* website, where the last two weeks' of audio dramas could be streamed. Two plays a week, every week, and a new Sherlock Holmes adventure once a month: That was a hell of a lot of material, and Mr. French himself appeared to bear most of the workload. Math was never my strong suit, but perhaps, I calculated, there might be room for my material to ease the great man's burden. If only I know the first thing about writing for the radio, which I did not.

Fortunately, Jim French and his colleague Larry Albert (A.K.A. Dr. John H. Watson) were sufficiently impressed, or at least persuaded by my *bona fides*, and provided me with several of Jim's scripts, through which I familiarised myself with the format. With this knowledge, and some advice from Bert Coules, mastermind of BBC Radio's complete Sherlock Holmes project, I was just about ready to go. Three-hundred or so radio scripts later, I'm still far from finished.

The majority of these scripts have been for *Imagination Theatre*: Episodes of *The Adventures of Harry Nile*, *Raffles the Gentleman Thief*, *Kincaid the Strangeseeker*, and my own creation, *The Hilary Caine Mysteries*. But my priority has always been the radio adventures of Sherlock Holmes. With Jim's superb example, and the note-perfect performances of John Patrick Lowrie and Larry Albert, writing these shows has never been a chore. It's almost a sin to accept payment for them, in fact, but I did, anyway. Being a part of these shows has meant that I've been able to seed certain ideas over the course of many years, such as the fate of Professor Moriarty's brother, Colonel James Moriarty, in 2005's *The Moriarty Resurrection*, which informed the motives of the third Moriarty brother (whose existence was established in *The Valley of Fear*) in 2017's four-part movie-length adventure, *The Moriarty Revelation*. It was John who suggested that I further explore the motives of the youngest Moriarty's mistress-cum-accomplice, Lady Susan for *Imagination Theatre*'s grand finale, *The Moriarty Conclusion*. I'm proud to say that the notion of a female criminal genius taunting Holmes from her cell in a mental institution was written before the final episode of *Sherlock* aired on BBC television, but you'll just have to take my word for it.

Then, of course, there is *Imagination Theatre*'s greatest achievement, *The Classic Adventures of Sherlock Holmes*: All sixty original tales, starring the same two lead actors throughout (John and Larry), and all dramatised by the same writer (whose name eludes me for the moment). It started simply enough, with a desire, in 2005, to adapt two stories that had rarely, if ever, been dramatised, *The Yellow Face* and *The Three Students*. But the experience inspired Jim and Larry, who encouraged me to continue, and to tackle the remaining fifty-eight tales. It took ten years before we finally arrived at our destination, but the achievement is one of which we are all justly proud. Our three-hour version of *The Hound of the Baskervilles*, in which I was permitted to make a fleeting appearance as Cartwright, the District Messenger, is a particular highlight. I'm not claiming that the entire production stood or fell upon the excellence of my performance, of course – that's for others to say.

But it *does* go without saying that while Jim French and *Imagination Theatre* could certainly have done it without me, I could never have done it without them. I am fortunate enough to have made great friends while making audio drama. God bless you all.

Matthew J. Elliott
July 2017

23

Foreword
by Dennis Bateman

"There's a scarlet thread of murder running through the colorless skein of life, and our duty is to unravel it."

How's that for a turn of phrase?

For many who choose the life of an actor, including me, nothing is more fascinating and fun than the opportunity to perform great lines of dialogue . . . solely with one's voice. It requires no expensive photos, make-up, hair, or costumes. Even one's age and waistline are of no consequence. And the medium of recorded voice creates an intimacy with one's audience that can't be replicated elsewhere. I think of it as a storyteller sharing a thumping good tale with a single rapt listener.

When I first met Jim French and Lawrence Albert and auditioned for *Imagination Theatre* nearly two decades ago, I knew it was a special organization: A national dramatic treasure where imagination is the key to experience . . . and one of the last of its kind in existence. Add the literary brilliance of Sir Arthur Conan Doyle and his faithful scribes in the Sherlock Holmes series, and the result is a trove of Victorian listening pleasure unsurpassed in audio drama.

Through decades of unstinting effort and dedication, the Jim French Productions company kept alive a precious and vanishing art, giving me, and many others, the rare opportunity to portray so many delicious characters – heroes, scoundrels, lovers, and rascals – that I couldn't begin to count them all. And I enjoyed being the series announcer as well! To Jim and Larry, I owe my thanks and undying friendship for what is truly a peak career experience.

I hope you treasure this collection as much as I relished being a part of it all.

This is Dennis Bateman speaking . . . .

Dennis Bateman
July 2017

24

Foreword
by Rick May
"Inspector Lestrade"

One of the great joys over the years as a voice actor has been the privilege of creating the characterization of Inspector Lestrade in so many Sherlock Holmes episodes. Thanks to diligent writing and direction, Lestrade didn't come off as a boor or incompetent, but rather closer to the sharper police inspector as visualized by Conan Doyle.

It turned out he was the perfect foil for Holmes and Watson. Yet, despite their somewhat cavalier attitude towards Lestrade, they still treated him with respect for the most part. This had such a positive effect on so many episodes and to my own interpretation. The entire experience has been a total joy.

Rick May
July 2017

Foreword
by David Natale

I was thrilled and chilled as a boy to take my AM transistor under the bed covers and listen to the CBS Radio Mystery Theatre. I dreamed of being a radio actor, but feared I would come of age too late. Then I found *Imagination Theatre*.

Jim French gave me roles that stretched my vocal, dialect, and acting skills to the utmost. Some of the best were from *The Further Adventures of Sherlock Holmes*.

There can be no greater proof to the veracity of Doyle's belief in "spirit writing" than these Holmes scripts. Jim scribes as if Sir Arthur himself had hacked into his computer from beyond the veil.

But in fact, the following tales are examples of the hard work and persistence of a living master who for years toiled to meet weekly recording session deadlines.

More amazing and hair-raising to me than revelations from a supernatural medium is Jim French's life of work in the medium of audio drama.

I hope you enjoy reading these plays as much as we did making them.

David Natale
July 2017

Recording
Imagination Theatre

Photos Courtesy of Larry Albert

Photo Courtesy of Larry Albert

Imagination Theatre's
Sherlock Holmes

ANNOUNCER: *The Further Adventures of Sherlock Holmes*, starring John Patrick Lowrie as Sherlock Holmes, and Lawrence Albert as Dr. John H. Watson.

MUSIC: *DANSE MACABRE* (UP AND UNDER)

The Blackmailer of Lancaster Gate
by M. J. Elliott

CHARACTERS

- SHERLOCK HOLMES
- DR. JOHN H. WATSON
- INSPECTOR LESTRADE
- MRS. HUDSON
- KATIE WHITEHALL – *A well-meaning cockney maid*
- THEODORE HARTNELL – *A man driven nearly mad by terror for his life*
- REUBEN FENSTER – *Apparently a kindly, slightly befuddled old gentleman*
- CABBIE – *A typical London cab driver*

SOUND EFFECT: OPENING SEQUENCE, BIG BEN

ANNOUNCER: *The Further Adventures of Sherlock Holmes*, starring John Patrick Lowrie as Sherlock Holmes, and Lawrence Albert as Dr. John H. Watson.

MUSIC: *DANSE MACABRE* (UP AND UNDER)

WATSON: (NARRATING) My name is Dr. John H. Watson, and I shared the adventures of Sherlock Holmes. It was in the late December of 1897 that our long-suffering landlady, Mrs. Hudson, met young Katie Whitehall while acting as chaperone at a dance for local domestics. When Katie recounted to her the curious goings-on at her place of employment on Lancaster Gate, Mrs. Hudson determined that the problem should be brought to the attention of her eminent lodger without delay.

MUSIC: OUT

MRS. HUDSON: Now you tell Mr. Holmes everything, Katie. Don't hold anything back. If anyone can deal with your predicament, it's my Mr. Holmes. Isn't that what I said, dear?

HOLMES: Mrs. Hudson, you're intolerably in the way.

MRS. HUDSON: Really, Mr. Holmes. Well, if a body's not wanted –

WATSON: I think what Mr. Holmes means to say, Mrs. Hudson –

SOUND EFFECT: DOOR SLAMS

WATSON: No supper tonight, Holmes. Er, now, Miss Whitehall –

KATIE: Call me Katie, Doctor.

WATSON: Very well. Katie, I understand that your problem concerns your employer.

KATIE: That's right, Doctor, Mr. Theodore Hartnell of Lancaster Gate. He's always been such a good employer, so kind. But that Mr. Fenster's driving him mad and I don't know what to do. I swear I don't!

HOLMES: Calm yourself, Miss Whitehall. Tell us first about Mr. Fenster.

KATIE: Well, sir, he arrived at the house one evening, about two months ago. He looked so kindly, with that bushy white hair and that smile, but as soon as Mr. Hartnell clapped eyes on him, I could tell there was no love lost between them.

WATSON: They were already acquainted?

KATIE: Yes, Doctor. I don't know how. Mr. Fenster just announced that he'd come to stay for an indefinite period and he'd be taking the master's bedroom.

HOLMES: Where does your employer sleep?

KATIE: On a cot in his study. It's the only room no-one's allowed to enter.

HOLMES: Not even Fenster?

KATIE: No, sir. Mr. Hartnell has interests in several companies, and he conducts most of his business from his study. I only go in there to deliver his meals.

WATSON: And what does Mr. Fenster do for a living?

KATIE: He mostly stays in his room, writing letters all day.

HOLMES: Letters? To whom?

KATIE: I can't say, sir. He insists on posting them himself. Oh, Mr. Holmes! I don't know what's going on in that house, but it's evil, I'm sure of it! Poor Mr. Hartnell won't do anything about it! When I confided in Mrs. Hudson, she was so sweet; I had no idea she was the landlady of a famous detective . . . .

WATSON: You did wisely allowing yourself to be guided by her.

HOLMES: If Mr. Fenster has been in residence at Lancaster Gate for the last two months, why should your concerns be any greater now?

KATIE: I . . . I only didn't mention it before because I don't know what it means, sir. A few nights ago, I saw Mr. Fenster arguing with a man out in the street. The argument got quite violent.

HOLMES: Could you hear what was being said?

KATIE: No, Mr. Holmes, they didn't raise their voices above a hiss.

WATSON: This other man – would you recognise if you saw him again?

KATIE: I don't think so, Doctor. It was too dark, and he was all bundled up. Such a thing happening so close to our door – it quite upset me.

HOLMES: I can imagine it would. If we were to call upon your employer this evening, would we find him at home?

KATIE: He never goes out in the evenings, Mr. Holmes. But I beg you not to tell him I sent you.

WATSON: We promise, Katie.

KATIE: Thank you both, sirs! I feel as though a weight has been lifted from my shoulders.

<u>SOUND EFFECT: SHE RISES FROM HER CHAIR</u>

WATSON: Allow me. Good-bye, Katie.

KATIE: Good-bye, Dr. Watson.

<u>SOUND EFFECT: HE OPENS AND CLOSES THE DOOR FOR HER. AS SOON AS IT SHUTS, HOLMES STRIKES A MATCH AND PUTS IT TO HIS PIPE</u>

WATSON: Holmes, if you won't smoke that foul tobacco in front of a lady, why can't you show me the same consideration?

HOLMES: (PIPE IN MOUTH) You know my ways, Watson. (HE TAKES A FEW PUFFS AND THE REMOVES PIPE) I'd be grateful for your views on this matter.

WATSON: This Fenster obviously has Theodore Hartnell under his thumb. Blackmail? That would explain the letters – demands sent to other victims, perhaps.

HOLMES: Based on what little information we have at present, that may be a sound deduction.

WATSON: Yes, well, no doubt we'll know more when we speak with Hartnell.

HOLMES: I'm still undecided as to whether or not we should go.

WATSON: But you just said . . . .

HOLMES: If he is in Fenster's power, it will be well-nigh impossible to press Hartnell for details. Besides, if you are correct and this is nothing more than a vulgar blackmail case, I see little that would pique my interest.

WATSON: Very well. I must say, I don't envy you telling Mrs. Hudson that you're refusing to take the case.

(PAUSE)

HOLMES: You make a persuasive argument, Watson. Very well, we'll give Katie a head start before setting out ourselves. Bundle up warmly, old fellow. It looks like a bracing evening.

MUSIC: UNDERCURRENT

WATSON: The winter winds were so harsh they twice threatened to overturn the two-wheeler in which we travelled. When, at last, we arrived at Theodore Hartnell's address on Lancaster Gate, our client answered the door to us. Katie proved to be quite a talented actress, pretending not to recognise us in case her master happened to be listening. Holmes gave her one of his visiting cards, on the back of which he had written the word "*Blackmail*", and asked her to deliver it to Hartnell in his study.

MUSIC: OUT

SOUND EFFECT: (OFF MICROPHONE) KNOCK ON DOOR

HARTNELL: (MUFFLED) Yes, yes, come in.

SOUND EFFECT: (OFF MICROPHONE) DOOR OPENS

HARTNELL: What is it, Katie?

KATIE: A Mr. Holmes and a Dr. Watson to see you, sir.

HARTNELL: Well, send them away. Tell them I can't see anyone. Too busy.

KATIE: The gentlemen said I was to give you this sir.

HARTNELL: Eh, what this? I see . . . . Very well, girl. Show them in, then make yourself scarce.

KATIE: Very good, sir.

SOUND EFFECT: FOOTSTEPS MOVING ON MICROPHONE

KATIE: This way, gentlemen.

SOUND EFFECT: FOOTSTEPS ACROSS ROOM

KATIE: Mr. Sherlock Holmes and Dr. John H. Watson, sir.

SOUND EFFECT: DOOR CLOSES

HOLMES: Good evening, Mr. Hartnell.

HARTNELL: What the devil is the meaning of this?

HOLMES: You have a very fine jade collection, sir. A prideful thing.

HARTNELL: I am waiting for an answer.

HOLMES: It's my business, Mr. Hartnell, to be aware of that which others are not.

HARTNELL: And just what is it you think you know about me?

WATSON: That you are being blackmailed by a man named Fenster, who forced his way into your home two months ago.

HARTNELL: You, I take it, are Dr. Watson?

WATSON: I am.

HARTNELL: Well, Doctor, I've never heard a bigger pile of twaddle in my life! Reuben Fenster is my lodger. He has lived under this roof for the last three years – not two months. Your suggestion is nothing short of libellous!

WATSON: Then why does Mr. Fenster occupy your bedroom while you sleep in your study?

38

HARTNELL: I loathe spies, sir, loathe them. My reasons for sleeping in my study are medical in nature, but they are my own.

HOLMES: I supposed you might be fearful of intruders.

HARTNELL: (SUDDENLY SUSPICIOUS) Intruders?

HOLMES: Burglars, I should say.

HARTNELL: Then why say intruders?

HOLMES: Well, burglars intrude. I should have thought it would be a constant worry to a gentleman with so exceptional a collection of jade pieces. This one, for example, is Fei Tsui, I think. I'm surprised that you display such a valuable jewel on such a dull plinth –

HARTNELL: Kindly do not touch my possessions! Mr. Holmes, you have burst into my house uninvited and unwelcome. You have proceeded to spew lies concerning my friends, and have generally behaved in a most ungentlemanly fashion. I insist you both leave immediately.

HOLMES: Very well, Mr. Hartnell. If you wish to call upon me, you have my card.

SOUND EFFECT: HARTNELL STAMPS TO THE DOOR OF THE STUDY AND FLINGS IT OPEN

HARTNELL: Get out, the pair of you! Out of my study and out of this house!

SOUND EFFECT: HE SLAMS THE DOOR

WATSON: Well, Holmes, did that go better than you anticipated or worse?

HOLMES: I think we're expected to find our own way out.

SOUND EFFECT: THE SCRATCHING OF A KEY IN THE LOCK

HOLMES: Look, Watson. It appears that Mr. Hartnell has another visitor. One with his own key.

SOUND EFFECT: FRONT DOOR OPENS ONTO LONDON STREET. BACKGROUND NOISES, WHICH STOP AS FRONT DOOR CLOSES

HOLMES: Mr. Reuben Fenster, I presume?

FENSTER: My name, sir. I apologise if we've met before, I'm afraid I don't . . . .

HOLMES: I am Sherlock Holmes, and this is my colleague, Dr. John Watson.

WATSON: Good evening, Mr. Fenster.

FENSTER: Good evening to you both, gentlemen. Oh! Ah! Sherlock Holmes, did you say?

HOLMES: Is something amiss, Mr. Fenster?

FENSTER: No, I don't believe so. I suppose that when one hears the names of Sherlock Holmes and Dr. Watson, one always expects some dreadful villainy to be afoot. It must be very tiresome for you. Are you friends of Mr. Hartnell?

WATSON: Acquaintances.

FENSTER: I am very sorry to see that you are leaving, gentlemen. I should have liked to hear about some of your adventures. I'm afraid my own life is very dull by comparison.

HOLMES: Perhaps we shall meet again soon. Good evening, Mr. Fenster.

MUSIC: SHORT BRIDGE

SOUND EFFECT: QUIET LONDON STREET BACKGROUND, STRONG WINDS

WATSON: Not a cab in sight! There's a rank just 'round the corner, I think.

HOLMES: Perhaps a walk in the fresh air will help me think.

WATSON: Fresh? Holmes, it's practically freezing! I'll be surprised if there isn't snow tonight. Anyway, what's there to think about?

HOLMES: A malevolent force is at work in that house, Watson, but I'm uncertain of its true nature. I only hope the moment of clarity doesn't come too late . . . . Tell me, what was your impression of Reuben Fenster?

WATSON: Too good to be true, I thought. That kindly nature is obviously an act.

HOLMES: I found him very interesting, particularly his right shirt-cuff.

SOUND EFFECT: A CAB APPROACHES

WATSON: There's a cab, Holmes, I'm not waiting a minute longer! Cabbie, over here!

MUSIC: GRIM UNDERCURRENT

WATSON: (NARRATING) When, at last, we arrived back at our Baker Street digs, I retired to bed, leaving Holmes coiled up in his favourite armchair, consuming ounce after poisonous ounce of his favourite coarse tobacco as he studied the snowflakes falling past our window at an ever-increasing rate. It was not yet light when I was awakened from my slumber by a tugging at my shoulder.

MUSIC: OUT

HOLMES: Watson! Watson, wake up!

WATSON: (DROWSY) Holmes, what's the matter? Is there a fire?

41

HOLMES: A telegram from Inspector Lestrade. We must return to Lancaster Gate at once. Reuben Fenster has been strangled in his bed.

MUSIC: UNDERCURRENT

SOUND EFFECT: FADE IN TROTTING HORSE PULLING CAB UNDER

MUSIC: OUT

WATSON: That's quite a crowd around the house!

HOLMES: Pull up here, driver!

SOUND EFFECT: CAB HALTS IN LONDON STREET WITH SEVERAL MURMURING VOICES

WATSON: Look, Holmes. There's Lestrade, standing in the doorway.

HOLMES: Here you are, my man. Something for your trouble.

CABBIE: Bless you, Squire!

SOUND EFFECT: THEY ALIGHT FROM THE CAB AND STRIDE TO THE DOOR

HOLMES: Lestrade!

LESTRADE: You got here sharpish, gentlemen! This is a bad business.

WATSON: What, exactly, has happened?

LESTRADE: A passer-by saw the front door open. The alarm was raised, and this Fenster was found dead in his bed. The whole house must have been asleep when it happened.

HOLMES: Was a weapon used?

LESTRADE: Just the killer's bare hands. Nasty. See the scratches around the keyhole? He picked the lock in order to gain entrance to the house.

HOLMES: May I? (A PAUSE WHILE HE EXAMINES THE LOCK) Ah, yes.

LESTRADE: Shall we go inside, if you're finished, Mr. Holmes?

HOLMES: Of course, Lestrade.

SOUND EFFECT: FRONT DOOR SHUTS

LESTRADE: See these footprints heading up the stairs? They don't match the shoes of Fenster or the lodger.

WATSON: It's Mr. Hartnell who's the owner of the house. Fenster was his tenant.

LESTRADE: Really? I've only had a brief word with this Hartnell. Took ages for the maid to wake him, and a right state he's been in ever since. Practically tearing his hair out.

WATSON: Well, since the murderer came from outside, it appears as though the bundled-up man Katie saw is our only real suspect. Eh, Holmes?

HOLMES: (LOST IN THOUGHT) I'm sorry, Watson. What were you saying?

LESTRADE: Sounds like you two know a lot more about this case than I do, though I don't know why that should surprise me.

WATSON: Well, Inspector, it appears that Reuben Fenster was a blackmailer, and that he had the owner of this house, Mr. Theodore Hartnell, in his power.

HOLMES: Is the body still here, Lestrade?

LESTRADE: No, sir. It was removed about quarter-of-an-hour ago.

HOLMES: (TUTS) I want to take a look at the murdered man's room. Watson, try and get what you can out of Hartnell.

LESTRADE: You'll find him in the study, Doctor.

HARTNELL: (FADE IN: WEEPING UNCONTROLLABLY)

WATSON: Compose yourself, Mr. Hartnell! This behaviour is not seemly.

HARTNELL: Go to the devil!

KATIE: Please, Mr. Hartnell, listen to Dr. Watson. He and Mr. Holmes have lots of experience of dealing with criminals. Whatever's happened here, they'll get to the bottom of it.

HARTNELL: (WAILS AGAIN)

WATSON: (GROANS. THEN, LOW) Katie, come over here. (PAUSE) I'm not easy in my mind about your staying here after what's happened.

KATIE: (LOW) I appreciate your concern, Doctor, but surely the danger's passed now.

WATSON: Then why is your master even more upset than he was before the murder? No, I'm still not satisfied. You'd be safer somewhere else.

KATIE: If Mr. Hartnell is in danger, then I have to stay. That's why I came to you for help in the first place. I can't leave him now.

WATSON: I see. Of course. You're a brave girl, Katie.

SOUND EFFECT: MUFFLED BY THE CLOSED DOOR, TWO PAIRS OF FEET DESCEND THE STAIRS

WATSON: That'll be Holmes and Inspector Lestrade. Come along.

SOUND EFFECT: WATSON OPENS THE STUDY DOOR

WATSON: Any luck, Holmes?

HOLMES: I'm afraid there's nothing more to be learned here.

KATIE: Do you think so too, Inspector?

LESTRADE: I'm bound to say I agree with Mr. Holmes, Miss. If the dead man was a blackmailer, there's no trace of any such material upstairs. It's possible though that the killer took it all away with him, so he was either a victim or a competitor. If you'll take me to your master, I'll inform him of the situation, and then I'll be off myself.

KATIE: If you'll follow me, sir.

SOUND EFFECT: LESTRADE AND KATIE ENTER THE STUDY, SHUTTING THE DOOR BEHIND THEM

WATSON: Well, Holmes, are you any closer to a solution?

HOLMES: I have a notion, Watson, but at present it is too . . . fantastic to be credited.

MUSIC: UNDERCURRENT

WATSON: (NARRATING) The next morning, I was surprised to find that Holmes seemed to have no intention of leaving Baker Street to pursue his enquiries. Instead, he paced the room in an agitated fashion, like some caged beast.

MUSIC: OUT

WATSON: Holmes, do sit down. Lestrade will be here soon enough.

HOLMES: What makes you think I'm waiting for the inspector?

WATSON: I haven't worked at your side all these years without learning to tell when you're being mendacious. I know your ways, remember.

HOLMES: Then I really must try harder in future.

WATSON: You were plotting something last night, and Lestrade – who's a terrible actor, by the way – was in on it.

HOLMES: Not all of it, Watson, by any means.

WATSON: I notice you couldn't tell me. I think I deserve a little better at your hands.

HOLMES: My apologies, Watson. The truth is . . . I won't be happy in my own mind until I know the results of Lestrade's work.

WATSON: You doubt your own conclusions?

HOLMES: Oh, every link is sound, of that I'm certain. But the solution is almost too incredible to be believed.

WATSON: Why not sit down and tell it to me?

HOLMES: Very well. Help yourself to a cigar, old man. This might take a while.

SOUND EFFECT: HE SITS, WATSON TAKES A CIGAR FROM A BOX AND LIGHTS IT

HOLMES: Now, in order to make sense of the events of the last two days, it is necessary to understand two things: Firstly, that we have uncovered not one but two plots, diametrically opposed to one another; and secondly, that it was *Hartnell*, not Fenster, who was the blackmailer of Lancaster Gate.

WATSON: Hartnell! But Holmes, the man was terrified!

HOLMES: And with good reason. He had only one victim, you see, a powerful and dangerous individual, who could never be safe so long as Hartnell had a hold over him.

HOLMES: So Fenster played no part in the drama whatsoever? How can that be?

HOLMES: Fenster was part of a plot, but he was entirely ignorant of his role. Theodore Hartnell was in fear of his life, and did his best to put up as many barriers as possible between himself and

46

his blackmail victim. I think it very likely that the two of them never actually met.

WATSON: Good Lord! Holmes, I believe I see it now. It's monstrous!

HOLMES: Everything Hartnell told us about his houseguest was true, but he omitted one important detail. Fenster did indeed come to live at Lancaster Gate three years ago, as a lodger. But without his knowledge, he was to appear to the outside world to be master of the house.

WATSON: That was the mistake Lestrade made.

HOLMES: He came and went while Hartnell never left the house, and at night he slept in the master's bedroom.

WATSON: And if anything were to happen to Fenster, Hartnell would have time to flee.

HOLMES: And that, I imagine, is exactly what he did earlier this morning.

WATSON: I can see why you thought the whole thing unbelievable, Holmes.

HOLMES: Actually, Watson, that was the more straightforward portion of the puzzle, the first of our two plots. The unbelievable part is yet to come.

SOUND EFFECT: THE DOORBELL RINGS

HOLMES: That will be Lestrade, I'll wager.

WATSON: Holmes, calm down. Even you can't tell that from the ring of the bell. Perhaps Mrs. Hudson is entertaining.

HOLMES: That has never been my experience.

SOUND EFFECT: A RAP AT THE DOOR

HOLMES: Come in!

MRS. HUDSON: Mr. Holmes! Inspector Lestrade is here with Katie!

HOLMES: Very good, Mrs. Hudson.

MRS. HUDSON: It's not good at all, Mr. Holmes – Katie's in handcuffs!

MUSIC: STING

LESTRADE: By rights, we should be down at the Yard now, but I thought you'd appreciate reading these, Mr. Holmes.

SOUND EFFECT: LESTRADE HANDS HOLMES A SHEAF OF PAPERS, AND HE LEAFS THROUGH THEM

HOLMES: (A SATISFIED CHUCKLE)

LESTRADE: Are they what you expected?

HOLMES: They are more than satisfactory, Inspector.

LESTRADE: This proves Sir Norris' guilt beyond a doubt.

WATSON: I don't wish to appear dense, but who is Sir Norris?

KATIE: (HER ACCENT IS NOW REFINED, HER TONE BITTER) Sir Norris Whitehead, Dr. Watson. My father.

WATSON: Katie?

HOLMES: Watson, may I introduce Miss Katherine Whitehead, daughter of the noted industrialist Sir Norris Whitehead, and without doubt the most calculating villainess to have tested my wits in many a year. I think, perhaps, you're due an explanation.

LESTRADE: Me, too. There's still a great deal about this case that isn't clear to me.

KATIE: You do surprise me.

48

LESTRADE: That's enough of that, miss.

HOLMES: Some years ago, Hartnell came into possession of papers – these papers * –

SOUND EFFECT: * AS PER DIALOGUE, HE HOLDS UP PAPERS

HOLMES: – proving that in former times, Sir Norris Whitehead was an agent of the criminal organisation controlled by Professor Moriarty. In spite of Hartnell's precautions, Sir Norris somehow discovered his address, and sent his own daughter to work at the house on Lancaster Gate as maid. The second plot I was telling you about.

WATSON: But she must have realised that Hartnell, not Fenster, was the owner of the house. Surely there was no need to kill the lodger. She could just have located the papers, taken them, and disappeared.

KATIE: Why not ask her? I am still here, Doctor. I could hardly be anywhere else thanks to these.

SOUND EFFECT: SHE RATTLES HER HANDCUFFS

KATIE: The papers were obviously somewhere in the study, but Hartnell practically lived there. I only saw the inside of the place when I brought him his meals.

HOLMES: Although, as it turned out, his hiding place was the simplest part of the entire problem.

KATIE: Oh?

HOLMES: I was struck by the fact that he kept his most precious jade on a very ordinary pedestal. It seemed to me that he was more protective of the plinth itself.

KATIE: (CATCHING ON) Because it was hollow and the papers were inside it! (GROANS)

HOLMES: What better hiding place for such a valuable item than beneath another, more obviously valuable item?

LESTRADE: So why was Fenster killed if they were after Hartnell and those papers?

HOLMES: Because it was convenient. Watson, do you recollect my gambit in the Irene Adler affair?

WATSON: Of course. You created a false alarm of fire, and in her panic she rushed straight for the sliding panel, behind which she kept the compromising photograph of His Majesty.

HOLMES: Sir Norris and his daughter concocted a deadly variation on my original scheme. Why not just scare Hartnell into revealing his hiding place?

KATIE: My father is a businessman. He considered the loss of one insignificant life an acceptable expense. You see, Mr. Holmes, we could never have done this without you.

HOLMES: A fact that gives me no comfort, Miss Whitehead. You let your father into the house last night. I examined the scratches he made on the front door. No pick ever went inside that lock.

WATSON: And I suppose making Mrs. Hudson's acquaintance and gaining an interview here was all part of this same plan.

HOLMES: But not a dignified part. Our role was simply to act as glorified messenger boys, and to corroborate Miss Whitehead's version of events. If the famous Sherlock Holmes says that Fenster was a blackmailer who got what he deserved, then it must be so.

WATSON: Holmes has never counted modesty among the virtues, Inspector.

HOLMES: Police attention then focused upon the dead man, leaving you to go to work on Hartnell, who slept through the entire incident, thanks to the sleeping draught placed in his evening meal.

WATSON: You wanted to be on hand to play on his fears, taunting him about Holmes's dealings with criminals.

KATIE: I'm glad I neglected to pay you, gentlemen; I expect I would be due a refund now.

HOLMES: After our departure, you ingratiated herself with your employer sufficiently to learn his immediate plans. Which were, Lestrade?

LESTRADE: Turned out Hartnell had an account with the Capital and Counties Bank in the name of "Arthur Wontner". He planned to withdraw as much money as possible before leaving London.

HOLMES: And once he had gone, Miss Whitehead here informed her father where he might catch up with his tormentor.

WATSON: The blackmailer, the papers, and the money, all at the same time, and all for the cost of a life.

LESTRADE: But while Sir Norris was following Hartnell, I was following him, and I was able to nab both of them at the same time! Thanks for the tip, Mr. Holmes.

KATIE: If you are quite finished congratulating yourselves, gentlemen, I believe I would like to join my father at Scotland Yard . . . . Mr. Holmes, perhaps you would do me one small favour.

HOLMES: That very much depends upon the favour, Miss Whitehead.

KATIE: Tell me where I miscalculated. I thought my plan was perfect.

HOLMES: There's no such thing as the perfect murder, Miss Whitehead, but you came as close as any. It was your great misfortune that we encountered Reuben Fenster on the doorstep at Lancaster Gate yesterday evening. Watson, with what hand did he raise his hat to us?

WATSON: Umm . . . his right. You mentioned something at the time about his right shirt-cuff, Holmes.

HOLMES: There were no ink-stains, as one would expect to find on the cuff of the inveterate letter-writer. If your claim that Fenster spent all his days writing letters, apparently to blackmail victims, was a lie, then why not all of it?

KATIE: And that led you to the truth?

HOLMES: The lie concerning the stranger in the street did that. It differed from all your other untruths in that it involved someone outside the house. Now, why was that?

KATIE: You appear to have all the answers, Mr. Holmes.

HOLMES: You wished to give the impression that Fenster had an unseen enemy who might do him harm. To my everlasting regret, the truth didn't occur to me in time to save his life.

KATIE: It was necessary if I was going to save my father.

HOLMES: But you haven't, Miss Whitehead. And now a man is dead. And in a very short time, justice will demand the taking of two more lives, your father's and your own. Was it really worth it?

MUSIC: *DANSE MACABRE*

WATSON: This is Dr. John H. Watson. I've had many more adventures with Sherlock Holmes, and I'll tell you another one . . . *when next we meet!*

MUSIC: (FADE OUT)

The Adventure of the Forgotten Throne
by Gareth Tilley and Lawrence Albert

CHARACTERS

- SHERLOCK HOLMES
- DR. JOHN H. WASON
- MYCROFT HOLMES
- PRINCESS KATRINA – *Young Intelligent with something of an educated Germanic accent, speaks English with British inflections. She is confused and frightened at her loss of memory. She's used to being in control.*
- STOCKLASA – *A large dark man, not well educated, used to using his size to get what he wants*
- GRIGGS – *Young street wise cockney lad. Very sharp*
- COUNT VICTOR VON SCHRIEBER – *Highly educated, with same accent as Princess. A romantic, very much in love with Katrina. Prone to rash actions*
- CONSTABLE JENKS – *Young, brave, kind and quite the admirer of Sherlock Holmes*
- BEGGAR – *Heavy drinker, missing teeth, smells bad*

SOUND EFFECT: OPENING SEQUENCE, BIG BEN

ANNOUNCER: *The Further Adventures of Sherlock Holmes*, starring John Patrick Lowrie as Sherlock Holmes, and Lawrence Albert as Dr. John H. Watson.

MUSIC: DANSE MACABRE (UP AND UNDER)

WATSON: My name is Doctor John H. Watson, and it is my great pleasure to recount to you an adventure of my good friend Sherlock Holmes that involved a brush with Royalty. My story begins on the third of April 1897. I recall that it had been a typically blustery spring, so upon arising on that particular morning, I was pleased to see that the foul weather had finally abated. And that being the case, following breakfast I popped out to obtain my usual weekly sundries, such as tobacco, pipe cleaners, and other effects. I was just crossing the street in front of 221b with my purchases when a large, four-horse, closed black carriage raced past me at a high rate of knots and nearly ran me over. Then, as this juggernaut swerved sharply to avoid an oncoming brougham, the right side door sprang open and a woman fell out of the carriage onto the street, severely striking her head on the pavement. I immediately rushed over to see if she was all right.

MUSIC: OUT

SOUND EFFECT: CITY STREET

KATRINA: (MOAN)

WATSON: (NARRATING) As I drew closer, I could see she was a petite young woman with a most charming face that was slowly being marred by the blood coming from a rather nasty wound on the left side of her head. Since I was without my medical bag, I applied my linen handkerchief to the injury.

KATRINA: (MOAN)

WATSON: There, there, my dear. Lie still.

KATRINA: (Moan)

STOCKLASA: (OFF MICROPHONE) You there! Leave her alone!

WATSON: (NARRATING) I looked away from the stricken woman and saw that the careening carriage had stopped further down the street. Rapidly approaching us, on foot, was a giant hulk of a man with a harsh scowl on his heavily bearded face. From his dress, I took him to be the driver.

STOCKLASA: Get away from her!

WATSON: My good man, this woman needs medical attention!

KATRINA: (MOAN)

WATSON: It's all right. I'm a doctor. Try to remain still.

STOCKLASA: She is only a maid. Do not waste your time on her. Let me have her.

WATSON: Nonsense. She must not be moved until I'm satisfied as to the extent of her injuries.

STOCKLASA: You interfering busybody! I have no time for this. Give me the woman or I will –

CONSTABLE: (OFF MICROPHONE) 'Ere now! What's all this about, then?

WATSON: Ah, Constable Jenks. Just in time.

STOCKLASA: (ANGRY) You'll pay for this meddling!

SOUND EFFECT: MAN WALKING AWAY RAPIDLY AND STARTING CARRIAGE *

CONSTABLE: * Good morning, Dr. Watson. What happened? Was that big bloke givin' you trouble?

WATSON: This young woman fell from that four-wheeler you see the, umm, big bloke climbing onto. I'd think we'd better take her to my rooms where I can examine her properly.

CONSTABLE: Righto, Doctor

WATSON: Can you walk, my dear? Its not far.

KATRINA: (WEAKLY) I think so.

MUSIC: VIOLIN BRIDGE

SOUND EFFECT: DOOR OPENS

WATSON: Right in here.

CONSTABLE: Will you be needin' me any longer, Doctor?

WATSON: No thank you, Jenks, I think I can handle it from here. However, on your way out, would you explain what happened to Mrs. Hudson and ask her to come up with some hot water?

CONSTABLE: Yes, sir, my pleasure. I hopes the little lady will be all right. You let me know if I can be any further assistance.

WATSON: Yes, I will, Jenks, and thank you again.

CONSTABLE: Think nuthin' of it, Doctor. Just doing me duty. My best to Mr. Holmes.

WATSON: Umm, Jenks – Mrs. Hudson?

CONSTABLE: Oh, right sir. Cheerio, then.

SOUND EFFECT: DOOR CLOSES

WATSON: All right, now let's get you onto the sofa where I can have a good look at you.

KATRINA: Thank you. You have been very kind.

HOLMES: (MOVING ON MICROPHONE) Well, Watson, and who's our guest?

WATSON: A patient. She fell into my path, so to speak.

HOLMES: Yes, I happened to glance out the window in time to see that part of the drama. Really Watson, you must learn to antagonize ruffians closer to your own size.

SOUND EFFECT: WOMAN SITTING DOWN

KATRINA: (Moan)

HOLMES: Will she be all right?

WATSON: I haven't been able to do a proper examination as yet. How are you feeling now, my dear?

KATRINA: Much better thank you.

WATSON: Good. We'll soon have you on your feet again.

KATRINA: And may I know the name of my rescuer?

HOLMES: He is Dr. John H. Watson. I am Sherlock Holmes. And you are?

KATRINA: Me? I am . . . I am. I . . . I can't remember! (A LITTLE UNNERVED) I can't remember! What's wrong? Why can't I remember who I am?

MUSIC: STING

KATRINA: (A BIT FURTHER ALONG IN BUILDING TOWARD HYSTERIA) I can't remember who I am! I can't remember who –

WATSON: There now, my dear. Don't let yourself get worked up. You've sustained a head injury, and a temporary loss of memory is not an uncommon result of such things.

HOLMES: What *can* you recall?

WATSON: Holmes, this can wait until the girl has rested.

KATRINA: No, no, he is right, I must try. I feel it is important that I regain my memory as soon as possible. (PAUSE) . . . . I remember being in a large old house . . . and . . . two men, one young and one older. The young one is quite handsome and . . . seems very concerned about my well-being. The older man is enormous with . . . a . . .

WATSON: . . . Large black beard?

KATRINA: Yes, yes, that is correct! They blindfolded me and tied my hands.

HOLMES: I thought as much. I assume you noticed the red welt marks about her wrists, Watson . . .

WATSON: Well, actually no, I was a bit preoccupied with her head.

58

KATRINA: (REMEMBERING) I must have been taken outside . . . .

HOLMES: Yes, to get you into the carriage, no doubt. Go on.

KATRINA: We were going at a great rate of speed, and something in my mind told me that I didn't have much time to effect an escape. The rope was not too thick, and I was able to loosen the knot with my teeth.

HOLMES: Very resourceful.

KATRINA: I removed the blindfold, and I was attempting to open one of the carriage's windows to shout for help when the vehicle swerved. I was thrown against the door, the lock gave way and –

HOLMES: – And out you tumbled into the arms of my dear colleague, and your knight in shining armor.

WATSON: Really, Holmes.

HOLMES: The question now is threefold: Who are you, who were those men, and why were you so shamefully treated by them? As to the first: Although your accent has definite Germanic undertones, I can't quite place the dialect. Your English is excellent, so you have therefore been well educated in that language, at least.

WATSON: (NARRATING) Holmes then began to question the young lady in several different languages, including one or two I couldn't place. In each case, she responded without hesitation in the same tongue. He then made a minute examination of her hands.

KATRINA: What are you doing, Mr. Holmes?

HOLMES: In some cases, the hands can be a clearer roadmap to the life history of an individual than many a written biography.

WATSON: The driver of the four-wheeler tried to convince me she was someone's maid.

HOLMES: Ha! An obvious lie. Her hands reveal little acquaintance with manual labour. She is fluent in many languages; so has obviously received excellent tutoring.

WATSON: Well, her dress alone was enough to tell me she was no one's maid.

HOLMES: Quite. It's most singular. Many of the finer ladies of London have gold woven into their lace, but not on such a lavish scale. It must be worth a small fortune. (ALMOST TO HIMSELF) Her poise, the accent, the clothes . . . Yes that's it! Watson pass me my scrapbook of the noble houses of Eastern Europe.

SOUND EFFECT: FOOTSTEPS ACROSS ROOM AND BOOK PULLED OUT OF CASE

WATSON: Here you are.

HOLMES: Thank you.

SOUND EFFECT: FLICKING THROUGH PAGES

HOLMES: (UP) The morning papers are still on the table behind you. Be a good fellow and read the headline from the front page of *The Times*.

SOUND EFFECT: RUSTLE OF NEWSPAPER

WATSON: Is this it? *"Another Royal assassination in the Kingdom of Liechtenstein."*

HOLMES: Yes. Summarize it for me, will you?

WATSON: Well, (SMALL PAUSES) It says that, umm, King Nicolas IV has been killed by a bomb thrown into his open carriage, and that the young Princess Katrina is now to inherit the throne.

HOLMES: Hmm.

WATSON: However, it appears she's gone missing, umm, presumed to have eloped with her lover, the Count Victor von Schreiber.

KATRINA: (TO HERSELF) Von Schreiber . . . .

HOLMES: Fascinating. Liechtenstein has a constitutional monarchy. However, the royals have been rather vocal in defending the rights of the populous against the new laws enacted by their Prime Minister, Johann Reichmann

WATSON: Didn't he cancel elections this year under some pretence of needing emergency laws passed regarding state security?

HOLMES: I believe so. He's also cultivated a Secret Police that is notoriously cruel. A-ha! I have her.

WATSON: Have whom? (REALIZATION) You don't mean . . . .

HOLMES: I knew I'd seen her before. Here, take a look for yourself Study this picture from *The Illustrated London News* I've pasted on this page. We are in the presence of royalty, Watson.

WATSON: (PAUSE) Good heavens. Eighteen years old, black hair, blue eyes, a highly accomplished linguist and equestrian . . . .

HOLMES: Yes, I believe it also says she was nearly killed in a riding accident when she was thirteen. The horse fell on her.

WATSON: Eh?

HOLMES: Surely you noticed her slight limp?

WATSON: Yes, but how did you know she had a limp? You haven't seen her walk without my support.

HOLMES: I didn't need to. Her shoes show the pattern distinctive to more heavy use of the right side.

KATRINA: May I see the photograph?

WATSON: Of course. There you are.

KATRINA: That is I?

HOLMES: Her Royal Highness, Princess Katrina of Liechtenstein.

KATRINA: Katrina . . . .No, it doesn't sound familiar.

WATSON: I'm sure it will in time. Well, Holmes, what next? Shall we contact the police?

HOLMES: I think not. This is a matter for my brother, Mycroft. I'll wire him immediately. Then it's to the streets for us, old fellow. We must act quickly if we are to get to the bottom of this affair. Mrs. Hudson can look after the princess while we're out.

WATSON: Very well.

HOLMES: Your Highness? Before we go, I'd like one more piece of information. After you were placed in the carriage, how long was it before you broke free?

KATRINA: I believe it was about fifteen minutes, Mr. Holmes.

HOLMES: Good. Thank you. Come, Watson! The game's afoot!

MUSIC: VIOLIN BRIDGE

SOUND EFFECT: CITY STREET

WATSON: Here's the place, Holmes. You can still see some blood on the pavement where she struck her head.

HOLMES: And the carriage was coming from the south. But which way did it go after Jenks arrived on the scene?

WATSON: I thought you said you watched the "drama" from the window?

HOLMES: Yes, but the carriage itself was out of view from my vantage point.

WATSON: Well, I'm afraid I was too preoccupied to notice.

HOLMES: Pity. Ah, that beggar across the street may be able to help us.

WATSON: But he's blind.

HOLMES: Come along, Watson. Don't dawdle.

SOUND EFFECT: FOOTSTEPS CROSSING STREET

BEGGAR: (OFF MICROPHONE) Penny for the blind.

HOLMES: There you are, my good man.

SOUND EFFECT: DROPPING OF CHANGE

HOLMES: How careless of me. I've emptied my purse on the pavement. (PAUSE) There I think I've got it all.

SOUND EFFECT: WALKING AWAY

WATSON: (HUSHED) Holmes you left a sovereign on the pavement.

HOLMES: (HUSHED) Patience Watson, patience. Ah, he's gone for it!

SOUND EFFECT: TWO MEN WALKING

HOLMES: Not so blind as to not see a sovereign.

BEGGAR: What! Oh, all right, you caught me, guv'nor.

HOLMES: You can keep the coin if you give me some information.

BEGGAR: (SUSPICIOUS) What sort of information?

HOLMES: Did you see the large closed black four wheeler with a red band and gold trim pulled by three roans and one grey, that was racing through here about an hour ago?

WATSON: I didn't notice all those things.

HOLMES: Not terribly surprising, Watson, when there's a pretty face about. (TO BEGGAR) Well?

BEGGAR: I did, sir. It was tearing along at such a rate it was hard to miss.

HOLMES: And after the driver's little set-to with my friend here, did you see which way it went?

BEGGAR: Down the street it went, like Lucifer his-self was drivin' it.

MUSIC: UNDERSCORE

WATSON: (NARRATING) We made our way across London, and by asking local traders, beggars, and street urchins, we finally tracked down the house where the princess's journey may have started. It was in a distinctly unsavory part of London.

MUSIC: OUT

SOUND EFFECT: EXTERIOR AMBIENCE. URBAN AREA

HOLMES: Not exactly a place one would expect to find royalty, eh Watson?

SOUND EFFECT: OPENING IRON GATE AND TWO MEN ON GRAVEL PATH

WATSON: There's a carriage 'round the side.

HOLMES: Let's have a look.

SOUND EFFECT: WALKING FROM THE STREET TO THE SIDE OF THE HOUSE

WATSON: Well, it looks like the one I saw this morning. It's got the red band and gold trim you mentioned. What do we do now?

HOLMES: First, we must be certain that this is our quarry's lair.

WATSON: And how do we accomplish that?

64

HOLMES: Yes, how? A-ha! Look across the street, Watson. Do you see those rubbish bins in front of that alley entrance?

WATSON: What? Umm, yes I see them.

HOLMES: Very good, I want you to go and hide yourself down behind them in such a way that you'll be able to clearly see the front door of this house.

WATSON: What on earth for?

HOLMES: No questions, old fellow. Time is of the essence. (REMOVING HAT AND COAT) Here take my hat and coat. Now, off with you!

SOUND EFFECT: STREET NOISES CONTINUE UNDER NARRATION

WATSON: (NARRATING) By this time in my association with Holmes, I'd learned that it would have been futile to ask for any further explanation. So without another word, I turned and made my way across the street to the rubbish bins and, after making certain I was unobserved, bent down behind them. I'd no sooner gotten myself into an acceptable position than I saw a filthy, disheveled, and obviously drunken ruffian stagger up the front stairs of the place and ring the doorbell. In quick order, the door was thrust open and the drunkard found himself confronted by the huge figure of the very man we were looking for.

By this time, I'd realized the drunken sot was Holmes. I couldn't hear what he was saying to the bearded giant, but it was clear that whatever it was, it was causing the fellow to grow increasingly agitated. I fully expected to have to leave my hiding place to come to Holmes's assistance when suddenly, the brute turned his head as if in response to something or someone within the house.

Then, without warning, he was gone and the door closed. Holmes stared at the barred entrance for a few moments. With a shrug of his shoulders, he turned and staggered back down the steps to the street. He then made his way toward my place of concealment. I stayed hidden, not wanting to show myself until Holmes said it was safe. But instead of stopping, he spoke to me as he passed by.

HOLMES: Don't show yourself for five more minutes, Watson. Then follow me 'round the corner.

SOUND EFFECT: FADE ON STREET NOISES

HOLMES: (OFF MICROPHONE) Over here, Watson.

SOUND EFFECT: FOOTSTEPS. (MOVING ON MICROPHONE) WATER SPLASHING FOR WASHING UP

WATSON: Good grief, Holmes. You look a fright.

HOLMES: The result of a necessary improvisation. I trusted that whomever answered the door would see only the filth I'd quickly dashed over myself and not the man beneath. That, and a swallow of brandy from a flask I had the on my person, settled the picture of the sot come-a-begging.

WATSON: And you did all of this in the brief time it took me to hide myself? Amazing.

HOLMES: Hmm. I must say, though, this particular clay is proving devilishly hard to remove. Oh well, this will have to do. Hand me my coat, will you, old fellow?

WATSON: Yes, of course. (DOING SO) So, Holmes, we're now certain that's the place. What made him close the door so suddenly?

HOLMES: All in good time, old chap. In the meantime, that house needs watching. Ah, here's luck. (CALLING) You, boy! Come here!

GRIGGS: (OFF MICROPHONE) You callin' me? Blimey, it's Mr. 'Olmes.

HOLMES: Watson, say hello to Griggs, one of the newest members of the Baker Street Division of the detective police force.

WATSON: You mean the Irregulars?

GRIGGS: Yes, sir, that's us. What's doin' Mr. 'Olmes?

HOLMES: Are there any of the other lads in the area?

GRIGGS: Yes, sir. Curly's 'cross street by that sweet shop, and a few of the others are about.

HOLMES: Excellent. I have a certain house that needs keeping an eye on. To each boy taking a watch, I'll pay half-a-crown a day, but no more then two boys per time period. I'll want the second lad there to run to the telegraph shop and wire me at Baker Street immediately if the occupants look like they're leaving. It's the large brown two-story around the corner, with the black and gold iron-gate to the left side.

GRIGGS: We'll need a few bob to pay for the telly-gram.

SOUND EFFECT: COINS BEING DROPPED

HOLMES: Right, This should cover it. Now off with you.

SOUND EFFECT: FOOTSTEPS RUNNING OFF

HOLMES: Now, Watson, be a good fellow and flag down a cab. We must return to Baker Street with all speed and see if Mycroft's appeared.

MUSIC: UNDERSCORE

WATSON: (NARRATING) By the time we caught a hansom and arrived back at 221b, it was dark. Mycroft Holmes had not yet arrived, so I asked Mrs. Hudson to bring up a light supper. While we'd been gone, that estimable lady had done an excellent job of cleaning and bandaging the princess' head wound. Holmes paced about the room like a caged tiger, his entire being focused on the problem that lay before us

MUSIC: OUT

HOLMES: Ah, ha! I recognise that authoritative pull on the cord anywhere.

SOUND EFFECT: OPENING DOOR

HOLMES: (CALLING) Well, Mycroft you've finally left the comfort of your club.

SOUND EFFECT: HEAVY FOOTSTEPS MOVING UPSTAIRS

MYCROFT: (OFF MICROPHONE MOVING ON) Yes, and it better be worth it. You know I don't travel well.

HOLMES: I hope your twenty-minute ride wasn't too uncomfortable.

SOUND EFFECT: STEPS STOP. DOOR CLOSES UNDER DIALOGE

HOLMES: Now, brother, let me introduce . . . .

MYCROFT: Ah, Princess Katrina! What a pleasure to see you again. The last time we met, you couldn't have been older than fourteen. On the Royal visit of '83, I believe.

KATRINA: I am sorry, sir, but I don't remember. I have lost my memory. See this bump on my head?

MYCROFT: How unfortunate. What's all this about, Sherlock? Your wire was sorely lacking in details.

HOLMES: Can we entrust you to look after the princess?

MYCROFT: Of course. Given the current political climate in Liechtenstein, her safety is paramount. I've little doubt that their Prime Minister Reichmann is behind the death her brother, and quite probably her parents as well.

KATRINA: (SHARP IN TAKE OF BREATH) Oh my . . . .

MYCROFT: Oh, please forgive my lack of tact, Your Highness. Mind you, Sherlock, I shall have to inform my higher-ups.

HOLMES: (PLAYFULLY) Really. I thought you had no "higher-ups".

WATSON: (TAKEN ABACK) The Queen and the Prime Minister, Holmes.

HOLMES: Oh, yes, of course.

MYCROFT: Now, tell me, how did you meet?

HOLMES: Watson found her.

MYCROFT: Really?

HOLMES: Yes, she fell from a carriage straight into his lap.

WATSON: We believe she was being kidnapped.

MYCROFT: Interesting. The last word I had on her was in regards to her so-called elopement to this country with her lover, the Count Victor Von Schreiber. We thought she was in the country, but weren't completely certain.

HOLMES: There are dark dealings going on here, brother, and I mean to discover their depths.

MYCROFT: I'm sure you do. But may I remind you, Sherlock, as you go about your investigations in your usual athletic fashion, that the handling of this matter could have important international repercussions.

HOLMES: Quite. However, at the moment I have urgent business to attend to in Fleet Street. Oh, and Watson – be ready to rise early tomorrow. We need to leave here no later than six o'clock. And don't forget that service revolver of yours. It may be needed.

MUSIC: UNDERSCORE

WATSON: (NARRATING) There was an excitement and gleam it Holmes's eye that I knew meant he felt the case was coming to a head. However, I was exhausted from the day's activities and went straight to bed shortly after the princess and Mycroft Holmes took their leave. I awoke early and, following a hurried breakfast, I went with my friend back to the dark old house we'd visited the day before.

MUSIC: OUT

SOUND EFFECT: EXTERIOR AMBIENCE. URBAN AREA, EARLY MORNING

HOLMES: Good morning, Griggs. Any sign of activity?

GRIGGS: Not as ya can tell, guv. I did a bit of askin' around, an' there's just two blokes what's livin' in the place, a Fancy Dan and his servant.

HOLMES: Excellent. You've done a fine job. I need one more errand done before you can have your half crown. Deliver this to the house. You'll know in what manner.

SOUND EFFECT: PASSING OF NEWSPAPER

GRIGGS: Yes, sir.

MUSIC: VIOLIN BRIDGE

WATSON: Holmes?

HOLMES: Umm?

WATSON: Why are you going to all this trouble? I mean, wouldn't it have been simpler just to have told your brother where these men are and have him take care . . . .

SOUND EFFECT: SHOT FIRED IN HOUSE ACROSS STREET

HOLMES: Quick, Watson to the house!

MUSIC: STING

70

SOUND EFFECT: TRYING FRONT DOOR *

WATSON: * The door's locked.

SOUND EFFECT: RAPID KNOCKING ON DOOR *

HOLMES: * Strike me for a fool! I should have foreseen this as a possibility! Open up!

SOUND EFFECT: DOOR BEING UNLOCKED

HOLMES: Have your revolver ready, Watson.

WATSON: Right

SOUND EFFECT: DOOR OPENS

VICTOR: Yes? How can I help you gentlemen?

HOLMES: Drop the pistol!

SOUND EFFECT: GUN DROPPED TO FLOOR

VICTOR: Am I under arrest?

WATSON: There was a shot. Is anyone injured?

VICTOR: He's through here.

SOUND EFFECT: THREE MEN WALKING INTO ROOM

VICTOR: I think he's still alive.

STOCKLASA: (WEAKLY) My shoulder . . . .

WATSON: Here, Holmes. Take my pistol. Now, let's have a look.

STOCKLASA: I remember you. The busybody . . . .

WATSON: Keep still.

HOLMES: (PAUSE) Well, Watson?

WATSON: He'll live, if he doesn't bleed to death before we can get him to hospital.

HOLMES: You're fortunate, Count Von Schreiber. A murder charge would not have helped your cause.

VICTOR: How did you know my name? And what do you know about my "cause", as you call it?

HOLMES: I am Sherlock Holmes, and it is my business to know such things.

VICTOR: Explain.

HOLMES: Very well. When you heard of the death of her brother, King Nicolas, you reasoned that Princess Katrina's life was in grave danger. After all, she was now heir to the throne. I submit that you wanted to continue your elopement incognito, but she would have none of it. Now that her brother was dead, she determined to return to Liechtenstein. The people needed her. But you could not bear the thought of her being murdered, so you hit upon a plan to kidnap her for her own protection. Am I correct so far?

VICTOR: This viper, Stocklasa, this villain your friend is trying to save, tricked me into abducting the woman that I love. He knew I needed time to convince her that returning home was the worst possible thing she could do. He said he had a friend here in England who could look after her. But she loves her country passionately and would never concede to going into hiding willing. So we hatched a scheme to kidnap her. (FORCEFULLY) He told me the plan had worked perfectly and she was safe!

HOLMES: But then you discovered she hadn't been taken to safety after all.

VICTOR: The fool unwittingly handed me that information this morning with my breakfast. He doesn't read English, you see. I saw how I'd been manipulated into helping place my darling in the very danger I was trying to save her from. I knew now that this fiend was working for the Secret Police. I confronted him. He grew angry and tried to attack me, but I was already prepared . . . .

STOCKLASA: You might as well have killed me. My life is over. Once it is learned how I failed in my mission . . . .

HOLMES: Your life is not over yet if you agree to help the British authorities.

STOCKLASA: What do you mean?

HOLMES: You give them the names of all of those in England who were to help you spirit the princess back to Liechtenstein, and your government need never know of your whereabouts ever again.

MUSIC: TRANSITION

WATSON: (NARRATING) Next day, we received news at 221b from Mycroft, saying the princess had fully recovered her memory and was now returning to Liechtenstein under armed guard with the Count. They had managed to patch up their differences, and I dare say that he had done a lot of growing up over last couple days. Stocklasa was in protective custody and revealing vital information regarding the Liechtenstein Secret Police.

MUSIC: OUT

WATSON: You never did tell me what it was you gave Griggs to deliver to the Count.

HOLMES: Here. Take a look for yourself.

SOUND EFFECT: RUSTLING OF NEWSPAPER

WATSON: It's the front page of yesterdays *Times*. Is that all?

HOLMES: Look at the article in the lower left hand corner.

WATSON: Let's see *"Police foil royal kidnap plot. Scotland Yard has announced that they have Princess Katrina of Liechtenstein in their protection after a failed kidnap attempt by that country's Secret Police. The Yard has issued the description of a man they would like to interview in connection with the crime. He is said to be of heavy build, with black beard and foreign accent. An imminent arrest is expected."*

HOLMES: I had Griggs replace the real font page with this one. I gambled that a brute like Stocklasa couldn't read our language and would simply serve the paper to his master with the morning meal.

WATSON: That was why you went to Fleet Street – to have this made up.

HOLMES: Excellent reasoning, Watson, since that is where most of London's newspaper are published. A friend at *The Times* simply redid a small portion of the genuine paper and produced this single special edition.

WATSON: But why, Holmes? Why all this charade, when all you needed do once we found the Count and Stocklasa was to turn the information and the princess over to Mycroft and let him handle it from there.

HOLMES: Ah, old friend. For a mind such as mine, it is the game that keeps it from stagnating. And every once in a great while, when an innocent's life or freedom is not at stake, it is taking a commonplace crime such as this one and adding *soupçon* of style to enhance the challenge, a small twist to give my adversary something to ponder during the long nights in his prison cell. In this case, don't believe what you read in the newspapers.

WATSON: (DRYLY) Especially if you're a criminal and the author is Sherlock Holmes.

MUSIC: *DANSE MACABRE* IN AND UNDER

WATSON: This is Dr. John H. Watson. I've had many more adventures with Sherlock Holmes, and I'll tell you another one *. . . when next we meet!*

<u>MUSIC: UP AND OUT</u>

The Adventure of the Aldgate Noose
by Matthew Booth

CHARACTERS

- SHERLOCK HOLMES
- DR. JOHN H. WATSON
- INSPECTOR LESTRADE – *A Scotland Yard Inspector, forthright, honourable. Not stupid, but steps behind Holmes*
- EMILY COMPTON – *Proud, virtuous, caring, slightly naïve*
- JAMES DACRE – *Handsome, persuausive, loyal, arrogantly intelligent*
- WICKHAM – *A bank manager, efficient, pompous, morose*

SOUND EFFECT: OPENING SEQUENCE, BIG BEN

ANNOUNCER: *The Further Adventures of Sherlock Holmes*, starring John Patrick Lowrie as Sherlock Holmes, and Lawrence Albert as Dr. John H. Watson.

MUSIC: *DANSE MACABRE* (UP AND UNDER)

WATSON: (NARRATING) The year 1888 was a busy one for my friend, Sherlock Holmes. Among those cases I have for that year is the singular tale of the Aldgate Noose, and the tragic story of Miss Emily Compton. It was a spring afternoon when the affair began —as so many of his cases did — with a knock at the door of our sitting room in Baker Street, and our introduction to the young lady herself who, I remember, showed great signs of agitation.

EMILY: I apologize, Mr. Holmes, for intruding on you at such short notice.

HOLMES: My dear Miss Compton, you will find no more informal household in all London than my own. There is a problem which confronts you?

EMILY: I hardly know where to begin.

WATSON: May I suggest that you compose yourself, take your time in arranging your thoughts, and give as many details as possible? Perhaps some coffee would assist.

EMILY: Thank you, Dr. Watson. That would be most welcome.

SOUND EFFECT: WATSON POURS THE COFFEE AND HANDS THE CUP OVER

WATSON: There.

EMILY: Thank you.

HOLMES: Admirable. And now perhaps we may proceed to the core of the matter.

EMILY: Of course. The reason for my concern is Edward, my brother, Mr. Holmes. He retired to bed last night as usual, but this morning . . . there was no trace of him.

WATSON: He may have simply gone out early.

EMILY: That's what James said when I told him.

HOLMES: James?

EMILY: James Dacre, Mr. Holmes. My *fiancé* of two years.

WATSON: I wonder that Mr. Dacre is not with you today, Miss Compton.

EMILY: I asked him, Doctor, but he refused. He is wary of me wasting the time of such a person as you, Mr. Holmes.

SOUND EFFECT: HOLMES LIGHTS HIS PIPE

HOLMES: Those in genuine need of my services seldom waste my time, Miss Compton. If the matter is of sufficient interest, I am here to be used.

78

EMILY: I hardly dared hope for such kindness. (PAUSE) I fear for Edward, Mr. Holmes. I have heard nothing from him for almost six hours. It is so very unlike him.

HOLMES: You have not seen him since he retired to bed last night?

EMILY: No; that was around ten o'clock. We live together in a fairly proud house left to us jointly by our parents. Last night, Edward declared that he was very tired and desired to retire to his room. That was the last I saw of him.

WATSON: What happened this morning, when your brother's absence was noted?

EMILY: When Edward did not appear for breakfast, I went to his room. I knocked and went in.

HOLMES: It was not locked?

EMILY: No. His bed was empty, but the bedsheets were disheveled and there was an impression of his body on the mattress.

WATSON: Indicating that he either slept in the bed for a time – or else wished to make it appear so.

HOLMES: Possibly; very possibly. It is certainly a suggestive case. Why should a man retire to bed but simply vanish before morning?

EMILY: He wouldn't just leave without saying a word and not be in touch like this. I know my brother well enough.

WATSON: Of course you do.

EMILY: Yesterday, I saw a strange man, staring up at the house. He didn't approach, but he appeared to be watching the bedroom windows. Then, he simply vanished.

HOLMES: Indeed. (WITH ENERGY) Well, there is nothing to be gained by sitting here talking. This is a time for action, Miss Compton, and I fear we must invade your property and examine your brother's room, in the hope some clue may come to light.

SOUND EFFECT: A DISTANT CLOCK CHIMING FOUR

HOLMES: Judging from his room, your brother was a man of extremely tidy habits, Miss Compton.

EMILY: Edward has always been a methodical man.

WATSON: It is evident that his bed has been slept in, as you said previously, Miss Compton.

SOUND EFFECT: A KNOCK AT THE DOOR

DACRE: Sorry to intrude, Emily, but I wondered if our guests would like some tea.

EMILY: Mr. Holmes, this is James Dacre, my *fiancé*. I asked him to be here for your arrival.

DACRE: Pleasure to meet you, Mr. Holmes.

HOLMES: You have injured your hand, sir.

DACRE: Oh, it is nothing. A graze from my own foolishness. But you are here about Edward. I'm sure there's nothing to worry about. Edward's not one to get himself lost.

HOLMES: Nevertheless he has vanished, Mr. Dacre. Can you suggest anything which might explain his disappearance?

DACRE: I can think of nothing.

EMILY: He has appeared distracted recently, don't you think, James? Normally, he was so placid and soothing. Of late, I have noticed him staring into the distance with an abstract expression on his face.

HOLMES: When did you first notice this, Miss Compton?

EMILY: In the last week or so, Mr. Holmes. One morning at breakfast, he almost scalded himself on the coffee pot, so wrapped in his own thoughts was he.

WATSON: Did you not ask him the reason for his anxiety?

EMILY: Of course, Dr. Watson. But he simply smiled and assured me I was not to concern myself. Edward never liked to think of me worrying.

DACRE: Which is why he would be ashamed of himself for causing you to behave as you are now. I tell you, Emily, there is nothing to fear. There is a rational explanation for this, and when he comes home, Edward will give it to us.

HOLMES: What is Mr. Compton's professional capacity?

EMILY: He is on the board of Wickham and Compton.

WATSON: The bankers? I didn't realize you were connected with them, Miss Compton. My apologies.

DACRE: Emily's father and Alistair Wickham founded the bank twenty years ago.

EMILY: After his death, father was anxious that Edward follow in his wake.

HOLMES: Is it possible that his professional life might have caused the anxiety of which you speak?

EMILY: It is possible, but as I have said, I have no notion of the cause of his concern.

DACRE: I've a good mind to give Edward a thrashing for the trouble he is causing.

WATSON: (DISAPPROVING) That would be one solution to the problem, certainly.

HOLMES: I wonder, Miss Compton, if you would object to leaving Dr. Watson and me in this room for the purposes of examination.

EMILY: Certainly, Mr. Holmes, if you wish it.

HOLMES: Purely to minimize any disturbance of the evidence, you understand.

EMILY: Of course.

SOUND EFFECT: THEY LEAVE THE ROOM, AND CLOSE THE DOOR BEHIND THEM

HOLMES: (SUDDENLY EAGER) What do you make of it, Watson? Does anything strike you about this room?

WATSON: Only, as you say, how tidy it is. I wish you'd take a leaf out of this chap's book and give the same attention to Baker Street.

HOLMES: I tidied away those papers you complained about last week.

WATSON: Tossing them from the centre of the room into a corner does not constitute tidying them away.

HOLMES: Save your recriminations for later, Doctor, if you don't mind. For now, concentrate your energy on devising an explanation as to why a man might disappear in the night — and yet leave his waistcoat, watch, and socks behind.

WATSON: Good Lord! So he has. Neatly folded on the bedside cabinet.

HOLMES: Does it suggest to you that the man left in a hurry? If not, then a close examination of the window sill may convince you, if taken in tandem with the folded clothes.

WATSON: I don't follow.

HOLMES: Look here.

HOLMES: You see that small chip in the glass?

WATSON: Somebody threw something up at the window!

HOLMES: Precisely, Watson! Gravel from the driveway below the window, in all probability. There are remnants on the sill itself, I perceive.

WATSON: Someone stirred Edward Compton from his bed by throwing gravel at his window. Seeing who it was, he dressed hurriedly and left. That would explain why his room was unlocked this morning too.

HOLMES: Excellent, Watson! We might venture further, however. Judging by the fact that this window is not closed properly, I should say that Compton opened the window to have a brief interview with this nocturnal visitor.

WATSON (SADDENED WHISPER): And it would be someone he knew, clearly. Perhaps the man Miss Compton saw staring up at the house?

HOLMES: Possibly. The thing takes shape, Watson.

SOUND EFFECT: A RING AT THE BELL AND MUFFLED VOICES BELOW

WATSON: Hello, what's that commotion?

SOUND EFFECT: THE DOOR OPENS

HOLMES: Lestrade!

LESTRADE: Mrs. Hudson said you were here, Mr. Holmes.

HOLMES: You have been to Baker Street? It must be a matter of some urgency to bring you here after me.

LESTRADE: I was going to ask you to accompany me to this very house, Mr. Holmes. I had no idea you would be here already.

WATSON: What has happened, Inspector?

LESTRADE: I take it you are investigating Edward Compton?

HOLMES: You have news of him?

LESTRADE: I think I can save you some work, Mr. Holmes. Edward Compton has been found in a rented room in Aldgate.

WATSON: (SADDENED WHISPER) Oh, no.

HOLMES: Go on, Lestrade.

LESTRADE: He has committed suicide, Mr. Holmes. He has hanged himself from a brass hook in the ceiling.

MUSIC: STING, THEN UNDERCURRENT

WATSON: (NARRATING) The rented house in Aldgate was clearly rundown, with mildew on the windows and no carpets on the stairways. We found ourselves outside the room itself, and Holmes examined the lock on the door, which had been badly damaged.

MUSIC: OUT

LESTRADE: We were obliged to force the lock, Mr. Holmes. The room itself was locked.

HOLMES: No key?

LESTRADE: None yet found. It's one of the more puzzling details.

HOLMES: Let us enter the room, Lestrade.

SOUND EFFECT: THEY ENTER AND WALK OVER THE BARE FLOORBOARDS INTO THE ROOM

WATSON: Good God.

HOLMES: Stood on the chair and kicked it away, I presume, Inspector.

LESTRADE: It looks that way, doesn't it? No idea why he has neither socks nor waistcoat on.

HOLMES: I can explain that to you later. For now, we must examine this room and its tragic occupant.

WATSON: Can't we get him down first? He still deserves some dignity, for God's sake.

HOLMES: In time, Watson. The truth must come first. Lestrade, I see that he has tied the end of the rope to this bar across the window.

LESTRADE: To anchor himself, Mr. Holmes.

WATSON: What is so bad that it can drive a man to this?

LESTRADE: Edward Compton took this room a week ago from the landlord who let us in. He signed an agreement with him, which is how we got his name and address.

HOLMES: A week ago? That would mean he took this room at the same time his sister noticed a change in his behaviour.

WATSON: You think there is a connection?

HOLMES: There is a curious coincidence of dates, if nothing else.

LESTRADE: But why should a man go to the trouble of hiring a room in order to do himself in? Why not just do it at home?

WATSON: Perhaps, Lestrade, he had some compassion for his sister's feelings. I shouldn't want my sister to be the one to find me hanging in my bedroom.

HOLMES: Quite so. And the fact that the room was taken a week ago suggests that Compton desired some place of solitude to think about things. It is not so very unusual. (A BEAT) What is unusual, however, is the key.

LESTRADE: I knew you would think so. It's a question to be answered. If a man commits suicide in a locked room, you'd expect the key to be on the inside of the door, wouldn't you?

WATSON: Someone took it away, obviously.

LESTRADE: Exactly. But why?

HOLMES: It was certainly a very queer thing to do. For now, Inspector, I think our friend the doctor is correct and that we should take the body down. Lend a hand will you, Watson?

SOUND EFFECT: THEY TAKE THE BODY DOWN, THE ROPE STRAINING WITH THE WEIGHT, THE MEN GRUNTING WITH THE EFFORT

HOLMES: Lay him on the floor here. Now, Lestrade, let me examine that noose.

LESTRADE: Certainly, Mr. Holmes. There you are.

WATSON: Look at those wounds around his neck. (TO HIMSELF) My God.

HOLMES: There is nothing very singular about this noose. A fairly professional attempt however. Stout rope. There may be some clue in that, Lestrade. (SOMETHING STRIKES HIM) Hello.

LESTRADE: What is it?

HOLMES: There is a small quantity of dried blood on this rope. Most curious.

WATSON: (NOTICING SOMETHING) Holmes . . . .

HOLMES: You consider this to be a simple suicide, Lestrade?

WATSON: (MORE URGENCY) Holmes . . . .

86

LESTRADE: I don't see that it can be anything else.

WATSON: It is nothing less than murder, gentlemen, I can promise you that.

HOLMES: Watson?

WATSON: This man no more killed himself than you or I, Holmes. A genuine hanging, especially with a noose like that one, would not have given these results.

LESTRADE: What are you talking about?

WATSON: The man's neck isn't broken. A genuine hanging, with a stout noose like that one, would break the neck instantly. This man has been strangled by hand.

LESTRADE: Are you sure?

HOLMES: Watson's medical qualifications are beyond doubt, Lestrade. This is a fascinating development. Most gratifying.

WATSON: (APPALLED) But it's murder, Holmes!

HOLMES: (TO HIMSELF) It explains the absence of the key most satisfactorily. If the man was murdered, his killer could lock the door and take the key. It becomes not a curious mystery, but a fundamental error. Well done, Watson, capital work!

LESTRADE: But if Edward Compton was strangled to death, how on earth did the killer manage to string him up like that? And why go to all that trouble to make it look like suicide?

HOLMES: Questions which we shall have answered as soon as possible, Lestrade. For now, we must hunt for a particularly cunning killer.

MUSIC: STING

WATSON: (NARRATING) It was late afternoon when we reached the offices of Wickham and Compton. We were shown at once to Alistair Wickham, the senior partner, whose bowed shoulders and pinched eyes showed of a life bending over accounts' books and ledgers. Holmes broke the news of his former employee's death and stated the reason for our visit.

WICKHAM: A tragedy of course, Mr. Holmes, but I can hardly say I am surprised. Young Compton was not in the same class as his father, alas.

HOLMES: How so, Mr. Wickham?

WICKHAM: Young Edward was a common thief, sir! Large quantities of reserve have been siphoned off over the last two years or so.

WATSON: By Edward Compton?

WICKHAM: It took me a long time, Dr. Watson, but I managed to get him in the end. These * are his vault keys.

SOUND EFFECT: * JANGLING KEYS ON A KEY RING

WICKHAM: I took these from him only yesterday. You see there, Mr. Holmes, on the end?

HOLMES: Moulding clay. He was making impressions of the vault keys.

WATSON: The fool.

WICKHAM: I have no doubt my exposure of his crime led to his suicide, Dr. Watson, but I must confess that it will not lie heavily on my conscience. I am a man of honour. Kingsley Compton and I built this bank from scratch, and I won't allow any man to take it from me in disgrace.

WATSON: I can well understand that. But about the suicide –

HOLMES (QUICK INTERRUPTION): Mr. Wickham! Pride is a quality of which every man is guilty, and a characteristic which can blind us to the truth.

WICKHAM: What do you mean by that, sir?

HOLMES: You owe Miss Emily Compton an apology for the distress you caused her brother, and you owe him one for the wrong you do him now.

WATSON: Holmes . . . ?

WICKHAM: What is the meaning of this, Mr. Holmes?

HOLMES: Edward Compton was innocent of any charge you level against him. He was as honourable and proud of his name as you are yourself. Good day, sir.

<u>SOUND EFFECT: HOLMES WALKS OUT OF THE ROOM AND SLAMS THE DOOR BEHIND HIM. BUSY STREET OUTDOORS</u>

WATSON: Holmes, what did you mean by all that?

HOLMES: Precisely what I said. Come, Watson, we must return to the home of Miss Emily Compton. There is further work to be done there.

<u>MUSIC: BRIDGE</u>

HOLMES: My deepest sympathies, Miss Compton. It is painful news.

EMILY: Perhaps I knew in my heart he was dead. But I do not accept that he killed himself. I will not.

DACRE: What other explanation, dear Emily?

EMILY: Oh, James, I –

HOLMES: Murder, sir. Murder is the other explanation. And the true one.

DACRE: Who on earth murders a man by hanging him? It doesn't make sense.

WATSON: He was strangled, not hanged. The hanging was staged.

89

HOLMES: Mr. Dacre . . . Who was your accomplice? Who was the man who stared up at the house yesterday, and who was in this plot with you?

EMILY: Mr. Holmes?

DACRE: What are you talking about? Are you mad?

HOLMES: It was clear from the first that Mr. Compton had been decoyed away. His bed and clothes showed as much. In addition, there is a chip in the window pane of his bedroom and gravel on the sill, which indicate that he was roused from his sleep by someone from outside.

WATSON: But it was someone whom he knew. The man who stared up at the house was a stranger. Miss Compton said that herself, and so it could not have been he who threw gravel at the window.

HOLMES: Compton was decoyed away to the flat in Aldgate which had, unknown to him, been taken in his name. There, he was murdered. By you and this accomplice of yours, Mr. Dacre.

WATSON: Why go to all the trouble of hiring the room, Holmes? Why not do it here?

HOLMES: They dared not run the risk of waking Miss Emily. They needed a place of solitude to carry out their work. It could, after all, be explained as a refuge of a desperate man, who did not wish his family to discover his body. But the truth was that Mr. Dacre and his confederate needed privacy to commit their crime. But you took the key to the room away with you, sir, thus exposing the suicide as a fraud. It was impossible that the key would be missing in a genuine suicide attempt.

WATSON: You staged the suicide to divert suspicion away from yourselves.

DACRE: This is fanciful. Even if I were involved, what makes you think there was a third person? And why would I do such a thing?

90

HOLMES: Even a strong man would struggle to pull a grown man up to the ceiling on a rope, single-handed.

WATSON: Of course! There had to be someone to take the weight of the corpse. It took three of us to get it down, so the work must have been hard.

HOLMES: Which would explain how you came to graze your palm, Mr. Dacre. Your accomplice heaved Compton onto his shoulders, whilst you pulled the noose tight and secured it. The weight of the corpse took the skin off your palm.

DACRE: This is nonsense. You can't prove a word of it.

HOLMES: There are corresponding blood stains on the noose, Mr. Dacre.

EMILY: But why, Mr. Holmes? I don't understand.

HOLMES: This man has been your *fiancée* for two years, Miss Compton. For the same length of time, money has been siphoned out of your father's bank. I have no doubt that the two events are connected.

DACRE: Damn you . . . .

HOLMES: Last week, Alistair Wickham – believing that your brother was a thief – confronted him, and threatened exposure. The vault keys your brother possessed showed evidence of having been duplicated.

WATSON: But they were duplicated for you, Mr. Dacre, for your own purposes.

HOLMES: Why should a partner in the bank, who owns his own keys, need to have duplicates made for himself? There is no conceivable reason. He would be unlikely to give his keys up to any third person, however, and so would make copies.

WATSON: But when Compton was confronted with his crime, and possible ruin . . . .

DACRE: He threatened to expose us.

EMILY: You were going to rob him? All this time, you were planning to rob him?

DACRE: You're rich, Emily. You always have been. But me? I've never had any more than I could barely survive on. You've no idea what it means to see your parents starve so that you can eat. None at all. I tried to make my way in the world, but it was hard. Then I met you and I thought things might change.

HOLMES: How did you get Compton to co-operate with you against his own firm?

(PAUSE)

EMILY: Why are you looking at me like that, James? What are you saying?

HOLMES: He made threats against you. To force your brother, to blackmail him, into compliance.

EMILY: No!

WATSON: Look at his eyes, Miss Compton. It is all there.

EMILY: You coward! You would have had it all when we married anyway. Even if you only loved my money and not me . . . . Why could you not wait instead of all this?

HOLMES: His greed took over. He could not wait for marriage or honest inheritance through you.

DACRE: I have pride, gentlemen. I didn't want to live off a woman. What sort of man would that make me?

HOLMES: A more honourable one than a thief and a murderer.

EMILY: And a liar. You have ruined me, James. I cannot bear to look at your face.

HOLMES: Your accomplice . . . ?

DACRE: I tell my own tales, Mr. Holmes, but I don't tell anybody else's. If you want him, you find him. I am sure your famous powers will help you.

HOLMES: Scotland Yard's files and Miss Emily's description of him will assist far more than any contribution I may make.

DACRE: You saw him?

EMILY: Yesterday. Staring up at the house.

DACRE: The bloody fool! (A BEAT) His name is Stock. Freddy Stock. I've known him for years. I promised him half of what I could get if he would help me.

WATSON: Do you have any regret about all this? Any at all.

DACRE: No more than any other man in this world. Why should I suffer when others flourish?

EMILY: And Edward? Branded a thief and a suicide? What of him?

DACRE: I am sorry for that. It was desperation, no more.

HOLMES: Many men are desperate in a cruel world, Mr. Dacre. It is how you manage that desperation that brings honour and dignity. Edward Compton should serve as a lesson to you with regard to both qualities.

(LONG PAUSE)

EMILY: I never realized how naive I was until today.

WATSON: Do not let it taint any future you may have, Miss Compton. There is goodness in this world if you choose to seek it.

EMILY: Thank you, Doctor. And thank you, Mr. Holmes.

HOLMES: I am only sorry that we could not bring a happier solution to your door.

EMILY: I sought the truth, Mr. Holmes, not happiness. I am content with the truth as it is.

SOUND EFFECT: SHE LEAVES THE ROOM

WATSON: A brave girl, Holmes.

HOLMES: I did not notice, Watson. She is a mere factor in the problem.

WATSON (NARRATING): But I think he *had* noticed. I tried to see a glimpse of the heart behind the mind, but it was too far hidden beneath the mask. We stayed with her for half-an-hour more, before Lestrade came to take charge. Then, we passed from that house of grief into the pale sunlight of the spring day.

MUSIC: *DANSE MACABRE*

WATSON: This is Dr. John H. Watson. I've had many more adventures with Sherlock Holmes, and I'll tell you another one *. . . when next we meet!*

MUSIC: (FADE OUT)

The First Mate's Jacket
by J.R. Campbell

CHARACTERS

- DR. JOHN H. WATSON
- CONSTABLE HENRY – *A young, likable police officer serving in the Irish port of Queenstown*
- SHERLOCK HOLMES
- MARY RANSTEAD – *A petite, delicate American woman, recently widowed by a tragedy at sea*
- MR. LANSING – *An elderly clerk with a formal bearing, but suffering a weakness for gossip*
- CLUNEY – *A large, rough sailor from America*

SOUND EFFECT: OPENING SEQUENCE, BIG BEN

ANNOUNCER: *The Further Adventures of Sherlock Holmes*, starring John Patrick Lowrie as Sherlock Holmes, and Lawrence Albert as Dr. John H. Watson.

MUSIC: *DANSE MACABRE* (UP AND UNDER)

WATSON: My name is Dr. John H. Watson, biographer and confidante of the consulting detective Sherlock Holmes. Over the years, many have found it strange that I do not covet my friend's unique deductive abilities. Perhaps, knowing Holmes as well as I do, I am more aware than the general public of the high cost Holmes pays for his skills. To a detective, distrust and suspicion are useful tools. For those of us concerned with matters such as family and friends, they are demons to be shunned. Perhaps no case demonstrated this difference between Holmes and I better than the matter of the first mate's jacket. Holmes had arranged to meet me on a street corner in the Irish port of Queenstown, but I was late . . . .

MUSIC: OUT

HENRY: Here he is now, Mr. Holmes.

WATSON: Holmes, sorry I'm late. I'm afraid there was a medical emergency.

HOLMES: (SNIFFS) A medical emergency?

WATSON: Yes, down by the docks. A rather extraordinary event, I –

HOLMES: Indeed. A most extraordinary medical crisis. One that requires you to linger in the warmth of the Bellavista Hotel, sipping brandy in a lady's chambers while Constable Henry and I braved the elements without benefit of your company.

HENRY: Now Mr. Holmes, I'm sure that's not true. The doctor wouldn't just abandon us. Tell him, Doctor. Tell him he's wrong.

WATSON: I – well, that is, uh –

HOLMES: Come now, Watson, cat got your tongue?

HENRY: Well now, that's a surprise. Tell me Mr. Holmes. However did you know all that?

HOLMES: A simple matter of observation and deduction. Note his right pant leg, the discoloration above the hem. Obviously he has stepped in salt water, placing him down by the docks. Just as apparent is the fact that the fabric has dried, indicating the doctor has been indoors. But where? For that we must rely on our sense of smell. Do you not perceive the lingering scent of a woman's perfume about the doctor?

HENRY: (SNIFF, SNIFF, SNIFF)

HOLMES: It is, I must confess, a scent unfamiliar to me, but unmistakably expensive. This places him at the Bellavista Hotel, the only dockside establishment fit for such clientele. For

97

evidence of brandy, one need only look at the doctor's left shirt cuff. The doctor is, I assure you, not normally so careless with his drink. One can only assume there was some matter – some excitement – which caused him to spill brandy on himself.

WATSON: Now, Holmes, I must protest –

HENRY: Remarkable, Mr. Holmes, quite remarkable.

HOLMES: A trifling matter, I assure you. Note his coat. You see how the left side is noticeably drier than the right? No doubt hung over a chair with the left side closer to the fire. It should be possible to calculate the length of time Watson spent in the lady's company by –

WATSON: Holmes! Let me explain.

HOLMES: If you feel you must.

WATSON: Everything you've said is true –

HENRY: A-ha!

WATSON: However, none of it is as you make it seem. I was passing the docks early this morning when I noticed a group of men gathered on a pier, staring out into the downpour. Naturally I asked them what they hoped to see. They claimed someone had glimpsed a small dory coming in.

HENRY: A dory? In this weather?

WATSON: Precisely my reaction. My knowledge of the sea is limited, but it was plain even to me that so small a craft was unsafe in this dreadful weather. I waited with the others and, after some time, we saw them, two figures struggling towards safety in a small rowboat. It was obvious they were at the end of their strength. Some of the men hurried into a boat of their own, rowed out, and towed them back to the pier.

HOLMES: And in the boat?

WATSON: Two survivors of the *Canning's Pride*, a schooner out of St John's. One large, blond fellow called Cluney, the ship's first mate. The other survivor was Mrs. Mary Ranstead, a petite woman nearly frozen from her ordeal. I stepped into the boat and carried the poor woman onto the dock. There was a measure of water in the boat's bottom, it was then my foot was soaked.

HOLMES: Did Mrs. Ranstead have a bag with her?

WATSON: Nothing at all, Holmes. The poor thing has lost everything. According to Cluney, the ship went down last evening and only the two of them escaped in time. If it wasn't for the lighthouse –

HENRY: That'd be the lighthouse at the old head of Kinsdale.

HOLMES: Thank you, Constable. Watson, please continue.

WATSON: There's not much more to tell. You've deduced the rest. I took Mrs. Ranstead to the Bellavista Hotel and arranged for lodgings. She was so pale and trembling, chilled to the bone. I stoked the fire until the room was a furnace, had her change into dry clothes, and bundled in blankets.

HOLMES: You offered her brandy?

WATSON: Yes, both to warm her and to ease the haunted look in her eyes. She's lost everything, Holmes. Her husband was intent on relocating to England. Everything they owned was on that ship.

HOLMES: Tragic. The dry clothes – provided by the hotel I assume?

WATSON: Yes.

HOLMES: Did the establishment provide any other essentials?

WATSON: A hot meal and the lodgings. Oh, and the brandy. What difference does –

HOLMES: Forgive me Watson. You know I am prone to odd curiosities. So, you left Mrs. Ranstead to find us?

WATSON: Only to be accused of being some sort of Lothario.

HOLMES: Indeed. I should have known better. Can you forgive me?

WATSON: Well, the evidence did seem against me. Of course I forgive you, Holmes. I did get away as soon as my conscience allowed. I hope Mrs. Ranstead is doing better.

HOLMES: I insist we return to the hotel and check on this unfortunate woman.

WATSON: I would feel better if I saw her before we leave.

HENRY: Well, gentlemen, if you've no further need of me –

HOLMES: I've not forgotten my promise to you Constable. Your assistance has been invaluable and, I seem to recall, I promised to stand you a pint. The weather seems likely to keep the villains of Queenstown indoors and out of trouble. You simply must come with us. Once Watson is satisfied his patient is out of danger, we'll share a drink together.

HENRY: I wouldn't say no to that.

HOLMES: Then it's agreed. Watson, let us attend your patient.

MUSIC: BRIDGE

SOUND EFFECT: WATSON KNOCKING ON DOOR

MARY: Come in.

SOUND EFFECT: HOTEL DOOR OPENING

MARY: Dr. Watson, how good to see you again.

WATSON: Just wanted to check and see – Oh, hello. I'm sorry, I didn't mean to interrupt.

LANSING: Not at all, Doctor.

MARY: Mr. Lansing has come to ask me some questions about, about . . . .

WATSON: There, there, Mary. It's all right.

LANSING: I've come to take a statement on behalf of the Maritime – Oh, good afternoon, Constable.

HENRY: Good afternoon.

MARY: What's this? I'm not in any sort of trouble, am I?

WATSON: Goodness no. The constable is here with me and my friend, Sherlock Holmes.

HOLMES: Mrs. Ranstead, Dr. Watson has told us of your tragic accident. You've lost so much.

MARY: Yes. Every penny we owned was aboard that ship. I don't know what will become of me.

HOLMES: And, of course, your husband lost as well. Such a tragedy.

MARY: Yes.

HOLMES: Watson, the Constable and I shall wait for you in the hall. I'm certain Mrs. Ranstead could use your support during her deposition. Again, Mrs. Ranstead, please accept our condolences.

MARY: Thank you, Mr. Holmes.

SOUND EFFECT: HOLMES AND HENRY LEAVE ROOM AND CLOSE DOOR

LANSING: Now then, Mrs. Ranstead, in your own words could you describe the events leading up to your arrival in Queenstown this morning?

101

MARY: Of course. Well, my husband insisted we travel by schooner, said he didn't trust the air aboard the big liners. He'd been born in England, you see, and, having made his fortune, was anxious to return to his boyhood home. So we booked passage aboard the *Canning's Pride*.

WATSON: You're doing very well, Mary.

MARY: Thank you, Doctor. Well, our passage was uneventful until, until –

WATSON: Courage, Mary, courage.

MARY: Last night, as the sun set, the weather turned foul. I couldn't sleep. The rough seas frightened me, so I made my way up on deck. As I stood there, watching the rain, I heard this enormous crash.

LANSING: Did you, by chance, see anything?

MARY: No, I didn't, but the ship had just come out of a steep wave and, after the crash, we started to tilt to one side.

LANSING: Listing. When a ship tilts, they say it's listing.

MARY: If you say so, Mr. Lansing. As you can imagine, I was quite frightened, and I started back down to my cabin. The first mate, Mr. Cluney, found me and ordered me into the lifeboat. If not for him, I've no doubt I would have perished beneath the waves. It was Cluney who put me in the lifeboat and lowered it into the water, but by that time, the *Canning's Pride* was, was – gone.

LANSING: I see.

MARY: It was dark and raining and the waves towered over us. It was horrible, so cold and wet, but Cluney kept pulling on the oars. I was certain we would not survive, but then we saw the light.

LANSING: That would be the lighthouse?

MARY: Yes. Please, if you see Mr. Cluney, thank him for me. The man is a hero. I owe him my life.

LANSING: Of course, Mrs. Ranstead. Have you anything to add to your account?

MARY: No, I'm sorry. That's all I remember.

LANSING: Very well. Thank you, Mrs. Ranstead.

WATSON: Have they any idea what caused the sinking?

LANSING: Well, between you and me, Mr. Cluney testified there was some cargo improperly secured in the ship's hold. A great iron stone, a sacred relic of the Beothuck people. Cluney says he drew the Captain's attention to it, but the Captain just laughed and accused Cluney of believing in heathen superstitions. Cluney suspects the stone broke lose during the rough seas and burst through the vessel's hull. The poor souls didn't have a chance –

MARY: (SOBS)

LANSING: Excuse me if I've said too much.

WATSON: That's all right. We appreciate your candor.

LANSING: If it would help, ma'am, I could make inquiries with the insurance company.

MARY: Thank you Mr. Lansing. Most considerate of you. And you, Dr. Watson, thank you for your gallantry. I mustn't keep you. I know you've friends waiting.

WATSON: I'm afraid Holmes and I are leaving this evening. You have my card though. Be sure to contact me when you've settled.

MARY: Thank you, Doctor.

SOUND EFFECT: WATSON OPENS DOOR, LEAVES HOTEL ROOM

WATSON: Listening at the keyhole, Holmes?

HOLMES: I felt it safest. Tell me, Constable, what do you make of Mrs. Ranstead's tale?

SOUND EFFECT: THE THREE MEN WALK DOWN THE HALL

HENRY: A tragedy, plain and simple.

HOLMES: Indeed. And you, Watson?

WATSON: I'm forced to agree with the constable. Holmes, what are you –

SOUND EFFECT: HOLMES STOPS SUDDENLY, THE OTHERS STOP WITH HIM

HOLMES: Watson! Look there! Unless I miss my guess it is the valiant first mate, Mr. Cluney.

WATSON: Yes that's him. Looks as if he's taking up lodgings across the street.

HOLMES: So it appears. Constable Henry, observe the man's jacket. Tell me what you see.

HENRY: Well sir, not much to tell. It's a pea-coat – many sailors favor them. Soaked right through, but that's to be expected. Quite worn. It's seen better days –

HOLMES: Worn how, exactly?

HENRY: Well, there's that burn on the shoulder by the neck.

WATSON: Yes, I see that too.

HOLMES: And what do you suppose would cause such a burn?

HENRY: Difficult to say –

WATSON: A rope! A rope passed across his shoulder. The better to lower a heavy burden.

HOLMES: Very good, Watson.

HENRY: Well, what of it? He did lower the lifeboat with Mrs. Ranstead in it.

HOLMES: I doubt he lowered her quickly enough or far enough to account for such a burn. Nor is it likely the first mate signed up for a crossing in so shabby a jacket.

WATSON: An incident aboard the ship?

HOLMES: Perhaps, Watson, perhaps. Constable, I believe I promised you a pint.

HENRY: If you insist, sir.

HOLMES: And afterwards, I have another small task for you. Our work this morning earned a feather for your cap, Constable. Would you care to earn another tomorrow?

HENRY: Really, Mr. Holmes?

HOLMES: I've no doubt of it. Watson, we will need lodgings for another night. And Watson –

MUSIC: UNDERCURRENT

HOLMES: – I would prefer not to rest under the same roof as the unfortunate Mrs. Ranstead.

MUSIC: OUT

HOLMES: Watson, time to wake up.

WATSON: (GRUNTS, ROLLS OVER)

HOLMES: Come, Watson! The game's afoot!

WATSON: Wha – What's that Holmes? What time is it?

105

HOLMES: Early. We have some distance to travel before the dawn finds us. Bring your revolver, Watson, I fear we've strayed into troubled waters.

WATSON: Holmes, I've no idea what you're talking about. Good Heavens, what's that smell? You've been smoking that rough-cut tobacco again.

HOLMES: Yes.

WATSON: All night? Holmes, what problem torments you so?

HOLMES: Not a problem, Watson. Rather, it is a solution I am struggling to avoid. I am troubled by suspicions I cannot dismiss. If I am right, there is a cruelty in these events rivaling anything in our experience.

WATSON: Won't you explain? Really, Holmes, you can be damned frustrating at times.

HOLMES: It is possible I am afflicted by a dark fancy, suffering delusions wrought from my morbid imagination, and you can best assist me by maintaining an opinion untainted by my unwholesome suspicions. The day's events may yet reveal a flaw in my reasoning. Tonight, perhaps, I'll speak of the fears which chill me now and we'll share a laugh at my expense.

WATSON: If you insist, Holmes.

HOLMES: We've a short sea journey ahead of us. Best bring your jacket. And Watson – your service revolver. Do not forget!

MUSIC: UP AND UNDER

WATSON: And so I followed Holmes down to the docks. Constable Henry, his eyes bleary but his uniform crisp, hailed us from the deck of a local fisherman's boat. Holmes was quite pleased with the constable for arranging passage on the vessel, and he hopped eagerly aboard. The sinking of the *Canning's Pride* was still fresh in my thoughts, however, and it took me a moment to summon the courage necessary to step onto that swaying deck. Stars shone brightly above us as we left the harbor.

MUSIC: OUT

SOUND EFFECT: SEA SOUNDS, GULLS, AND WAVES

HENRY: Here we are, Mr. Holmes. Everything just as you said it would be.

HOLMES: Excellent. Watson, help me launch this rowboat.

WATSON: We're going ashore?

HOLMES: Try to contain your disappointment. Now, lift –

SOUND EFFECT: BOAT BEING LIFTED, THE SPLASH OF THE BOAT'S LAUNCH, THE THREE MEN CLIMB INTO THE BOAT

HOLMES: Thank you, Captain. Your help is very much appreciated. Constable? Watson?

WATSON: Yes, Holmes?

HOLMES: Row.

SOUND EFFECT: SOUNDS OF ROWING

HOLMES: Now, Constable, describe how you came upon this location.

HENRY: Well, sir, you said it would be best to look from the water, so I had the Captain take me for a sail last evening. I told him what I was looking for, and he brought me straight here. Sure enough, it was all just as you said it would be. Empty cove, no one about, in sight of the lighthouse, and within rowing distance of the harbor.

HOLMES: And the buoy?

HENRY: Just as you predicted. The Captain wasn't happy to see it. Said it didn't belong there.

HOLMES: You didn't let him tamper with it, did you?

HENRY: No, sir. I remembered what you told me.

HOLMES: Is there a road nearby?

HENRY: Not here, but there is a path over in the next cove.

HOLMES: Over there, gentlemen. We'll pull the boat ashore and hide it in those bushes.

WATSON: Hide from whom?

HENRY: That seems a fair question.

HOLMES: I expect First Mate Cluney will arrive by boat while the morning is still new. If he suspects we are here, he will flee and we will be forced to give chase. Our task will be simpler if we hide ourselves away until the proper moment.

WATSON: Here we are.

SOUND EFFECT: MEN SPLASHING INTO WATER AND PULLING BOAT ASHORE

HOLMES: Good, but let's turn the boat around. When the time comes, we'll need to be quick. It will be a race, but our side will have the advantage.

SOUND EFFECT: BOAT IS TURNED

HOLMES: Excellent. Now we wait.

MUSIC: BRIDGE AND UNDER

WATSON: Holmes entertained Constable Henry with the tale of the boat race on the Thames which resulted in the capture of the notorious felon Jonathan Small. Holmes had not yet finished the story when a rowboat appeared.

MUSIC: OUT

WATSON: Holmes –

HOLMES: Yes, there's our quarry now. Has he seen us? Apparently not. Good.

HENRY: Mr. Holmes, shall we –

HOLMES: Patience, Constable, patience.

WATSON: What's he doing with that buoy?

HOLMES: Tidying up after himself. You recall the buoy does not belong here.

HENRY: It looks heavy.

HOLMES: Indeed, see how he rocks his little boat? Not a gentle man, our Mr. Cluney. It puzzled me Watson, the stain on your trouser hem. One expects a boat lost in a downpour to collect a measure of water –

WATSON: Yes?

HOLMES: – but salt water? I would have expected any seawater taken on during the lifeboat's launch to be diluted by rainwater. Yet the stain was quite distinct. On the other hand, look how Cluney handles that rowboat. Not hard to imagine him taking on seawater lowering a weight overboard. Still, it's a question of timing, isn't it? Our moment is nearly upon us. I suggest we make ready.

SOUND EFFECT: HANDS SHIFT THE GROUNDED BOAT

HOLMES: Almost. Better to let Mr. Cluney expend his strength lifting rather than rowing. (PAUSE) Gentlemen – *Now!*

SOUND EFFECT: BOAT LAUNCHED, OARS ROWING

HENRY: He's seen us!

109

HOLMES: But he dares not release the buoy. He knows we'll take it if he does. Look at him pull that rope. Faster, gentlemen, faster. We've got him now!

HOLMES: (SHOUTING) It's too late, Mr. Cluney! Put down that oar!

WATSON: Drop your weapon, Mr. Cluney, or I will be forced to shoot you!

CLUNEY: Curse you all!

HOLMES: Your knife, too. The one hidden in your boot. Over the side with it.

CLUNEY: (GRUMBLES)

HOLMES: Constable, you may arrest this man.

HENRY: Begging your pardon, Mr. Holmes. What's the charge?

HOLMES Murder, Constable Henry. Nothing short of murder.

WATSON: Cluney glared back at me as I watched him over my revolver's barrel. The look in the sailor's eyes convinced me that, should my pistol waver, he would shed as much blood as necessary to make good his escape. Constable Henry stepped into the boat, ready with a set of manacles to take the first mate into custody.

110

SOUND EFFECT: SOUNDS OF THE SEA, HENRY STEPPING INTO BOAT, THE RATTLE OF MANACLES

HENRY: Now don't give me any trouble.

WATSON: If he does, it will be his last act in this world.

HOLMES: One moment, Constable. Mr. Cluney, would you be so kind as to remove your jacket?

CLUNEY: What?

WATSON: You heard him. Take off your jacket. Now.

SOUND EFFECT: A JACKET IS REMOVED

HOLMES: And your cap.

SOUND EFFECT: A CAP HITS THE BOTTOM OF THE BOAT

HOLMES: Thank you. Constable, you may proceed.

SOUND EFFECT: MANACLES FASTENED

HOLMES: Well, Mr. Cluney. Anything to offer in your defense?

CLUNEY: You can't pin nothing on me!

HOLMES: We shall see, Mr. Cluney, we shall see.

HENRY: It's a chest.

WATSON: What's that?

HENRY: Tied to the buoy. The weight Cluney was pulling from the water. It's a chest. Should I open it Mr. Holmes?

HOLMES: No need, Constable. It contains Mrs. Ranstead's lost fortune. All those pennies she lost to the deep.

111

HENRY: You mean Cluney stole that poor lady's fortune as their ship sank? Why you –

CLUNEY: I didn't steal anything!

HOLMES: I'm afraid he's telling the truth. He may be a murderer, but he's no thief.

WATSON: I don't understand.

HOLMES: All will be made clear shortly. Watson, it seems you're our closest match to Mr. Cluney. Our work here is only half done. A small deception may hurry the end of this matter. If you would put on Cluney's coat and cap.

WATSON: Of course, Holmes. But why?

HOLMES: Cluney did not come here alone. A confederate waits for him in the next cove. Disguised as Cluney, you're to wait in the boat while Constable Henry and I secure the prisoner ashore. We'll then make our way overland to the next cove. Provided the confederate is distracted by Cluney's apparent return, the Constable and I should be able to approach undetected.

WATSON: Sounds reasonable. Best if you take the revolver then.

HOLMES: Certainly not! Watson, you must be on your guard. Cluney is dangerous, but his confederate is even more deadly. Keep your pistol to hand and do not hesitate to use it. The constable and I shall reveal ourselves once you reach the shore. Be careful, Watson!

MUSIC: UNDERCURRENT

WATSON: I watched as Holmes and Constable Henry proceeded with the plan, my imagination running wild with the warning Holmes had imparted to me. What manner of monster waited for me in the next cove? Pulling up the jacket's collar, tugging the cap low over my eyes, I took up the oars and rowed. The weight of my revolver was heavy in the jacket pocket. Rounding into the cove, I glimpsed a distant figure on the shore.

Quickly I turned my face away to preserve my disguise. As I neared the shore, to my surprise, I recognized the voice calling to me. The voice of Mary Ranstead!

MUSIC: OUT

SOUND EFFECT: SOUNDS OF THE SEA, ROWING

MARY: Hurry, my love. Hurry!

SOUND EFFECT: OARS STOWED, THE BOAT SLIDES ASHORE

MARY: Almost done. Just bring the chest over to the cart.

HOLMES: (SHOUTING FROM A DISTANCE) You will drop that pistol, Mrs. Ranstead! It cannot save you now!

MARY: Cluney, hurry! I – Dr. Watson!

HOLMES: (SHOUTING, CLOSER) Drop your weapon, Mrs. Ranstead!

WATSON: You'd better do as he says, Mary.

MARY: But – how? I don't –

HOLMES: Mrs. Ranstead!

SOUND EFFECT: PISTOL DROPPED ON SHORE

HOLMES: A wise choice, Mrs. Ranstead. Constable, your second arrest of the day. Same charge as Cluney.

MARY: It was Cluney! He forced me to –

HOLMES: You may want to save this story for the trial, Mrs. Ranstead. I've no doubt Mr. Cluney is already rehearsing his testimony. Constable?

SOUND EFFECT: MANACLES FASTENED

113

MARY: (SWOONS)

HENRY: She's fainted, Mr. Holmes.

HOLMES: Yes, she's had a trying day.

WATSON: Holmes, I think it's time you told us what all this is about.

HOLMES: Yesterday, when you arrived late, I was troubled by the scent of perfume. The scent was stronger than a casual encounter suggested. When you spoke of the shipwreck I deduced you had given your jacket to the shivering Mrs. Ranstead and thus unwittingly scented your coat.

WATSON: I did give her my coat.

HOLMES: Of course you did, but you see where that leaves us? Mrs. Ranstead claimed to be adrift at sea for well over nine hours, drenched by rain and spray. There was no perfume in her hotel room. I checked. How is it possible then that she retained enough perfume to transfer the scent to your coat? I knew she was lying, but why? What difference would it make if her ship sank that morning or the previous evening?

WATSON: Unless –

HOLMES: Exactly, Watson! Unless she wished to disguise how far out they were when the ship met its fate. It wasn't until I saw the first mate, and the burn on his jacket, that a possible motive for Mrs. Ranstead's deceit presented itself. The list of items heavy enough to cause a rope to burn a coat in such a matter is small, and gold tops that list.

WATSON: You're saying Mrs. Ranstead and Cluney sank the ship in order to steal her husband's fortune?

HOLMES: Precisely.

HENRY: But Mr. Holmes, how's that possible? I mean, there's just the two of them against the crew and passengers.

HOLMES: A simple matter, Constable. Have you ever traveled by schooner? A long central corridor lined with doors, doors which open inwards to keep the passage clear. A single length of rope strung between those doors would trap everyone inside their cabins. Finding Cluney in the corridor, rope in hand, might raise suspicion, but the petite Mrs. Ranstead? With everyone locked in their cabins, the first mate and Mrs. Ranstead had the run of the ship.

WATSON: Sink the ship, hide the money, and come back for it the next day.

HOLMES: I suggest, Constable, you drag the waters of the cove where we arrested Cluney. The wreckage of the *Canning's Pride* waits for you there. The Royal Navy's deep-sea divers will, no doubt, recover some impressive evidence for the trial.

HENRY: But Mr. Holmes, the perfume? Why would Mrs. Ranstead put on so much perfume before sinking the ship?

HOLMES: An indiscreet question, Constable. Mrs. Ranstead found herself in desperate need of an ally and, apparently, was willing to take whatever action necessary to secure one. Perhaps she hoped the perfume would disguise the unfortunate consequences of her alliance. I trust I need not describe these sordid events any further?

WATSON: And to think I felt sorry for that woman. How many people did she murder?

HOLMES: According to last night's paper: Eight. Three crew and five passengers – including her husband, of course.

WATSON: I should have realized –

HOLMES: My dear Watson, it is simply not in your nature to question why an attractive woman smells so lovely. It hampers your abilities as a detective, but makes you a far better husband than I could ever hope to be.

MUSIC: *DANSE MACABRE*

WATSON: This is Dr. John H. Watson. I've had many more adventures with Sherlock Holmes, and I'll tell you another one *. . . when next we meet!*

MUSIC: (FADE OUT)

The Hudson Problem
by Jeremy B. Holstein

CHARACTERS

- SHERLOCK HOLMES – *Consulting Detective*
- DR. JOHN H. WATSON – *Medical Doctor and Holmes's right-hand man*
- MRS. HUDSON – *Holmes and Watson's housekeeper*
- INSPECTOR LESTRADE – *Scotland Yard detective. Brash*
- MRS. ALLARD – *Young woman, uneducated*
- STEPHAN PEARLMAN – *Young man, educated*
- INSPECTOR GREGSON – *Scotland Yard detective. Level-headed*
- POLICEMAN – *All business*

SOUND EFFECT: OPENING SEQUENCE, BIG BEN

ANNOUNCER: *The Further Adventures of Sherlock Holmes*, starring John Patrick Lowrie as Sherlock Holmes, and Lawrence Albert as Dr. John H. Watson.

MUSIC: *DANSE MACABRE* (UP AND UNDER)

WATSON: (NARRATING) My name is John H. Watson, and it has been my pleasure to share and chronicle the adventures of Sherlock Holmes. In the years since our adventures first saw print in *The Strand* magazine, much has been written about my celebrated friend, but little about those who helped in his investigations. One such overlooked participant was our long suffering landlady, Mrs. Hudson. Many have marveled at her tolerance of my friend's peculiar habits, habits which included chemical stains upon the woodwork and the firing of a pistol within the confines of our rooms. My answers to these questions have always been vague to protect Mrs. Hudson's privacy, but now, with the passage of time and her kind permission, I am finally able to reveal the truth.

MUSIC: OUT

118

WATSON: (NARRATING) It was in the summer of 1882, shortly after we had first moved into our rooms at 221b Baker Street, that the feud between Holmes and Mrs. Hudson began.

SOUND EFFECT: CHEMICAL HISSING. BANG! A DOOR BEING OPENED

MRS. HUDSON: Saints alive, what was that awful noise?

HOLMES: Stop! Stay where you are, Mrs. Hudson, if you value your life! The fumes from this beaker can be quite hazardous.

MRS. HUDSON: Are those my carpets? You've ruined my carpets!

HOLMES: Carpets can be replaced, but this experiment is absolutely vital! My investigation depends on it!

MRS. HUDSON: Oh, no, Mr. Holmes! You're not getting out of this one so easily. I'll expect full payment for the carpet at the end of the month, or I'll throw you out myself!

HOLMES: Watson, please show Mrs. Hudson out of our private lodgings.

WATSON: I'm sorry, Mrs. Hudson. When he gets like this, there's no reasoning with him.

HOLMES: I heard that.

MRS. HUDSON: He's the most infuriating man, Doctor. You're a gracious tenant, but that Mr. Holmes! Well! I certainly hope he isn't going to ask me for a reference with his next landlady!

WATSON: (NARRATING) I tried to talk to Holmes about being more considerate of Mrs. Hudson, but he would have none of it. And so their feud continued. I began to wonder if Mrs. Hudson would carry through with her intention to evict my friend, and me along with him, when fate intervened. It was the morning of September the 27th, and I was about on my morning constitutional. Upon my return to Baker Street, I was startled to see a police coach outside our rooms, and none other than Mrs. Hudson being ushered into its cabin!

SOUND EFFECT: RUNNING FOOTSTEPS

WATSON: Mrs. Hudson! Mrs. Hudson!

MRS. HUDSON: Oh, Doctor Watson! This is madness!

POLICEMAN: Quiet. That's enough talk.

WATSON: Where are you taking her?

POLICEMAN: The Yard, of course. You can speak to her there. Driver!

SOUND EFFECT: THE CRACK OF A WHIP. HORSE HOOVES AND WHEELS ON COBBLES AS THE COACH PULLS AWAY

WATSON: (NARRATING) I rushed up the stairs and burst into our rooms.

SOUND EFFECT: DOOR OPENING

WATSON: Holmes!

HOLMES: No need to shout, Watson. I'm right here.

WATSON: It's Mrs. Hudson, Holmes! They've arrested her!

HOLMES: Yes, I observed the entire affair through the window. The crass efficiency of Scotland Yard never ceases to amaze me. The butcher was only murdered an hour ago.

WATSON: What are you talking about? What butcher?

HOLMES: Why, Mrs. Hudson's butcher, of course. Kenneth Allard. He was found dead in his shop this morning. Stabbed, I believe.

WATSON: And they think Mrs. Hudson killed him?

HOLMES: Evidently.

WATSON: It's just not possible!

HOLMES: Not only is it possible, my dear Watson, it is indeed probable. Had you taken the time to observe, you would have seen the blood stain on Mrs. Hudson's dress as she was arrested.

WATSON: That could be anything.

HOLMES: And the note found clutched in Allard's hand with Mrs. Hudson's name scrawled upon it?

WATSON: Now how on earth did you know about that?

HOLMES: Scotland Yard needs to teach its officers not to boast about evidence to suspects.

WATSON: We have to help her!

HOLMES: "*We*" do not have to do anything, Watson. You are free to do as you wish. I shall be staying right here. I have vital research which requires my attentions.

WATSON: You can't be serious. This is a woman's life!

(PAUSE)

HOLMES: I suppose my experiments can wait a few hours. But no more than that.

WATSON: Then you'll accompany me to Scotland Yard?

HOLMES: Not yet, Watson. The scene of the crime first, I fancy. The trail is getting cold, while Mrs. Hudson isn't going anywhere.

WATSON: (NARRATING) And so we set out to the butcher's shop of Mr. Kenneth Allard, situated on a secluded street right around the corner from 221b. As we approached, we saw a familiar face standing guard at the shop's open door.

HOLMES: Gregson, my dear fellow. It's good to see you. We haven't run into you since that business over on Brixton Road.

GREGSON: Ah, it's you Mr. Holmes. I half wondered if you'd be turning up, what with your landlady being a suspect.

WATSON: Yes, she's already been taken to the Yard.

GREGSON: Has she now? That would be Lestrade's doing. Always rushing to conclusions, that one.

WATSON: Lestrade? It was Lestrade that had Mrs. Hudson arrested?

HOLMES: Now, now, Watson. Let us not jump to conclusions without all the facts. What happened here, Gregson?

GREGSON: See for yourself, Mr. Holmes.

WATSON: (NARRATING) Gregson ushered us inside the tiny shop, where the poor Mr. Allard lay slumped over his counter, a cleaver driven into the square of his back. The scent of blood hung heavier over that room than almost any other I can remember.

HOLMES: Has anything been touched?

GREGSON: I couldn't say, Mr. Holmes. I've been asked to guard the scene, and wasn't personally involved in the investigation. I'm just waiting for the medical examiner, but he's busy with an accident over near Piccadilly.

WATSON: Do you see something?

HOLMES: Difficult to say, Watson. A herd of buffalo could not have left more of a trail than the official force.

GREGSON: This was Lestrade's investigation, sir. It was his responsibility to preserve the scene.

HOLMES: Still, it is clear from what remains of the evidence that Mrs. Hudson is innocent. She could not have committed this crime.

WATSON: Holmes, that's marvelous!

GREGSON: Begging your pardon, Mr. Holmes, but what evidence has Lestrade overlooked?

HOLMES: Observe the proximity of the body to the wall. There is little space between the two, meaning that only one person could stand behind the counter at a time. A blow powerful enough to penetrate a man's back outright would require the killer to stretch his arm back – thus – and forward – thus – in a chopping motion. There is simply no room behind the counter to accommodate two people, victim and murderer, let alone allow for the swinging of a cleaver. It is physically impossible.

WATSON: Perhaps he was struck from behind elsewhere and staggered over to the counter before he died?

HOLMES: Now, now, Doctor. Remember your medical training. A blow such as this would sever the vertebral artery, causing considerable loss of blood.

WATSON: And yet, there is no corresponding blood pool beneath him! Yes, I see!

GREGSON: Likely this pool of blood here, Mr. Holmes, over by the front door.

HOLMES: Which means?

GREGSON: That his body was moved after he died.

HOLMES: Excellent, Gregson! There's hope for you yet. Our poor Mrs. Hudson just does not have the physical strength to move the remains of our Mr. Allard, whose weight I would estimate to be roughly two hundred and eleven pounds. No, make that two hundred and thirteen.

WATSON: It still doesn't exonerate her, though. There's still the matter of the fresh blood-stain on her dress, and the note with her name clasped in Mr. Allard's hand.

HOLMES: Yes, those facts are troubling. Is that the note on the counter?

GREGSON: I would assume so.

HOLMES: Mixed in among the other receipts. My, my. Lestrade was certainly in a hurry to make his arrest.

GREGSON: It's more than just that, gentlemen. Look at this calendar here behind the till. You'll note the name marked and circled on every Thursday.

WATSON: (READING) *"Martha Hudson"*. Good Lord!

HOLMES: Yes. Written by a right-handed man with a tendency to leave a tail on the letter *"o"*. Most distinctive.

GREGSON: It seems pretty clear that these two were on more than just casual terms.

HOLMES: Yes, no doubt you're right, Gregson. Where can we find Lestrade?

GREGSON: Well, if he's already arrested your Mrs. Hudson, then he'll have taken her to the Yard to process.

HOLMES: Then our next stop will be Scotland Yard. Come, Watson.

WATSON: (NARRATING) We emerged from the butcher's shop and out in the welcome fresh air. Holmes hailed a cab and we were finally on our way to the Yard. Twenty minutes later, we stood before the desk of Inspector Lestrade.

LESTRADE: You're wasting your time, Mr. Holmes. You may have gotten lucky on that Brixton Road business, but this time out we've got the murderer dead to rights. A witness saw Mrs. Hudson leave Allard's shop, and no one else entered before the body was discovered half-an-hour later.

HOLMES: Who am I to argue with the official force?

LESTRADE: Really. I thought for sure you were here to persuade me that Mrs. Hudson didn't kill her lover.

WATSON: Her lover? Who, Allard? Isn't that a bit presumptuous, Lestrade?

LESTRADE: Not at all, Doctor. We've got a witness.

HOLMES: Allard's widow.

LESTRADE: Now how the blazes did you know that?

HOLMES: I didn't, although it seemed probable. May I speak with her?

LESTRADE: Hmm. Well, I suppose I could do you a favor, Mr. Holmes, and show you how we do things in Scotland Yard. I was just beginning my interview with her when I was informed of your arrival. She's waiting for me in the interrogation room.

WATSON: (NARRATING) Lestrade ushered us into a small room, dimly lit. A lovely woman sat there, dabbing her eyes with her kerchief. My heart went out to her beauty.

LESTRADE: Now then, Mrs. Allard. Please continue your story.

ALLARD: Who are these men?

HOLMES: My name is Sherlock Holmes. This is my colleague, Doctor Watson.

WATSON: My deepest sympathies on your loss, madam.

ALLARD: Thank you, Doctor. You're most kind.

LESTRADE: Mr. Holmes and Doctor Watson have been of some minor assistance to the force in the past, madam. He's asked to sit in on your interview.

ALLARD: Fine, as long as we can get this over with quickly. I need time to mourn for my husband.

LESTRADE: Of course, madam. Of course. Now, you were about to tell me what you saw this morning.

ALLARD: Well, we live about the shop, Kenneth and me. Kenneth left to open the shop around half-past-seven this morning, and I set about tidying our place up a bit. It was a lovely day, so I left the window open, to air out the place, you know. That was how I come to see her entering the shop, just past nine.

LESTRADE: Martha Hudson.

ALLARD: That's her. 'Bout ten minutes later, I saw her leave. When no more customers showed, I thought I'd take Kenneth down a nice cup of tea. That's when I found . . . I found . . . (SHE BREAKS DOWN CRYING)

WATSON: There, there, my dear woman.

LESTRADE: Madam, if this is too difficult, we can wait until you've composed yourself . . . .

ALLARD: No, please, Inspector. Let's get this over. I need to be strong. For Kenneth.

LESTRADE: Tell us what you saw.

ALLARD: I saw him, my Kenneth, slumped over his counter, a cleaver in his back. And there, clutched bright as day in his hand, a note with her name on it. His killer!

HOLMES: Can you think of any reason that Mrs. Hudson would want to kill your husband?

ALLARD: I certainly can, Mr. Holmes. She fancied him! Most customers are in and out of Kenneth's shop. Not her. She'd always linger, chatting him up, batting her eyes at him. I seen her.

WATSON: But if that's true, why would she want to kill your husband?

ALLARD: Because I confronted him about it, that's why! Just last night! He promised me he'd talk to her, warn her off, and she killed him for it!

LESTRADE: There's your motive, Mr. Holmes.

HOLMES: You said no customers entered the shop after Mrs. Hudson. How can you be certain of that fact?

ALLARD: Kenneth kept a bell on the front door, and I'd hear it ring for every person that'd enter or leave the shop. That damn bell drives me crazy. Drove me crazy, I mean. (BEGINS TO CRY AGAIN, BUT KEEPS SPEAKING) When she left the shop, the bell rang, and I didn't hear it ring again until I found him. Oh, Kenneth!

LESTRADE: I think we've heard enough. Thank you, Mrs. Allard.

HOLMES: Just two more questions, if I may. You said your husband affixed a bell to the front door. Is there a back door as well?

ALLARD: Of course. But Kenneth keeps it locked at all times.

LESTRADE: We checked that, Mr. Holmes. Firmly fastened from the inside.

HOLMES: Very good, Lestrade. Just one last thing, then. I've inscribed a phrase from my favorite poet on this piece of paper. Could you read it to me, Mrs. Allard?

SOUND EFFECT: RUSTLING PAPER

ALLARD: I'm sorry, sir. I never did learn my letters. That was always more Kenneth's area.

HOLMES: I see. Then we shan't take up any more of your time.

WATSON: Again, you have our deepest sympathies.

LESTRADE: I expect you'll be wanting to see your Mrs. Hudson now, for all the good it'll do you. You'll find her in holding. Just tell the guard at holding you're there as my guest. He'll let

127

you through. Now come, Mrs. Allard. I'll see you out of the station.

ALLARD: Thank you, Doctor. Thank you, Inspector. Mr. Holmes.

WATSON: (NARRATING) Holmes and I made our way down a set of stairs, and before long we stood in front of a dingy cell. Mrs. Hudson sat behind the bars amidst a crowd of women. Upon spotting us, she rushed forward.

MRS. HUDSON: Mr. Holmes! Doctor Watson! Thank the Lord you're here!

WATSON: How are you holding up?

MRS. HUDSON: Oh, not well, Doctor. They think I killed him! They think I killed that poor sweet Mr. Allard!

WATSON: We all know that's not true.

MRS. HUDSON: Bless you for saying so, but I've heard the inspector's so-called "evidence". It really doesn't look good for me.

HOLMES: You shall be free by tomorrow evening . . .

MRS. HUDSON: Mr. Holmes!

HOLMES: . . . provided you can clear up one or two points. Let us begin with Mr. Allard. Were you romantically involved with him?

MRS. HUDSON: How dare you! How can you even ask me that question? I honor my husband's memory and will 'til I die!

HOLMES: It is the lynchpin of the evidence against you.

WATSON: Please, Mrs. Hudson. He's only trying to help.

(A SILENT MOMENT)

MRS. HUDSON: Mr. Allard and I were friends, nothing more, no matter what anyone might say.

HOLMES: By *"anyone"*, you are referring to his wife.

MRS. HUDSON: I'm not one to gossip, but there was trouble in that marriage. Mr. Allard didn't say as much, but a woman knows.

HOLMES: I see. And the blood on your dress? How did that come about?

MRS. HUDSON: Oh, that. It's the new girl I hired, that Mrs. Turner. She was carrying a bowl for the blood-pudding and tripped. Spilled all over both me and the carpet, she did. Honestly, I don't know where that girl's head is.

HOLMES: And why did you not wash the blood off your clothing?

MRS. HUDSON: Priorities, Mr. Holmes! I could wash my dress or I could wash the carpet. My clothes I can replace, but that carpet was my mother's! I was just finishing scrubbing it down when the inspector knocked on the door.

HOLMES: Very good. Thank you, Mrs. Hudson. Now, come, Watson. My experiments have been neglected for long enough.

MRS. HUDSON: But Mr. Holmes! What you said, about my being free by tomorrow evening? Did you really mean that?

HOLMES: My good woman, I am a man of my word. I shall expect supper on my table by seven.

WATSON: (NARRATING) We made our way back to Baker Street, where Holmes's chemical experiment had congealed into a bold shade of purple.

HOLMES: Ah, excellent! Success, Watson! Success!

WATSON: If you say so.

HOLMES: This is a further refinement of my experiment at Barts, an effort to differentiate the blood of humans from the blood of animals.

WATSON: Holmes, I'm sure it's a marvel of science, but what about Mrs. Hudson? However will you prove her innocent by tomorrow?

HOLMES: Tomorrow evening, Watson. Let us not rush things.

WATSON: But the only other suspect is his wife, and the same evidence which exonerates Mrs. Hudson rules her out as well! If the body really was moved . . . .

HOLMES: Which it was.

WATSON: All right, but Mrs. Allard is even more frail that Mrs. Hudson! There's no possible way she could have moved her husband's body onto the counter!

HOLMES: Excellent, Watson! Really, you excel.

WATSON: Then the killer of Mr. Allard is still at large.

HOLMES: Precisely. Which is why I shall now be leaving. There is still work to be done to tie the threads of this case together. Please be here at quarter-to-ten tomorrow morning, and don't be surprised if Inspector Gregson is here as well. Oh, and Watson?

WATSON: Yes, Holmes?

HOLMES: Make sure to have your revolver ready.

SOUND EFFECT: A DOOR SHUTS

WATSON: (NARRATING) And with that he was off, dashing down the seventeen steps and out onto the cobbles of Baker Street.

MUSIC: STING

WATSON: (NARRATING) Holmes did not return that night, nor had his bed been slept in the next morning when I arose. Mrs.

Turner brought me a tolerable breakfast, although it was not up to Mrs. Hudson's excellent standards. I wondered how Holmes intended to prove Mrs. Hudson's innocence. His deductions at the crime-scene all seemed true enough, but those same deductions exonerated the only other suspect in the case. Without another neck to hang the noose around, Mrs. Hudson would almost certainly stand trial for Mr. Allard's murder. Around twenty-to-ten, the bell rang and Mrs. Turner showed Inspector Gregson up into our flat.

WATSON: Ah, Gregson. Good to see you.

GREGSON: And you, Doctor. Is your Mr. Holmes about?

HOLMES: I haven't seen him yet this morning, although he told me to be here by quarter-to-ten.

GREGSON: He told me much the same. Do you have any idea what this is about?

WATSON: Not really, except that it's almost certainly connected to that Allard business.

SOUND EFFECT: BELL RINGING

WATSON: Ah, that will be Holmes now.

SOUND EFFECT: DOOR OPENING

HOLMES: Ah, you're both here. Excellent. Now, listen to me carefully. We have little time to prepare. Watson, I need you to conceal yourself by the front door. Gregson, kindly hide in the other room, but be sure to leave the door open! I may need you at a moment's notice.

SOUND EFFECT: BELL RINGING

HOLMES: Dang and blast, he's here early! Quickly, gentlemen! Quickly!

SOUND EFFECT: SCUFFLING FEET. FEET ON STAIRS. DOOR OPENING

131

HOLMES: Yes?

PEARLMAN: Are you Mr. Holmes?

HOLMES: I am.

PEARLMAN: I'm here about the position. My name is Stephen Pearlman, and I was told to apply in person at this address.

HOLMES: Quite right. Come in, sir. Come in.

PEARLMAN: I hope I'm not here too early.

HOLMES: Not at all, not all. I like a man who doesn't make me wait. If I like your penmanship, the job's as good as yours.

PEARLMAN: Penmanship, sir?

HOLMES: Certainly. I can't hire you as my bookkeeper without a good look at the ledger you keep, now can I? There's a quill and paper at the desk. If you would transcribe this sentence please, we'll see if you meet my qualifications.

PEARLMAN: (READING) *"Thus my hands did roam."* Is this poetry, sir?

HOLMES: A favorite quote of mine. If you please, Mr. Pearlman. Sit down.

SOUND EFFECT: A CHAIR BEING DRAGGED ACROSS THE FLOOR

HOLMES: You'll find the inkwell to your left.

PEARLMAN: I'm right-handed, sir.

HOLMES: Oh dear, how silly of me! There you are, your inkwell in easy reach. Now please, dip you pen, and . . . .

SOUND EFFECT: PEN SCRATCHING ON PAPER

PEARLMAN: Is that satisfactory, sir?

HOLMES: Most satisfactory. Gregson, if you please?

GREGSON: Mr. Stephen Pearlman . . .

PEARLMAN: (YELLING) What is this?

GREGSON: . . . I arrest you in the name of Queen Victoria!

<u>SOUND EFFECT: SCUFFLE</u>

HOLMES: Watson! He's making a break for it!

WATSON: Stop right there! I assure you, sir, this revolver is armed, and I am an expert shot.

PEARLMAN: Yes. Yes, I believe you are. Very well, gentlemen. I shall come quietly.

HOLMES: Take him down to the Yard, will you, Gregson? Watson and I will tidy up here and join you shortly.

GREGSON: And what shall I charge him with, Mr. Holmes?

HOLMES: Why, with the murder of Kenneth Allard, of course! And while you're at it, you might want to pick up his widow as well. She was Mr. Pearlman's accomplice.

PEARLMAN: No. No, it was all me! Alice had nothing to do with it!

HOLMES: Sir, the game is finished. I know everything. How else do you think I was able to trap you?

GREGSON: Come along, you.

<u>SOUND EFFECT: DOOR OPENING</u>

HOLMES: Well, Watson. All in all a satisfying conclusion. Gregson and I shall have words with Lestrade and Mrs. Hudson will be home by supper as promised.

WATSON: Holmes, you never cease to amaze. However did you find Stephen Pearlman?

HOLMES: Patience, Watson. Let us begin at the beginning of the chain rather than its end. I admit that the circumstantial evidence against Mrs. Hudson did steer me toward a hasty conclusion, something I shall have to avoid in the future. The blood on her dress combined with the note in the dead-man's had did paint a powerful picture, exactly as it had been designed to do. We were meant to think that Mr. Allard, in the last seconds of his life, scrawled the name of his murderer on a scrap of paper before expiring. That much might be plausible. But couple that with the image of that same murderer walking calmly down Baker Street, covered in blood, and failing to change her clothing in the hour or so before she is arrested. Well. You begin to see where this line of reasoning falls apart.

WATSON: But Holmes, the blood came from Mrs. Turner! There's no way the murder, or murderers, could have known about that.

HOLMES: An accident, then, but one which both Scotland Yard and I foolishly latched onto. Need we dwell upon my faults, or may I continue?

WATSON: No, no. Continue, by all means.

HOLMES: The vital clue was the note, of course, or more specifically the writing upon it. One only had to look at the receipts by the till to see that they had been written in a different hand. If we assume the receipts were written by Mr. Allard himself, then it must have been someone else that wrote the note naming Mrs. Hudson.

WATSON: Ah, I see! That's why you asked Mr. Pearlman to transcribe the poetry! You wanted to see a sample of his handwriting to see if it matched the note! But why that phrase . . . . What was it again?

HOLMES: *"Thus my hands did roam"*. An anagram, Watson. Remove the words *"my"* and *"did"* and we are left with *"thus hands roam"*. Rearrange the letters and you have . . . .

134

WATSON: "*Martha Hudson*"! Of course!

HOLMES: Precisely.

WATSON: So Mr. Pearlman killed Mr. Allard and scrawled the name Martha Hudson on the receipt, placing it in Allard's hand to implicate her.

HOLMES: The calendar as well. The handwriting on both is a perfect match.

WATSON: But why? And how did you come to find Mr. Pearlman?

HOLMES: We'll come to the "why" presently, but let us now consider our interview with Mrs. Allard. From that I gleaned two vital pieces of information. The first was that Mrs. Allard was clearly lying about how she discovered her husband's body. Surely you can see the flaw in her story, Watson?

WATSON: Her story did sound a bit odd, but I'm afraid I don't see the clue.

HOLMES: The bell, Watson! The bell! Remember how Mrs. Allard insisted that Mrs. Hudson had been the last person to enter the shop as the bell had not rung since her departure? Yet when we arrived the door was propped open!

WATSON: I assumed that Scotland Yard had propped it open during their investigation.

HOLMES: Yet the pool of blood found by the door was undisturbed. Conclusion? The door was propped open *before* Mr. Allard was killed, not *after*. This makes his wife's story impossible. Clearly she was lying, which implied she knew the truth about her husband's death. Still, she could not be the murderer herself, as she could not have moved Mr. Allard's body. Couple this with the second piece of information, that Mrs. Allard was not capable of writing the note herself, and we are left with the inescapable conclusion that another must have been involved.

WATSON: Good Lord!

HOLMES: The murderers went one step further, though. Seeking to supply a motive, they also inscribed Mrs. Hudson's name on the calendar, implying more than a professional relationship between herself and Mr. Allard.

WATSON: An implication further confirmed by Mr. Allard's widow.

HOLMES: It was Mrs. Hudson herself who suggested the final piece of the puzzle. She said 'I'm not one to gossip,' which gave me an idea. It was to that end that I disguised myself and went down to the local Baker Street pubs to obtain some information.

WATSON: To get some local gossip, as it were.

HOLMES: There were rumors about Mrs. Hudson and Kent Allard – that much Lestrade had right. But I also inquired about Mr. Allard and his wife, and was none too surprised to hear that the two had been squabbling for months. Mrs. Allard had even been seen out and about accompanied by a young gentleman. The rumor was that Mr. Allard was none too pleased.

WATSON: I should say not!

HOLMES: I hit several pubs, but at my third I had a stroke of luck. Who should I find drinking but Mrs. Allard herself!

WATSON: Did she recognize you?

HOLMES: Perhaps had she been sober, but after three pints of bitters? I should say not. Besides, I flatter myself that even you might not recognize me in my workman's disguise.

WATSON: Now, really.

HOLMES: I struck up a conversation, and mentioned I was looking for a young man to maintain my books. I implied that I was desperate, and would pay twice the going rate for a qualified applicant. I told her that I'd be holding interviews at 221b the following morning at ten o'clock, and that if she knew anyone who might be interested, they should apply in person at this very address.

WATSON: Do you mean to say that the young man seen accompanying Mrs. Allard was Stephen Pearlman?

HOLMES: None other. With Mr. Allard out of the way, there was nothing to prevent their romance and eventual marriage. Mrs. Allard had been feeding the rumor mills around the neighborhood for months about her husband's interest in Mrs. Hudson. Once they felt that seed of doubt had been well planted in the neighborhood, it was only a matter of time before she could convince Pearlman to remove his rival for her affections.

WATSON: By Jove! That's positively cold-blooded!

HOLMES: Indeed.

WATSON: Well, Holmes, it seems you've wrapped it up rather nicely.

HOLMES: Thank you, Watson.

WATSON: But there is one point. How did you know that Stephen Pearlman was a bookkeeper?

HOLMES: Every profession has its unique qualities, Watson, and book-keeping is no exception. A bookkeeper's obsession with numbers tends to affect the way they write their prose. Take note of the way in which Mr. Pearlman forms the letter 'o' in Mrs. Hudson's name. Do you see the tail attached to the character? That is most commonly seen in a bookkeeper's ledger. It seemed entirely probable that the murderer of Kenneth Allard was a bookkeeper by trade. And a right-handed one at that.

WATSON: So you invented this fake job interview to lure the man here.

HOLMES: And told the one person I was sure had a motive in Kent Allard's death. The rest was just a matter of waiting for my prey to enter my trap.

WATSON: (NARRATING) After a visit to Scotland Yard, and a talk with a very frustrated Inspector Lestrade, Holmes and Gregson were able to secure Mrs. Hudson's release. Stephen Pearlman and Alice Allard were both arrested and charged with Kenneth Allard's murder. That night, Holmes and I sat down to a fantastic meal prepared by a very relieved Mrs. Hudson.

SOUND EFFECT: CLINKING SILVERWARE

WATSON: Mrs. Hudson, you've outdone yourself.

MRS. HUDSON: Thank you, Doctor. It isn't every day a woman gets out of prison, you know. Seemed a good a night as any to celebrate. Mr. Holmes, I just wanted to say thank you. You've not been the easiest tenant, 'tis true, but I'd not be a free woman tonight if it wasn't for you.

HOLMES: Well. Speak no more of it. Let us enjoy this feast, and look forward to many more in Baker Street.

WATSON: (NARRATING) And we did. Things were never the same between Holmes and Mrs. Hudson. Holmes continued his eccentric habits, and Mrs. Hudson continued to scold him, but there was always an understanding between them from that day forward, an understanding which continued long after Holmes left Baker Street for the Sussex Downs.

MUSIC: *DANSE MACABRE* (UP AND UNDER)

WATSON: This is Dr. John H. Watson. I've had many more adventures with Sherlock Holmes, and I'll tell you another one . . . *when next we meet!*

MUSIC: (FADE OUT)

The Tollington Ghost
by Roger Silverwood

CHARACTERS

- SHERLOCK HOLMES
- DR. JOHN H. WATSON
- INSPECTOR LESTRADE
- CABBIE
- CRAMPHORN – *Butler to Lord Tollington*
- LORD TOLLINGTON – *In his sixties or older. Posh, very English*
- CURATE – *Thirties, gentleman, quietly spoken*
- JOSIAH DEEP – *Undertaker, broad Scotsman*

SOUND EFFECT: OPENING SEQUENCE, BIG BEN

ANNOUNCER: *The Further Adventures of Sherlock Holmes*, starring John Patrick Lowrie as Sherlock Holmes, and Lawrence Albert as Dr. John H. Watson.

MUSIC: *DANSE MACABRE* (UP AND UNDER)

WATSON: (NARRATING) My name is Doctor John H. Watson, and it was my privilege to share in the adventures of Sherlock Holmes. It was just after Christmas in 1899 that we were summoned to Carlisle, to Tollington Hall, by our old ally and occasional adversary, Inspector Lestrade. In his telegram, he stated that he'd appreciate our assistance with a most unusual case that was baffling the local police. Scotland Yard had been called in to investigate the death of a guest of Lord Tollington. It mentioned that a dead body had vanished from a locked room. We arrived late in the afternoon, absolutely chilled to the bone.

MUSIC: (FADE OUT)

LESTRADE: Ah, there you are, Mr. Holmes. So good of you to come. And you Doctor Watson.

WATSON: Lestrade.

HOLMES: Yes, Inspector. Now, what is it that makes you need my services so urgently this stark winter's day in the middle of nowhere?

LESTRADE: What I have to tell, Mr. Holmes, is impossible! I must say, I can't make head nor tails of it.

HOLMES: Please try, for all our sakes.

LESTRADE: Well, yes. The facts unfold like this: For his entertainment, Lord Tollington had a houseful of guests over Christmas, and during the jollifications, there was talk about the ghost that haunts the house. You will have heard of it – the Tollington Ghost, probably the most famous ghost in the world.

HOLMES: My agency is founded upon rationality, Lestrade.

WATSON: I wouldn't be so dismissive, Holmes. I've heard of it. It is well documented.

HOLMES: Remember my motto, Watson: *"No ghosts need apply at 221b."* Please continue, Lestrade.

LESTRADE: Well, for a bet, a man well known for his outrageous eccentricities, Wellington Pinchbeck by name, declared that he didn't believe that ghosts existed, and that to prove it, he bet his Lordship a hundred guineas that, not only would he spend the night in the room where the ghost was supposed to appear, but that, if he could find a corpse, any corpse, he would do it in company with a corpse in an open coffin.

WATSON: Good Lord!

LESTRADE: Mr. Pinchbeck was quite a one for his outrageous eccentricities. I had known him slightly. I've been in his company several times at the giant August Bank Holiday parties for police orphans he used to support in Hyde Park these past few years.

HOLMES: From your use of the past tense, I take it all did not end well for Mr. Pinchbeck. Please go on, Inspector. You have my full attention.

LESTRADE: Well, by a private arrangement with the local undertaker, the body of a vagrant, who was to have been buried the following day, was delivered into the room in a coffin. Then Wellington Pinchbeck, apparently to much hilarity, was locked in the room at ten o'clock that night. Some of the guests took it in turns to stay outside the room and make sure he didn't attempt to pick the lock or find any other way of escape. Then at nine o'clock the following morning, his Lordship, the undertaker, and his Lordship's butler, unlocked the room in company with many of the guests to discover that the corpse of the vagrant had disappeared, and in the coffin in its place was the dead body of Wellington Pinchbeck.

WATSON: How grotesque!

HOLMES: Well, our first step is clear: We must see the room, Lestrade.

LESTRADE: Indeed. His Lordship has given me possession of the key. Please follow me, gentlemen.

SOUND EFFECT: KEY INSERTED IN LOCK, TURNED IN LOCK. HEAVY DOOR SOUEAKING OPEN. SEVERAL ECHOING FOOTSTEPS. (DIAGLOGUE ECHOES THROUGHOUT SCENE)

LESTRADE: Here we are. As you can see, a big room, but with only the one door and the one window.

WATSON: Mm. And not much in the way of comfort.

LESTRADE: No. Just a make-shift bed, a chair, a table, and two trestles on which the coffin rested. You'll note, gentlemen, that the trestles were positioned next to the bed. A great joker was Wellington Pinchbeck!

WATSON: A damned fool, if you ask me. What are all those huge stone statues all the way round the room?

142

LESTRADE: Figures of all the previous Lord Tollingtons. The present holder of the title is the thirteenth.

WATSON: Huh! Thirteenth! An ominous number.

HOLMES: Only to the superstitious, Watson, and I credit you with more sense than that. Who made the discovery in the morning?

LESTRADE: First at the door were Lord Tollington, the butler, Cramphorn – an entirely dependable man, if you ask me – and the undertaker, Josiah Deep. But they were also in company with many of the other guests. Cramphorn had a breakfast tray for Mr. Pinchbeck, and was prepared to assist Josiah Deep to remove the coffin containing the vagrant to the hearse, which was waiting to go straight to the church for the funeral.

HOLMES: I see. They searched this room, of course.

WATSON: It doesn't appear that there's anywhere to search.

HOLMES: In time, Doctor, in time. The search, Lestrade?

LESTRADE: They found nothing. They reported the situation to his Lordship, who summoned the Carlisle police. They came immediately, but found . . . nothing.

HOLMES: Has the vagrant's body turned up anywhere?

LESTRADE: No. That's the mystery. That, and who killed Wellington Pinchbeck. And why.

WATSON: And how.

HOLMES: Mm. And where is the body of Wellington Pinchbeck now?

LESTRADE: In Josiah Deep's funeral parlour.

WATSON: I don't mean to complain, Holmes, but it's freezing in here.

HOLMES: Indeed it is. We need dally here no longer. We must visit Josiah Deep's funeral parlour immediately.

(DIALOGUE ECHO ENDS)

MUSIC: SHORT BRIDGE. DISSOLVE INTO . . . .

SOUND EFFECT: CARRIAGE ROLLING ALONG AND TROTTING HORSES. GENTLE BREEZE BLOWING

CABBIE: (AWAY FROM MIKE) Whoa there! Whoa there! Steady there.

SOUND EFFECT: CARRIAGE AND HORSES STOP

CABBIE: Here we are, gentlemen. Josiah Deep's funeral parlour.

WATSON: I say, Holmes, look at that. (READS) *"Josiah Deep and Son. Funeral Parlour, Coffin Maker, To the Gentry"*.

LESTRADE: Thank you, cabbie. Wait for us here.

SOUND EFFECT: CARRIAGE DOOR CLOSES

CABBIE: Right, sir.

WATSON: (CHUCKLING) Coffin maker to the gentry? Hmm.

HOLMES: Come along, Watson.

LESTRADE: Somebody is just coming out through the door.

SOUND EFFECT: DOOR CLOSING

LESTRADE: I wonder if that's Josiah Deep?

SOUND EFFECT: FOOTSTEPS ON GRAVEL

HOLMES: His dress would seem to discount that possibility, Lestrade. He appears to be a man of the cloth.

WATSON: Good evening, sir.

144

SOUND EFFECT: FOOTSTEPS ON GRAVEL STOP

CURATE: Oh. Good evening, gentlemen.

HOLMES: Good evening, Rector.

CURATE: Not yet "Rector". Just a humble Curate, I fear, in the service of the Lord. Excuse me, gentlemen. I have not seen you round these parts. Have you recently moved here? Should I be calling on you and welcoming you and your families to the parish of Little Tollington, and hopefully counting you among my congregation at the church of Saint Peter?

HOLMES: I think not, Curate. But thank you. We are guests of Lord Tollington and staying a day or two at Tollington Hall.

CURATE: Oh? Ah yes. You must be the policemen investigating the death of Mr. Wellington Pinchbeck. Strange business. My name is Striker. I wonder if you could help me? I am trying to construct an appropriate service of burial for the poor man. I have chosen the *Psalms* . . . the Twenty-third . . . "*The Lord is my Shepherd, I shall not want*" is always appropriate, and perhaps the Hundred-and-fifty-forth . . . "*Let him come with cymbal, drum, and fife*". Hymns are easier to choose. I let Mr. Moffatt, the organist, have the last word there. But mourners will expect a homily . . . and I don't know the first thing about the poor man . . .

HOLMES: I should speak with Lord Tollington. What he doesn't know about Wellington Pinchbeck, I'm sure he would be able to find out from Pinchbeck's acquaintances.

CURATE: A good idea, Mr. Holmes. I will contact him forthwith. Thank you.

HOLMES: Please excuse us. We must press on.

CURATE: Delighted to have met you, gentlemen. Goodnight.

WATSON: Goodnight.

LESTRADE: Goodnight.

SOUND EFFECT: FOOTSTEPS ON GRAVEL. KNOCKING ON DOOR

LESTRADE: Let's hope Josiah Deep hasn't retired to bed.

HOLMES: Funeral Directors are expected to keep odd hours – People often choose the most inconvenient time at to die.

WATSON: That is so.

SOUND EFFECT: DOOR OPENS

DEEP: Ah! Josiah Deep at your service, gentlemen. What can I do for you? (MOURNFULLY) Are you looking for a coffin? Have you need for a funeral? (TRAGICALLY) I am very sorry about your sad loss.

LESTRADE: I am Inspector Lestrade from Scotland Yard, and this is Sherlock Holmes and this is Doctor Watson.

DEEP: Not *the* Sherlock Holmes.

WATSON: The very one.

HOLMES: And *the* Doctor Watson.

WATSON: Thank you, Holmes.

DEEP: Very pleased to meet you, gentlemen. Come in. Come in.

SOUND EFFECT: DOOR CLOSES. CUT GENTLE BREEZE

HOLMES: Thank you.

WATSON: Hmm. (ASIDE) It's very dark in here.

HOLMES: Mr. Deep, I understand that you delivered a corpse to Tollington Hall for an overnight stay, intending to collect it the following morning.

DEEP: That is correct. It's not against the law, is it? He was a vagrant. He was to have been buried by the Parish. It was a charity case. The cost would have been borne by the ratepayers of Lower Tollington if Lord Tollington had not offered — out of the goodness of his heart — to pay for a brand new shroud, a second hand coffin with four new brass handles with sixteen screws, a sprig of holly, the hire of two horses with refluffed plumes, and the hire and washing and polishing and use of my brand new glass-sided hearse, recently imported from Bohemia.

LESTRADE: Losing a body is a serious offence.

DEEP: With respect, Inspector, I didn't lose him. You must talk to his Lordship about that.

HOLMES: Where is the body of the poor chap now?

DEEP: I don't know. Nobody knows. It's the biggest mystery since Jack the Ripper and the Whitechapel Murders. All I know is I delivered the body in a pine coffin to Tollington Hall at nine o'clock that evening, and when I came the following morning, prepared to take the vagrant straight to the Church for the Curate to bury him, the body in the coffin was not him at all, but that of the gentleman, Wellington Pinchbeck.

HOLMES: Well, where are the last remains of Wellington Pinchbeck now?

DEEP: Standing behind you.

WATSON: (ALARMED) What? Standing!

DEEP: In that pine coffin leaning against the wall. It's one of our finest caskets. The fine inlaid gold lettering in copper-plate on the lid was done by my own fair hand. Aye.

LESTRADE: (READING) *"Wellington Pinchbeck, 1842 TO 1899. R.I.P."*

DEEP: It's a work of art, isn't it?

HOLMES: Mr. Deep, I would like to see the corpse.

147

DEEP: Of course, of course.

HOLMES: Thank you.

DEEP: I'll take the lid off. He looks quite respectable now.

SOUND EFFECT: LID OF COFFIN LIFTED OFF

DEEP: Look ye. I'll bring a candle over. What do you think?

WATSON: (GASPS – AMAZED) I say, Holmes.

LESTRADE: (AMAZED) Good gracious.

DEEP: I can remove the pennies now.

SOUND EFFECT: TWO COINS RATTLE TOGETHER AND DROP IN POCKET

DEEP: There. Yes. (CLOSE TO MICROPHONE) You see, how I've filled out his cheeks with sawdust . . . and it's amazing what you can do with a little cochineal, isn't it? . . . A bit of soot . . . and talcum powder and starch . . . I believe I have made him look more human than he did in real life. Yes?

LESTRADE: (SHUDDERS ASIDE) I've seen better in "The Chamber of Honors".

HOLMES: Lestrade, you knew Wellington Pinchbeck? Would you say that that is his body?

LESTRADE: Oh yes. Without doubt, Mr. Holmes. Without any doubt at all. That's Wellington Pinchbeck, all right.

HOLMES: Mr. Deep, do you have the death certificate.

DEEP: Indeed I do. It's here.

HOLMES: Would you please be good enough to let Doctor Watson peruse it.

DEEP: Of course, of course.

WATSON: Thank you.

HOLMES: What does it say, Watson?

WATSON: Mm. Wellington Pinchbeck . . . December 28th, 1899. Heart failure . . . pneumonia . . . Hmm. Signed by Septimus Flynn, D.M., Dublin-London Road, Carlisle.

HOLMES: Are you satisfied, Watson?

WATSON: It looks all right to me, Holmes.

HOLMES: Well, what would cause heart failure?

WATSON: If he already had a weak heart, almost anything. I'm not surprised he caught pneumonia. These last few nights, it would be well below freezing in that room without heating at night.

HOLMES: Are you saying he died of natural causes?

WATSON: I'm saying it's *possible*, Holmes. *Only possible*.

HOLMES: Very well. If it *were* so, who removed the vagrant's body from the coffin?

WATSON: Good question.

HOLMES: In the middle of the night, did the dead vagrant obligingly remove himself from it and assist Pinchbeck to take his place? And then disappear into thin air? I think not.

MUSIC: UNDERCURRENT

WATSON: (NARRATING) We left Josiah Deep and took the cab back to Tollington Hall. I was tired, cold, and hungry. Holmes was irritable. He was always like that when he had a difficult case to deal with. He enjoyed the challenge, but he could be somewhat tetchy when he was making no progress. For me, I

149

couldn't make any sense of the case at all. Lestrade introduced us to Lord Tollington, then took his leave, as he had been called back to London on some other urgent police business. Lord Tollington was very kindly providing us with rooms in Tollington Hall, and what was even more welcome, he had invited Holmes and me to have dinner with him. We were enjoying the most delightful roast pheasant, with parsnips . . . .

MUSIC: OUT

TOLLINGTON: . . . You are both most welcome. I have your company to enjoy, and if you can solve the mystery, and find the murderer, Mr. Holmes, I shall be obligated to you.

HOLMES: You are most kind, Lord Tollington.

TOLLINGTON: (CALLING) Cramphorn!

CRAMPHORN: (AWAY FROM MICROPHONE) Yes, my Lord?

TOLLINGTON: A bottle of the '84.

CRAMPHORN: Very good, my Lord.

TOLLINGTON: Better put two more on ice. We must not stint our guests.

CRAMPHORN: Yes, my Lord.

WATSON: This is a grand meal, your Lordship. I give you thanks.

TOLLINGTON: My pleasure, Doctor.

HOLMES: Watson has been telling me about the Tollington Ghost. How long have you been aware of its presence?

TOLLINGTON: It's always been here. Even before I was born . . . my father spoke of it . . . .

HOLMES: And how and where does it manifest itself?

TOLLINGTON: It appears from the porter's pantry by the front door. That's why we always keep the room locked. I don't know if you can stop a ghost by locking a door, but anyway . . . It is the ghost of a Scottish piper, a friend of the Fourth Lord, who was passing through Carlisle on his way to Glasgow and was invited to stay the night. However, during the early hours, the night porter caught the man searching through his belongings in the pantry. Assuming he was an intruder, he hit him on the head with a lantern stand. The blow killed the soldier, and it subsequently turned out he was searching through his own trunk, looking possibly for some clothes, his bagpipes, or some whisky, for that's all there was in there. I've never seen the ghost, myself, but I have seen things move in response to its antics. I've heard it traversing the hall, and I have heard the pipes. You can sometimes, most unexpectedly, hear them played in the grounds, from the island in the loch, or even further away than that.

HOLMES: Most interesting, your Lordship.

TOLLINGTON: Ah good. Cramphorn's back – at last.

SOUND EFFECT: CORK POPS FROM A BOTTLE

WATSON: (BRIGHTLY) Oh, champagne. Our meals at Baker Street aren't quite as grand as this, eh Holmes?

HOLMES: Quite. Tell me, was this – er – Wellington Pinchbeck a friend of yours?

TOLLINGTON: I didn't know him very well, but I had heard he was excellent company, so I invited him to lighten our Christmas and entertain us, as we hoped to entertain each other. I didn't expect him to make a silly wager – which I couldn't get out of – that he would spend the night in the porter's pantry like that.

SOUND EFFECT: CHAMPAGNE POURED

WATSON: For a hundred guineas, your Lordship?

TOLLINGTON: That's right, Doctor.

CRAMPHORN: Champagne, my Lord?

TOLLINGTON: Yes, Cramphorn. . . . Mr. Holmes?

HOLMES: Thank you. And what can you tell us about the poor vagrant, whose remains have so mysteriously vanished.

CRAMPHORN: Sir?

WATSON Yes. Thank you, Cramphorn.

WATSON: (DRINKS) Ah. The '84. Unmistakable.

TOLLINGTON: Nothing, Mr. Holmes. Absolutely nothing. Josiah Deep was given the task of providing Wellington Pinchbeck with a corpse, and that he did. I saw the remains of the poor man in the coffin in a shroud, on its arrival at about nine o'clock that night. I have not seen anything of the corpse since.

HOLMES: Nor has anybody else. When I have finished this entirely delightful repast, your Lordship, I will retire to the porter's pantry. I will lock myself in, and I will take my pipe. I will need to beg a full box of matches from you, Watson.

WATSON: (ALARMED) Oh, no, Holmes. No.

TOLLINGTON: I would strongly advise against it, Mr. Holmes . . . considering what happened to Wellington Pinchbeck.

WATSON: You don't know what to expect. It could be very dangerous.

HOLMES: Dangerous or not, it will have to be done if we are to make any progress at all in solving this mystery.

MUSIC: UNDERCURRENT

WATSON: (NARRATING) Well, of course, despite my objections, Holmes got his own way. I was mightily apprehensive about the whole business . . . spending the night or even part of the night in that cold, inhospitable chamber on his own. I offered to join him, but he wouldn't hear of it. He went in with his pipe, tobacco pouch, and a full box of matches, just before midnight. I couldn't leave him and retire to my bed. Cramphorn furnished me with a blanket, a storm lantern, and a glass of port. Though very tired, I settled down in the hall porter's chair facing the door. I was very apprehensive, but I was warm and tolerably comfortable. I was determined to be on hand in case he required assistance. I was as prepared, as much as I could be, should the Tollington Ghost decide to show itself.

MUSIC: OUT

SOUND EFFECT: FADE UP CLOCK TICKING SLOWLY (HEAVY BREATHING, CLOSE TO MICROPHONE, THEN SNORING)

CRAMPHORN: (GENTLY) Now then, sir. Are you all right?

WATSON: (WAKING) Eh? What's this?

CRAMPHORN: Good morning, sir. I've brought you a pot of tea.

SOUND EFFECT: FADE OUT CLOCK TICKING SLOWLY

WATSON: (YAWNING) What? Who are you?

CRAMPHORN: Cramphorn, sir.

WATSON: Yes, of course. Cramphorn. What am I doing here?

CRAMPHORN: I've brought you a pot of tea, sir. It's eight o'clock. I thought you'd want to be wakened.

WATSON: Oh yes. Thank you. (REALIZING) Eight o'clock! Oh, my goodness! Where's Mr. Holmes?

CRAMPHORN: Haven't seen him this morning, sir.

WATSON: (HORRIFIED) Oh my goodness, he's . . . he must still be in there.

CRAMPHORN: Where, sir?

WATSON: In there . . . the porter's pantry. I must go in. Holmes said he only intended being in there for a couple of hours or so. Bring that lantern, will you.

CRAMPHORN: (NERVOUSLY) Oh, I don't think we should go in there, sir. It's still dark.

WATSON: (IMPATIENTLY) Oh, really . . . .

CRAMPHORN: (TENTATIVELY) Well, erm . . . Right. I'll follow you, sir.

WATSON: Hmm. The key's in the lock, Cramphorn. That's strange.

CRAMPHORN: I'm right behind you, sir.

SOUND EFFECT: KEY IS TURNED IN LOCK.

WATSON: It was locked? Who could have locked Holmes inside? I've been out here all night.

CRAMPHORN: (NERVOUSLY) You must have slept through it, sir.

WATSON: But Holmes had the key . . . took it in with him . . . so who?

SOUND EFFECT: HEAVY DOOR SQUEAKING OPEN.

WATSON: I only hope he's all right. (ECHOING) (CALLING) Holmes! (HAPPILY) Holmes, you old scallywag, you've had me worried. Where on earth have you been?

HOLMES: Where every sober and intelligent Englishman should be, of course, when the sun is set: In bed.

WATSON: Lucky you. I waited for you and . . . .

HOLMES: Yes, but when I came out of the porter's pantry, you were propped up in the chair fast asleep and you looked far too comfortable to disturb. So I bid you a passing goodnight and went up to my room.

WATSON: I never heard a thing. What time was that, pray?

HOLMES: It was eight minutes past two.

WATSON: So you were in there for over two hours. Did you see the ghost? Was there an appearance?

HOLMES: I did not. I experienced nothing ethereal whatsoever.

WATSON: (DISAPPOINTED) Oh. Well, did you discover anything?

HOLMES: I did, my dear friend. I did indeed.

WATSON: (BRIGHTLY) You found out *where* the dead body was hidden, and *who* dressed Wellington Pinchbeck in a shroud and put him in the coffin?

HOLMES: No. I did not discover how that came about.

WATSON: Well come along, Holmes. Don't tease me so. What did you find out?

HOLMES: I went to look for a concealed cavity, nook, room, or passageway, or any place where a body could have been hidden or removed.

WATSON: (EAGERLY) Ah. Yes.

HOLMES: Yes, Watson. I knew that the temperature in such a secret place, if one existed, would inevitably be different and would have caused a flow of air . . . even though it might have been very slight. With smoke from my pipe, I checked on all the seams and joints in the panelling, the floor, and the decor of the room . . .

155

WATSON: (ENTHUSIASTICALLY) Yes? Yes?

HOLMES: . . . and I can say, categorically, that there are positively no secret places where a body could have been concealed or transported.

WATSON: (DISAPPOINTED) Oh. Really! Ah. The window? Access must have been made via the window?

HOLMES: I'll wager that window has not been opened since Queen Victoria visited the Hall in 1849.

WATSON: (DISAPPOINTED) So what do you deduce from all that?

HOLMES: It's obvious. We have been misled.

WATSON: Misled by whom?

HOLMES: Of that, I am still in doubt. But the certainty that a body was not hidden or traversed through concealed places raises other trains of thought. I have two questions I must put to Lord Tollington. Come, let us find him . . . .

MUSIC: BRIDGE

TOLLINGTON: . . . Ask me anything at all, Mr. Holmes. I am just as anxious as the police to find out the truth.

HOLMES: Well, my Lord, I cannot help but wonder what happened to your last valet. I trust he must have left your employ at very short notice?

TOLLINGTON: You're quite right, Holmes. But how on earth could have known anything about my valet.

HOLMES: And your butler, Cramphorn, is filling his place. Willingly, nay, conscientiously – but not as efficiently?

TOLLINGTON: That's absolutely right, Mr. Holmes. Absolutely correct. But how could you possibly know that?

HOLMES: Your trousers, my Lord, if you will forgive me, have two parallel creases in them, which by common agreement among the Knightsbridge fashion *gurus* of the day, is one too many. No self-respecting valet would permit his master to appear in public in that way.

TOLLINGTON: (SURPRISED) Really? Mm. I didn't notice. But how did you know Cramphorn had executed the pressing?

HOLMES: Well, who else could it be? It was very likely, wasn't it? The fact that his eyesight is so weak tended to confirm it.

TOLLINGTON: (surprised) What? Well, yes. True, I knew he was having some difficulty with his eyes and had recently seen an optician, but how did *you* know . . . ?

WATSON: Yes, Holmes. Do explain . . . .

HOLMES: The champagne that we had at supper last night was not John de la Vere, 1884, but 1887. You asked Cramphorn for the '84, which is a little more acidic and nuttier than the '87. I took it that the reason for the error was Cramphorn's struggle with a dusty champagne label, a candle, and his weak eyesight in a dark cellar. I could conceive of no other explanation.

TOLLINGTON: Remarkable!

WATSON: Well done, Holmes.

TOLLINGTON: I must say, I wouldn't have known . . . .

HOLMES: Well, my Lord, what did happen to him?

TOLLINGTON: What? Oh yes. The valet. Well, I had to dismiss him. He was stealing.

HOLMES: Hmm. (PAUSE) Ah. Was his name Striker, by any chance?

TOLLINGTON: (AMAZED) How on earth did you know that, Mr. Holmes?

157

HOLMES: I didn't. But, last night, we met a confidence trickster of that name, posing as a curate, coming out of Josiah Deep's funeral parlour.

TOLLINGTON: Striker is Josiah Deep's brother-in-law!

HOLMES: Ah! (KNOWINGLY) The last piece in the puzzle. That explains everything!

WATSON: You didn't tell me he was a confidence trickster, Holmes. How did you find that out?

HOLMES: For one thing, he proposed to include *Psalm* number One-hundred-and-fifty-four at Wellington Pinchbeck's funeral.

WATSON: So?

HOLMES: Watson! Watson! Every self-respecting clergyman knows that there are only *one-hundred-and-fifty Psalms* in the book!

WATSON: Oh?

TOLLINGTON: (AMAZED) You never cease to amaze me, Mr. Holmes!

HOLMES: His dress as a curate was no doubt intended as a disguise. He called me, "Mr. Holmes", even though he pretended he did not know who we were. He was quizzing us to see how much we knew. A man who dressed up as a curate – with the aid of crude cosmetics and his brother-in-law's assistance – could just as easily dress up as a corpse.

WATSON: (IRRITABLY) Oh? Really, Holmes. I think it's dashed unsporting of you to keep that back.

HOLMES: (CHIDING) Watson! Watson! My good friend. I didn't know for certain . . . .

TOLLINGTON: Well, hadn't we better dash off and arrest Striker then . . . before he gets away?

HOLMES: There is no need. There is no crime.

158

TOLLINGTON: No crime? The man's dead.

HOLMES: Natural causes.

WATSON: Yes. That is so.

HOLMES: Heart failure, no doubt aggravated by the intake of alcohol, followed by pneumonia. It would be recorded as "accidental death".

TOLLINGTON: (AMAZED) What happened then, Mr. Holmes? What happened to the poor vagrant?

WATSON: I'm all at sea . . . I must say . . . .

HOLMES: There never was a vagrant. Wellington Pinchbeck boasted that he would spend the night in the porter's pantry in company with a corpse. Josiah Deep was approached to supply a corpse. His brother-in-law, Striker, heard of this, and – out of revenge – saw a golden opportunity to make mischief, and get back at his Lordship. He knew a substantial wager had been made. So Striker put himself up to be the corpse. Deep made him up to look the part and duly delivered him here in the coffin. During the night, Striker tapped on the coffin or sat up in it or performed some other manifestations and frightened poor Wellington Pinchbeck out of his skin. The shock killed him. Striker was in a predicament. The prank had turned to tragedy. He got out of the coffin, exchanged his shroud for the dead man's clothes, put Pinchbeck in the coffin, and waited until morning. When he heard the door opening, he hid behind one of the statues. All the attention would be on the dead man in the coffin. Striker was thus able to mingle with the guests and make his way unnoticed out of the room, while his brother-in-law, Josiah Deep, realising what had happened, was keeping the guest's attention, enabling Striker to get out of the house and away.

TOLLINGTON: (AMAZED) Mr. Holmes, I am truly amazed.

WATSON: You've done it again, Holmes. You've solved the unsolvable.

HOLMES: No, no.

WATSON: What about the ghost then? Is there really a Tollington Ghost?

HOLMES: Who knows, Watson? Who knows? There are things in this world that we cannot know . . . only time itself will reveal to us the absolute truth . . . .

MUSIC: *DANSE MACABRE*

WATSON: This is Dr. John H. Watson. I've had many more adventures with Sherlock Holmes, and I'll tell you another one . . . *when next we meet!*

MUSIC: (FADE OUT)

The Gastein Symphony
by Teresa Collard and John Patrick Lowrie

CHARACTERS

- SHERLOCK HOLMES
- DR. JOHN H. WATSON
- PAUL ROWLANDS – *Thirty years old, devoted to his wife and his music, and can't believe in his own stupidity*
- CHO PENN – *In his forties, is a wheeler-dealer with no conscience, but devoted to his daughter*
- PROFESSOR MARRYATT – *In his mid-fifties, is devoted to his students and will go to any lengths to make sure the needy get scholarships*
- JAMES DWIGHT KELLERMAN – *American in his fifties. Has made his money from oil. He is an idealist, philanthropist, and a realist*
- JEFFREY – *Innocent shop assistant in his twenties*
- WAITER

SOUND EFFECT: OPENING SEQUENCE, BIG BEN

ANNOUNCER: *The Further Adventures of Sherlock Holmes*, starring John Patrick Lowrie as Sherlock Holmes, and Lawrence Albert as Dr. John H. Watson.

MUSIC: *DANSE MACABRE* (UP AND UNDER). FADE TO . . . .

MUSIC: SCHUBERT'S "TROUT QUINTET" (UNDER)

WATSON: (NARRATING) My name is Dr. John Watson, friend and biographer of Sherlock Holmes. I had made comprehensive notes of the case I would come to call *The Gastein Symphony*, but Holmes never wanted the details to be made public – not while one of the main players was still living. However, all that changed a month ago, so I can now tell you how the case of one man's greed and another's obsessive desire led to undreamed – of success. Young Paul Rowlands called at Baker Street on a very inclement evening in the summer of 1890.

162

MUSIC: OUT

SOUND EFFECT: THUNDER IN THE DISTANCE. RAIN BATTERING AGAINST THE WINDOWS.

HOLMES: Sit down by the fire and dry out, Mr. Rowlands.

ROWLANDS: Thank you. And thank you, Mr. Holmes, for agreeing to see me. I must apologise for not making an appointment . . . .

HOLMES: Do not concern yourself But I would be quite interested to know what could be of such moment to bring a musician out on a night like this.

WATSON: Musician! How can you possibly know that, Holmes?

HOLMES: By this gentleman's reaction when he laid eyes upon my violin. He recognised it for a Stradivarius immediately. Would you care to examine it, Mr. Rowlands?

ROWLANDS: Why . . . why, thank you. I would indeed!

SOUND EFFECT: ROWLANDS PICKS UP VIOLIN AND TWANGS A FEW CHORDS

ROWLANDS: What a treasure, Mr. Holmes!

HOLMES: By the way you clasp the instrument, sir, you are no violinist. I hazard that you are a pianist and, unless I am very much mistaken, a composer.

WATSON: Now, Holmes, really –

ROWLANDS: Why, yes, Mr. Holmes. An unsuccessful composer, I'm afraid, but I have managed to earn a pittance by teaching *pianoforte* at the Conservatoire, of which Professor Marryatt is headmaster.

HOLMES: You are not totally unknown, Mr. Rowlands. My brother and I heard three of your piano sonatas played at St. James' Hall only last week.

163

WATSON: Oh. Well, then –

ROWLANDS: Yes. Well. A handful of sonatas will get me nowhere fast.

HOLMES: Hmm, Watson, I think our visitor needs a strong whisky to give him the courage to explain his misdeeds.

WATSON: Misdeeds? You may be jumping the gun, Holmes.

SOUND EFFECT: WATSON RISES, PICKS UP BOTTLE, AND POURS A DRINK

ROWLANDS: No, Doctor. Mr. Holmes is right. I am being blackmailed for being a stupid, unthinking ass. What I have done is unforgivable, utterly unforgivable! I dare not tell my wife what has occurred. It would really set her back. No, no, now is not the right moment. I have been thinking seriously about leaping off Tower Bridge rather than suffer further ignominy.

WATSON: Now, now, Mr. Rowlands. Here's your drink.

ROWLANDS Thank you, sir.

HOLMES: Your sin, Mr. Rowlands? Which of the Seven Sins have you committed?

ROWLANDS: I don't know how you would describe . . . plagiarism, Mr. Holmes. Theft, no doubt, or perhaps in this case simply greed. Avarice. But all for a good reason, I assure you.

HOLMES: Explain yourself.

ROWLANDS: I shouldn't have done what . . . what . . . This is not a good idea. I am sorry, Mr. Holmes, but I must leave. So sorry to have bothered you, but I –

SOUND EFFECT: ROWLANDS RISES AND WALKS TO DOOR

HOLMES: Sit down, Mr. Rowlands, and pull yourself together. Do you think that I would be standing here conversing if I believed you to be a criminal?

ROWLANDS: I . . . I . . . No, no, perhaps not. Very well. It all began innocently enough. Professor Marryatt, the present principal of the Conservatoire, knew that I needed extra . . . extra money. My wife, you see . . . Well, in any case, the professor asked me whether I would be prepared to compose a lullaby in the style of Mozart for a Mr. Cho-Penn, and to give his daughter piano lessons.

WATSON: Cho-Penn? An odd name.

HOLMES A Chinese name. Cho-Penn is an antiquarian book-seller, among other things.

ROWLANDS: Yes, he lives upstairs of his book shop. The lullaby was for his daughter, Maria, for her seventh birthday. But that was all a ruse, a sprat to catch a willing mackerel.

WATSON: You mentioned your wife.

ROWLANDS: Yes. My – my wife is quite ill and has recently taken a turn for the worse. The doctor suggested that a month in Brighton might be beneficial, but . . . but he made it clear that it would only be a temporary measure. I knew she was dying, and had learned that the only person in the world who could help her was Doctor Einz, in Switzerland. He specialises in . . . in . . . .

WATSON: Tuberculosis.

ROWLANDS: Yes, Doctor.

HOLMES: I see. How much did Cho-Penn pay for the lullaby?

ROWLANDS: Fifty pounds. It was enough to cover my wife's sojourn in Brighton, and she seemed to rally there. I was hopeful that she might – But once she returned to the filthy air in this city she . . . she . . . .

WATSON: She collapsed?

165

ROWLANDS: Yes.

WATSON: The curse of coal.

ROWLANDS: I continued to teach Maria. Shortly afterwards, I was waiting in Mr. Cho-Penn's music room for her to arrive home from school. I was seated at the Broadwood, that is, Mr. Cho-Penn's grand piano – a wonderful instrument, quite expensive, you know – when I noticed Schubert's "Duo for Two Pianos" lying open. It's an evocative work, open to improvisation. I was reading through it when Mr. Cho-Penn entered. He immediately locked the door.

HOLMES: Hmm. For him, it was the right moment and the right place. He offered you a further commission.

ROWLANDS: You're clairvoyant, Mr. Holmes. He offered me one-thousand pounds to compose a symphony. He would call it *The Gastein Symphony*, in the style of Schubert, based on his "Grand Duo for Two Pianos". He wanted me to write it . . . *sub rosa*.

HOLMES: Yes, of course.

ROWLANDS: On no account was I to mention it to Professor Marryatt, or even my wife because . . . because he already had an American buyer. Do you understand, Mr. Holmes?

HOLMES: I begin to.

ROWLANDS: My immediate reaction was to leap at the chance. Angela could go to Switzerland, you see, where Dr. Einz would perform a miracle! But, but I told him I wanted time to think. He gave me hours. The following morning, despite the need for secrecy, I determined to discuss the matter with Professor Marryatt. I was about to knock on his door when I heard raised voices. Mr. Cho-Penn was there, angrily accusing the Professor of attesting to my ability to compose the symphony, but that I was procrastinating.

HOLMES: (TO HIMSELF) Cho-Penn and Marryatt!

166

WATSON: So you refused the commission?

HOLMES: Oh, no, Watson! Cho-Penn knew that Rowlands was at his mercy. His wife needed urgent treatment in Switzerland.

ROWLANDS: Yes, Mr. Holmes. I had almost made up my mind to refuse the offer, but when I reached home that night, neighbours told me that Angela had been rushed to St Bartholomew's Hospital. That evening, I . . . I . . . I accepted the thousand pounds. The Professor gave me three days off in which to take Angela to Geneva. What else could I have done, Mr. Holmes? And yet – and yet how could I have done this?

MUSIC: SCHUBERT'S "GRAND DUO FOR PIANOS"

WATSON: But why commission music in the style of Schubert? Why not have an original work?

HOLMES: Surely you know, Watson, that Schubert manuscripts continued to be discovered years after his death. To the extent that, at times, it seemed as though he had never left us. And you must have read in *The Times* that during the past two years, Cho-Penn has made a fortune by auctioning rare music manuscripts at Christie's. Hmm? Ask yourself: How many of those manuscripts were genuine and how many forged?

WATSON: But who forges them?

HOLMES: Indeed. Wouldn't you say, Watson, that there is no better calligrapher in the world than the Chinese craftsman? It is an art in itself. They would need old paper, of course, and especially prepared inks. And who can produce antique looking paper?

WATSON: The Chinese!

HOLMES: Precisely.

WATSON: There must be profit in this business to go to such lengths.

HOLMES: Cost is no object when avid collectors have a target in their sights. Original Bach cantatas are making serious money these days. It was not two months ago that a volume of nine Mozart symphonies, not all copied in his own hand, fetched a very handsome sum. It seems to me, Mr. Rowlands, you are a composer who undervalues his talents. But I will endeavour to discover what hold Cho-Penn has on Marryatt.

ROWLANDS: I am lost, Mr. Holmes. I dare not share the problem with my wife. She is convalescing in Geneva, blissfully unaware of my disgraceful behaviour. I have already handed over the first three movements, but I can't bear to finish the work. I would rather burn it. Mr. Cho-Penn will swear to his American that Schubert composed it in –

HOLMES: *Austria*! When he was holidaying with his friend Vogl in the Gastein Mountains.

ROWLANDS: Yes. Schubert was a sad man, but a great one. I should not be plagiarising his work.

HOLMES: Fashioning a new work based on the themes of another composer is not plagiarism, Mr. Rowlands. Many great composers have done as much. What you are involved in is fraud. You repent your act. No one has been defrauded as yet. You've come to me. Why not go to the police?

ROWLANDS: I'm in it up to my neck, Mr. Holmes. I have already accepted the thousand pounds. I've already spent it. My reputation . . . I don't know what Mr. Cho-Penn might . . . might . . . But he's threatened – He is dead set on commissioning another work, this time by Scarlatti. If I don't write it, he swears he will tell this American collector, Kellermann I think is his name, that *The Gastein Symphony* is spurious and he must go straight to Scotland Yard.

HOLMES Hmm. A clever move, but he's obviously not a chess player. Are you still giving young Maria piano lessons?

ROWLANDS: Yes, I am. She already shows signs of becoming an excellent pianist.

HOLMES: When do you meet with her?

ROWLANDS: Friday afternoons at three.

HOLMES: Excellent! Check mate, in two days. Time enough in which to solve your problem.

ROWLANDS: Two days!

WATSON: Two days, Holmes?

HOLMES: Mr. Rowlands, you must arrive at Cho-Penn's book shop at five minutes past three on Friday. Precisely at five past three and carrying the final movement of the symphony with you. Can you complete it in that time?

ROWLANDS: I . . . I . . . .

HOLMES: Good man! Now tell me. Are all the rooms in Cho-Penn's house accessible?

ROWLANDS: Accessible? Why . . . yes. Yes, they are, as far as I know.

HOLMES: You're sure?

ROWLANDS: I think so. No, wait. There is one door leading off the main hall in which there is a keyhole but no doorknob.

WATSON: A basement, perhaps?

HOLMES: In all probability. Now, sir, forget about all this and concentrate on composing a grand finale. It is very important for your reputation that you lead us all to believe that the great man, himself, could have composed it. Return to your home, and prepare to leave for Switzerland in three days time.

ROWLANDS: Three days time! It's a dream, Mr. Holmes, but I will do exactly as you say.

HOLMES: May the muse be kind to you, Mr. Rowlands.

WATSON: At least it's stopped raining.

ROWLANDS: Goodnight to you both, and thank you.

<u>SOUND EFFECT: DOOR OPENS. ROWLANDS EXITS</u>

WATSON: Holmes, why on earth are you encouraging him to finish the work?

HOLMES: All will be revealed.

WATSON: There you go again. I do like to be kept in the picture.

HOLMES: Watson, tomorrow will be a busy day. First thing in the morning, we must call on Professor Marryatt at the academy.

<u>MUSIC: SCHUBERT'S "GRAND DUO FOR TWO PIANOS"</u>

<u>MUSIC: OUT</u>

MARRYATT: Good morning, gentlemen. Welcome to The Conservatoire. Pray be seated.

<u>SOUND EFFECT: CHAIRS BEING MOVED AND ALL THREE SIT DOWN.</u>

HOLMES: Thank you, Professor. I hope our visit has not inconvenienced you in any way.

MARRYATT: No, not in the slightest. My mornings are kept free for interviewing aspiring musicians.

HOLMES: Then I will come to the matter immediately. One of the members of your teaching staff is now giving *pianoforte* lessons to the daughter of a Mr. Cho-Penn.

MARRYATT: (COUGHS) Ah! Paul Rowlands. Indeed he is. Did Cho-Penn discuss the matter with you? Umm . . . . Ah, I believe he did. Yes.

HOLMES: You will forgive my asking, but were piano lessons the only reason for his visit?

MARRYATT: No. No, I believe he wanted to know about Rowlands' competence as a composer. He could have read the reviews of his latest work.

HOLMES: Sonatas, I believe?

MARRYATT: Yes. Quite nice. Well-crafted. Rowlands has real potential. Cho-Penn seemed to be interested in the possibility of a young composer producing a major concerto.

HOLMES: Or a symphony.

MARRYATT: Yes, Rowlands would leap at the chance. He needs the commission.

HOLMES: I am quite sure he would. Professor, I must congratulate you on the amazing number of original manuscripts you have in the academy library. Did you ever purchase any of these scores from Cho-Penn?

MARRYATT: Purchase? Oh, if only we had the money. No, quite the reverse, I'm afraid. On occasion we've had to part with treasures that have been left to us by generous benefactors. It is the only way we have to fund scholarships for promising students. The gifts come from all over the world. Just last year, on the death of Brahms, we received the original manuscript of one of his most delightful lullabies. That, I promise you, will never leave this building.

WATSON: Do wealthy collectors come knocking at the door?

MARRYATT: Andrew Carnegie. He's returned to Scotland, did you know? He often graces this building. But one of the wealthiest and, I have to say, the most generous is James Dwight Kellermann, from Richmond, in Virginia.

WATSON: Kellerman? Holmes, the same –

HOLMES: The same Kellerman who gives so generously to support orchestras in Chicago, New York, and London.

MARRYATT: Yes. He arrived in London last week and will be here this evening at a concert given by my students. Would you gentleman care to join us?

HOLMES: We would be delighted.

MARRYATT: I think Mr. Kellermann might enjoy meeting a consulting detective. Perhaps you and Dr. Watson could arrive early to savour a glass or two of excellent cognac prior to the performance.

SOUND EFFECT: STREET NOISES, HORSES' HOOVES AS CARRIAGES DRIVE BY

HOLMES: Well, Watson, what was your impression?

WATSON: Too effusive.

HOLMES: And a quick thinker who had no intention of discussing Cho-Penn. By maneuvering the conversation in the direction of tonight's concert, he believes that he has moved the target out of my range.

WATSON: Holmes, if you can spare me, I would like to dash home for a bit.

HOLMES: Certainly, my dear fellow. I am going to spend a couple of hours digging around in St Cecilia's Reference Library.

WATSON: Until tonight then!

SOUND EFFECT: VOICES IN THE GUEST SUITE AT THE CONSERVATOIRE. GLASSES CLINKING

WATSON: This is excellent malt, Holmes.

MARRYATT: Ah, there you are, Mr. Holmes. So glad you could make it. Let me introduce you to Mr. Kellermann.

KELLERMANN: Good evening, Mr. Holmes. And you, sir, are Dr. Watson, I presume?

WATSON: (LAUGHS) I am.

KELLERMANN: I never for one moment thought I would ever meet the most famous detective in Europe.

WAITER: Excuse me, Professor, but there is a Mr. Cho-Penn waiting downstairs to see you.

MARRYATT: (EMBARRASSED) Here, on such a night! Well he'd better be mighty quick about it.

KELLERMANN: Professor, he may be wanting a few words with me, as well. If so, I will see him after the concert.

MARRYATT: Very well! I'll give him the message.

KELLERMANN: Now, Mr. Holmes, my spies tell me you play the violin and actually own a superb Stradivarius.

HOLMES: My spies tell me that you are, at present, in the market for a work many musicologists, historians, and academics would dearly like to hear. Probably because they don't believe it exists.

KELLERMANN: (LAUGHS) Where and how have you picked up this slender thread?

WATSON: He's good at that sort of thing.

HOLMES: This afternoon, I spent some time in St Cecilia's Reference Library. On glancing through the Visitor's Book, I noticed that some months ago you had been researching the same subject.

KELLERMANN: If I ever have a problem to solve, Mr. Holmes, I know where to come and on whom to call!

HOLMES: You believe that Schubert composed not nine symphonies, but ten.

KELLERMANN: I think he did, yes.

HOLMES: How many of us long for just one more masterpiece from the hands of that young genius? Whilst in the library, I came across a copy of a letter written by Anton Ottenwalt in in which he mentions that Schubert was working on a symphony at Gmunden.

KELLERMANN: Yes, that it is why it is called the Gmunden-Gastein work.

HOLMES: Based on the "Grand Duo for Two Pianos".

KELLERMANN: Mr. Holmes, when I lay hands on this work, as I believe I will, you will be the first person to hear the good news.

HOLMES: Thank you. Tell me, have you ever commissioned a work in the manner and style of a great composer?

KELLERMANN: No, never. I have to have the genuine article.

HOLMES: Let us walk over to the window where we may be able to hear ourselves speak. I would like to put a hypothetical case to you. Watson, my friend, would you keep an eye out for Professor Marryatt. He hasn't told us yet where we are sitting.

SOUND EFFECT: SOUND OF TALKING FADES A LITTLE AS HOLMES AND KELLERMANN WALK OVER TO THE WINDOW

WATSON (NARRATING) It was a superb concert in which the young musicians gave all. Whatever the content of Holmes's hypothesis, it was not intended for Marryatt's ears, and I had not the slightest idea, until the following day, what was in the wind.

SOUND EFFECT: HOLMES PLAYING THE VIOLIN (UNDER)

WATSON: Holmes, Mary is expecting me to be back home tonight to welcome two of her distant relations. If I could find an excuse not to return, I would.

HOLMES: I am afraid, my dear fellow, you will have to do your duty. This case will have been proved to my satisfaction by late afternoon.

SOUND EFFECT: TWO CHORDS ON THE VIOLIN THEN HOLMES PUTS IT DOWN

WATSON: Sometimes, Holmes, I wish you would share your thoughts with me. I have not the slightest idea how you expect to clear Rowlands' name. As he says, he's in it up to his neck.

HOLMES: I want you on hand as an observer taking notes.

WATSON: Where?

HOLMES: An antiquarian book shop! This morning, while I am perfecting a disguise, I want you to go to the shop, get your notebook out, and write down the names of a few titles.

WATSON But what am I actually doing?

HOLMES: Making certain that a book on the Ming Dynasty dating from the 14th to the 17th century is not on the shelves. If Cho-Penn is keeping a watch on the books through the glass window in his office, you will become a known face.

WATSON: Why is that necessary?

HOLMES: This afternoon, we will both go to the bookshop. We will enter at five minutes to three. You must keep the assistant talking while I have words with Cho-Penn. I've instructed Rowlands to arrive at precisely five past three.

WATSON: Why?

HOLMES: Let's call it training in the ways of the world.

SOUND EFFECT: BELL CLANGS AS WATSON OPENS DOOR, ENTERS SHOP, AND WALKS AROUND. CLOCK STRIKES ELEVEN

JEFFREY: Good morning, sir! Are you looking for anything in particular?

WATSON: Yes, I am, I'd like to make a list of the various books you hold on bone operations.

JEFFREY: Are you a doctor, sir?

WATSON: I am.

JEFFREY: Wish you'd been around when my mother broke her knee.

WATSON: Why?

JEFFREY: The bloody doc – sorry sir, the doc didn't turn up until the next day.

WATSON: So gangrene had set in.

JEFFREY: Yes, sir. By then it was too . . . .

SOUND EFFECT: CHO-PENN OPENS HIS OFFICE DOOR AND SHOUTS

CHO-PENN: Jeffrey, I am still waiting to check this morning's takings.

JEFFREY: Sorry, sir, I will be with you in a shake of a lamb's tail.

WATSON: That's all right, You go ahead. I may be back later today.

WATSON: (NARRATING) That afternoon, at exactly five minutes to three, I once again entered the book shop. I followed a bearded fellow wearing horn-rimmed spectacles and a hat that had seen better days.

SOUND EFFECT: SHOP BELL RINGS AS SHOP DOOR OPENS

JEFFREY: Good afternoon, sir. You said you'd be back.

WATSON: Yes. Yes, I did.

HOLMES: Are you the manager of the establishment?

JEFFREY: Good God, sir. No!

HOLMES: No need to blaspheme. Tell the manager I wish to have a few words.

<u>SOUND EFFECT: OFFICE DOOR OPENS AND CHO-PENN ENTERS</u>

CHO-PENN: Come this way, sir. We can talk over here.

HOLMES: Are you Mr. Cho-Penn?

CHO-PENN: Yes, at your service.

HOLMES: Well, sir, I am on an impossible mission. Whilst at Leipzig University, I searched high and low for letters known to exist that relate to *The Gastein Symphony*.

CHO-PENN: *The Gastein*? I am afraid I don't stock rare letters.

HOLMES: Do you have manuscripts? For instance, Schubert's "Grand Duo for Two Pianos".

<u>SOUND EFFECT: CUPBOARD BEING UNLOCKED</u>

CHO-PENN: There you are, sir.

HOLMES: Good gracious! May I take it nearer to the light? My eyes are not as good as they were.

CHO-PENN: By all means, sir.

<u>SOUND EFFECT: CLOCK STRIKES THREE</u>

HOLMES: Oh dear. Not quite as lively as I had hoped.

CHO-PENN: I am sorry, sir.

HOLMES: Nevertheless, let me take another look.

CHO-PENN: Mr. Rowlands, you are late. You had better not keep my daughter waiting any longer.

HOLMES: Mr. Paul Rowlands?

ROWLANDS: Yes. Should I know you, sir?

HOLMES: Would you be so good as to show me the manuscript that you are carrying in your music case?

ROWLANDS: Mr. – Mr. Holmes?

CHO-PENN: What is going on, Rowlands? Do you know this man?

HOLMES: Sherlock Holmes, consulting detective.

CHO-PENN: Consulting – Well, whoever you are, the manuscript in that case belongs to me. I have paid good money for it.

HOLMES: Good money, but not as much as you would charge others, eh? Rowlands, open your music case.

SOUND EFFECT: OPENS CASE

HOLMES: Ah, the fourth and final movement of *The Gastein Symphony*.

CHO-PENN: As I told you, I paid a vast sum for it.

HOLMES: By Franz Schubert.

CHO-PENN: That's right.

HOLMES: But, look here. The ink is not yet dry. Surely Herr Schubert is not with us still?

CHO-PENN: What? No, no –

178

HOLMES: Ah, I see, you were having young Rowlands, here, make you a copy. But you have the original, I know. You're going to sell it to James Dwight Kellermann for twenty-thousand pounds.

ROWLANDS: Twenty-thousand pounds!

CHO-PENN: You know Mr. Kellerman?

HOLMES: I've made his acquaintance. I'd love to see the original manuscript. In fact, acting as Mr. Kellerman's agent, I'm afraid I must insist on it.

CHO-PENN: The original – ? I. . . I . . . Yes, of course. Jeffrey, go down to the basement and get the original –

HOLMES: Of the *fourth* movement.

CHO-PENN: The fourth –

HOLMES: But you can't quite do that, can you? Because the craftsmen you have working in your basement haven't had the time to draft it up yet, have they?

CHO-PENN: I paid this man a thousand –

HOLMES: You will get your thousand back. What you have to do now is close down your forgery operation immediately. Tomorrow, Inspector Lestrade will inspect the premises.

CHO-PENN: Mr. Kellermann is expecting to –

HOLMES: He is expecting us to take tea with him at four o'clock. Good-day, sir.

CHO-PENN: (FRIGHTENED) You mean he knows?

HOLMES: Oh, yes, he knows. Good afternoon.

SOUND EFFECT: DOOR OPENS AND ALL THREE EXIT

MUSIC: TRANSITION

179

KELLERMANN: Mr. Holmes, you have opened up a new vista. Why did I never think of commissioning a new work in the style of one of the great masters?

ROWLANDS: You are serious, Mr. Kellermann?

KELLERMANN: Indeed I am, Mr. Rowlands. As soon as you played the piano reduction for me, I knew I wanted it. I shall pay you twenty thousand for the symphony, and the London Philharmonic Orchestra will perform it in the Albert Hall on September the first.

ROWLANDS: This is beyond my wildest dreams. I shall join my wife in Switzerland immediately! But there is just one thing I feel should mention.

HOLMES: What's that, Mr. Rowland?

ROWLANDS: Professor Marryatt, I know, has been liaising with Cho-Penn, but everything the professor does is solely for his students. He has many more students on scholarships than at any other musical academy.

KELLERMANN: Both Mr. Holmes and I are aware of the Professor's devotion to the cause of the aspiring musician.

WATSON: Which is why my friend has asked me not to publish any records until after the Professor's death.

ROWLANDS: Thank you. Thank you, indeed.

KELLERMANN: Mr. Rowlands, enjoy Switzerland, but make sure you return to this country in September to hear the first performance of *The Gastein Symphony*.

ROWLANDS: Indeed I will!

(WATSON, HOLMES, AND KELLERMANN, LAUGH)

MUSIC: A SCHUBERT SYMPHONY OR SONATA

MUSIC: *DANSE MACABRE*

WATSON: This is Dr. John H. Watson. I've had many more adventures with Sherlock Holmes, and I'll tell you another one . . . *when next we meet!*

MUSIC: (FADE OUT)

The Curse of the Third Sign

by Jim French

<u>CHARACTERS</u>

- SHERLOCK HOLMES
- DR. JOHN H. WATSON
- ROBERT PAIGE – *A young suitor*
- CABBIE – *A typical London cab driver*
- HANLEY – *The Butler*
- SIR EDWARD DALRYMPLE
- SOPHIE DALRYMPLE – *Sir Edward's daughter*

<u>SOUND EFFECT: OPENING SEQUENCE, BIG BEN</u>

ANNOUNCER: *The Further Adventures of Sherlock Holmes*, starring John Patrick Lowrie as Sherlock Holmes, and Lawrence Albert as Dr. John H. Watson.

<u>MUSIC: *DANSE MACABRE* (UP AND UNDER)</u>

WATSON: (NARRATING) My friend Sherlock Holmes, although an enemy of all wrong-doers, was almost never interested in domestic squabbles which he occasionally was asked to investigate. "People should tend their own gardens," he would say, "and not run for help when weeds begin to grow." It wasn't surprising then, on a cloudless afternoon in July of 1887, that Holmes responded with the single word "*No*" to a telegram that came as he was basking in a wreath of pipe smoke, and appearing, for once, to be in deep contentment.

<u>SOUND EFFECT: BAKER STREET BACKGROUND</u>

WATSON: Just "*No*"? No explanation, Holmes? Seems a little short.

HOLMES: Why waste words on a lover's quarrel?

WATSON: Was that what the telegram was about?

HOLMES: Here, read it for yourself and see what you make of it.

SOUND EFFECT: TELEGRAM HANDLED

WATSON: (READS) *"Urgently request you investigate disappearance of my* fiancée *after misunderstanding. Will pay any fee for her safe return. Will you take my case?"* Signed *Robert D. Paige.*

HOLMES: Yes. Just throw it in the grate, Watson.

WATSON: I don't know . . . poor young fellow must be desperate to try enlisting Sherlock Holmes at *"any fee"*.

HOLMES: Let him use the police. He's already paying for their services, however incompetent they may be. And I certainly don't want it noised about that now I'm taking on lovers' spats. I won't turn my practice into a clinic for bleeding hearts!

WATSON: Yes, of course. Whatever you wish.

HOLMES: But you disapprove.

WATSON: No, I just happen to feel sympathy for a fellow who's desperate to find a missing loved one. As a matter of fact, I happen to have had some experience along those lines myself in years past.

HOLMES: Well then, there's the answer! Why don't *you* take his case?

MUSIC: UNDERSCORE

WATSON: (NARRATING) And after that, I'm sorry to say that he mooned in our rooms like the sun going behind a cloud. The next half-hour was spent in absolute silence, while Holmes riffled through some books and I read every word in the newspaper I had already perused the night before. Just as the stillness was becoming intolerable, from downstairs came the sound of the bell, Mrs. Hudson's steps to open the door, then a man's heavy tread on the stairs to our rooms.

SOUND EFFECT: KNOCK ON DOOR

HOLMES: He apparently didn't take *"No"* for an answer. (SHOUTS) Sherlock Holmes is not here! Kindly go away!

WATSON: Oh, Really, Holmes!

SOUND EFFECT: WATSON WALKS TO DOOR, OPENS IT

WATSON: Yes? May I help you?

PAIGE: I beg your pardon! The landlady said – that is, I thought –

WATSON: Are you Robert Paige, by any chance?

PAIGE: Yes! Here is my card. Are you Sherlock Holmes?

HOLMES: No, I am Sherlock Holmes. I take it you didn't receive my reply to your telegram?

PAIGE: I did, sir, but –

HOLMES: Was my wording unclear?

PAIGE: Not at all. But forgive me sir, I felt I must explain the circumstances that caused me to seek your help. I truly fear my *fiancée* has experienced some kind of shock that may have changed the direction of her life!

WATSON: Come in, Mr. Paige. I am Doctor John H. Watson, and I'll be glad to hear your story.

SOUND EFFECT: HE WALKS IN

PAIGE: You're very kind, Doctor, but I fear I need a detective.

SOUND EFFECT: DOOR CLOSES

HOLMES: Doctor Watson is far more experienced in matters of the heart than I am.

WATSON: You look a bit unsteady. Would you care for a drink?

PAIGE: Oh, no, thank you. I neither drink . . . . nor smoke.

HOLMES: But I do, so you may want to conduct your business outside where the air is more to your liking. Regents Park is only a quarter-mile away.

WATSON: *Holmes!*

HOLMES: Merely concerned for the comfort of your guest, Watson.

WATSON: Please have a seat, Mr. Paige. I'll be glad to hear your story.

PAIGE: Very kind of you, Doctor; I take it you know why I wired Mr. Holmes?

WATSON: You had an argument with your *fiancée* and now she's disappeared.

PAIGE: No, no! There was no argument! I'm sure it was just a misunderstanding, and it wasn't with my *fiancée*, but with her father.

WATSON: What happened?

PAIGE: It was this past Monday, the morning after I had had dinner with her and her parents. A note was delivered to my office. I brought it with me, if you'd care to read it.

WATSON: By all means.

PAIGE: Here.

WATSON: Hmm! Certainly short enough!

HOLMES: (OFF) Out loud, if you please, Watson.

WATSON: (READING) *"Robert: I am leaving the city. I shall always love you. Pray for me"*. And it's signed with the letter 'S'.

186

PAIGE: That stands for Sophie. Her name is Sophronia Dalrymple.

HOLMES: Dalrymple? Unusual name. Her father wouldn't be Sir Edward Dalrymple, the architect, by any chance?

PAIGE: Yes! Do you know him?

HOLMES: Only by reputation.

WATSON: What did you do after you received her note?

PAIGE: I went to her house immediately and their butler said the Dalrymples had left, and didn't say when they might be back.

WATSON: Did something happen at the dinner the night before?

PAIGE: I had never met Sophie's parents before, and of course I was nervous, but we had a lovely dinner, Mrs. Dalrymple was charming, and then Sir Edward showed me through their sumptuous home that he designed, and we wound up in his game room. He started reminiscing; he told me how he became an architect, and I told him my father had been a barrister in the firm I work for, and he asked for my card. Then he asked me what my middle initial stands for, and I told him the '*D*' stands for *Dunstan*. My full name is Robert Dunstan Paige. When I said that, his whole countenance changed. He looked at me oddly, and then he sank into a chair and his hands began to tremble! Finally, he said he was tired and needed to retire, so I said my goodbyes to Sophie and her mother and went home. And that was the last time I saw Sophie.

WATSON: How did you become acquainted with her?

PAIGE: Well, it happened this way. Nearly two years ago, a friend gave me a ticket to hear the young Polish pianist, Ignace Paderewski, at Covent Gardens, and I was seated next to a lovely young woman who was there with an older lady – her piano teacher as it turned out. As I sat down beside her, for just a moment our eyes met, and I felt an immediate attraction. I couldn't take my eyes off her! All through the first half, I would steal glances at her, and find her glancing at me! At the interval, we stayed in our seats rather than retiring to the lobby, and as we chatted we began to discover how alike we were – the same age, the same interests – it was uncanny! And after the concert resumed, our hands happened to touch, an then they brushed again, and this time I dared to take her hand, and you can imagine my thrill when I felt her delicate fingers entwine with mine! And from that moment on, I couldn't tell you a single note Paderewski played!. When the concert was over, she wrote her address on my program and I gave her my calling-card. We've been seeing each other as often as possible ever since. A year to the day after we met, I proposed and she accepted.

HOLMES: How old are you, Mr. Paige?

PAIGE: Why, I'm twenty-five. I see you're taking notes, Mr. Holmes. Does this mean that you'll help me after all?

HOLMES: We shall see. Are there any obstacles to your marriage?

PAIGE: None that I know of.

HOLMES: Perhaps a past commitment . . . ?

PAIGE: Neither of us have any past commitments.

WATSON: And your parents are agreeable to your plans to marry?

PAIGE: We haven't told them yet. Sophie thought it best to have all her social obligations settled before she leaves home. And I wanted to be sure my mother was in an agreeable state of mind to receive the news. Mother sometimes goes through – difficult moods.

WATSON: And what about your father?

PAIGE: He died seven years ago.

HOLMES: What was his name?

PAIGE: Trevor Paige. He was a barrister at the firm I later came to work for.

HOLMES: We shall do what we can. And we need to study Miss Dalrymple's note, if you'll leave it with us.

PAIGE: Of course, only please don't lose it. And you can't know how relieved I am that you will help me!

HOLMES: You will hear from us shortly.

SOUND EFFECT: HE STEPS TO THE DOOR AND OPENS IT

WATSON: Good day, Mr. Paige.

PAIGE: Good day, gentlemen. And thank you again.

SOUND EFFECT: HE STEPS OUT, DOOR CLOSES

WATSON: Well, Holmes?

HOLMES: The note interests me, and so does the sudden change in Dalrymple's manner. What do you see in it?

WATSON: The two must be connected. Read the note again.

HOLMES: *"Robert: I am leaving the city. I shall always love you. Pray for me."*

WATSON: By its brevity, she could have been extremely rushed, or possibly she wrote it in secret and didn't want her parents to read it.

HOLMES: Possibly. But what do you make of her salutation? *"Robert"*. Not *"Dear Robert"* or any other affectionate term; just *"Robert"*. Quite businesslike. Then she wrote, *"I am leaving the city."* If she knew where she was going, why not say so? Writing to her sweetheart, one would expect her to tell him where she was going, and when she expected to return.

WATSON: If she even knew those things.

HOLMES: Then she wrote *"I shall always love you"*. In popular literature, this would be a parting sentiment; something to be said in sadness to someone you don't expect to see again. And

189

her final line; *"Pray for me"* was that simply religious litany, or is she facing a serious problem that calls for prayer?

WATSON: Holmes! Do you know what it could be? The young lady may be ill, seriously ill! She might have some disease that took a sudden turn for the worse overnight, something that can't be treated in a London hospital! If that's the case, she and her parents might well have taken a boat to France to seek treatment! The French are far advanced in certain medical fields, and the cost of consulting a foreign specialist would be nothing for a wealthy man like Dalrymple.

HOLMES: Hmm. That could certainly explain why she wrote her note. But unfortunately, it still doesn't explain her father's reaction to the name "Dunstan".

WATSON: Then maybe there's no connection after all. Why don't I send a telegram to Robert Paige, asking him if Sophie ever mentioned having a serious medical problem?

MUSIC: UNDERCURRENT

WATSON: (NARRATING) So I sent Paige my question about Sophie's health. But instead of wiring me his reply, within the half-hour he was at our door!

MUSIC: OUT

SOUND EFFECT: DOOR CLOSES SHARPLY (BAKER STREET BACKGROUND)

PAIGE: (BREATHLESS) Forgive my intrusion, Dr. Watson, but your wire alarmed me! I must know what you've found out about Sophie! Is she ill?

WATSON: Calm yourself, Mr. Paige! I didn't mean to imply that she's ill. I only inquired about her health in order to dispose of one possible reason for her sudden departure. It seems reasonable that if she had to leave London so suddenly, there could have been a medical reason, and if that had been the case, it might explain why she wrote *"pray for me"*.

190

PAIGE: Yes, I see your reasoning. And I have been praying for her almost continuously since her note came, but to my knowledge, she enjoys excellent health.

WATSON: I'm delighted to hear it.

PAIGE: Is Mr. Holmes here?

WATSON: He's gone to do some research on your behalf. He said to expect him back around two.

PAIGE: Around two? I would wait for him, but I have to take an important deposition back in the office in half-an-hour. Will you let me know if he makes any progress?

WATSON: Of course.

MUSIC: UNDERCURRENT

WATSON: (NARRATING) After Paige left, there was nothing more for me to do until Holmes returned, so I took the opportunity to lie down on the sofa for a while to consider every possibility that could explain Sophie Dalrymple's mysterious leave-taking and how to find where she had gone. I had been occupied in this pursuit for only a few minutes, with my eyes closed to shut out distractions, when the next thing I knew, Holmes was standing over me.

HOLMES: Wake up, Watson! It's nearly six. We've missed our lunch and our tea.

WATSON: (WAKING) Umm, there you are, Holmes. Any news?

HOLMES: Bad news for Robert Paige. Sophie Dalrymple will not be marrying him.

MUSIC: VIOLIN STING

WATSON: Say that again, Holmes?

HOLMES: I said Sophie Dalrymple will not become Mrs. Robert Paige.

191

WATSON: Why? What's happened?

HOLMES: She and her mother are on a ship, bound for America!

WATSON: What? How do you know that?

HOLMES: I have a contact in the Passport Office. It seems Sir Edward exercised his influence and his cheque-book, and was able at the last minute to secure a first-class stateroom on the *Royal Jersey*, which was scheduled to sail from Southampton on Tuesday.

WATSON: They sailed without a word to young Paige at dinner the night before?

HOLMES: She and her mother may not have known they would be leaving the next day. If Paige's account of his conversation with Sir Edward was accurate, the entire complexion of his relationship with the Dalrymples changed when he uttered that name, *Dunstan*.

WATSON: Do you suppose someone named Dunstan was an enemy of the Dalrymples at some time in the past?

HOLMES: That's possible, but remember: All we know about Sophie is what Paige has told us. She may simply have had a sudden change of heart about marrying him and wanted to go as far away as possible, and her mother would naturally accompany her.

WATSON: What a blow to young Paige! I'm not looking forward to telling him.

HOLMES: And he has a thing or two to tell us. But right now, ask Mrs. Hudson to bring us our dinner while I wash London's grime from my face and hands and have a look at *The Evening Standard*.

WATSON: (NARRATING) And Mrs. Hudson, who was accustomed to our irregular hours, laid a table of cold pheasant, Stilton, and a loaf of fragrant bread hot from her oven. Holmes put down the paper and ate hungrily, more to replenish himself than to savor Mrs. Hudson's cooking. He finished well before I did, glanced at the clock, which was at half-eight, then he rose from the table.

MUSIC: OUT

HOLMES: Well, are you fortified enough to accompany me?

WATSON: Where are you going?

HOLMES: To visit Dalrymple.

WATSON: Tonight? Before dinner, you said he'd be back from Southampton tomorrow!

HOLMES: I said *by* tomorrow. There's a chance he's already returned. * I'll flag a cab while you do something about those flecks of cheese on your moustache.

SOUND EFFECT: * HURRIED STEPS TO DOOR, DOOR OPENS. BACKGROUND FADES OUT

(PAUSE)

SOUND EFFECT: FADE IN: HANSOM CAB UNDERWAY

WATSON: Before we ate, you weren't expecting Dalrymple until tomorrow, and now you think he's already returned? What changed your mind, the pheasant or the Stilton?

HOLMES: (GOOD CHUCKLE) Mark one up for you, Watson! No, as delicious as it was, our repast only satisfied my hunger and not my thinking. You'll recall that before we began dining, I was glancing at *The Evening Standard*? There was a small notice in the shipping news that caught my eye. *Royal Jersey*'s Monday sailing for New York was cancelled due to "*mechanical difficulty*" –

WATSON: What?

HOLMES: – so it is possible the Dalrymples turned round and took a train back to London last night, or stayed the night at a local inn and took an early train back this morning. Bradshaw's shows a northbound leaving Southampton at seven o'clock in the morning, arriving at Paddington at 11:45, and several more trains during the day.

WATSON: But if Dalrymple was trying to hide his daughter, there are many convenient places in this country where she might be hidden in perfect comfort without taking a sea voyage.

HOLMES: But much depends on whose plan it was to hide her from Robert Paige. Was it her father's? Or did she have a sudden change of heart? There's much we don't know.

WATSON: Have you been to Dalrymple's neighborhood before?

HOLMES: Never.

WATSON: Then how did you know where to direct the cabbie?

HOLMES: I make it my business to know every part of London, if not from experience, at least by location. *The Times* published an illustrated story about Dalrymple's town house when it was new, ten or fifteen years ago.

WATSON: Have you ever forgotten anything, Holmes?

HOLMES: Hmm. If I have, I can't remember what it was. Ah, we're there. (UP) This will do, driver.

SOUND EFFECT: HORSE STOPS. THEY EXIT THE CAB. QUIET NATURE SOUNDS

HOLMES: (TO CABBIE) We'll need you to wait, and we'll double your fare.

CABBIE: (OFF) Can't do it, guv'nor. No 'orse-drawn vehicles allowed to stand on this street. Sanitary reasons.

HOLMES: Then if you're told to move on, wait down at the corner in Coldridge Street and we'll find you. Come, Watson.

WATSON: These homes are like castles!

HOLMES: And the castle up ahead would be the abode of Sir Edward Dalrymple.

WATSON: You remember it from that old newspaper article? Amazing!

HOLMES: No, from the name carved on this stone gatepost.

WATSON: Oh. Heh-heh. "Dalrymple". Of course. Well, I see he has electricity.

HOLMES: And a telephone, if those wires are any evidence. After you.

SOUND EFFECT: THEY WALK UP SOME BRICK STEPS AND STOP KNOCK ON DOOR WITH A HEAVY KNOCKER

WATSON: What do you suppose it must have cost to build this place?

HOLMES: Estimating real estate values isn't among my talents. Ah, the butler approaches.

WATSON: What? How can you hear that?

HOLMES: I can't hear it, but I can see movement inside through a peephole disguised in this elaborate carving on the door.

WATSON: What? I don't see it.

HOLMES: It's hidden a bit higher than your eye level but visible to a person of my height. If you were to stand on your toes you could see it . . . but now that won't be necessary. Here he is.

SOUND EFFECT: BOLT SLIDES, BIG DOOR OPENS

HANLEY: Yes, gentlemen?

HOLMES: I am Sherlock Holmes and this is Doctor John H Watson. We are here to see Sir Edward Dalrymple. Our cards.

HANLEY: I'm sorry, gentlemen, but Sir Edward has retired for the night.

WATSON: Is he ill? I am a physician . . . .

HANLEY: No, he is not ill. He prefers to retire early.

HOLMES: Be good enough to give him our cards if you please, and tell him we shall call earlier next time.

HANLEY: Very good, gentlemen. Good night.

SOUND EFFECT: DOOR CLOSES

MUSIC: UNDERCURRENT

WATSON: (NARRATING) On our ride back to Baker Street, we had the cabby detour to the home address Robert Paige had written on his business card. There was no answer at his door. It had been a frustrating evening all around. I left Holmes going through some of his files, and I retired, suddenly lonely for my Constance, who was spending the month near Brighton for her health, which had been declining. I was in that twilight between consciousness and sleep, when I thought I heard the door to the stairway open and close, and low voices in the sitting room. I slipped my Eley's No. 2 into the pocket of my robe and stepped down to the sitting room. There, Holmes and Robert Paige were seated, face to face, in front of the fire in earnest conversation.

MUSIC: OUT

SOUND EFFECT: CLOCK

HOLMES: Ah, Watson. Our apologies for waking you.

PAIGE: It's my fault, Doctor. When I saw Mr. Holmes's note on my door, I flew here as fast as my feet would carry me!

HOLMES: When we stopped by on our way from Dalrymple's, Watson, I left a note saying he should come here no matter the hour. Perhaps I didn't mention it.

WATSON: You didn't; but now that you're here and I'm awake, what news do you have, Mr. Paige?

HOLMES: We both have news. I told him Sophie's voyage had been cancelled.

PAIGE: And then I told him – I've seen Sophie! She's in her house in Park Terrace!

WATSON: Did you talk with her?

PAIGE: No, no! I couldn't sleep for worrying about her, so — late as it was – I took a cab to Park Terrace and walked up and down, just to be on the street where she lived! She told me once that her bedroom was on the northwest corner of the second story, and to my relief, I saw her lamp was lit and there was someone in her room. There's a large chestnut tree outside her window, and I climbed it in hopes that somehow she hadn't gone after all, and miraculously, there she was!

WATSON: Did you make your presence known?

PAIGE: Oh, no! If I had been caught, I could be prosecuted as a Peeping Tom and my career would be through. I stayed on my perch for an hour, just thrilled to see her, but she was pacing back and forth, back and forth, obviously tormented! What I would have given to have stolen her away and awakened the nearest magistrate so we could be married!

HOLMES: Tell Dr. Watson about the origin of your middle name.

PAIGE: Dunstan is my mother's maiden name. My father chose it, and I was christened Robert Dunstan Paige.

WATSON: Then why did it alarm Dalrymple when he heard it?

PAIGE: I don't know, but I do have a theory. Perhaps some distant person with that same name could have been a threat to Sir

197

Edward at some time. I just want the opportunity to assure him that whatever the name means to him, he has no reason to fear. My mother is a Dunstan from some other branch of the family, or possibly not even from the same family at all!

HOLMES: And you shall have that opportunity tomorrow – correction, *today* – if Dalrymple is willing to see us.

MUSIC: EXCITING, OMINOUS BACKGROUND

WATSON: (NARRATING) The plan was, Holmes and I would return to Dalrymple's home and attempt to see him. If he refused, Holmes would swear out a complaint against him with the Metropolitan Police, charging that an adult woman was being held prisoner in her parents' home, and ask that Inspector Gregson, whom Holmes regarded as the most intelligent of the Scotland Yard detectives, be assigned to the case. But as it turned out, that wasn't necessary.

MUSIC: OUT

SOUND EFFECT: (OFF) DOOR OPENS, MAN WALKS TOWARD MICROPHONE

DALYRMPLE: (SLIGHTLY OFF MICROPHONE) I am Edward Dalrymple

HOLMES: I am Sherlock Holmes, and this is my associate, Dr. John H. Watson.

DALYRMPLE: And what is your purpose here?

HOLMES: We wish to assure you, first of all, that we come only with the hope of resolving a mystery.

DALYRMPLE: I know of no mystery.

HOLMES: *Dunstan.*

DALYRMPLE: (TIGHTENS) Where did you hear that name?

HOLMES: It is the middle name of our client, Robert D. Paige, as I think you know.

DALYRMPLE: He's your client?

HOLMES: A very earnest and honourable young man, if ever I saw one –

DALYRMPLE: I know who he is. So he sent you here?

WATSON: No one sent us here. We are here of our own accord.

DALYRMPLE: (PAUSE) All right, Hanley, we'll be in the drawing room.

HANLEY: Very good, sir.

DALYRMPLE: This way.

SOUND EFFECT: THREE MEN WALK, PAUSE. DOOR OPENS. WALK IN. DOOR CLOSES

WATSON: Let me compliment you on this magnificent home of yours, Sir Edward –

DALYRMPLE: My daughter has read some of your stories. She's told her mother about them, and I suspect she's read some of them, too.

WATSON: I can't tell you how gratified I am to hear that!

DALYRMPLE: I consider such things a damned waste of paper and ink. Now what do you know about Dunstan?

HOLMES: We know that Dunstan is Robert Paige's mother's maiden name, and we know that you knew that as well. We know that when you learned that Robert is her son, your entire manner changed. You sent Paige home, and hours later you took your wife and daughter away from London and booked passage for them on a ship sailing to America. But the ship didn't sail.

199

DALYRMPLE: What are you talking about? The ship sailed. I saw it leave Southampton myself!

HOLMES: You did not, sir. Its sailing was cancelled and your daughter is here!

SOUND EFFECT: (OFF) DOOR OPENS

SOPHIE: (OFF) Father, I heard someone at the door –

DALRYMPLE: Go back to your room, Sophronia!

SOPHIE: (MOVING ON) No! I heard Robert's name mentioned! Is he here?

DALRYMPLE: No, and I want you to leave this room right now! We are holding a private conversation! Now leave us!

HOLMES: It's a pleasure to meet you, Sophie. Robert has told us so much about you!

SOPHIE: Robert – ? Told you – ? Who are you?

HOLMES: I am Sherlock Holmes. This is Doctor Watson.

SOPHIE: Sherlock Holmes? Are you really?

DALRYMPLE: All right, I've had enough of your meddling! You two: Get out! Get out of this house before I ring for the police!

SOPHIE: Father, what are you doing?

DALRYMPLE Trying to protect you!

SOPHIE: No! They're not leaving!

DALRYMPLE: Get away from that door!

SOUND EFFECT: DOOR SLAMS SHUT

SOPHIE: No. I have a right to hear what they have to say!

200

DALRYMPLE: They'll say nothing more or I'll have them thown out!

SOPHIE: Then . . . Mr. Holmes . . . Doctor Watson . . . Robert has hired you?

WATSON: Yes. After he got your note, he rushed here to see *you*, but the butler said you were gone. There was no explanation –

SOPHIE: Yes, I was gone! And I couldn't give him an explanation, because I didn't know why my father put my mother and me on a ship in the middle of the night, saying he wanted to give us a holiday in America! It was a lie, and we knew it!

DALYRMPLE: I did it for your own good, Sophie. You must believe me! For your good! For your mother's good! If you understood what I've been living with – I had to stop you, Sophie! I couldn't let you marry him!

SOPHIE: You can't stop me!

DALYRMPLE: Listen to me! When you told me your plans to marry him, I had no objection. You're twenty-five. You should be married!

SOPHIE: But not to Robert!

DALYRMPLE: No, not to Robert.

SOPHIE: Why? Why? What has he done?

SOUND EFFECT: URGENT KNOCK ON THE DOOR, DOOR OPENS

HANLEY: Forgive me, sir, but Mr. Paige is at the door and he refuses to leave until you speak to him.

SOPHIE: Robert's here? Go let him in, Hanley!

DALYRMPLE: You'll do nothing of the kind, Hanley!

SOPHIE: Then I'll go to him! We'll elope!

201

DALYRMPLE: You can't! You'll bring disgrace down on our family!

SOPHIE: Go let him in, Hanley!

HANLEY: . . . Sir? What should I do?

DALYRMPLE: (LONG PAUSE) All right, let him in. And may God protect us!

MUSIC: STING

HANLEY: Mr. Paige, sir.

DALYRMPLE: All right, Hanley. That will be all. I'll call if I need you.

HANLEY: Yes, sir.

SOUND EFFECT: DOOR CLOSES

DALYRMPLE: I suppose you're proud of yourself, Paige.

PAIGE: Proud of myself? I seem to be carrying some evil around with me that's turned you against me!

SOPHIE: You're carrying no evil, my darling! When we're married, we don't ever have to listen to such foolishness again!

DALYRMPLE: You don't know! Neither of you know what you're doing!

SOPHIE: Then tell us!

(A LONG SILENCE)

HOLMES: Or shall I tell it? (PAUSE) Very well. Robert, your mother, Elsie Dunstan, at one time lived in the Dalrymple's house.

DALYRMPLE: That is a lie! She never lived in this house!

HOLMES: I didn't say she lived in this house. She lived in your *previous* house, before this house was built. She was a servant, a girl in her teens.

PAIGE: My mother?

DALYRMPLE: She was one of many servants. I'd forgotten all about her. She wasn't important at all.

HOLMES: But at one time, she was quite important. To you.

DALYRMPLE: All right, stop! That's enough!

PAIGE: Oh, no it isn't! I want to hear it all!

SOPHIE: And so do I!

HOLMES: It would be better if *you* told them, wouldn't it, Sir Edward? Why don't you have your butler bring your wife down as well, so the whole family can hear.

DALYRMPLE: My wife knows! (PAUSE) She's always known.

SOPHIE: Known what?

DALYRMPLE: That the young tart fancied me and wouldn't let me out of her clutches! I was just a young man myself . . . I'd had too much to drink one night . . . she threw herself at me . . . .

PAIGE: Just a minute! Who are you talking about?

DALYRMPLE: Elsie. Elsie Dunstan.

PAIGE: My mother?

DALYRMPLE: It was long ago.

HOLMES: Twenty-five years ago?

DALYRMPLE: Yes. . . . .Yes!

SOPHIE: Wait a minute! What are you telling us?

DALYRMPLE: Elsie gave birth –

SOPHIE: Oh, no!

DALRYMPLE: – To twins. She claimed they were . . . mine. But that couldn't be proved! It never could be proved!

HOLMES: But tell us what kind of twins they were.

DALRYMPLE: They're called . . . . Fraternal twins.

SOPHIE: Meaning they weren't identical?

DALRYMPLE: That's right. There was a boy . . . and a girl.

PAIGE: Oh my God.

DALRYMPLE: She was a loose woman! They could have been anyone's! I never loved her! I loved my wife! I told her so, over and over! But from that day on . . . . She's never let me forget!

SOPHIE: Then . . . she's not my mother?

DALRYMPLE: Listen to me, Sophie! When I learned Elsie was going to have a child, I paid for everything. I moved her out of our house and found her a decent home. When the babies were born, I had them placed for adoption. A young lawyer adopted the boy, and we adopted you. Your mother and I –

SOPHIE: Only she's not my mother! You're my father but my mother isn't . . . my mother!

DALRYMPLE: Never say that to her! It would break her heart! She's been as good a mother to you as if you were her own flesh and blood! She loves you! I – I love you!

PAIGE: And so where does that leave me?

DALRYMPLE Your father . . . your stepfather . . . adopted you. Gave you his name. But I never knew him. Never knew his name, never knew your name. You see, we adopted Sophie first, and we never visited the orphanage after that.

PAIGE: I see. And did you ever visit my mother after that?

DALYRMPLE: No.

PAIGE: Or me? Weren't you interested in seeing your son?

DALYRMPLE: I made a mistake. I went to church and asked to be forgiven, and I was forgiven, and in time . . . I forgot it and went on with my life. I never dreamed that my daughter and my son would ever meet!

SOPHIE: And fall in love.

PAIGE: Sophie . . . What can we do? (STRICKEN) What can we do?

WATSON: You can love each other as deeply as a brother and sister can love. When you are no longer young, you will still have that love, undimmed by time. What a gift that is! You will always be part of each other.

MUSIC: (UNDERCURRENT)

WATSON: (NARRATING) As Holmes and I rode back to Baker Street, he was silent for a long time. And then . . . .

HOLMES: Where did that come from? That wisdom, that counsel you gave to those poor young lovers?

WATSON: I don't know, Holmes.

HOLMES: Well . . . I think you do.

MUSIC: SEGUE TO *DANSE MACABRE*

WATSON: This is Dr. John H. Watson. I've had many more adventures with Sherlock Holmes, and I'll tell you another one . . . *when next we meet!*

MUSIC: (FADE OUT)

The Disappearance the Cutter *Alicia*
by John Hall

CHARACTERS

- SHERLOCK HOLMES
- DR. JOHN H. WATSON
- PONY TRAP DRIVER – *Forties, North Country Accent*
- CAPTAIN MOTT – *Eighties, Retired sea captain, North Country Accent*
- FISHERMAN – *Any age, North Country*
- MRS. BLAKE – *Thirties*
- MERRITT – *Thirties*

SOUND EFFECT: OPENING SEQUENCE, BIG BEN

ANNOUNCER: *The Further Adventures of Sherlock Holmes,* starring John Patrick Lowrie as Sherlock Holmes, and Lawrence Albert as Dr. John H. Watson.

MUSIC: *DANSE MACABRE* (UP AND UNDER)

WATSON: (NARRATING) In the summer of 1899, an investigation, which has no bearing on my present subject, took the two of us to Northumberland, a place which neither of us had visited before. The case which had originally taken us there was soon concluded satisfactorily, and for my part, I looked forward to returning to London. Holmes, however, seemed disinclined to hurry back, and over breakfast one morning I learned just why . . . .

MUSIC: OUT

HOLMES: It was at this time of year, Watson, and not so very many miles away, that the cutter *Alicia* disappeared some ten or twelve years back, in rather odd circumstances.

WATSON: Ah, yes, I seem to recall the case. Sailed into a small patch of mist, did she not, and never emerged?

HOLMES: Just so. I was consulted at the time.

WATSON: Oh?

HOLMES: Yes. (PAUSE) I was consulted at the time, but could not think of any possible explanation. I did not visit the scene, since a search had been made by the local fishermen and Coast Guard, and it seemed to me that where expert local knowledge had failed, I could not hope to succeed. I confess, I still cannot imagine what might have happened to the vessel.

WATSON: (LAUGHS) But, now you are here, you would like to investigate more thoroughly?

HOLMES: Well, then, quite frankly I would, although after this span of time, the trail, if ever there were one, will have gone stone-cold. Are you in any great hurry to return home?

WATSON: Not I. (NARRATING) It was true. We could return at any time, but such an opportunity might not occur again. I knew that Holmes was bursting to look into the problem, and I too found my curiosity piqued to be so close to the place where this very curious disappearance occurred. When breakfast was over, then, we paid our bill, took our bags – we both travel light – and set off in a hired pony and trap for the little fishing village, not many miles away, from whence the crew of the *Alicia* had been drawn.

SOUND EFFECT: PONY AND TRAP GOING ALONG ROUGH ROAD

HOLMES: You would have known the men who crewed the *Alicia*, driver?

DRIVER: I did, sir. It wasn't a large crew, two men and a boy. The skipper was a man named Allinson, and the mate was Josiah Merritt. Allinson's son, young Toby, was acting as third hand. Allinson and his wife had but the one child, and then Merritt, who was only twenty or so, had recently become engaged to be married to the sister of Allinson's wife, and indeed the wedding was set for a fortnight or so from the day the *Alicia* disappeared, so the tragedy was all the worse for that.

WATSON: Indeed. It is said lightly that "worse things happen at sea", and I have no doubt that the deeps hold many a tragic secret.

DRIVER: True enough, sir.

HOLMES: Thank you, driver. I had recalled the names, but had not realized that it was so close-knit a little band.

DRIVER: Aye, sir. Tragic, it was, for the families. Here we are, gentlemen.

SOUND EFFECT: TRAP RATTLES TO A HALT

HOLMES: Thank you, driver.

SOUND EFFECT: FISHING PORTS, SEAGULLS, ETC.

WATSON: First thing, find a place to stay, Holmes! With decent food.

HOLMES: Hmm. Now, Watson, you are, I know, an enthusiast for the sea stories of Mr. Clark Russell, and you have done a bit of sailing yourself, I believe, quite apart from your passages to India and the like?

WATSON: Oh, Oh, to be sure. Nothing like it, Holmes. A grand life, a man's life.

HOLMES: Well, then, in your expert opinion, why should a ship vanish from the surface of the sea?

WATSON: By sinking, of course. Rough weather, a capsize, that sort of thing. All too common, I fear.

HOLMES: It was a calm day, full summer, no wind to speak of. The local reports said as much, though indeed it was proved by the presence of that small patch of mist, which any wind would surely have dispersed.

WATSON: Collision, then? Another ship?

HOLMES: There were no reports of any collision, nor of another vessel missing. Visibility was good –

WATSON: But the mist?

HOLMES: Purely local, a small patch. And, apart from the fact that no other vessel was missing, no other vessel was even seen in the vicinity.

WATSON: There must have been some observer, though, Holmes, or the sighting of the *Alicia* going into the mist could never have been made?

HOLMES: Very good, Watson! I have a note in my memorandum book. Ah, yes. A man named Captain Mott is recorded as having reported seeing the vessel enter the mist patch. I have his address here, as well as his deposition, so I think we shall call upon him.

WATSON: He might be at sea.

HOLMES: No, for he was already described as "retired" when the vessel vanished.

WATSON: (LAUGHS) You appear to have all the relevant facts quite at your fingertips, Holmes.

HOLMES: (LAUGHS) Well, I knew when we first set out from Baker Street that we should be in the locality, and so it would indeed have been remiss of me not to have looked up the details of so intriguing a case. Captain Mott's house is on the North Cliff Road, and there is the north cliff, so this is evidently our way.

SOUND EFFECT: FOOTSTEPS ON ROUGH PATH

211

HOLMES: (THOUGHTFUL) No collision, and no wind to blow her violently off course. What else would there be to account for it?

WATSON: A collision, but with some sunken object perhaps, rather than a ship? Or perhaps some floating object, that flotsam or jetsam, the exact difference between which always seemed so important to one's schoolmasters?

HOLMES: A logical surmise. But the water there is relatively shallow, and there was no trace of any sunken object, either before or after the disappearance of the *Alicia*, which indicates that she hit nothing, and indeed that she did not sink for whatever reason. A thorough search was made.

WATSON: Was any debris found floating on the surface?

HOLMES: Not a matchstick.

WATSON: Hmm. It is a puzzle, Holmes.

HOLMES: Perhaps. But your expertise has narrowed it down considerably, has it not? There remain but two possibilities, surely.

WATSON: Which are?

HOLMES: Well, one is that this singular patch of mist had some of the qualities or properties which might appeal to Monsieur Jules Verne, or Mr. H.G. Wells – namely, that in some supernatural fashion, it caused the vessel to vanish utterly without trace.

WATSON: (DISMISSIVE) Impossible, Holmes!

HOLMES: I quite agree.

WATSON: And the other possibility?

HOLMES: Work it out for yourself, Watson.

WATSON: You mean – (BREAKS OFF, PAUSES) You mean that the *Alicia* simply sailed out the other side of the mist, unobserved?

HOLMES: It is surely the only explanation which makes any sense?

WATSON: But the testimony of this fellow, Captain Mott?

HOLMES: Ah, there you have me. Now, "Rose Cottage" was the address, and there is –

WATSON: – A cottage with a rather wind-swept rose tree creeping up it!

HOLMES: Just so.

SOUND EFFECT: KNOCK AT DOOR; LONG PAUSE, THEN DOOR CREAKS OPEN

WATSON; (NARRATING) After what seemed an age, the door was opened by a man who might have served for the model of every salt-water captain that ever sailed between the pages of boys' adventure books. He was bearded, and had a patch over one eye, and more tattoos that any man is decently entitled to carry. He was very old, nearer eighty than seventy, so I could quite see that he had been retired ten years or so ago. He looked from one to the other of us, a question in his one unpatched eye.

HOLMES: Captain Mott?

MOTT: Aye. Who, might you be?

HOLMES: My name is Sherlock Holmes. (WAITS FOR REACTION) And this is Dr. John H Watson.

MOTT: Never heard of you! And I've no need of a doctor, for all that I'm getting on a bit.

HOLMES: Indeed? But it was really in connection with the curious disappearance of the *Alicia*, some time ago now, that we wished to speak to you.

MOTT: Aye? The *Alicia*, you say?

HOLMES: You recall the matter?

213

MOTT: Indeed I do, sir. (MUSING) Aye, the *Alicia*. A few years ago, now, sir, but I remember it as if it was yesterday. (REMEMBERS HIS MANNERS) But here I'm keeping you standing on the doorstep! Come in, gents. Come in and take a seat.

MUSIC: BRIDGE

WATSON: (NARRATING) The old fellow ushered us into his little parlour, all glass floats and lobster pots, and waved us to chairs.

MOTT: Aye. I remember it like it was yesterday, it being so strange and all.

HOLMES: Where were you when the *Alicia* sailed into the mist?

MOTT: Why, here, sir. Looking out through – that.

WATSON: A telescope! And a powerful one, by the look of it. Let me see. Yes, a splendid piece of equipment!

MOTT: Eyes none too good these days, gents. Eye, I should say, for I've nobbut the one. Still, with that old spy-glass, I reckon I can see as well as another.

HOLMES: And your cottage is perched, as it were, almost on the very edge of the cliffs. As a viewpoint, it could hardly be bettered.

MOTT: You have the right of it, sir. There's not much I miss.

HOLMES: I am certain you do not. And, that day, you saw the *Alicia* sail into a patch of mist?

MOTT: Small patch, it were. Out there. By the shallows.

HOLMES: And then?

MOTT: And then nothing. Never came out again, did she?

WATSON: Did she not?

MOTT: Well, I never seed her come out. And then she vanished, didn't she? Stands to reason, if she vanished, it must have been in that mist.

HOLMES: You say you did not see her leave the patch of mist.

MOTT: No.

HOLMES: Ah, but did you look?

MOTT: How d'you mean?

HOLMES: Well, had you the patch of mist under observation at all times? How long did you continue to look at it, after the *Alicia* had sailed into it?

MOTT: Can't rightly say, sir.

HOLMES: Did you move the telescope to look for any other vessels, say, once the *Alicia* had gone from view?

MOTT: Oh, aye.

HOLMES: So you were not actually observing the patch of mist the whole day?

MOTT: Oh, not the whole day. But long enough.

HOLMES: What o'clock was it?

MOTT: About dinner time, sir.

HOLMES: The evening?

MOTT: No! Dinner time. What you'd call "luncheon". Noon, near enough.

HOLMES: And you missed your luncheon, your dinner, I mean, that day, in order to scan the deeps?

MOTT: Not me! I've a good appetite, better than many a young one.

215

HOLMES: Did you eat your dinner in here? At your spy-glass?

MOTT: (SCORNFUL) Not a bit of it. I may be only an old sailing man, but I have my standards. I eats my dinner in the kitchen, at the table.

HOLMES: So you left your vantage point for long enough to eat your meal.

MOTT: Oh, aye.

HOLMES: Well, thank you very much, sir. You have been most helpful.

MOTT: A puzzle and all, isn't it? The *Alicia*, I mean? Her vanishing like that?

HOLMES: It is indeed. Thank you again, sir. We must bid you good day.

WATSON: (NARRATING) We took our leave of Captain Mott, and made our way down towards the little fishing village. Holmes turned to me with a smile.

HOLMES: Well, Watson?

WATSON: Well, Holmes, despite the assurances of that delightful old fellow, it seems pretty clear that the *Alicia* might easily have sailed on unobserved. But none the less, that does not tell us what happened to her.

HOLMES: No, but it does enable us to eliminate one possibility, that of the supernatural, does it not? It gives us a course, as it were, by which to steer.

WATSON: I trust there will be no more nautical metaphors in this case, Holmes?

HOLMES: It is said that the sea is in every Englishman's blood.

WATSON: (IGNORES THIS) And in any event, we had already eliminated the supernatural.

WATSON: True. So what does that leave?

HOLMES: It leaves the *Alicia* sailing into the mist, and out again. But what became of her then?

HOLMES: Ah, that is a puzzle. Where did the crew take her?

WATSON: Why should they take her anywhere, Holmes?

HOLMES: They must logically have taken her somewhere!

WATSON: No, no. I meant, rather, why should they have taken her somewhere special, as it were? They may just have sailed to their usual fishing grounds.

HOLMES: Not that, for there were other boats in the fleet out there, and they never saw the *Alicia* at their usual marks.

WATSON: Hmm. Well, then, they may have tried a different spot, somewhere new which they thought would give a good catch?

HOLMES: Plausible. And then?

WATSON: Then – well, they may have just sunk. Out of sight of land. Out of sight of even the good Captain Mott!

HOLMES: Sunk? How, precisely?

WATSON: Collision? Oh! No, for you said that no other vessel was missing, or involved in any accident. But what of some vessel which no-one knew was there?

HOLMES: Possible. But unlikely, surely? Unregistered, and crewed by men none of whom had a family, loved ones, to report their loss?

WATSON: Hmm. A ship of foreign registry?

HOLMES: I believe I said that I looked into the matter as best I could, at the time. That was one of the things I could check, and did. As also pleasure craft, yachts, Her Majesty's Navy.

WATSON: Hmm. (PAUSE) I know – a whirlpool!

HOLMES: A whirlpool?

WATSON: (DOUBTFUL) Or a water-spout.

HOLMES: Or a sea-serpent? The Kraken? A shoal of mermaids?

WATSON: (OFFENDED) No need for cheap sarcasm, Holmes! Just trying to help, after all.

HOLMES: It won't do, Watson. These waters may not be as busy as the English Channel, but still there are fishing boats, larger vessels bound to and from the Baltic, or Scandinavia. Any vagaries of weather, any freak of the tide, would be noticed.

WATSON: I suppose so.

HOLMES: The crew of the *Alicia*, then, deliberately sailed her to where they would not be known.

WATSON: But that could be anywhere, Holmes. The Baltic. Scandinavia, even. Possible, with a well-found boat and a stout crew.

HOLMES: Possible, but improbable. Even France, relatively close, would present them with practical difficulties.

WATSON: The language, for instance?

HOLMES: Just so. And the very unfamiliar way of life. No, it was for somewhere in England that they were bound. And somewhere not too far, either, or I miss my guess.

WATSON: And why that? Why not the Thames, say? London?

218

HOLMES: (THOUGHTFUL) They knew these waters, you see, Watson. Their local fishing grounds, their familiar marks. What did these men know of the Wallet, or the Maplin Sands?

WATSON: That makes sense. But then, Holmes – they could not have gone anywhere *too* familiar, or they would have been seen. Recognized.

HOLMES: That, too, makes much sense. Very well, we have defined the problem very neatly, you and I. All that remains –

WATSON: – Is to find the solution.

HOLMES: Exactly. And here we are at the quayside, which is where we must start looking. A local boatman. That is our first objective.

WATSON: The fellow there, mending the nets? He looks pretty well encrusted with the local barnacles.

HOLMES: Hmm. Good day, my man!

FISHERMAN: Good day, sir.

HOLMES: Any chance of hiring you and your boat for a short voyage?

FISHERMAN: How short?

HOLMES: Oh, a couple of hours. Half a day, at most.

FISHERMAN: Sight-seers, are you? Trippers?

HOLMES: Just so.

FISHERMAN: Not much call for pleasure cruises here, sir. Not sure –

HOLMES: Perhaps this might help?

SOUND EFFECT: CHINK OF COINS RATTLED IN THE HAND

FISHERMAN: Oh, well, sir. My little boat's just down here, if you and the other gentleman would care to step along?

MUSIC: HORNPIPE, FADING OUT QUICKLY

SOUND EFFECT: CREAK OF SAILS, SEAGULLS, ETC

FISHERMAN: Once round the lighthouse, is it, gents?

HOLMES: Where is the nearest port?

FISHERMAN: Just left it, sir!

HOLMES: (LAUGHS) No, the next one. North or south?

FISHERMAN: South, sir. North, there's nothing until you reach Scotland. And that's sailing against wind and tide.

HOLMES: South, then. The nearest landfall?

FISHERMAN: That'd be Seawall, sir. Fifteen miles off. You want to go there?

HOLMES: In that direction. Is there nowhere you might beach a vessel before there?

FISHERMAN: (DOUBTFULLY) There's Smuggler's Bay, sir. Five mile this side of Seawall.

HOLMES: Ah-Hah!

FISHERMAN: But the tide's awkward there, sir. Many an old smuggler been sunk there, plying his trade.

HOLMES: Very well. Seawall it is, then. And perhaps you could point out this bay as we pass it?

FISHERMAN: Right you are, sir.

HOLMES: Is there a railway station at Seawall?

FISHERMAN: (LAUGHS) No railway station before Newcastle, sir. (PAUSE) But there is a halt up on the moors. Ten miles off.

<u>SOUND EFFECT: SMALL SEAPORT</u>

HOLMES: Are you ready for a ten mile walk, Watson?

WATSON: I'm ready for my dinner! Your theory, I take it, is that these men sailed the *Alicia* here, then took the train?

HOLMES: Most likely they landed at that Smuggler's Bay, sunk the boat, and took to their heels over the moors. Ten miles is nothing to a fit man.

WATSON: Even less to a fit cab-horse! And look – isn't that the same fellow we hired this morning? (CALLS OUT) I say!

DRIVER: Hello again, gents! Had I known you was bound for Seawall, I'd have brought you here direct!

HOLMES: Be that as it may. Do you know the railway halt, up on the moor?

DRIVER: Know it, sir? I'm bound there now, to meet the express. Got a parcel to collect.

HOLMES: The express?

DRIVER: Southbound express, sir. A funny place for it to stop, middle of nowhere, but the halt serves the big house, you see. Sir George, he's a director of the railway company.

HOLMES: I see. Are there many trains?

DRIVER: Just two per day, sir. Northbound at five-thirty-two in the morning, southbound express to Sheffield at four-twenty-nine in the afternoon. Climb aboard, gents, if you're wanting the train, for I'm off!

<u>SOUND EFFECT: STEAM TRAIN COMPARTMENT</u>

221

HOLMES: We have made good time. We shall be in Sheffield in a few minutes.

WATSON: And then?

HOLMES: And then we shall see where our luck takes us.

WATSON: Luck? You used not to rely upon "luck", Holmes!

HOLMES: (LAUGHS) Well, in this case, it is pretty much all we have. But the Goddess of Chance has served us well so far, has she not?

WATSON: (SKEPTICAL) Has she?

HOLMES: Well, if the *Alicia* was sailed as we think –

WATSON: "*We*", Holmes?

HOLMES: As *I* think, then. And if the men did take a train – and that seems logical – they did so in the daytime. Ergo, they took this train, and they arrived, as we are arrived, in Sheffield. Come along!

SOUND EFFECT: BUSY RAIL STATION. PASSENGERS ALIGHTING

WATSON: There are many "if's" in your thesis, Holmes. And if – *if* – you are right, what then? It was a decade ago, after all. And this is one of the busiest rail junctions in the north of England. If they had come here, they might have taken a connecting train to anywhere. Even to London, for I see there is one on an hour's time. I suggest we find a restaurant, and take that train ourselves. Do you see a restaurant anywhere?

HOLMES: I see that there are plenty of trains to London, so that we need not hasten. And I see a large and garish poster, advertising, "*Cheap, Clean, Good Rooms To Let*".

WATSON: Holmes, the poster is brand new!

222

HOLMES: Agreed, but there were very likely rooms to let at the same address a decade ago. Let us examine this poster a little more closely.

SOUND EFFECT: PAPER SCRAPED WITH A FINGERNAIL

WATSON: (HORRIFIED) Holmes, what on earth are you doing? Defacing railway property is a serious crime. You could be liable to a few years penal servitude.

HOLMES: Nonsense. A small fine, at most. A-ha! You see. Watson? The new poster has merely been glued over the old ones. A modern palimpsest, my boy! And more useful than many a medieval court roll, for it shows that there were rooms to let at the same address some time ago, although the landlord's name is different. Well, what do you say?

WATSON: I say that of all the preposterous theories you have put forth, this takes the cake! And not merely the cake, but any chance of my dinner, to boot! But – (RESIGNED) we might as well play it out to the bitter end. What's the address? "Knife-grinders' Alley". Hmm. Sounds insalubrious enough. (CALLS OUT) Cab!

SOUND EFFECT: CAB RATTLES TO A HALT

HOLMES: Thank you, driver!

SOUND EFFECT: CAB RATTLES OFF. KNOCK AT DOOR. DOOR OPENS

HOLMES: Good morning, madam. Mrs. Blake, is it not? We saw your advertisement at the rail station.

MRS. BLAKE: I'm sorry, gentlemen, but I have no rooms free just at the moment. If you like, I can give you another address, a very nice place –

HOLMES: No, no. It was not a room we were wanting. But I fear that you can scarcely be expected to help us in our investigation, for you cannot have been running this house ten years ago? You are too young, I fancy.

MRS. BLAKE: Thank you, sir. But I assure you that I was here ten years ago, and more. My mother had the place then, but I helped her, in the kitchen and what have you. Then I met Joe, my husband, I mean, and we more or less took over the running of it, with Ma being ill. She died some four years ago now.

HOLMES: Ah. I'm sorry to hear it. Joe, you say? Joseph, that is?

MRS. BLAKE: No, sir, Josiah.

HOLMES: Ah, yes. Josiah Merritt, of course.

MRS. BLAKE: Blake, sir.

HOLMES: Of course. How very silly of me. Tell me, would it be too much to ask for a word with Mr. Blake? Is he in the house now?

MRS. BLAKE: He is, sir. If you'll wait in the parlour, I'll call him.

SOUND EFFECT: FOOTSTEPS. DOOR OPENS AND CLOSES

HOLMES: We appear to be in luck, you see, Watson.

WATSON: It may be a mere coincidence of given names, though. The surname is different, after all. And –

SOUND EFFECT: DOOR OPENS

MERRITT: (SLIGHTLY SUSPICIOUS) You wished to see me, sir?

HOLMES: In private, if we may. Mrs. Blake, I wonder –

MRS. BLAKE: I'll be in the kitchen, Joe.

SOUND EFFECT: DOOR CLOSES, NOISILY

HOLMES: Now, Mr. Josiah Blake. Or should I say Josiah Merritt? I saw a photograph taken of you some time ago, and you have changed remarkably little in the meantime. Quick, Watson! He's –

WATSON: He's fine, Holmes.

BLAKE: Aye. Just a bit shocked, sir, that's all. How did you find me? Did they send you?

HOLMES: (GENTLY) No-one has sent us, I assure you. And no-one need ever know what is said in this room. But you left some questions unanswered when you vanished all those years ago.

WATSON: And a grieving family.

MERRITT: (SKEPTICAL) Grieving family? (THEN ANGRY) Why the devil d'you think we ran away in the first place, you great dunce?

WATSON: I really have no idea, sir. Perhaps if you were to explain the matter to us, without descending to personalities?

HOLMES: (SOOTHING) That is an excellent notion.

MERRITT: Well, maybe so. You'll understand, if you know the truth. Allinson was the owner of a little fishing boat, the *Alicia*, and I'd learned my sailing from my father, in a little village a few miles up the coast. Then, when I was old enough, I set off to seek my fortune, as you might say, and walked down the coast. I met Allinson on the dockside, and we got to talking, and the upshot was that he offered me both a job going mate with him, and lodgings, for they had a spare room. It seemed ideal, and I moved my bits of gear in right away. Well, I soon worked out that something was wrong with the pair of them. Oh, Allinson was all right. You couldn't ask for a finer skipper or a better friend. And the lad, Toby, he was first-class too. It was the wife that was the cause of all the trouble. She was the daughter of an old lady who lived a couple of doors away – the father had cleared out, he was nobody's fool! Well, the old lady had a tongue like the worst sort of fishwife, and the daughter wasn't far behind. She scolded poor old Allinson something terrible. And she drank.

WATSON: Good Lord!

MERRITT: Aye. And when the daughter stopped, the mother came in. There was another daughter, a younger one – and don't ask me just how it happened, gentlemen, or I couldn't tell you, not to this day – but I found myself engaged to this other daughter, and the old lady set fair to running my life. Running it? *Ruining* it, more like. Well, you don't like talking of these things, but with being out at sea so much together, we couldn't rightly help mentioning it now and again. One day we were in the pub, and maybe we'd had one too many – you know how it is – and Allinson, he's pretty well in tears. "You don't know the half of it, Joe," he tells me. "She drinks, and she hits the boy, and I'm sure there are other men. And what's more, her sister encourages it, and she's every bit as bad herself, if not worse," he goes on. Well, the wedding was only three or four weeks off, so you can imagine how that sounded to me! I got cold feet, and no mistake. "Tom," I say to him, "I'm scared, pal. What am I to do?" and he looks at me, and he says, "What gets to me is the boy. You and me, we're grown men, we ought to be able to handle it, but the boy's only young. Delicate, like. He takes it to heart. Tell you what," he says, half joking, "we could run away to sea!"

HOLMES: And you did?

MERRITT: To be brief, we did, sir. Oh, we talked, and we hesitated. But both of us had set our minds to it. All upon. We couldn't quite bring ourselves to do it, though, until one day we decided that we'd let Toby have the last word. Allinson asks him, "Would you like to sail off to a new life?" And the boy, he says, "Australia, father?", him having always had a fancy to go there. Tom says, "Yes, Australia if you like, but it'd just be the two of us, or three if Joe wants to come as well." And the boy thinks a moment and then nods his head.

HOLMES: You beached the boat, took the train, and arrived here?

MERRITT: When we got here, we were tired out. We saw the address of this place at the station. Tom and Toby, they stayed the one night and then moved on. I had a postcard from them, from London. I don't know if they ever got to Australia, I hope so.

HOLMES: And you stayed here, of course?

MERRITT: I met Violet, that first night, and I was taken with her at once. And I could see she felt the same way about me. The old lady – Violet's mother, I mean – was running the place then, but she was getting on, and not too well. She'd been looking for a handyman to do a few little repairs, so I offered to help out a bit, and one thing led to another. (PAUSE) Well, gentlemen, you've heard my story. What action do you propose to take?

HOLMES: You have committed no crime, of course.

WATSON: I suppose there might be grounds for an action for breach of promise of marriage. But only if they catch up with you!

MERRITT: "If"? You won't –

HOLMES: No, sir. We shall not. Come, Watson. Good day, Mr. – ah, *Blake*.

SOUND EFFECT: DOOR OPENS AND CLOSES. FOOTSTEPS

WATSON: A very lucky day's work, Holmes. Reliant upon much coincidence!

HOLMES: Oh, I don't know. We followed the trail, and we were rewarded. A modicum of chance, I agree, but even had we not actually run into Merritt, we should none the less have demonstrated what might easily have happened. (PAUSE) If we can find a cab, we can catch a London train in less than twenty minutes, and be back in Baker Street for dinner.

MUSIC: *DANSE MACABRE*

WATSON: This is Dr. John H. Watson. I've had many more adventures with Sherlock Holmes, and I'll tell you another one . . . *when next we meet!*

MUSIC: (FADE OUT)

The Mystery at Mandrake's Circus
by Gareth Tilley

CHARACTERS

- SHERLOCK HOLMES
- DR. JOHN H. WATSON
- HANS THE CLOWN – *Fifties, Chirpy, Gullible, Simple Man, Working class English Accent*
- CHARLES MANDRAKE – *Circus owner, Ringmaster, Theatrical English Voice*
- ANNIE EVANS – *Working class, Circus Girl*
- PRINCESS AYESHA – *Mysterious and commanding voice, Foreign Accent*
- HERCULES THE STRONGMAN – *Deep Voice*
- CROWD No's 1 and 2

(COLD OPENING)

SOUND EFFECT: FORTUNE TELLERS TENT. JANGLE OF CHIMES

HANS: Princess Ayesha, I heard you wanted to see me?

AYESHA: Yes Hans, I did. Come in and be seated, won't you?

HANS: I'd rather stand, if it's all the same to you.

AYESHA: There's no need to be afraid. Please – come and sit in the chair.

HANS: So you can do your . . . business?

AYESHA: If by "business", you mean read your future . . . .

HANS: My mother, bless her soul, told me never to listen to gypsy fortune tellers . . . .

AYESHA: I am no gypsy, Hans. I am a princess.

HANS: From where exactly?

AYESHA: I am a direct descendant from Cleopatra. Do you know who she was?

HANS: (UNCERTAIN) I've heard of her . . . .

AYESHA: Then you'll know she was the greatest Queen of Egypt. Come now, Hans. Sit here so I may talk with you.

HANS: If I must.

SOUND EFFECT: MOVEMENT OF CHAIR

HANS: Though why you'd want to see someone like me, I don't know.

AYESHA: I have seen the future Hans. *Your* future.

HANS: And what does that mean?

AYESHA: I mean just as I say.

HANS: You can really see into the future?

AYESHA: A nonbeliever, such as you, couldn't begin to imagine the powers I hold.

HANS: But I thought the crystal ball was just part of the act.

AYESHA: No Hans, it is no act. With this crystal ball, I can see images from the past, present, and even the future.

HANS: Then you'll tell me about Annie? She's so pretty, but I don't think she's as sweet on me as I'm on her.

AYESHA: I've not summoned you here to talk of love.

HANS: Then what is it?

AYESHA: There are clouds on your horizon, Hans.

HANS: Clouds? What kind of clouds?

AYESHA: Come. Show me your palm.

HANS: It's a bit dirty, mind. I've just been cleaning out the lions.

AYESHA: It is of no matter. (WHILST EXAMINING HAND) Yes, yes, it is as I thought. You see this line here?

HANS: Yes.

AYESHA: That is the line of your life. It shows how long you will live.

HANS: Does it?

AYESHA: And you see this break in the line?

HANS: There, you mean?

AYESHA: It is as I feared . . . .

HANS: Well, what is it?

AYESHA: Your life, Hans, is about to be cut tragically short.

HANS: Now hold on a minute. That can't be right. I'm as fit as a fiddle, see?

AYESHA: Your health has nothing to do with it. The palm never lies.

HANS: Yes, but . . . .

AYESHA: You must listen to me, Hans. What I say is the truth.

HANS: How – How long have I got then?

AYESHA: Let me see your hand again . . . . (TUTS)

231

HANS: Is it bad?

AYESHA: You have no more than a matter of days.

HANS: Days? Are you sure?

AYESHA: There can be no doubt.

HANS: And there's really nothing I can do?

AYESHA: No, I see no possible . . . . Wait a moment!

HANS: What is it?

AYESHA: Yes, there might be a way. See how this line crosses the line of life here and then curves round to cross it again?

HANS: Is that important?

AYESHA: This line represents a person. Someone who can bridge the gap between the two parts of your life, the here and now and your possible future.

HANS: They can prevent my death?

AYESHA: I believe so.

HANS: You must tell me who it is!

AYESHA: That will be difficult. It will require the most delicate of readings.

HANS: Please, you must try and find out who it is.

AYESHA: Very well. We will consult the crystal ball first. You must place your hands on either side. Good. Now close your eyes and concentrate. Think of the stars and moon, for they are the future . . . Concentrate, Hans . . . .

HANS: I'm trying, Princess . . . .

AYESHA: Ah yes. The clouds are clearing. Yes, I see patterns forming. It is a man you seek.

HANS: What can you tell me about him?

AYESHA: Ah, he is both brave and cunning.

HANS: Cunning?

AYESHA: Yes, but not evil. He works for the forces of good.

HANS: A policeman?

AYESHA: No, I sense he works outside of official organizations.

HANS: You mean an amateur?

AYESHA: Ah, I see him more clearly now. He has a great brow and prominent forehead. This man is a great thinker. His mind is his weapon.

HANS: I know who you're talking about – It's Mr. Sherlock Holmes!

AYESHA: And you feel that in your heart?

HANS: Yes . . . yes, I think so.

AYESHA: Then he is the man you seek.

HANS: What should I do when I find him?

AYESHA: First you must take a sign.

HANS: A sign?

AYESHA: Yes, you must show him this . . . .

SOUND EFFECT: RUSTLE OF PAPER

HANS: A poster for the circus?

AYESHA: Then bring him to me. I shall explain what needs to be done.

HANS: Right. I'll go and fetch him straight away.

AYESHA: Wait! Before you go, there is something you must know. No one must hear about this, you understand?

HANS: Yes.

AYESHA: When you bring Sherlock Holmes to me, no one must know who he is. Do you hear?

HANS: If you think it's important.

AYESHA: It is vital, for your very life depends on it.

HANS: Then no one will find out. Not from my lips.

AYESHA: Then go, Hans, and bring Sherlock Holmes back to me as soon as you can!

(INTRODUCTION)

SOUND EFFECT: OPENING SEQUENCE, BIG BEN

ANNOUNCER: *The Further Adventures of Sherlock Holmes*, starring John Patrick Lowrie as Sherlock Holmes, and Lawrence Albert as Dr. John H. Watson.

MUSIC: *DANSE MACABRE* (UP AND UNDER)

WATSON: (NARRATING) My name is Doctor John H. Watson, and I shared the adventures of Sherlock Holmes. The case I am about to relate occurred in the summer of 1895 and began, like so many, on a seemingly quiet and peaceful morning at our Baker Street lodgings. Mrs. Hudson had cleared away the breakfast leftovers, and Holmes was enjoying a pipe while I thumbed through the mornings newspapers. It has long been a maxim of Holmes's that – however great an author's imagination – truth is always more curious than fiction. As such, it had become a form of game for me to choose a seemingly mundane article, and for Holmes to try to prove it improbable in nature.

MUSIC: OUT

<u>SOUND EFFECT: BAKER STREET. RUSTLE OF PAPER. PAUSE. THEN . . . .</u>

WATSON: A-ha! I have one!

HOLMES: Really?

WATSON: At the very bottom of page ten.

<u>SOUND EFFECT: RUSTLE OF PAPER</u>

HOLMES: Where, exactly?

WATSON: Second column in. A man's been executed at the prison on Devil's Island. I ask you, Holmes – What could be more commonplace than that?

HOLMES: I must admit executions are by no means unusual there –

WATSON: I'd say they aren't. The place houses some of France's worst criminals.

HOLMES: – but in this case I think you've failed to note the man's name.

<u>SOUND EFFECT: RUSTLE OF PAPER</u>

WATSON: "The Jackal". I grant you it's a little strange, but not so outlandish for a murderer.

HOLMES: Then perhaps you're unaware of his role at the prison?

WATSON: Why don't you enlighten me, Holmes?

HOLMES: Like most institutions of its kind, the executioner is drawn from the ranks . . . .

WATSON: He was the prison executioner?

HOLMES: Indeed he was.

WATSON: Why should he do that? Surely it would make him the most hated man on the island?

HOLMES: Because the position also provides certain privileges. In fact, it was jealousy over his taking the role which led to an attack by a fellow prisoner.

WATSON: Attack?

HOLMES: And during the altercation, he killed his assailant – which is why he was guillotined.

WATSON: I still don't find the affair that remarkable.

HOLMES: Not when his first job as executioner was to build a new guillotine for the prison? Now I ask you, Watson, how many men can claim to have been killed by an instrument of their own design?

WATSON: How do you know all this, Holmes?

HOLMES: Yesterday's *Le Figaro* had a more detailed write-up. He was an interesting fellow, "The Jackal". You know, I sometimes wish the English criminal classes could emulate his flair . . . .

SOUND EFFECT: RING OF BELL INTERRUPTS

HOLMES: It seems we have a visitor. Perhaps you'd see who it is, Doctor.

WATSON: You mean question them on the doorstep?

HOLMES: Your eye is getting better. Why, only last week you sent away the Dowager Duchess of Devonshire without me having even to ask.

WATSON: You didn't fancy finding her lost Pekinese then?

HOLMES: It is not my area of speciality. What I'm after is something to challenge the intellect . . . .

WATSON: I'll go and open the door, then.

<u>SOUND EFFECT: A COUPLE OF FOOTSTEPS, THEN OPENING DOOR</u>

WATSON: (OFF MICROPHONE) Good morning.

HANS: (OFF MICROPHONE) Morning, sir. I've come to see Mr. Sherlock Holmes, if I may.

WATSON: (OFF MICROPHONE) You have an appointment?

HANS: (OFF MICROPHONE) No, sir, I can't say I have. I came in a huff, you see. It really is most important.

WATSON: (OFF MICROPHONE) In what way is it important?

HANS: (OFF MICROPHONE) It's a matter of life and death.

WATSON: (OFF MICROPHONE, CALLING) Holmes?

HOLMES: Yes, Watson, show him in.

<u>SOUND EFFECT: CLOSING DOOR AND COUPLE OF FOOTSTEPS</u>

WATSON: (ONTO MICROPHONE) This is Mr. Holmes.

HOLMES: And the gentleman who showed you in is my colleague, Doctor Watson.

HANS: I'm pleased to meet you both. My name is Hans Fredericks. But please, call me Hans. Everyone else does.

HOLMES: (FINDS IT UNUSUAL CALLING SOMEONE BY FIRST NAME) Er, very well . . . Hans. Do have a seat.

<u>SOUND EFFECT: SCRAPE OF CHAIR</u>

HANS: I'm sorry about arriving uninvited like this. I came here in such a rush . . . .

HOLMES: From a circus, I believe?

HANS: Why yes, that's right. Do you possess the same powers as Princess Ayesha, Mr. Holmes?

HOLMES: Princess Ayesha?

HANS: She's our fortune teller.

HOLMES: What I possess is the power to observe, Mr. Freder – er, Hans. The piece of dung stuck to the side of your shoe for instance. Taken in conjunction with the traces of sawdust, the inference is clear – elephant dung, I suggest . . . .

WATSON: But you also find elephants in the zoo, Holmes.

HOLMES: True, but the hint of greasepaint around his collar indicates a circus entertainer, does it not?

HANS: Then you did nothing psychic after all.

HOLMES: There is nothing that cannot be deduced in the presence of sufficient evidence.

WATSON: Perhaps you could tell us why you've come to consult Mr. Holmes?

HANS: It's the fortune teller at Mandrake's Circus.

WATSON: The Princess Ayesha you mentioned?

HANS: That's right. She said my life is in danger.

HOLMES: From what?

HANS: She didn't say.

HOLMES: Then how can she be so certain?

HANS: Prince Ayesha sees all, Mr. Holmes.

HOLMES: How convenient for her.

WATSON: Hans, how did she tell you about this danger?

HANS: Well, first she read my palm . . . .

HOLMES: She read your palm? Is that all?

HANS: Oh, no. She used her crystal ball, too.

HOLMES: Saints preserve us!

WATSON: (INTERJECTS) If I may clarify. This Prince Ayesha read your palm . . .

HOLMES: And used a crystal ball, Watson.

WATSON: . . . and used a crystal ball, and told you your life was in danger.

HANS: She said only Mr. Holmes here could save my life and I must go to him at once.

WATSON: And that's all she said?

HANS: Oh, no, of course not.

HOLMES: Ah, perhaps we are getting to the heart of the matter.

HANS: Here. She told me to give you this.

SOUND EFFECT: RUSTLE OF PAPER

HOLMES: (MUSING) Hmm . . . What do you make of it, Watson?

WATSON: It's a poster for Mandrake's Circus. Your circus, of course.

HANS: That's right.

WATSON: It shows a bare-chested knife-thrower and a girl tied to a wheel. Very colorful. At the bottom is the itinerary – first London, then Amsterdam, followed by London again, then Copenhagen . . . .

HOLMES: In short, it's a perfectly ordinary circus poster.

WATSON: I should say so.

HOLMES: And so would I. (ANNOYED) Really, sir, I don't take kindly to people wasting my time like this.

HANS: But she said I'd die if you didn't help me!

HOLMES: Then let me assure you, your life is considerably safer than the knife-thrower's assistant.

HANS: But Princess Ayesha –

HOLMES: (ANNOYED) Princess Ayesha be hanged! Unless you can give me a logical and coherent reason as to why you might die, I cannot be expected to assist you.

HANS: Yes, but –

HOLMES: Now if you don't mind, I am really very busy.

HANS: Of course . . . .

SOUND EFFECT: A COUPLE OF RAPID FOOTSTEPS, AND THEN OPENING DOOR

HOLMES: (MOVING OFF MICROPHONE) You know your way out, I trust.

HANS: Goodbye, then, Doctor.

WATSON: It was a pleasure to meet you, Mr. Fredericks.

SOUND EFFECT: A COUPLE OF FOOTSTEPS

HOLMES: (OFF MICROPHONE) And good-day to you, sir.

HOLMES: (ONTO MICROHPONE) I ask you, Watson, have you ever heard such nonsense in all your life?

WATSON: (DISAPPOINTED IN HIM) Holmes, only a moment before he arrived, you demonstrated how strange life can be. Would it really have been so much trouble to follow the matter up?

HOLMES: Oh, don't worry; I'll follow the matter up all right.

WATSON: Ah!

HOLMES: I've got a good mind to pay this Princess Ayesha a visit and tell her to stop sending every Tom, Dick, and Harry my way.

WATSON: (MOVING OFF) If you don't believe in prophecies, perhaps you'd better take a look out of the window.

HOLMES: (ONTO MICROPHONE) What have you seen?

WATSON: That man with the stick – he started following Hans just after he left us.

HOLMES: Are you sure?

WATSON: Quite sure.

HOLMES: Watson, do you know who that is?

WATSON: I can't say I do.

HOLMES: His name is "Silver" Wilkins. It just so happens that he's one of the biggest dealers in stolen goods in Limehouse.

WATSON: Then perhaps there is some truth in what our friend had to say after all.

MUSIC: STING

WATSON: (NARRATION) We donned our hats and headed out immediately. It soon became apparent that both Hans and his shadow, "Silver" Wilkins, were heading to Hampstead Heath. When we arrived, we found that, instead of the usual gathering of nannies with their perambulators, dog walkers, and other lovers of the great outdoors, the whole of the common had been taken over by a great circus. Crowds had gathered from near and far to enjoy the entertainment, and an atmosphere of high revelry filled the air. In all the hustle and bustle, it wasn't long before we lost sight of our quarry. Holmes and I decided to separate and double our chances of finding Hans all the more quickly . . . .

SOUND EFFECT: FAIRGROUND NOISE AND BUSTLE IN BACKGROUND

MANDRAKE: Roll up, roll up! Step this way to see intrigues that will amaze and delight. Roll up to witness wonders that will astound and astonish. You sir! Can I interest you in a ticket for the Big Top tonight?

WATSON: Er, no thank you.

MANDRAKE: Think of your grandchildren, sir, and of the marvels you'll be able to tell them you saw. Hercules the Strongman, who bends iron bars with his own bare hands. There's Vittoria the Circus Belle. (HUSHED) I tell you sir, you've never seen anything as pretty as her before . . . .

WATSON: No, really. Not now, thank you.

MANDRAKE: You know where to find me if you have a change of heart.

WATSON: I'll bear it in mind.

MANDRAKE: (MOVING OFF MICROPHONE) Roll up, roll up! Step this way . . . .

WATSON: (PUSHING THROUGH CROWD) Excuse me . . . Excuse me . . . .

ANNIE: Ow, do you mind?

WATSON: I'm sorry, madam. I do beg your pardon . . . .

ANNIE: I should think so, too, treading on a girl's toes like that!

WATSON: I do apologise. It's just that I didn't see you . . . .

ANNIE: That's alright. No harm done, I suppose.

WATSON: You're sure you're not hurt?

ANNIE: I'm alright, Mister, I promise.

WATSON: It's Doctor, actually. Doctor John Watson.

ANNIE: (LIGHTLY) I thought doctors were supposed to *cure* people, not *hurt* them!

WATSON: That is the general idea.

ANNIE: Annie Jones is my name, but you can call me Annie if you like. Everyone else does.

WATSON: Well, thank you, Annie. It's more than I deserve for my unchivalrous behaviour.

ANNIE: I suppose the circus can feel a little crowded if you're not used to it. It took me awhile when I started here, I can tell you.

WATSON: You work here?

ANNIE: Why don't you come over to the Big Top later and see the show?

WATSON: If I have time. I've always enjoyed the circus. It must be an exhilarating life here.

ANNIE: I'd say it is. Especially when you're the knife thrower's assistant.

WATSON: The knife – You don't mean someone actually throws knives at you?

ANNIE: That's just what I mean!

WATSON: Then you must have nerves of steel, Annie.

ANNIE: They blindfold me first, silly. The way I see it, I'm being paid just for keeping still.

WATSON: That's one way of looking at it, I suppose. Or perhaps *not* looking at it, in your case.

ANNIE: I've only been hit once. (SAUCILY) As you're a doctor, I'll show the scar, if you like.

WATSON: Well, er, I'm not sure if that would be . . . .

ANNIE: I'm only pulling your leg silly. Look, it's here on my finger.

WATSON: Ah, yes, I can see it. You know, I had thought –

ANNIE: Oh, I know what you thought, Doctor! Now you'll have to excuse me, I really should be going.

WATSON: Annie? Before you do, I wonder if you could help me. I came here with a friend, you see, and we're looking for someone. His name is Hans Fredericks. I believe he's an entertainer.

ANNIE: Oh, if it's Hans you're after, why didn't you say? His caravan's that one over there.

WATSON: Thank you, Annie. You know, it's not often I get to steal a march on my friend, but on this occasion I fancy I might have beaten him.

244

ANNIE: (OFF MICROHONE) Ta-ra, then, Doctor. Perhaps I'll see you later.

WATSON: Goodbye, Annie, and thank-you for your help.

SOUND EFFECT: A COUPLE FOOTSTEPS ON GRASS

WATSON: (TO SELF) Let's see now, this was the one she pointed to . . . .

SOUND EFFECT: KNOCKING ON WOODEN CARAVAN DOOR

WATSON: Hans, are you there?

SOUND EFFECT: OPENING CARAVAN DOOR

HOLMES: Come on in, Watson.

WATSON: Holmes, you're already here, then?

HOLMES: Why don't you join us?

MUSIC: BRIDGE

SOUND EFFECT: INSIDE CIRCUS CARAVAN

HANS: I'm sorry if it's a little cramped, Doctor. You'll have to take a seat where you can.

SOUND EFFECT: COUPLE OF FOOTSTEPS ON WOODEN CARAVAN FLOORBOARDS

WATSON: Thank you, Hans. Have you been here long, Holmes?

HANS: He only just arrived. I must admit, I was rather taken aback when I opened my door.

WATSON: I can well imagine.

HOLMES: After discussing matters with Doctor Watson here, felt I was a little hasty about sending you away like I did . . . .

HANS: I can see it must have sounded a little strange.

HOLMES: There are a couple of points I'd like to go over with you, if you don't mind.

HANS: Ask whatever you like, Mr. Holmes.

HOLMES: Firstly, before you spoke to Princess Ayesha, you had no idea your life might be in danger?

HANS: I'll say I didn't! When she told me, you could have knocked me over with a feather.

HOLMES: And then she sent you to me . . . .

HANS: With the poster for our circus.

HOLMES: Did you notice anything unusual about the poster?

HANS: In what way?

HOLMES: It is your standard advertising poster, I presume?

HANS: That's right.

HOLMES: And has anyone else spoken to you since you saw us?

HANS: Only Mr. Mandrake.

WATSON: The circus owner? I think I've met him – rather an insistent fellow.

HANS: He's our ringmaster and manager. He wondered where I'd been all morning.

WATSON: And what did you tell him?

HANS: The truth, of course. He was like you, Mr. Holmes – told me I shouldn't worry about such things.

246

HOLMES: How many people know that you came to consult me?

HANS: Only Mr. Mandrake. And Princess Ayesha, of course.

HOLMES: Good. The fewer people who know about my involvement, the better.

HANS: Then you really think my life is in danger after all?

HOLMES: That, Hans, is precisely what Doctor Watson and I intend to find out.

MUSIC: BRIDGE

WATSON: (NARRATING) Holmes and I threaded our way through the crowds. It wasn't long before we came upon an intriguing-looking tent dressed with Oriental symbols. A board outside proclaimed Princess Ayesha's talent for contacting departed loved ones, fortune telling, and myriad other mystical abilities. We slipped through the curtains to find a veiled lady dressed in a fine costume and jewels. With the slightest movement of her hand, she bade us to take a seat.

SOUND EFFECT: FORTUNE TELLERS TENT

ANNIE: (ANNIE PRETENDING TO BE PRINCESS AYESHA, MIMICKING HER ACCENT) I sense you wish to learn from the wisdom of the spirits.

HOLMES: We'd certainly like to ask you a few questions, Princess Ayesha.

ANNIE: Naturally. People come from far and wide to seek my powers.

HOLMES: Perhaps we should introduce ourselves first. This is . . . .

ANNIE: (INTERRUPTS) No, you don't need tell me . . . (PAUSE. THEN, AS IF SENSED) You are a medical man, are you not?

WATSON: How did you know that?

HOLMES: Really, there are countless signs. That iodine stain on your cuff for a start.

ANNIE: So you are an unbeliever.

HOLMES: If your features weren't covered by a veil, I could make equally trivial deductions about you, madam. Or should I address you as "Your Highness"?

ANNIE: You mock me. But ask yourself this: Would a mere stain tell me his name is . . . (PAUSE) *John Watson*?

HOLMES: My colleague and I are not without fame in certain quarters.

ANNIE: Then allow me to further demonstrate my powers.

SOUND EFFECT: SHUFFLE OF CARDS

ANNIE: These are no ordinary cards. They are cards of the Tarot. They can be used to see your past, present and future. Doctor, will you take a card?

WATSON: As you wish, madam.

ANNIE: Remember. You must choose carefully. These cards may change your life forever.

WATSON: I'll have this one.

SOUND EFFECT: FLICK OF CARD

ANNIE: You have drawn *The Clown*. Ah, this card represents a man – a man you have been searching for.

WATSON: We were searching for one of the entertainers, weren't we, Holmes?

HOLMES: And who sent him to our door in the first place?

ANNIE: Now choose another card.

ANNIE: Ah, *The Princess*. There was a woman . . . yes, someone who helped you find your clown . . . .

WATSON: As it happens there was a girl . . . .

HOLMES: I would expect nothing else of you, Watson.

ANNIE: Now take a final card, Doctor, and choose most carefully of all, for this will show your future.

WATSON: Very well, I'll have this one.

SOUND EFFECT: FLICK OF CARD

ANNIE: *The Couple*. This card can mean only one thing.

WATSON: Which is?

ANNIE: You will be married before the end of the year.

WATSON: Again?

HOLMES: I think this has gone far enough. I don't know who you are, but I want to be taken to see the real Princess Ayesha at once.

ANNIE: And just what do you mean by that?

HOLMES: Every professional fortune teller knows the correct names for the Tarot Cards.

ANNIE: And you claim I do not?

HOLMES: This card is known as *The Fool* – not *The Clown*. This is *The High Priestess*. And finally, this card is *The Lovers* – not *The Couple*.

WATSON: I think someone's been having a joke at our expense – haven't they, Annie?

249

ANNIE: (NORMAL VOICE) I'm sorry, Doctor. When I saw you coming, I couldn't resist it.

WATSON: You know, I only spotted that scar on your finger when you turned the last card. And, of course, you're the only woman at the circus who might know my name.

HOLMES: I take it you know the lady?

WATSON: Sherlock Holmes, allow me to introduce Miss Annie Jones, knife thrower's assistant . . . and accomplished practical joker.

ANNIE: I'm pleased to meet you, Mr. Sherlock Holmes.

WATSON: Annie, you might have gathered we're looking for Princess Ayesha. Do you know where she is?

ANNIE: Can't help you there. All know is she left the circus earlier today.

HOLMES: For where, precisely?

ANNIE: Not sure. Mr. Mandrake told me she'd gone and asked if I'd stand in for her.

HOLMES: I see. And where might we find Mr. Mandrake?

ANNIE: Right now he'll be over at the Big Top. The show starts in half-an-hour – I should be getting over there, too.

MUSIC: BRIDGE

SOUND EFFECT: INSIDE CIRCUS BIG TOP. NOISE OF SETTLING CROWD IN BACKGROUND

HOLMES: Excuse me, madam. Thank you.

WATSON: These are our seats, Holmes. I must say, they give us a fine view of the ring.

HOLMES: It's a view of Mandrake I'm after.

WATSON: You sound very certain.

HOLMES: I have a theory, Watson, that's all.

WATSON: Well?

HOLMES: You must realize that whoever Princess Ayesha is, she took a lot of effort to get that circus poster to our door.

WATSON: But Hans said it was just an ordinary poster.

HOLMES: Yes, Watson, and that is the most remarkable thing about it.

WATSON: Really, Holmes, must you be so paradoxical? How can something ordinary be remarkable?

HOLMES: Do you remember the circus itinerary on the poster?

WATSON: Let me see now . . . There was Amsterdam and Copenhagen. Yes, and London was mentioned a couple of times, too.

HOLMES: And what do Amsterdam and Copenhagen have in common?

WATSON: Well, they're all reasonable-sized cities for one . . .

HOLMES: Yes . . . ?

WATSON: . . . and they're both famed for their art and jewelry trades . . . .

HOLMES: Quiet, Watson. I think it's about to begin.

SOUND EFFECT: RIPPLE OF APPLAUSE AND HUSH OF CROWD

MANDRAKE: Ladies and gentlemen! Boys and girls! Welcome to the greatest show on earth! I am your ringmaster, Charles

251

Mandrake, and I have personally selected the greatest talents the world has seen for your delectation and entertainment. Allow me to present . . . *Hercules the Strongman*!

SOUND EFFECT: RIPPLE OF APPLAUSE

MANDRAKE: . . . Who can bend iron with his own bare hands!

SOUND EFFECT: RIPPLE OF APPLAUSE

MANDRAKE: *Carlos the Knifethower* . . . .

SOUND EFFECT: RIPPLE OF APPLAUSE

MANDRAKE: . . . and his assistant, *Miss Annie Jones*!

SOUND EFFECT: RIPPLE OF APPLAUSE

WATSON: (NARRATING) We made our way to the back of the Big Top and watched a succession of entertainers enter and then exit, once their turn was done. Hans arrived with a group of fellow clowns and was greeted to great cheers by the crowd. Annie's act was last, and as far as I could tell from the applause, no blood was spilled. Finally, once the show was over, Mandrake made his way from the tent. And when he did, he was quickly surrounded by a small crowd of angry members of the troupe.

SOUND EFFECT: OUTSIDE THE BIG TOP

HERCULES: Where is she, Mandrake?

MANDRAKE: Where's who, Hercules?

HERCULES: Princess Ayesha.

MANDRAKE: I've already told you. She left us this morning.

HANS: And we don't believe you.

HOLMES: (CLOSE TO MICROPHONE) It seems events have overtaken us, Watson.

ANNIE: Hans is right. She wouldn't just go without saying goodbye.

HANS: So where is she, Mr. Mandrake?

MANDRAKE: Look here, I really don't know.

HERCULES: Don't make me beat it out of you, Mandrake.

MANDRAKE: Now, Hercules . . . there's no need for violence . . . .

CROWD No. 1: I know where she is. I saw him take her to his caravan this morning.

ANNIE: Is this true?

MANDRAKE: Well, as it happens, she did come round, yes.

CROWD No. 2: She didn't look like she wanted to go to me.

HANS: Let's go to his caravan and take a look . . . .

MANDRAKE: No really, I must protest . . . .

HANS: And bring him with us, Hercules. He's got some explaining to do.

MUSIC: BRIDGE

WATSON: (NARRATING) We followed the crowd over to Mandrake's caravan, which he opened most unwillingly. On the floor, gagged and bound, was Princess Ayesha. Holmes quickly untied her.

SOUND EFFECT: OUTSIDE CIRCUS CARAVAN

HOLMES: How is she, Watson?

WATSON: She seems none the worse from her experience.

AYESHA: (BREATHING HEAVILY) Are you Mr. Sherlock Holmes?

HOLMES: Indeed I am.

AYESHA: Then you got my message.

HOLMES: Yes, Hans proved to be an admirable agent, even if I failed to see the significance of the poster at first.

AYESHA: Then you know?

HOLMES: That Mandrake has been using the circus for smuggling stolen goods in from the Continent?

AYESHA: Yes. I caught him one night passing the goods to his contact here in London.

HOLMES: "Silver" Wilkins, no doubt.

AYESHA: It was too dangerous for me to go to the police, so I had to trick Hans into making you come and see me.

HANS: But why didn't you just tell me what was going on?

AYESHA: I didn't want to put your life in danger too, Hans.

MANDRAKE: Now wait a moment. You've no proof of any of this . . . .

HOLMES: It seems you have two choices, Mr. Mandrake. You can either make a confession and come with us, or we can leave you with your friends here and allow them to dispense their own form of justice.

HERCULES: Leave him to me, Mr. Holmes. I'll make him pay for what he's done to the Princess.

HANS: Yes, it's not right to tie the Princess up like that.

ANNIE: What did you plan to do with her? Do her in so you could carry on with your smuggling?

MANDRAKE: Mr. Holmes . . . you wouldn't leave me at their mercy would you?

HOLMES: Come along, Watson. I think it's time for us to go.

MANDRAKE: All right, all right, I'll confess! Just don't leave me alone with them . . . .

WATSON: All right, everybody. You can leave the matter with us. We'll see that justice is done. You can count on that.

AYESHA: Thank you, Mr. Holmes. I knew for certain I could rely on you.

HOLMES: You did?

WATSON: Of course she did, Holmes. It was written in the stars.

MUSIC: *DANSE MACABRE*

WATSON: This is Dr. John H. Watson. I've had many more adventures with Sherlock Holmes, and I'll tell you another one . . . *when next we meet!*

MUSIC: (FADE OUT)

A Case of
Unfinished Business
by Steven Philip Jones

<u>CHARACTERS</u>

- DR. JOHN H. WATSON
- MRS. TURNER
- LOT MORRILL
- MYCROFT HOLMES
- SHERLOCK HOLMES (AS *JOHN REEVES*)
- INSPECTOR LESTRADE
- WALTER SIMONSON
- ENGINEER
- FIREMAN
- PORTER

<u>(COLD OPEN)</u>

<u>SOUND EFFECT: TRAIN STEAM WHISTLE SCREAMS AND THEN ECHOES AWAY. (BACKGROUND) TRAIN TRAVELS</u>

ENGINEER: Look at that gauge. Best take on water at the next signal.

FIREMAN: (APPREHENSIVE) What do I say? They ought to put a water trough along this cutting. Save time.

ENGINEER: Oh, go on. You just don't like to stop in this trench.

FIREMAN: Why should I? The walls are too steep. You can't even see the sun at noon. It's not safe. (QUIETER) Being too close to the mine and all.

ENGINEER: Did you just hear yourself?

FIREMAN: Everyone knows about Blue John Gap.

ENGINEER: You mean those fairie tales? Like the one where a big old boogey carries sheep into the mine when there's a full moon?

FIREMAN: And that doctor? He died of fright after trying to kill something there!

ENGINEER: So you say. I heard he was a lunger on borrowed time. I've been driving the Derbyshire to London line since '68, and . . . . (PAUSE) What are you looking at?

FIREMAN: Something's moving along the ledge.

ENGINEER: You mean up where you can't even see . . . ?

FIREMAN: (INTERRUPTS, PETRIFIED) The tracks! Look out!

SOUND EFFECT: LOTS OF GUNFIRE IN DISTANCE

ENGINEER: (ALARMED) The brakes!

SOUND EFFECT: WHEELS SQUEEL FROM SUDDEN BRAKING. STEAM WHISTLE SCREAMS. SQUEALS AND SCREAM FADE INTO SILENCE

(INTRODUCTION)

SOUND EFFECT: OPENING SEQUENCE, BIG BEN

ANNOUNCER: *The Further Adventures of Sherlock Holmes*, starring John Patrick Lowrie as Sherlock Holmes, and Lawrence Albert as Dr. John H. Watson.

MUSIC: *DANSE MACABRE* (UP AND UNDER)

MUSIC: (FADE TO . . . .)

MUSIC: MELANCHOLY MUSIC (UP AND UNDER)

WATSON: (NARRATING) It was that dreadful May of 1891. After the events at the falls of Reichenbach, I took a short leave from my practice. Mycroft Holmes had requested me to organize

258

Sherlock Holmes's papers and put Baker Street back in order after Moriarty's attempted arson. The busy work occupied my mind, but also prevented me from moving past the tragedy.

MUSIC: (FADE OUT)

SOUND EFFECT: (BACKGROUND) BAKER STREET'S TICKING CLOCK. WATSON IS PUTTING ROOM INTO ORDER. MRS. TURNER KNOCKS ON DOOR

TURNER: (CALLING THROUGH DOOR) Dr. Watson?

SOUND EFFECT: WATSON WALKS TO DOOR AND OPENS IT

WATSON: Hello, Mrs. Turner. Is Mrs. Hudson back?

TURNER: I fear not, sir, but I'm not surprised. She was so upset about what happened to Mr. Holmes and the fire (PAUSE) Oh, but you have the place looking much better!

WATSON: Thank you. It hasn't been easy. You've been most kind to watch the house while she's away.

TURNER: She'd do the same for me. But there's a gentleman here who says he's an old friend of yours. He went to your home and Mrs. Watson sent him here.

WATSON: "Old friend"?

TURNER: The name on his card is *Lot Morrill*. He says he went to university with you. (LOWERS VOICE) He's an American.

SOUND EFFECT: (BACKGROUND) TICKING CLOCK FADES OUT. RESTAURANT NOISES UP AND UNDER. (BACKGROUND) PEOPLE CHAT, GLASSES CLINK, UTENSILS CLATTER

MORRILL: I'm sorry I called at a bad time, John.

WATSON: On my oath you haven't. This breakfast is doing me wonders. Now . . . what's it been, Lot? Twelve years?

259

MORRILL: (TIRED) About that, although Barts seems a lifetime ago.

WATSON: And I've kept track of you in the Colonies.

MORRILL: (CHUCKLES) "The Colonies"? You snob!

WATSON: I'm not! Your work on intubation with O'Dwyer at St. John's Hospital for Sick Children? Revolutionary!

MORRILL: I only assisted Joseph. No glory in that, but plenty of satisfaction. Speaking of which, I've kept track of you, too. (PAUSE) My condolences on Mr. Holmes.

WATSON: Yes. He was the best man . . . the wisest man I've ever known.

MORRILL: (RATTLED) Yes. A very appropriate quote. I'm . . . I'm sure Plato could not have held Socrates . . . in any higher esteem . . . than you did Sherlock Holmes.

WATSON: (CONFUSED) I'm sorry. Did I say something wrong?

MORRILL: What? No! I'm just peckish. Where's that waiter?

SOUND EFFECT: RESTAURANT NOISES FADE OUT. DIOGENES CLUB. PORTER'S FOOTSTEPS APPROACH MYCROFT HOLMES

PORTER: (WHISPERS) Mr. Holmes? You've a visitor with a message he claims is of the first importance. He is waiting in the Stranger's Room.

SOUND EFFECT: MYCROFT STANDS, WALKS TO STRANGER'S ROOM, OPENS AND CLOSES DOOR

MYCROFT: Yes, what is it? (GASPS) Sherlock!

HOLMES: Good afternoon, Mycroft.

MYCROFT: What in Heaven's name are you thinking? Coming to the Diogenes Club? You're known here!

HOLMES: But Sherlock Holmes isn't here. (DISGUISES VOICE) I'm John Reeves, a cabbie baring a vital missive, sir.

MYCROFT: From the land beyond the mists, no doubt.

HOLMES: (DEADLY SERIOUS) Could any missive be more vital?

MYCROFT: Fine. What is it?

SOUND EFFECT: HOLMES'S VOICE UNDER AS HE TALKS

HOLMES: Well, brother, earlier today I . . . Reeves . . . was working along the Strand.

SOUND EFFECT: FLASHBACK: LONDON STREET SOUNDS (UP)

MORRILL: (CHIPPER) That meal was an absolute tonic! Simpson's is better than I remember!

WATSON: Yes, it's still one of my favorite restaurants. It's nice that some things haven't changed. (HAILING A CAB) Cabbie! (TO MORRILL) Game for a tour of our old haunts?

SOUND EFFECT: HORSE'S HOOVES CLOP AS HANSOM CAB APPROACHES AND STOPS

HOLMES: (AS JOHN REEVES, TO HORSE) Hold up, Caprice. (TO WATSON AND MORRILL) Where to, gents?

MORRILL: (TO WATSON) Well, if you're really up for it, John, I would like to . . . . (INTERRUPTED)

BACKGROUND: LESTRADE CALLS IN DISTANCE

LESTRADE: Doctor Watson!

MORRILL: Who is that? A colleague of yours?

WATSON: (ANNOYED) In a manner of speaking.

MORRILL: (CONCERNED) Oh, a Scotland Yarder. Rough looking sort.

SOUND EFFECT: LESTRADE REACHES WATSON AND MORRILL

WATSON: Lestrade is that. (TO LESTRADE) Inspector.

LESTRADE: Sorry to bother you. If it weren't important . . . .

WATSON: (INTERRUPTING) You wouldn't intrude, I'm sure.

LESTRADE: Can you come with me? Official business.

WATSON: Now? What could involve me that . . . ?

LESTRADE: (INTERRUPTING) I have a four-wheeler waiting.

MORRILL: (TIRED) Go on, John. They must need you.

WATSON: I'm sorry, Lot. I'll pay the cab in case you can use it.

MORRILL: No, please. I can walk. I'm just up the street at the Charing Cross Hotel, and the sun feels good.

WATSON: Certainly. Dinner tonight?

MORRILL: Sure. (TO LESTRADE) A pleasure, Inspector.

LESTRADE: Same to you, sir.

SOUND EFFECT: LESTRADE'S VOICE AND LONDON STREET SOUNDS FADE OUT AS LESTRADE TALKS

LESTRADE: This way, Doctor.

SOUND EFFECT: END FLASHBACK. QUIET OF DIOGENES STRANGER'S ROOM

MYCROFT: (COYLY) So you followed Dr. Watson and Lestrade?

HOLMES: No. Why would I?

MYCROFT: To see where they went.

HOLMES: Unnecessary. I knew their destination as well as you do, so I took the precaution of following Dr. Morrill. His visit to Watson could have just been a coincidence, but I felt it wise to verify.

MYCROFT: (CURIOUS) And did Morrill return to his hotel?

HOLMES: Without detour, but for two shillings another cabbie is doing Reeves the favor of watching the hotel in case Morrill leaves. "An ounce of prevention . . . ."

SOUND EFFECT: MYCROFT INHALES DEEPLY THEN EXHALES

MYCROFT: (TIRED OF GAMES) All right, I have no more energy to bandy words. Surely you see this is my first respite since Professor Moriarty's death.

HOLMES: I do. I'm afraid it was one matter to predict that human criminal nature would swiftly fill the vacuum of the Professor's former empire.

MYCROFT: Experiencing it . . . along with the aftershocks it is sending through three continents . . . is quite another. It's like going to war. (TETCHY) Blast it, you're supposed to be on your way to Tibet!

HOLMES: And abandon a colleague in peril?

MYCROFT: Oh, Sherlock, if that's your important message, I promise you, Dr. Watson is not in peril. You don't need to hang about playing guardian angel.

HOLMES: Actually, I've been "playing guardian angel" for your right-hand man, Walter Simonson, although he always communicated to me under the *nom de plume* . . . .

MYCROFT: (INTERRUPTING) Hush! Even here the walls may have ears!

HOLMES: Oh, Mycroft, surely you see that the time has passed for worrying about that.

MUSIC: MELANCHOLY MUSIC (UP AND UNDER)

WATSON: (NARRATING) Waiting inside the four-wheeler for Lestrade and I was a tall wiry man, early thirties, with hazel eyes, and hair and mustache blond enough to pass for white.

MUSIC: (FADE OUT)

SOUND EFFECT: HORSE'S HOOVES AND STREET NOISES

LESTRADE: Dr. Watson, may I introduce my friend, Walter Simonson.

WATSON: How do you do?

SIMONSON: (SLIGHT SWEDISH ACCENT) I can't tell you how much I've looked forward to talking with you in person. I only wish Mr. Holmes could be here, too.

WATSON: (CONFUSED) Have we corresponded?

SIMONSON: We haven't, but I corresponded four times with Mr. Holmes using the name "Fred Porlock".

WATSON: (CAN'T QUITE RECALL) "Porlock?" (REMEMBERS) The Birlstone murder! You tried to warn Holmes about it!

SIMONSON: Before I tried to warn him off of it. (CHUCKLES) Your persistence nearly got me drawn-and-quartered.

WATSON: Yes. Holmes said you were an informer working closely with Professor Moriarty.

SIMONSON: Actually, I infiltrated Moriarty's organization in '86 for the British Government under the *aegis* of Scotland Yard's Special Branch. There were times, though, that I felt Justice might be better served by informing Mr. Holmes rather than my

264

superiors about information I learned, but only if he had no idea what I was truly about. But now, Doctor, I need your help.

WATSON: Why, certainly.

SIMONSON: Thank you. Before I explain, though, allow me to beg your patience a few more minutes.

SOUND EFFECT: HORSE'S HOOVES AND STREET NOISES FADE OUT

WATSON: (NARRATING) The Clarence cab soon stopped at a four-storey house on Wigmore Street where Simonson rented a suite on the third floor. Lestrade warned me this was the scene of a crime with a body in the sitting room. I was more than a little surprised as I saw no constables.

SOUND EFFECT: DOOR TO SIMONSON'S SUITE OPENS. SIMONSON, WATSON, AND LESTRADE ENTER

LESTRADE: (TO WATSON) There you are, Doctor.

SIMONSON: We have no idea who he is, but we found a garrote, a neddy, concealed knives, and a Colt revolver on him. Things being as they are, we're assuming he's an assassin who was in Moriarty's employment.

SOUND EFFECT: WATSON EXAMINES THE BODY

WATSON: No indications of a struggle or violence. (PAUSE) Everything suggests he's only been here a few hours. (PAUSE) Looks like he was enjoying some of your brandy, Mr. Simonson.

SIMONSON: Oh, Walter, please. Judging by the level in that carafe, my guess is he had two full glasses.

SOUND EFFECT: WATSON PICKS UP CARAFE AND SNIFFS

WATSON: (TO HIMSELF) Smells all right, I suppose. (SNIFFS AGAIN)

LESTRADE: That's a nerve. Enjoying your spirits while waiting to kill you.

SOUND EFFECT: WATSON PUTS DOWN CARAFE

WATSON: (TO LESTRADE) Why no constables, Inspector?

LESTRADE: Unadvisable under the circumstances, but these premises are being watched.

SIMONSON: Expediently apprehending Moriarty's associates takes precedence over proper police protocol. In fact, we are sworn to secrecy regarding this matter.

WATSON: I see. And you'd prefer me examining the body rather than calling a coroner?

SIMONSON: Yes . . . but also . . . well, not all of the Professor's associates were willing ones. Among other means, Moriarty used blackmail and extortion, such as purchasing incriminating debts to manipulate people in high positions of corporate and political power. Now someone intends to expose them and inflict widespread harm.

SOUND EFFECT: WATSON GRUNTS, AGHAST

WATSON: The more I learn about the Professor, the more I see why Holmes would sacrifice himself to destroy the man.

SIMONSON: It was Mr. Holmes who informed the government about this plot just before you two went to the Continent. Considerable resources are being dedicated to prevent it, but now my superior needs to see a file Mr. Holmes kept with his casebooks and indexes.

WATSON: Oh, dear. Holmes kept all that in a large tin box he used to store in his bedroom. But it's not there now, and I have no clue where he put it.

SIMONSON: That's all right. Mr. Mycroft has the clue.

WATSON: Pardon?

266

SIMONSON: Mr. Holmes gave his brother a clue to the box's location. A clue to be revealed to you if circumstances dictated.

WATSON: What if I don't understand the clue?

SIMONSON: Let's find out. The message from Mr. Sherlock Holmes is: "*Not papers. And then my fee.*"

SOUND EFFECT: PAUSE

WATSON: (ANNOYED) Oh, for Heaven's sake.

LESTRADE: Doctor?

WATSON: I wrote an account of one of Holmes's investigations titled "A Case of Identity" where I referenced an earlier investigation, "A Scandal in Bohemia."

LESTRADE: The one about Irene Adler and the King of Bohemia? I like that one. She was more than a match for Holmes!

WATSON: And he admired her for it. Remember, Holmes even requested a photograph of Miss Adler from the King.

LESTRADE: Oh, I see! Holmes wrote where to find this box on the back of that photograph!

WATSON: No. (TO SIMONSON) Walter, I must return to Baker Street.

SIMONSON: Let's go. The four-wheeler is still waiting.

WATSON: Just a moment. Once we're there, I wish to go inside alone. For my own reasons.

SIMONSON: All right.

WATSON: But before we leave, tell me everything you know about this body.

SIMONSON: I did. I give you my word.

WATSON: So you have no idea who put hemlock in the carafe?

LESTRADE: What's that?

SOUND EFFECT: LESTRADE PICKS UP CARAFE AND SNIFFS

LESTRADE: (CONTINUED) This brandy smells all right.

WATSON: I suppose. (TO SIMONSON) Walter, prior to this morning, when were you last here?

SIMSONSON: Yesterday afternoon. And the brandy was fine then, or I wouldn't be talking to you now. The body was here when I returned, so I contacted Lestrade. He's my Scotland Yard liaison.

LESTRADE: (TO WATSON) How can you be sure there's hemlock in here without an analysis?

WATSON: I can't. It could be something similar . . . say curare . . . but that has a bitter taste and this man drank two full glasses. What's more, hemlock contains coniine. Just 0.1 grams can be fatal, and its effects would have been abetted by brandy's natural inebriant action and ability to depress the motor function of the cranio-spinal axis.

LESTADE: Fair enough. Sounds like a quick and painless death.

WATSON: Relatively, yet unpleasant. He probably felt cold, but wouldn't know why, then numb starting with his extremities. Eventually, he wouldn't have been able to move and died alone trapped in that chair. Before paralysis set in, however, it looks like he walked around a bit attempting to warm up. That explains these fresh flecks of dried mud about the floor.

SIMONSON: Actually, that might have been me when I came back.

WATSON: Really? I thought I saw mud on his boots.

SOUND EFFECT: WATSON EXAMINES DEAD MAN'S BOOTS

WATSON: (CONTINUED) Yes. Look here. This mud is the same yellowish brown color as what's on the floor.

SIMONSON: (INTRIGUED) Hold on a moment.

SOUND EFFECT: SIMONSON GOES TO HIS BEDROOM AND COMES BACK OUT

SIMONSON: (CONTINUED) I haven't cleaned these boots yet, and they're covered in the same color mud.

LESTRADE: Where from?

SIMONSON: Blue John Gap. It's a Derbyshire mine. Been abandoned for years. Locals claim it's the lair of a beast or creature.

WATSON: I read about that in *The Times*! Fascinating story! Those folktales got stirred up again recently by a . . . umm . . . Dr. Hardcastle. I recall he passed away from phthisis, which he insisted was aggravated after hunting some primordial monster back into the mine.

SIMONSON: You have a good memory. What Hardcastle actually found was an outpost for Moriarty's organization that was playing up the legend to keep people away from the mine, going so far as making it look like the thing was nicking sheep whenever there was a full moon.

LESTRADE: Sounds like an excuse for free mutton to me.

SIMONSON: Waste not, want not. Moriarty's men arranged things to look like the doctor treed the monster in the mine but it doubled-back on him, then told him to get busy dying or they'd save him the effort.

WATSON: That's outrageous!

SIMONSON: That's Moriarty idea of poetic justice. But what comes around goes around. When news of the Professor's death and the search for his associates reached Blue John Gap, his men realized it'd be dicey fleeing by road or countryside. So they

269

opted to commandeer a train they could ride into London. Once there, they could scatter into the East End and escape England by ship.

WATSON: (BEGRUDINGLY) A sound plan.

SIMONSON: Sound enough that when word of it reached London, I had no choice but to lead a posse that arrived just as Moriarty's men were moving in to seize the train.

SOUND EFFECT: MEMORY VOICES: REPEAT FIREMAN AND ENGINEER FROM EARLIER

FIREMAN: The tracks! Look out!

SOUND EFFECT: LOTS OF GUNFIRE IN DISTANCE

ENGINEER: The brakes!

SOUND EFFECT: (BACKGROUND) GUNFIRE CONTINUES

SOUND EFFECT: SIMONSON SPEAKS IN PRESENT

SIMONSON: (CONTINUED) Moriarty's men fled back to Blue John Gap to make a last stand. We didn't disappoint them.

SOUND EFFECT: GUNFIRE ENDS

SIMONSON: (CONTINUED) That's where I picked up this mud.

WATSON: So this stranger had to have been there, but had sense not to return to the mine. He must have recognized you and found a way to London to confront you.

LESTRADE: Only to poison himself. Word about you must have also got back to London, Walter, and another of Moriarty's gang poured hemlock or whatever in this carafe. How could they know about this fellow's intentions? I'd say you had two near-misses this day

SIMONSON: (MOSTLY CONVINCED) I suppose you're right.

WATSON: (NARRATING) I must confess I was generally satisfied with Lestrade's hypothesis as well. So we returned to Baker Street and I went inside alone. The thought of rummaging through Holmes's things in front of anyone struck me as too severe a violation of his privacy.

MUSIC: (FADE OUT)

SOUND EFFECT: WATSON'S FOOTSTEPS APPROACH, HE OPENS DOOR INTO BAKER STREET SITTING ROOM

WATSON: (THINKING OUT LOUD) All right, where is it? With your tobacco in your Persian slipper? Perhaps the coal-scuttle with your cigars and pipes?

SOUND EFFECT (BACKGROUND): WATSON SEARCHES THE PERSIAN SLIPPER AND COAL-SCUTTLE

WATSON: (NARRATING) In "A Case of Identity", I referenced "A Scandal in Bohemia" as "*the case of the Irene Adler papers*". However, Holmes was commissioned to retrieve a *photograph* of the King of Bohemia with Miss Adler, a slip Holmes often enjoyed chiding me about.

SOUND EFFECT: WATSON STOPS SEARCHING

WATSON: (TO HIMSELF) Not here. (PAUSE) Think, John. Think like Holmes. You'd put it somewhere sensible but inconspicuous . . . like . . . a pocket of one of your dressing-gowns? Or on the deal table, lost in plain sight amongst the chemistry equipment?

SOUND EFFECT (BACKGROUND): WATSON SEARCHES DRESSING-GOWNS AND DEAL TABLE

WATSON: (NARRATING): That photograph of Miss Adler given to Holmes was a reward he had requested on the spur of the moment. The actual fee paid by the King was in the form of a gold snuff-box with a large amethyst on its lid. That's where Holmes left how to find the file. Inside that gold box.

SOUND EFFECT: WATSON STOPS SEARCHING

WATSON (THINKING OUT LOUD) Blast it! Where is it? Peoples' lives are depending on this! (PAUSE) I've been through your papers and put back your belongings. Where else would you . . . (REALIZATION) Yes.

SOUND EFFECT: WATSON WALKS TO HOLMES'S DESK

WATSON (NARRATING) The last place I would have searched was Holmes's desk to the side of the sofa. Except for retrieving his personal casebook, I had had no intentions of going through its drawers, believing it was Mycroft's place to attend to Holmes's most personal items.

SOUND EFFECT: WATSON OPENS TWO DRAWERS AND STOPS

WATSON: Eureka! (NARRATING) I opened the lid. Poked through the powdered tobacco. Nothing. I poured out the tobacco, pried out the bottom, and found a key, most likely to a bank deposit box, judging by its appearance!

SOUND EFFECT: WATSON HURRIES DOWN STEPS TO FOYER

WATSON: (CALLING OUT) Mrs. Turner? I'm going out! Can you . . . .

SOUND EFFECT: WATSON STOPS RUNNING IN FOYER

WATSON (CONTINUED, STARTLED) Mrs. Turner, come here!

SOUND EFFECT: MRS. TURNER HURRIES INTO FOYER

TURNER: (WORRIED) What's wrong? Are you all right?

WATSON: (FEIGNING CALM) When was the foyer last swept?

TURNER: Early this morning.

WATSON: Has anyone else been in here since Lot Morrill?

TURNER: Only that one policeman, Lestrade. (PAUSE) Oh, look at all that mud on the mat. I'll shake it clean.

WATSON: (GLUMLY) That's all right. It doesn't matter now.

TURNER: Doctor?

WATSON: I'm sorry I startled you, Mrs. Turner. Would you please lock Mr. Holmes's rooms for me? I have an appointment.

MUSIC: UP AND UNDER

WATSON: (NARRATING) I gave the key to Walter and Lestrade, confident their resources would divine the bank box it opened. Then I took a hansom to the Charing Cross Hotel, where I paid the cabbie to wait.

MUSIC: (FADE OUT)

SOUND EFFECT: WATSON KNOCKS ON MORRILL'S DOOR

WATSON: Lot?

MORRILL: (THROUGH DOOR) Come in. I've been waiting.

SOUND EFFECT: WATSON OPENS AND CLOSES DOOR. MORRILL TAKES A DRINK FROM A GLASS

MORRILL: (CONTINUED) Afternoon. Or should I say good evening? Time does fly. I'd offer you a drink, but I'm afraid I just finished the last of it.

WATSON: (REALIZING) You did what? No!

SOUND EFFECT: WATSON RUSHES OVER AND GRABS GLASS

WATSON: Hemlock?

MORRILL: Perceptive. Same old John. You gave me quite a turn when you paraphrased Plato this morning. Coincidences like that always pester me. I don't believe in them. I'd rather think everything happens for a reason.

SOUND EFFECT: WATSON PUTS GLASS ON A TABLE

WATSON: Well, this isn't going to happen! Not while I can stop it!

MORRILL: You can't. I'll be dead before you can scrounge anything to use for artificial ventilation, and we both know that's the only way to sustain life until the affects of coniine poisoning wear off. So, please, grant me a final request. Sit down and talk with me one last time.

WATSON: (STUBBORN) Lot!

MORRILL: (MORE STUBBORN) John.

SOUND EFFECT: WATSON SITS

WATSON: (FRUSTRATED) Why?

MORRILL: You'll find a letter on the bedside table that explains all this. Just in case. You can give it to your colleague, Lestrade. Now, did I ever tell you about my family?

WATSON: Just that your father died and your mother remarried.

MORRILL: That's more than I tell most folks. In a nutshell, my father was a farmer in the Delaware Valley. A good man. Honest. Strong. A Confederate captain named Harsh Washburne killed him near the end of the War. Harsh had taken a fancy to my mother, and she returned the feelings. Only my mother and I knew about the murder, and I never could get myself to hate her enough to make her suffer by taking Harsh away from her.

WATSON: (SINCERE) I'm so sorry.

SOUND EFFECT: MORRILL STRETCHES HIS FINGERS AND LEGS

274

MORRILL: I'm starting to get numb. Best hurry.

WATSON: Lot, please! I can . . . .

MORRILL: (INTERRUPTING) Do nothing, John! (CALMER) I assume Lestrade took you to Simonson's flat?

WATSON: Yes.

MORRILL: I figured. I'd say it was a coincidence, but . . . .

WATSON: You don't believe in them.

MORRILL: You know, there wouldn't have been an opportunity for any coincidences if I had just left England this morning. But I knew there was no escaping this. So I paid my call on you. (HAPPY) It's really good to see you again.

WATSON: The dead stranger? That is Washburne?

MORRILL: Oh, yes. Like I told you this morning, my mother died suddenly two weeks ago. Harsh never considered the consequences of that. I was finally free to avenge my father. His murder has been within a hand's reach of my thoughts for most of my life. I couldn't live with myself if I did nothing, but now that I've done, it I still can't live with myself. I'm a doctor. "Do no harm."

WATSON: I . . . I don't know what to say.

MORRILL: You don't have to say anything. That's the wonder of friendship at times like these. (Shiver) I'd ask for a blanket, but it'd do no good.

WATSON: (NEEDING TO KNOW) Lot, are you . . . were you ever part of Moriarty's gang?

MORRILL: No. That was Harsh. Worked for Moriarty for years.

WATSON: As a paid killer?

MORRILL: And a good one. Give him his due. But the War also taught him how to lead men. Plan and execute raids. I suppose he'd have turned that training to crime on his own. Like Frank and Jesse James did. (SHIVERS) Moriarty paid him so much money. My mother thought I should be grateful to them both. My father could never have paid for my medical education.

WATSON: You would have found a way.

MORRILL: (SINCERE) Thanks. That means a lot. Coming from you. (SHIVERS) Harsh and my mother moved to Matlock. Last winter. So he could run things at Blue John Gap. Then she died. I couldn't get here in time for her funeral. Harsh thought it natural I'd want to visit her grave. That was only one reason I came.

WATSON: By the time you arrived, Washburne must have been trying to find a way to get his men out the country.

MORRILL: He'd already decided to steal the train. I thought, "If he's killed doing that, that's Providence. "Murmur not at the ways of Providence." I went along with him to the Gap that morning. We made plans to meet in Montenegro. I'd avenge my father there, though I told Harsh I'd get him back to America. Instead, Harsh came back to the mine. He'd recognized Simonson. Wanted blood. I helped him get to London. Helped him find Simonson's place. Then . . . when his guard was finally down . . . I poisoned him. Watched him die. (EMOTIONS OVERWHELM HIM) I wish I could say I'm sorry. Why can't I say I'm sorry?

WATSON: Because you're not a liar, and where it really counts you're still a good man. (PAUSE) Lot? (PAUSE) Lot!

SOUND EFFECT: WATSON GETS UP AND EXAMINES MORRILL

WATSON: (CONTINUED) Oh, Lot. And now you're gone, too.

MUSIC: MOURNFUL TRANSITION MUSIC

SOUND EFFECT: WATSON APPRAOCHES, WALKING FROM HOTEL TO HIS WAITING HANSOM CAB. (BACKGROUND) STREET SOUNDS. SIMONSON PAYS COINS TO CABBIE

SIMONSON: (TO CABBIE) There you are. And fair warning. Make sure you deliver that message. (TO WATSON) Hello, Doctor. You've caught me in the act of commandeering your cab.

WATSON: Hello, Walter. Why didn't you come up with Lestrade?

SIMONSON: No time. On my way out of the country until all of Moriarty's gang are in a salt box. Orders from my superior. For my own good, he says. This isn't my style, but what choice do I have? Not ours to reason why.

WATSON: Yes. *Mea gloria fides.* [1] Will you be away long?

SIMONSON: I hope not, but who can ever say how long a war will go on? (PAUSE) I am sorry about your friend.

WATSON: Yes. I've been hearing that a lot lately.

SIMONSON: I'm afraid life is like that sometimes.

WATSON: Lestrade mentioned you were able to use that key. Hopefully that will speed the war along.

SIMONSON: Hopefully.

WATSON: I'd be honored if you visit me when you get back.

SIMONSON: (DELIGHTED) I'll do that. And I'd be honored if we could share this cab.

WATSON: I'd like nothing better.

HOLMES: (AS REEVES) Taking you back to Baker Street then, sir?

SOUND EFFECT: WATSON CONSIDERS THAT FOR A MOMENT

WATSON: No. No, it's time you take me home to Paddington.

HOLMES: As you say.

SOUND EFFECT: WATSON AND SIMONSON GET INTO CAB AND HOLMES SNAPS REIGNS FOR HORSE TO MOVE

HOLMES: (CONTINUED) Off with you, Caprice.

SOUND EFFECT: HORSES' HOOVES

HOLMES: (TO HIMSELF IN HIS OWN VOICE) Good old Watson.

MUSIC: *DANSE MACABRE*

WATSON: This is Dr. John H. Watson. I've had many more adventures with Sherlock Holmes, and I'll tell you another one . . . *when next we meet!*

MUSIC: (FADE OUT)

NOTE

1 - *"Fidelity is my glory"*

278

The Singular Affair at
Sissinghurst Castle
by David Marcum

CHARACTERS

- SHERLOCK HOLMES
- DR. JOHN H. WATSON
- DRIVER
- STANLEY CORNWALLIS
- PHILO T. BURKE
- CONSTABLE WAGNER
- REPORTERS No's 1, 2, and 3

SOUND EFFECT: OPENING SEQUENCE, BIG BEN

ANNOUNCER: *The Further Adventures of Sherlock Holmes*, starring John Patrick Lowrie as Sherlock Holmes, and Lawrence Albert as Dr. John H. Watson.

MUSIC: *DANSE MACABRE* (UP AND UNDER)

MUSIC: OUT

SOUND EFFECT: WAGON WHEELS AND HORSE WALKING STEADILY

WATSON: Holmes, I appreciate the chance to get out of London for the day, and Kent is certainly lovely in the spring, but you don't always have to be so mysterious. Why are we here?

HOLMES: We are going to Sissinghurst. Do you know of it?

WATSON: Not at all, I'm afraid.

HOLMES: I received a letter several days ago from the owner of Sissinghurst Castle and the surrounding farm, a Mr. Stanley Cornwallis.

WATSON: And what does Mr. Cornwallis require from Mr. Sherlock Holmes?

HOLMES: He is being bothered by a treasure hunter.

WATSON: Treasure? In Kent? I might believe that about some of the areas along the coast, with their centuries of smuggling and the occasional shipwreck. But deep in the heart of the county? Not likely.

HOLMES: There is more than one kind of treasure, Watson. It was only a few months ago that I told you about Reginald Musgrave at Hurlstone, and the recovery there of the lost crown of the former King of England.

WATSON: As I recall, King Charles's crown was hidden at Hurlstone during the reign of Cromwell during the Commonwealth. Does Cornwallis suspect something similar is at Sissinghurst?

HOLMES: No, he believes exactly the opposite. He is certain that there is *nothing* hidden at the house. The estate apparently has some connection with events relating to those muddled times of transition between Mary and Elizabeth. It is a common story in that area, but there has never been any hint of treasure.

WATSON: Then why is there a treasure hunter?

HOLMES: Several weeks ago, an American arrived in Sissinghurst who has repeatedly insisted on searching the buildings and grounds for something of value. So far, Mr. Cornwallis has denied him any access. However, it seems that, in spite of his initial disbelief, Mr. Cornwallis did become more interested in whether there is any truth to the American's claims.

WATSON: And so he communicated with you?

HOLMES: He wrote, asking if I would be interested in doing some research to determine if there was any possibility of truth in the matter. I replied, and then I devoted part of a day in the reading room at the British Museum. Although there is some local historical significance to Mr. Cornwallis's farm, I found no evidence of anything relevant to a treasure at Sissinghurst.

WATSON: They why have we traveled down here?

HOLMES: I was ready to relay my results to Mr. Cornwallis when this morning's wire arrived. Something seems to have happened that made our presence necessary. As you can see, the message is rather vague as to details.

WATSON: (READING) *"Come at once. Situation becoming intolerable. Please wire details of arrival. Cornwallis"*. (NORMAL VOICE) Vague, indeed. It could be anything from an unpleasant encounter with the American, to murder.

HOLMES: Well, perhaps not murder. If it was that, Cornwallis might have used stronger language than to simply call the situation *"intolerable"*. (LOUDER) Driver, what can you tell us about this area?

DRIVER: Not much to tell, sir. There's the village, and the main farm. It's well run, it is. The farmhouse is very nice. And then there's the old house beside it. Hundreds of years old, it is, but it's mostly fallen down now. Some calls it a castle, maybe because it has something of a tower, but it's really naught but an old house.

HOLMES: Did anything interesting ever happen there?

DRIVER: Not much. Of course there was "Bloody" Baker.

HOLMES: I learned something of the fellow during my researches. A fellow with the appellation "Bloody" certainly sounds somewhat interesting, eh, Watson? Driver. What can you tell us of this man?

DRIVER: Not much, sir. Baker were a Catholic man, back during the reign of Mary. He was the owner of Sissinghurst then, and he made it his business to make life hell for the Protestants living around here. That's about all I know for sure, but I've heard about him all my life.

DRIVER: There's Sissinghurst. We're nearly there now, sirs.

MUSIC: SHORT BRIDGE

CORNWALLIS: Mr. Holmes? I am Stanley Cornwallis. Thank you
for coming. I apologize for not sending a carriage to the station.
I have been too distracted by today's events.

HOLMES: It is quite all right, Mr. Cornwallis. We arranged for
transportation. I have brought Dr. John Watson with me. He is
an experienced investigator as well, and often accompanies me.

(AD-LIB: GENERAL GREETINGS: NICE TO MEET YOU,
ETC.)

HOLMES: What are the events today to which you referred?

CORNWALLIS: Come this way, gentlemen, around to the back of
the house.

SOUND EFFECT: FOOTSTEPS THROUGH GRASS OR ALONG
WALKWAYS

CORNWALLIS: (SLIGHTLY WINDED) Is Dr. Watson aware of
the reason I originally wrote to you?

HOLMES: Somewhat. However, I have not revealed to him as yet
the little bit of information that my researches revealed.

CORNWALLIS: (IRATE) I have not received a report from you,
either, Mr. Holmes. Did you find any indication whatsoever that
there might be some sort of treasure at Sissinghurst?

HOLMES: None whatsoever. While there appears to be a long
history to the place, there is nothing monumentally outstanding,
and certainly nothing that makes this small byway any more
interesting than countless other villages across Britain.

CORNWALLIS: (AGITATED) Then why would that insane American do *that*?

WATSON: Oh . . . my.

HOLMES: Is this what you meant, Mr. Cornwallis, when you wired that the situation was becoming "intolerable"?

CORNWALLIS: Of course that's what I meant. This situation! That American! It's all intolerable. And I want you to gather evidence to stop it. I will prosecute him, sir. I will! I wired for you as soon as we found this, and I have sent for the law as well. The man will pay!

WATSON: Your stone terrace, Mr. Cornwallis. It's . . . it's been nearly destroyed. Almost all of the stones are overturned –

HOLMES: What indication do you have that the American is responsible for this? Did you perhaps catch him in the act?

CORNWALLIS: No, no. It was this way when we came out this morning. He did it during the night. I'm sure he did it. He has been pestering me for weeks to dig on the grounds for his ridiculous treasure. When I said no, he obviously came back on his own and did this.

WATSON: And you say that you have called for the police?

CORNWALLIS: Actually, I did not notify them immediately. My first thought was to send for you, Mr. Holmes. I sent one of the farm hands into the village to send a wire. He waited for your reply, and then returned here. Later, I thought to send my man back for the constable, but I neglected to tell him to meet your train.

WATSON: (TO HIMSELF) That explains why there was no one to meet us at the station.

HOLMES: Perhaps we could go inside while we wait for the constable to arrive, and you can tell us about this American. We can discuss the history of this estate and why there might – or might not – be any treasure at Sissinghurst.

MUSIC: SHORT BRIDGE

WATSON: Have you ever seen any indication of anything that might be considered treasure here?

CORNWALLIS: No, Dr. Watson. The property has been in my family for many generations, and there has never been anything like that here.

WATSON: Was there ever any evidence of visits here by royalty? Did anyone in your family ever travel or have adventures in foreign lands which might have given them an opportunity to obtain a treasure?

CORNWALLIS: There is a rumor that Edward I stayed here in the village in the early 1300's, but if so, he would certainly not have hidden a treasure here.

WATSON: No, that can't be it.

CORNWALLIS: And of course, there was Sir John Baker, who owned the house in the early 1500's, and was left two-hundred pounds by Henry VIII, in spite of Baker's noted pro-Catholic beliefs.

HOLMES: Ah, yes, "Bloody" Baker. He is the center of your American's treasure theories. What can you tell us of him?

CORNWALLIS: Why, that is Sir John, over there, in that painting over the fireplace.

WATSON: (MUTTERING) Grim looking fellow. (LOUDER) But overall he does not seem very threatening. Certainly not worth the name "Bloody" Baker.

HOLMES: Hmm. (READING) *"Sir John Baker. 1488 to 1558"*. (NORMAL VOICE) Long lived for his time. As I understand it, he was quite a successful man in this region.

CORNWALLIS: Yes, he was. Although he was fiercely pro-Catholic, Sir John enjoyed an excellent relationship with King Henry VIII, in spite of Henry's strong anti-Catholic beliefs.

HOLMES: In fact, I learned that during the time King Henry was taking so many estates, churches, and monasteries from pro-Catholic citizens and redistributing them to his friends and cronies, he actually gave many properties to Sir John, who ended up owning a number of manors and farms scattered around this area of Kent.

CORNWALLIS: Peacefully, I might add.

WATSON: But there was nothing bloody about any of that! Was there ever any indication of Baker showing excessive violence toward the local Protestants?

CORNWALLIS: None, Doctor. He questioned them, and often they had their property taken from them, but I have never heard anything that would lead to the name "Bloody" Baker.

HOLMES: As I understand it from your original letter, it is the claim of the American treasure hunter . . . I'm sorry, what was his name again, Mr. Cornwallis?

CORNWALLIS: Burke. Philo T. Burke.

HOLMES: Ah, yes. Peculiar name, isn't it, Watson? It is the claim of Mr. Burke that during this time Sir John Baker took something of great value from one of the local families and hid it here at Sissinghurst. During the confusion following Queen Mary's death, the item was never recovered. And soon after, Sir John died, and his secret with him.

CORNWALLIS: That is Burke's assertion, yes. However, there is no basis for such a fabrication. The local families have never mentioned any lost treasure, nor have they ever listed the theft of a treasure amongst their grievances against Sir John.

HOLMES: This location has spent the better part of the last thousand years in relative ease and peace. Even the tensions between

Catholics and Protestants in the area never achieved any great level of bloodshed.

CORNWALLIS: Would you be willing to present your evidence to Burke? Excellent!

<u>SOUND EFFECT: CARRIAGES ARRIVING OUTSIDE (MUTED)</u>

CORNWALLIS: That will be the constable. Will you relate to him as well what you have told me?

HOLMES: Of course.

<u>SOUND EFFECT: CURTAINS PULLING BACK AND WINDOW OPENING</u>

CORNWALLS: Look out there! That's not the constable! It's Burke, with several carriages of rough-looking men with him!

<u>MUSIC: SHORT BRIDGE</u>

<u>SOUND EFFECT: QUICK FOOTSTEPS ACROSS GRAVEL</u>

CORNWALLIS: Burke! What is the meaning of this? I have told you that you are not allowed on my property!

BURKE: (AMERICAN ACCENT) Good morning to you, Mr. Cornwallis. I realize that we have had some disagreements in the past, but we cannot let something like that stand in the way of the historical find of the century! Just think, sir – when the truth is revealed, your little castle here will be the destination point of visitors from both Europe and America!

CORNWALLIS: Leave! Leave now! The law will be here soon, and then I will have you arrested! Do you think you can get away with vandalizing my property and trespassing? I will have you arrested and then deported!

BURKE: I don't think we've had the pleasure, gentleman. My name is Philo Burke, of Cleveland, Ohio. I'm sure Mr. Cornwallis has told you about me.

CORNWALLIS: Yes, I have. They are here because of *you*! They can debunk your whole treasure theory. This is –

HOLMES: (INTERRUPTING) We have been doing been doing some research for Mr. Cornwallis in London. He is correct. There is no evidence of any historical event here that would indicate the presence of treasure.

BURKE: Of course that is what the official records would say. If there was a conspiracy to conceal the fact that "Bloody" Baker had hidden a treasure here, he would have covered his tracks well.

(AD-LIB: THE MEN OF THE PRESS MUTTERING TO THEMSELVES)

BURKE: (LOUDER) Boys, I've looked at the same papers in London that this gentleman is referring to, and I can tell you that there is more to it than he thinks. In fact, *(Lowering voice)* I was even able to find a coded message contained in the papers, which is what led me to search under the flagstone terrace behind the house!

CORNWALLIS: You destroyed that terrace! It has only been there for thirty years, since the current house was built. It wasn't even there when Sir John lived here!

BURKE: Mr. Cornwallis, I do not know if you are truly ignorant of the historical nature of what is hidden here, or if you yourself are part of the conspiracy to keep the truth hidden. But I tell you that the truth must come out, and you cannot stop it! I have brought these fine men of the press with me today, to assure that the truth will be told. For too long the secret has been kept! Come with me, boys!

SOUND EFFECT: MULTIPLE FOOTSTEPS ACROSS GRAVEL (FADING)

BURKE: (FADING) Follow me behind the house. Whatever it is, it's been buried for over three hundred years. It's time to bring it out into the sunshine!

HOLMES: (LOW VOICE, BUT STILL NEARBY) What do you say to a day in Kent, Watson?

WATSON: (LOW VOICE) Kent sounds wonderful. If we don't get killed in the crossfire. I assume you didn't want Burke to know you are a detective.

HOLMES: (LOW VOICE) Exactly. Burke may or may not have heard of me, but I want to see what his game is for a while, and the best way to do that is to let him play it out. The terrace is already damaged. A little more destruction cannot hurt it too badly. Let us see what Mr. Burke has planned for us.

MUSIC: SHORT BRIDGE

HOLMES: Hurry, Watson, let us hear what Mr. Burke is saying to the press.

BURKE: (VOICE BECOMING LOUDER – SPEAKING TO THE PRESS) As you can see, I was unable to finish my search of the terrace last night. I was interrupted and forced to flee when I thought I was about to be discovered. Of course, I will recompense Mr. Cornwallis for the cost of repairs to his terrace.

CORNWALLIS: You certainly will!

BURKE: However, I feel that once the treasure is recovered, he will be so grateful that he will understand why this was necessary, and he may not even ask for any compensation.

REPORTER #1: And what is your deal in all this, Mr. Burke? If they find a treasure, you don't get to keep it.

BURKE: Certainly not. My only interest is in the advancement of historical knowledge.

REPORTER #2: How did you get onto it? Being from Ohio and all?

BURKE: I came across some old documents, which made references to other documents. I followed the trail, using the specialized knowledge I have acquired from a lifetime of study, until I found conclusive proof of the Sissinghurst Treasure.

289

REPORTER #3: (SLIGHTLY OFF IN THE DISTANCE) Oi! What's this?

HOLMES: (SOFTLY) I believe we are about to see Mr. Burke's surprise, Watson.

REPORTER #2: It's a skeleton! Down in the hole underneath this terrace stone!

REPORTER #3: This stone wasn't flipped like all the others. I was just looking to see what was underneath. And – oh my God! The back of his bloody head's been knocked in!

REPORTER #1: Let me see!

REPORTER #2: Get out of the way, you!

BURKE: Well, I had not expected this. No, sir. Had you, Mr. Cornwallis? Did you perhaps know what we would find?

CORNWALLIS: (STUNNED) No. No, of course not.

HOLMES: And what did you expect, Mr. Burke?

BURKE: Well, sir, to be honest, I did not rightly know. Treasure of some sort, of course, perhaps a chest, but I never expected to find a murder!

WAGNER: (FADING IN) Murder? What's this about a murder? How was this found, sir?

CORNWALLIS: Constable Wagner! It's about time you arrived.

REPORTER #2: It's a skeleton. Underneath this paving stone.

WAGNER Any idea who this might be?

290

CORNWALLIS: None. This terrace is only thirty or so years old. There is no indication that there has ever been a treasure here, contrary to Mr. Burke's wild claims. Let alone a skeleton. This gentleman will tell you. He has researched the matter.

WAGNER: And your name sir? You look familiar to me. Wait, aren't you —

HOLMES: Might I speak with you in private for a moment?

WAGNER: Why, um, certainly.

SOUND EFFECT: FOOTSTEPS ACROSS GRAVEL (FADING)

REPORTER #1: (YELLING) Mr. Cornwallis! Do you care to give a statement about this gruesome discovery?

REPORTER #2: (ABRASIVE) Mr. Cornwallis, sir! Do you know which member of your family killed this man and hid his body under the terrace?

REPORTER #3: (LOUDER) Do you feel that it is now the right time to reveal the location of the treasure?

CORNWALLIS: Burke! This is all your fault! I'll –

SOUND EFFECT: FOOTSTEPS APPROACHING ACROSS THE GRAVEL

WAGNER: (LOUD) You people. I want your names and which paper you are with. Then I want you to clear off out of here. Return to the village, and don't leave until I tell you so. (NORMAL TONE) Mr. Cornwallis, I am going to leave the remains here under your responsibility until I can return. Mr. Burke, you will return to the village with me.

BURKE: (ANGRY) Wait! You cannot simply go off and leave this find unprotected. We don't know how it got here. His family may have had something to do with it. You may get back and the treasure may be gone! Or the bones!

WAGNER: Sir, there are a number of witnesses who have seen the skeleton, most of them reporters that you brought here yourself. Too many people have seen this. I do not think that anything will happen here while I'm gone, and I trust these men to watch over things until I get back. Gentlemen, until I return, good day.

SOUND EFFECT: FOOTSTEPS ACROSS GRAVEL (FADING)

CORNWALLIS: Mr. Holmes, what does it all mean? Is it possible that "Bloody" Baker was not the innocent man your researches showed?

HOLMES: Perhaps you should go inside and rest, Mr. Cornwallis. Dr. Watson and I will be responsible for the skeleton until the return of Constable Wagner.

CORNWALLIS: Yes, of course. Thank you, Mr. Holmes.

SOUND EFFECT: FOOTSTEPS ACROSS GRAVEL (FADING)

HOLMES: What do you make of it, Watson?

WATSON: This is certainly no murder, is it?

HOLMES: As I'm sure you can see, the bones are clean and white. More importantly, they were obviously once *wired together*. What does this suggest?

WATSON: This fellow has, until recently, been the resident of some sort of teaching facility, perhaps a hospital. I imagine, from his excellent condition, that he has not been dead and preserved for too many years, and that he certainly has not been in this hole for very long.

HOLMES: No, not for more than twelve hours or so, I would say. The bones are extremely clean, and there is no sign of discoloration from exposure to the soil or the groundwater. In addition, the sides of the hole are still quite vertical, and there has been no creep or collapse of the walls.

WATSON: But why was he placed here? I assume that Burke is behind this.

HOLMES: Oh, of course he is. Obviously, he came out here last night and buried the bones under a flagstone large enough to cover a skeleton before he replaced that stone and proceeded to disrupt a number of others. Then, as we saw a few minutes ago, he let someone else make the discovery, creating the shocking effect that he was attempting.

WATSON: But surely he realizes that a cursory examination would show that this skeleton is of very recent origin?

HOLMES: Possibly. It may be that he has such a low opinion of the country constabulary that he believed the skeleton's condition would not be noticed. Or more probably, he does not care. He intentionally made sure there were reporters here, and he seemed pleased that they were writing down everything they saw and heard.

WATSON: When you referred to this as Burke's surprise, did you know exactly what was going to be found?

HOLMES: Not at all. But when Burke arrived with the reporters, I realized that he had probably hidden something that he wanted to be found in front of witnesses. However, I did not know what form the item would take.

WATSON: But what about the hole in the skull?

HOLMES: It simply adds to the effect. I'm sure the hole was knocked there by Burke to give the initial impression that the fellow had been murdered. If you look, you can see that the exposed cracked edges around the hole are clean and white, even cleaner than the surface of the skull, indicating that the wound is of recent origin.

WATSON: So all this has been arranged for some reason as a show for those reporters brought down by Burke.

HOLMES: Exactly. Although I am not quite certain of his motive at this point, I believe that we shall have to give Mr. Burke a little more line in order to set the hook before we can reel him in.

WATSON: And the constable? Did you make him aware of all this?

HOLMES: I did. He appeared to recognize me, and was in fact about to identify me when I stopped him. I quickly explained to him what we have seen about the age and provenance of the skeleton, as well as Burke's apparent actions in the matter. He immediately picked up on what I was telling him, and he agreed that we should allow Mr. Burke to act out his little drama for a while.

WATSON: I see. In that way, we might have something more against him than a simple charge of terrace vandalism. As it stands now, Burke could simply claim it was a joke, make restitution or pay a small fine, and disappear without the real reasons behind this ever becoming known.

HOLMES: And now let us go inside, where you can check on Mr. Cornwallis, and I can smoke a pipe or two until Constable Wagner returns.

MUSIC: SHORT BRIDGE

WATSON: Cornwallis finally dropped off to sleep. The poor man is a nervous wreck. I'm afraid that if this continues, he'll suffer a case of brain fever.

HOLMES: And what news do you have for us, Constable Wagner?

WAGNER: The village doctor is outside, loading the skeleton. He has confirmed that is it is simply a medical exhibit, and not a murder victim.

HOLMES: And the laborers you brought with you? Can they be discrete?

WAGNER: I've sworn these men to secrecy. Burke is being watched by one of my men at the local inn. He's been holding court with those reporters, spinning one wild theory after another.

WATSON: I can just imagine.

WAGNER: By the time I left, he had one going where "Bloody" Baker had kidnapped half the countryside at one time or another during Queen Mary's reign, holding them for ransoms until the families gave him their valuables.

WATSON: Oh my Lord.

WAGNER: He's even saying that Mr. Cornwallis will be putting this place up for sale soon in order to get away from the horrible reputation that this place has acquired.

WATSON: You can't be serious.

WAGNER: He's hinting darkly that the place is haunted. The reporters are eating it up. They're already clogging up the local telegraph office, passing on these stories to their newspapers.

HOLMES: I am sorry that we must let Burke continue to play out this nonsense until we can discover his true motives. It is going to cause a certain amount of distress for Mr. Cornwallis before it's all over.

WATSON: (SOFTLY) That is for certain.

HOLMES: However, as I told Watson, it will be better if we can arrest Burke for more than simple vandalism. Do you suppose that you could get a few wires off for me without alerting the reporters?

WAGNER: Of course. The telegraph agent is my brother-in-law.

HOLMES: Stress the urgency of these. The longer this goes on, the more mess Mr. Cornwallis will have to deal with.

WAGNER: Certainly, sir. I'll let you know if I hear anything. I'll be back out first thing in the morning.

SOUND EFFECT: FOOTSTEPS ACROSS ROOM (FADING). DOOR SHUTS

WATSON: What now, Holmes?

HOLMES: Now, old friend, we wait.

MUSIC: SHORT BRIDGE

WATSON: (NARRATING) The next morning, the sun was quite high in the sky, and still there was no word from Constable Wagner, either of news regarding Burke's activities in the village the night before, or answers to Holmes's telegrams. And as for Holmes? He was becoming quite impatient.

HOLMES: Blast! Wagner seemed quite intelligent, Watson. I cannot understand why we have heard nothing!

WATSON: Perhaps he has nothing yet to tell. And if that gaggle of reporters is still in the village, he has no doubt had other matters to deal with.

HOLMES: Possibly, possibly. Ah, Mr. Cornwallis. How are you feeling this morning?

CORNWALLIS: Not well, Mr. Holmes. Not well at all. All night I tossed and turned, wondering what that man Burke will come up with next. What can be his purpose in all this?

HOLMES: I hope to have an answer for you soon. Ah, I perceive that Constable Wagner has arrived. Hopefully, he has some news.

SOUND EFFECT: FOOTSTEPS ENTERING THE ROOM

WAGNER: The story is in all the papers, I'm afraid, sir. Have a look at these, the latest editions down on the London train this morning.

SOUND EFFECT: NEWSPAPERS RUSTLING

HOLMES: What of the replies to my telegrams, constable?

WAGNER: I have them right here, sir.

CORNWALLIS: (GROANS) Treasure! They all have stories about the estate being filled with buried treasure. We shall be overrun!

WATSON: Secreted fortunes, bloody murders. There are speculations enough here to fire any boy's wildest dreams. This paper even hints that there are lost entrances to a vast underground cavern on the estate, filled with hoards of gold and jewels.

WAGNER: And what of this one? It speaks of the tower, which it says was designed with hidden passages and booby traps for the unwary.

WATSON: Look here! This reporter speculates that "*Mr. Cornwallis intends to sell the estate and leave the country, due to the fact that the* foully murdered victim *found under the* ancient flagstone terrace *is such an embarrassment to the family that he can no longer stand to remain in England.*"

CORNWALLIS: This states that I was aware of the murdered victim, as well as many others hidden around the estate, and that I will flee from the authorities before I can be questioned – or jailed!

WAGNER: Mr. Burke has spread it around that he will be exposing another surprise here today at eleven a.m. Mr. Cornwallis, I'm afraid that the reporters will be coming back here then. It appears that half the village will be joining them.

CORNWALLIS: Oh my.

WAGNER: My men and I will be here, but I'm afraid there aren't enough of us to stop them. We will arrest as many as we can, if you'd like, but I cannot do anything until they actually trespass on the property.

CORNWALLIS: Of course, of course. Thank you.

HOLMES: Based on the information in these wires from America, you *can* arrest Burke, however.

WAGNER: Yes, sir. Anytime you say. And a good thing, too. I simply wanted to speak with you about it first.

HOLMES: Excellent. Watson, will you hand me that Bradshaw from that shelf behind you? Thank you. Would you care to examine the telegrams while I ascertain today's train schedule?

HOLMES: There is a train at eleven a.m, departing for London. An amazing coincidence, wouldn't you say? Exactly the time everyone will be gathering here at the Sissinghurst house.

WATSON: Perhaps we should be at the station then.

HOLMES: Quite.

CORNWALLIS: What? Won't you be here at eleven when Burke and the reporters come back? I don't understand.

HOLMES: I believe that the reporters will be here without Mr. Burke, and without him to provide any entertainment, I feel that they will soon become disinterested and leave. In the meantime, Mr. Burke will probably be attempting to slip out of town on the first train of the morning.

CORNWALLIS: What?

HOLMES: I am still not entirely certain as to Mr. Burke's reasons for creating this entire production, although certain aspects of the matter are becoming clear. However, yesterday, through the kindness of Constable Wagner and his brother-in-law, I cabled several acquaintances of mine in the United States, particularly a police officer in Cleveland, Ohio. What he replied about Mr. Philo T. Burke was of some interest indeed.

WATSON: These cables make interesting reading. Confidence man. Thief. Forger. Murderer. A very wanted man in America. It was rather careless of Mr. Burke to reveal his true name and place of origin, wasn't it?

WAGNER: Once they found out where he was, the Americans then wired me as well as Mr. Holmes here to hold Burke until they can send someone after him. Should be here in about a week.

298

HOLMES: Do you have enough men to keep an eye on the reporters, as well as making sure that Burke cannot slip away?

WAGNER: As soon as I got this information, I quietly sent to surrounding areas, requesting some additional constables. Burke's under observation in the village by my men, but right now it's not a problem. He's still sitting around, feeding whatever crazy stories that he can think of to those reporters.

HOLMES: When the time comes to travel out here from the village, he will certainly arrange for the reporters to go on ahead of him. Then he will quietly slip away to the train station and head back to London.

WAGNER: That's the way I see it. Of course, we will prevent him.

HOLMES: Mr. Cornwallis, we must leave you now to stop Mr. Burke. Rest assured that this matter will soon be concluded.

MUSIC: SHORT BRIDGE

SOUND EFFECT: TRAIN STATION. A TRAIN IS PREPARING TO DEPART

WATSON: (SOFTLY) There he is. On that bench on the up-side of the platform.

WAGNER: (SOFTLY) I see him.

HOLMES: (NORMAL TONE) Mr. Burke? A moment, if you please?

BURKE: (NERVOUS) Hmm? Is there a problem, gentlemen?

WAGNER: There doesn't need to be. Mr. Philo T. Burke, of Cleveland, Ohio, I place you under arrest.

BURKE: Oh, no, you don't!

(AD-LIB: SCUFFLE)

BURKE: (ANGRILY, OUT OF BREATH) What are you anyway? One of those Scotland Yarders?

HOLMES: I am Sherlock Holmes.

BURKE: (A BEAT) Heard about you. In fact, someone I met over here, never mind who, warned me not to get tangled up with you. I thought this far out in the country I would be safe. Never had a chance, did I?

WAGNER: Come on, get him to the station.

MUSIC: SHORT BRIDGE

BURKE: Search my bag all you like, gentlemen. There's nothing criminal in there.

HOLMES: Nothing but these newspapers and handwritten sheets, Burke.

BURKE: Those? They're nothing. Just some harmless scribbling. Certainly nothing illegal about them.

WATSON: What are they, Holmes?

HOLMES: See for yourself.

SOUND EFFECT: PAGES RUSTLING

WATSON: Why, each one of these is a handwritten draft, describing the upcoming sale of the Sissinghurst farm and castle.

WAGNER: Sale? How can he plan a sale of something that he does not own?

HOLMES: They are all very similar, having only slight variations from one another. Obviously the sheets were rough drafts of some sort of prospectus. Notice the numerous scratched out words, as if Mr. Burke had tried differing combinations before settling on phrasing that pleased him.

WAGNER: But what is the purpose, Mr. Holmes?

HOLMES: I am not completely certain, but I believe that I have a reasonable understanding of Burke's plan. It fits his background as a confidence man and trickster. Correct me if I'm incorrect, Mr. Burke.

BURKE: I've done nothing wrong here.

HOLMES: Burke had researched and found a likely spot in Sissinghurst. The place was old, but there never was any reason to think that treasure had been hidden there. However, there was enough history to the place that stories of treasure could be fabricated, at least long enough to serve Burke's purpose. And of course, there was the association with the fascinating "Bloody" Baker.

WAGNER: But where's the crime? If it hadn't been for those telegrams, we wouldn't have had reason to arrest him, except for a petty charge of vandalism. What did he gain from all of this?

HOLMES: After picking Sissinghurst, Burke showed up and began to make himself a nuisance to Mr. Cornwallis. His plan was to continue that for a few weeks until he could stage the incident with the reporters, the terrace, and the skeleton. I expect that when you got here, Mr. Burke, you did not know exactly where or how the incident would take place, but I'm sure you had the skeleton with you, as you looked for a likely spot. Did you buy the skeleton, Mr. Burke, or did you steal it from a medical school or hospital?

BURKE: This is your tale, Mr. Holmes. I'm simply an innocent victim.

WATSON: So it was his intent all along to create a story that would grab the imaginations of the reporters. He made it seem as mysterious and exciting as possible, throwing in hidden treasure, an unexpected dead man, and hints of hauntings and conspiracy.

HOLMES: What he was after, of course, was to have numerous stories about the incident in as many different newspapers as he could find. He never intended that the story should hold up to any kind of close scrutiny. He planned to be gone as soon as possible, and he didn't care if the exact origins of the skeleton were quickly discovered.

WATSON: Of course. As long as he had the newspapers containing the stories of treasure and a possible sale of the estate, he would be able to carry out the rest of his plan.

WAGNER: So after he left for London on this morning's train –

HOLMES: He would wait there for a few days, seeing if any other useful newspaper articles were printed that might add to the recently fabricated treasure legends of Sissinghurst Castle. He would buy up as many old copies of today's newspapers as he could reasonably carry, for future use.

WATSON: Then, after returning to America –

HOLMES: After returning, he would have printed a series of brochures, false deeds, and other bogus documents, each implying that he was the agent responsible for selling the Sissinghurst estate. He would let on that people in England were reluctant to buy the estate, possibly afraid of ghosts.

WATSON: By showing a number of legitimate British newspapers, each with stories verifying Burke's claim that the estate was for sale and why, he could sell the estate over and over again to gullible American investors.

HOLMES: Exactly.

WATSON: Each would think they were getting the place at a bargain, and not only acquiring an actual English estate with a castle, but also a property fairly loaded with hidden treasure and an interesting ghostly history.

HOLMES: Of course, after each false sale, he would simply move on and try the same thing in a different town. Is that substantially correct, Mr. Burke?

BURKE: You're the one telling it. I'm just listening. So far, all you can charge me with is vandalism of Cornwallis's terrace, and you'd have to prove that. What difference does it make if I decided to leave town? And maybe I just bought all those newspapers because I thought it was an interesting story.

SOUND EFFECT: CHAIR MOVING BACK AS BURKE STANDS UP

BURKE: So unless you can do better than that, gentleman, I am going to depart.

HOLMES: I don't think so, Mr. Burke. You were a little careless in telling me that you were from Cleveland, Ohio. I wired to some professional acquaintances there about you. Your history is an interesting one. Apparently your violent attack on one of the city's most prominent citizens, which caused you to flee America late last year, is still the subject of much discussion there.

BURKE: It's a lie!

HOLMES: The man later died. The Cleveland police were quite pleased to know that you are here, and they are sending someone to retrieve you, even as we speak.

(AD-LIB: SCUFFLE)

WAGNER: (WINDED) Put him in a cell. He's the guest of Her Majesty now, until his own people come to fetch him.

MUSIC: SHORT BRIDGE

SOUND EFFECT: TRAIN TRAVELING AT A STEADY SPEED, OCCASIONAL WHISTLE

WATSON: Poor Mr. Cornwallis. I fear that he will be bothered by the aftermath of this affair for years to come.

HOLMES: Perhaps. He is certainly fearful that people will be trespassing on the estate, digging and looking for treasure, and

303

then bringing suit against him if they somehow fall and hurt themselves in the process.

WATSON: Well, I hope it doesn't turn out that way. And after all, you were able to give the reporters most of the facts, and Constable Wagner will be telling them the rest of the story.

HOLMES: Hopefully the whole matter will die a quick death. (A BEAT) Watson, would you enjoy attending a concert tonight, when we arrive back in London? They are playing German music, which I find especially appealing.

WATSON: Certainly.

HOLMES: Good. Then I believe we shall just have time for me to tell you of an investigation I conducted not long after I entered private practice in London. It was on an estate similar to Sissinghurst, in central Norfolk.

WATSON: Really?

HOLMES: Unlike Sissinghurst, however, this estate did indeed reveal a singular treasure, which we might, if you are interested and not too busy, go to see tomorrow at the British Museum.

MUSIC: *DANSE MACABRE*

WATSON: This is Dr. John H. Watson. I've had many more adventures with Sherlock Holmes, and I'll tell you another one *. . . when next we meet!*

MUSIC: (FADE OUT)

The Beast of Hyndford
by Iain McLaughlin, Claire Bartlett,
and John Patrick Lowrie

CHARACTERS:

- SHERLOCK HOLMES – *Consulting detective*
- DR. JOHN H. WATSON – *Loyal friend*
- REVEREND PATRICK MORRIS – *Minister in Hyndford. Mid-thirties*
- ELIZABETH MORRIS – *Married to Reverend Morris. Thirty-ish*
- MRS. PRIDDY – *Housekeeper to the Morris family. Fifties*
- IRENE – *Local widow. Twenties*

SOUND EFFECT: OPENING SEQUENCE, BIG BEN

ANNOUNCER: *The Further Adventures of Sherlock Holmes*, starring John Patrick Lowrie as Sherlock Holmes, and Lawrence Albert as Dr. John H. Watson.

MUSIC: *DANSE MACABRE* (UP AND UNDER)

MUSIC: OUT

WATSON: (NARRATING) There are few subjects in this world upon which I would claim that my dear friend, Sherlock Holmes, lives in ignorance. And fewer still upon which I would claim a greater knowledge and experience. However, the fairer sex is one such subject – although, as I have oftentimes noted previously, Holmes never fails to surprise me.

SOUND EFFECT: TICKING CLOCK.

WATSON: Take your time, my dear.

ELIZABETH: Thank you, Doctor Watson. You are very kind.

HOLMES: On occasion, too kind, I would venture.

WATSON: Pay him no heed. Take your time, and tell us what brings you to Baker Street.

ELIZABETH: I have thought for many days of how I could say this, but now that I am here I find the words slow to come.

HOLMES: The facts will be sufficient, Mrs. . . . ?

ELIZABETH: Morris. Elizabeth Morris. My husband is the vicar in Hyndford. A small town just outside of London.

HOLMES: I know of it. Fourth stop on a thrice daily service from the Liverpool Street Station. Please continue.

ELIZABETH: This is a delicate subject, Mr. Holmes. One I am not entirely comfortable discussing with anyone.

HOLMES: If you will not discuss it, I do not see how I can help you.

WATSON: Take your time, Mrs. Morris, and be sure, nothing you say here will leave these rooms. Of that you have our assurance.

ELIZABETH: Thank you, Doctor. My husband and I have long held the dream of becoming parents. We have been married now for nine years and we have, as yet, no children.

WATSON: That is unfortunate, but hardly uncommon.

ELIZABETH: Three years ago, I was blessed to find myself with child. Finally. It was something we had prayed for. It was the happiest time of our lives. My husband and I . . . we were both overwhelmed by the good wishes of the people of Hyndford. People can be so kind, can't they?

WATSON: Indeed they can.

HOLMES: Although it is notable that people rarely arrive at our door to tell us of kindness.

WATSON: Sadly that is true. Please continue, Mrs. Morris.

307

ELIZABETH: Seven months into my time, I began to feel such pain. There was . . . I do not need to go into detail on such a delicate thing with a medical man such as yourself, Doctor Watson. The fact is that my child did not go to term and was lost to us. Since then, we have hoped for another child. Hoped desperately, but to no avail. My husband has been kind, but I know that in spite of his kindness, there is a terrible disappointment, and that makes his kindness all the more heartbreaking.

WATSON: I'm so terribly sorry.

ELIZABETH: Patrick tells me that it is the Lord's work. That such great decisions belong only to God. And I had believed him.

HOLMES: Why do you not believe him now?

ELIZABETH: I did not say that.

HOLMES: Indeed you did. By inference, if nothing else.

WATSON: Why did your opinion change?

ELIZABETH: This will sound strange. It sounds unbelievable to me every time I think of it, but I must tell you. We are an old village and we have many old superstitions, one of which is that those living in my house are cursed. Of course, no-one can remember where and when the rumours began, and few other than the most easily influenced of the village pay them heed.

HOLMES: Yet still you are here. Are you easily influenced, Mrs. Morris?

ELIZABETH: Normally, I would say not. But some months ago, I began . . . I began to sense that . . . something . . . something was happening . . . in our home.

HOLMES: "Something" is of no use or interest to me. You must be more precise. I require detail. Facts are the currency of my profession.

WATSON And manners the currency of a gentleman, Holmes. Continue, please, Mrs. Morris.

ELIZABETH: Yes. I'm sorry . . . I . . . I was alone at home one night. Patrick was visiting a parishioner, the niece of our housekeeper, Mrs. Priddy. Her niece is a widow, poor thing, who was left with a young child to raise on her own. Anyway, I was alone and I began to hear . . . a sound. It was distant, like the moaning of a poor tormented soul. The moaning continued for a long time that night. I was quite on edge, but when Patrick returned, he could hear nothing, and I dismissed it as imagination. But a few days later, Patrick was again out visiting parishioners, and again I heard the moaning. But this time it was louder and more prolonged. And as it reached its loudest, I felt the house become suddenly cold and the lamps in the front parlour were all blown out by a sudden wind, even though the doors and windows were all closed. When my husband returned, I began to tell him of what had happened, but I could see in his reaction that he did not believe me. He is a man of God. He cannot contemplate that our house would be plagued by such things. We are on consecrated ground.

HOLMES: Your house is close to the church?

ELIZABETH: No more than thirty yards. The church grounds are quite large. There are several cottages on the far side of the church. Patrick uses them for the poor and disadvantaged of our parish. We have the elderly couple whose farm burned, Mrs. Priddy's niece with her baby, Mrs. Garritty with her two boys. Tear-aways, both of them.

HOLMES: Are you trying to tell me that all these good parishioners moan like tormented souls?

ELIZABETH: What? Why, no, Mr. Holmes –

HOLMES: Then why do you mention them?

ELIZABETH: Why? I –

HOLMES: When I said facts are the currency of my profession, perhaps I should have been more expansive. So I shall amend my earlier comment and say "pertinent facts". Is that more helpful to you?

WATSON: Holmes –

ELIZABETH: I apologise, Mr. Holmes.

HOLMES: Pray continue.

ELISABETH: Yes. Well, as I said, my husband would not hear talk of any malignant spirit. And yet, night after night, I have heard this unearthly moaning, seen the candles quelled, and had the stench of decay fill my home. But that was not the worst. I had almost become used to it. Then . . . then it was three years to the day since my dream of holding my child was taken from me. That was the first time I heard it.

WATSON: Heard what?

ELIZABETH: I was in the parlour. I heard the moan and the chill, as I had many times before. But this time, I heard something else. As the lights were extinguished, I heard the cry of an infant. It was in distress. I could hear it in no other room in the house, nor could I hear it outside. Only in the parlour – the parlour in which I had been sitting when I collapsed before my child was taken from us. Mr. Holmes, I fear that I am being haunted . . . haunted by the spirit of my own dead child.

SOUND EFFECT: A CART ON A STREET. RURAL. RAIN FALLING HEAVILY

WATSON: Holmes, I have to say that I was surprised when you agreed to assist this unfortunate woman.

HOLMES: Indeed, Watson?

WATSON: I had expected you to send her on her way with a pithy comment. (IMITATING HOLMES) "If your problem is medical, may I suggest my friend, Doctor Watson. If you are ailed by a spiritual matter, I recommend that you seek refuge with your clergyman husband."

HOLMES: You think me so callous?

WATSON: I know you have little truck with the spiritual world and the resurrectionists.

HOLMES: Hmm. So you think we're off to do battle with ghosts and demons?

WATSON: I'm sure I don't know what we might be facing.

HOLMES: My mind was in want of a burden to carry. Monotony is dangerous to me. You know that.

SOUND EFFECT: DOOR OPENS

MRS. PRIDDY: Off you go. And stay indoors out of this rain, girl.

IRENE Yes, Auntie.

SOUND EFFECT: FOOTSTEPS RUNNING AWAY IN THE RAIN

MRS. PRIDDY: May I help you, gentlemen?

ELIZABETH: (EXCITED) Mr. Holmes, Doctor Watson. You came.

HOLMES: Did you doubt that we would?

ELIZABETH: I am aware of how unlikely a tale I told you, Mr. Holmes. I would not have borne you any ill-will had you chosen not to respond to it. Please come in.

WATSON: Thank you, Mrs. Morris.

ELIZABETH: Mrs. Priddy, some tea, please.

MRS. PRIDDY: As you wish. Ma'am.

ELIZABETH: Mr. Holmes, Doctor Watson, the parlour is this way.

SOUND EFFECT: FOOTSTEPS

WATSON: I'm surprised you still come to this room so readily.

ELIZABETH: I am not a coward, Doctor. I would be lying if I said I do not feel a chill each time I come in here, but far less so during the day. Even one so cold and wet as this.

HOLMES: You have never experienced any of these unusual phenomena in the hours of daylight?

ELIZABETH: Never, Mr. Holmes. Always, it waits until I am alone. Even when my husband is out, I am never alone during the day. Mrs. Priddy, our housekeeper, is always here, and a vicar's house is rarely without visitors.

HOLMES: And no-one else has seen or heard anything untoward?

ELIZABETH: No-one at all.

HOLMES: Interesting.

ELIZABETH: Is it?

HOLMES: I was referring to your house.

ELIZABETH: "Interesting" is hardly the word a woman would most like to hear with regards to her house, Mr. Holmes.

WATSON: Etiquette is hardly Holmes's speciality, I'm afraid.

HOLMES: Quite true. Watson is far more socially adept than I. Tell me of the house. What is its history? When was it built?

ELIZABETH: I cannot say. According to the townsfolk, the church and its buildings have simply always been here.

HOLMES: I would prefer something more precise than local lore.

ELIZABETH: I have no doubt that the exact dates will be available in the church records. At least those that were not destroyed in the Reformation.

WATSON: I would never have guessed it was so old.

ELIZABETH: Parts of the house were built only fifty years ago, but this side – the parlour, the kitchen, and so on, date back long before.

HOLMES: So it was a Catholic church?

ELIZABETH: I presume so. I imagine we are fortunate it is still here. So many religious buildings were torn down.

WATSON: It was a brutal time. Hundreds of clergymen were tortured and even murdered for their beliefs.

HOLMES: Indeed. Tell me, do you know the fate of the local priest here during the Reformation?

ELIZABETH: I do not, Mr. Holmes. I must admit that I have taken precious little interest in the history of the parish. The present needs of the area offer plenty enough challenges to occupy us constantly.

HOLMES: You mentioned parish records. Would they be here?

ELIZABETH: Some are in my husband's study, I believe.

HOLMES: Show them to me.

ELIZABETH: I never enter my husband's study, Mr. Holmes. We have an agreement. He never enters my kitchen or the small parlour where I entertain my visitors, and I never linger in his study.

WATSON: I assure you, Holmes would not ask for these records unless it was important.

ELIZABETH: Well, all right, then. It will be something of a thrill to finally break the agreement. I have often told Patrick that he should keep his study tidier.

WATSON: I have often told Holmes the same.

ELIZABETH: The study is this way.

ELIZABETH: This is it.

SOUND EFFECT: A DOOR CREAKS OPEN. A RATTLE OF CUPS APPROACHES

MRS. PRIDDY: Mrs. Morris?

ELIZABETH: Just put the tea in the parlour please, Mrs. Priddy.

MRS. PRIDDY: (POINTEDLY BUT NOT UNKINDLY) Very wise, ma'am. The Reverend would not appreciate cups near his papers.

ELIZABETH: I know, Mrs. Priddy. We will be careful, I assure you.

MRS. PRIDDY: With your permission, Mrs. Morris. I'll return a shawl to my niece. She left it here, silly girl.

ELIZABETH: Of course, Mrs. Priddy.

SOUND EFFECT: DOOR CREAKS AND CLICKS SHUT

ELIZABETH: As you will see, my husband is something of a collector of books. Finding the information you seek may prove more difficult than I had imagined.

WATSON: This is a remarkable collection.

HOLMES: And not so randomly arranged as you imagine. They're alphabetical.

WATSON: I don't think so, Holmes. Look at the . . . .

HOLMES: When translated into Latin, the titles are arranged alphabetically.

ELIZABETH: That would not surprise me. Patrick is quite a scholar.

HOLMES: The parish records . . . . Yes, here they are. Bound ledgers. In chronological order. How is your Latin, Watson?

WATSON: Not as good as yours, obviously.

HOLMES: Nonsense. You start with the oldest. I'll start with the most recent.

SOUND EFFECT: HEAVY LEDGERS MOVED. OPENED

WATSON: This one is from before the Reformation. As is the next. It talks of loyalty to Rome.

HOLMES: Everything is here. Births, deaths, marriages. Hmm. This might be instructive.

SOUND EFFECT: LEDGERS MOVED

WATSON: This one is still too early. Oh.

HOLMES: What is it?

WATSON: It seems Geoffrey Cobb married three times in the space of three years. Busy fellow.

ELIZABETH: Perhaps a sad one, too, Dr. Watson. One thing I do know of the town is that there were great outbreaks of disease which claimed many lives.

WATSON: So I see. In 1472, an outbreak of . . . from the details here . . . I would say influenza . . . the outbreak took almost half of the village.

SOUND EFFECT: PAGES TURNED

WATSON: The original building here became an infirmary. (READING) "*They came to the house of the Lord seeking solace, and within the shadow of His house they were taken to His mercy.*"

ELIZABETH: They died here? In this house? How many?

WATSON: Dozens . . . Influenza is a terrible thing.

HOLMES: But it does not haunt a woman with her dead child. We require something singular. Something pertinent to this case.

SOUND EFFECT: PAGES FLICKED

HOLMES: I find nothing in this volume.

SOUND EFFECT: BOOK PUT DOWN, ANOTHER TAKEN FROM A SHELF

HOLMES: Perhaps this shall be more productive.

WATSON: Holmes, here's something interesting. Catherine Hudd, a woman of previously good character, whose four children aged from three months to five years were all taken to the Lord's bosom by the illness, had her soul corrupted by evil. She issued a curse upon the priest and the followers of God, wishing death upon the priests, the people, and the children who had survived. Her soul was purified by burning at the stake.

ELIZABETH: After losing four children!

WATSON: The legend of the curse on the parish grew when a priest was found dead on his altar with signs of terror upon his face. Well, that could have been anything. A heart failure is often accompanied by an expression of fear.

HOLMES: I have something, Watson. (READING) *"Two Catholic friars, aware of the order of his Gracious Majesty, King Henry, chose to ignore his break with the dishonourable false church of Rome, and continued to preach a Catholic mass in violation of both the King and God's true law of the new Church of England. For this transgression, they were condemned to a traitor's death."*

ELIZABETH: Traitor's death?

HOLMES: Hanged, drawn, and quartered. A brutal punishment invented for the Scottish rebel, William Wallace. A criminal is hanged until near death before being disembowelled while still alive. The body is then cut into –

WATSON: Holmes! There's a lady present.

HOLMES: A lady whose question I was answering.

ELIZABETH: Thank you, Doctor Watson, but I did indeed ask.

HOLMES: Here . . . (READING) *"The condemned priests, refusing to recant their heresy, were doomed to die. The first did continue to profess treason and heresy until gagged so that even his screams were not heard as just and right sentence was carried out. But the second priest, held captive within the priory, escaped, as if into thin air. The priest's escape caused such outrage that the homes of those suspected of Papish Sympathies were set to the torch. Over one hundred souls – men, women and children – burned as the Roman influence was purged."*

ELIZABETH: How horrible!

HOLMES: Certainly a reason that legends of spectral occurrences would grow.

SOUND EFFECT: FOOTSTEPS APPROACHING

PATRICK: Elizabeth? What is happening? Why are you in here?

ELIZABETH: Patrick! I did not expect you to return so quickly.

PATRICK: Evidently. Please tell me who these gentlemen are and why you are in my study.

ELIZABETH: Patrick, they have come to help us.

PATRICK: By talking of spectral happenings? Poppycock. Elizabeth, I have told you that there is nothing to these tales. They are from a superstitious time. Gentlemen, I must ask you to name your business here.

ELIZABETH: I asked them to come.

WATSON: My name is Doctor John Watson and this is –

PATRICK: A doctor? Are you a doctor of the mind, sir?

WATSON: Well, I . . . .

HOLMES: Do you think your wife needs such a doctor?

PATRICK: She does not require institutionalisation in a Bedlam, if that is your question.

WATSON: An evaluation with which I heartily concur.

PATRICK: But you must see how unlikely these thoughts of an unseen mystic presence are.

ELIZABETH: I'm sure you will see the irony in a man of God making that assertion.

PATRICK: The two are completely different, Elizabeth. Your comparison is . . . is unworthy.

ELIZABETH: I'm sorry, Patrick, but something is happening in this house and you won't take it seriously.

PATRICK: I *do* take this seriously, Elizabeth. I also take your well-being seriously.

ELIZABETH: As do I. That is why I sought the assistance of these gentlemen.

PATRICK: Without discussing the matter with me first?

ELIZABETH: Because you will not discuss the matter.

PATRICK: Because there is nothing to discuss!

ELIZABETH: There is *everything* to discuss!

MRS. PRIDDY: May I get you and your guests anything, sir? Madam?

ELIZABETH: You are returned, Mrs. Priddy.

PATRICK: And you are a reminder that these gentlemen are indeed guests.

HOLMES: Guests who should trouble you no longer this evening, I think. This is a matter that would be better discussed in private between you both.

PATRICK: Thank you, Doctor . . . .

HOLMES: My colleague is the doctor. I can claim only rudimentary medical knowledge. My friend, however, is as fine a practitioner of medicine as you can hope to meet.

WATSON: Thank you, old fellow.

HOLMES: Reverend, might I suggest that my friend and I retire to our lodgings for the night and return in the morning?

ELIZABETH: You would leave me without investigating the matter further?

HOLMES: We will return tomorrow, I assure you. You have the word of Sherlock Holmes on the matter.

PATRICK: *The* Sherlock Holmes?

WATSON: I assure you, there is only one Sherlock Holmes.

SOUND EFFECT: FOOTSTEPS

ELIZABETH: Mr. Holmes, I beseech, you. You cannot leave!

HOLMES: It is for the best. Come along, Watson. Reverend, would you have any objections to Watson and I returning through your churchyard? I have an interest in the growth-rate of mosses.

PATRICK: Of course –

ELIZABETH: You said you would help me, but you talk of mosses?

HOLMES: Watson, come along.

319

ELIZABETH: Mr. Holmes? Doctor Watson? Please? You must help me!

PATRICK: Elizabeth, calm yourself. Please.

ELIZABETH: You cannot simply abandon me!

HOLMES: We shall return in the morning.

ELIZABETH: No! Please!

PATRICK: Elizabeth. Please be calmed. Please.

SOUND EFFECT: DOOR CLOSES. FOOTSTEPS

WATSON: Holmes, have you taken leave of your senses? First you insist upon this trip, which I believe to be utter folly, and then you abandon that poor woman to her hysteria. At least as a physician, I could have helped her with that.

HOLMES: I assure you, Watson, that I have done a good deal worse to her. And before the night is done, we may do worse still.

WATSON: (NARRATING) Holmes left me at the inn in which we had taken rooms and told me he would be gone for the rest of the afternoon, but that I should be ready to go out when he returned. The inn had a small but comfortable common room with a fireplace, and I passed a few pleasant hours there going over my notes and catching up on a back issue of *The Lancet* which I had thought to bring with me. The crackling of the fire on the hearth made a warm counterpoint to the wind-born spatters of rain assailing the window panes. It was long past supper when my friend finally returned, but he was as good as his word, and we went out again right away.

SOUND EFFECT: OWL HOOTS. NIGHT SOUNDS. WIND BLOWS IN TREES. RAIN FALLING

WATSON: When you told Mrs. Morris that we would return, I confess that I did not expect it to be in the middle of the night,

HOLMES: Hardly the middle of the night, Watson. It is scarcely nine o'clock.

WATSON: Well, it's as dark as the middle of the night and just as miserable. Why are we hiding in the bushes anyway?

HOLMES: I should imagine that even you could hazard a guess as to that.

WATSON: Well, obviously we don't want to be seen. But by whom?

HOLMES: By anyone.

WATSON: There are certainly enough people awake to see us. Lights in the Morris house, lights in the houses on the far side of the church . . . . Sensible people are clearly staying indoors. At the moment, I wish we were more sensible.

HOLMES: Do you intend to complain all night?

WATSON: That depends on how long we are stuck in these damnable wet bushes.

HOLMES: A-ha!

WATSON: What? Oh, I see. There are lights coming on in the church.

HOLMES: I thought as much. I was sure it would happen. Come, old fellow. We must be quick.

WATSON: We can't go calling on the reverend at this time of night. It's not decent.

HOLMES: The evil afoot in this house is not decent, Watson. (SHARPLY BUT QUIETLY) Don't knock!

SOUND EFFECT: DOOR TRIED GENTLY

WATSON: Locked?

HOLMES: Yes.

SOUND EFFECT: RATTLE OF KEYS

WATSON: Holmes, what are you doing? To enter any house unbidden is unacceptable, but a minister's home? It's intolerable. It's like invading the sanctity of a church.

HOLMES: Then I suggest you say a silent prayer for my soul.

SOUND EFFECT: CLICK. DOOR OPENS

HOLMES: Follow me.

SOUND EFFECT: DOOR OPEN, CLOSES. CLINKING OF CHINA

HOLMES: It sounds like Mrs. Morris is in the kitchen.

WATSON: It could be Mrs. Priddy.

HOLMES: I very much doubt it. We must secrete ourselves.

SOUND EFFECT: CLINKING OF CHINA

HOLMES: This way. Here.

WATSON: Holmes, this is an unacceptable intrusion. We shall be lucky to avoid a night in the local cells for this.

HOLMES: Quiet. These heavy drapes should hide us well.

SOUND EFFECT: CLINKING OF CHINA. WIND WHIPPING BY OUTSIDE. THE CRACKLE OF A FIRE. TEA BEING POURED. A CREAKING SOUND.

ELIZABETH: Patrick? Is that you? Mrs. Priddy?

SOUND EFFECT: A HOLLOW, EERIE HOWLING. VAGUELY DEMONIC, OTHERWORLDLY

WATSON: (WHISPERED) What the deuce is it?

322

HOLMES: I am more concerned with where it comes from.

WATSON: Can you smell . . . .

HOLMES: Decay? Yes . . . .

SOUND EFFECT: THE HOWLING SOUND BECOMES LOUDER

ELIZABETH: I do not fear you! Whatever you are, I do not fear you!

SOUND EFFECT: THE HOWLING BECOMES LOUDER. THE FIRE CRACKLES

HOLMES: I thought as much.

ELIZABETH: I do not fear you! God will protect me!

SOUND EFFECT: ANOTHER SOUND. THE CRY OF A BABY, DISTANT, HEARD THROUGH THE UNEARTHLY HOWLING

ELIZABETH: (BREAKING) I do not fear you! I shall never fear my own child!

SOUND EFFECT: SOUND GROWS

WATSON: We must help her, Holmes. I cannot bear to see her in such distress.

HOLMES: Her distress will be far worse if we move from this place too soon.

SOUND EFFECT: HELLISH CRYING AND HOWLING GROWING

ELIZABETH: I do not fear my child!

SOUND EFFECT: THE SOUND IS NOW INTENSE, THE FLAMES BILLOW BRUTALLY. THE CHILD'S CRY IS LOUDER

WATSON: The fire, Holmes!

HOLMES: I see it. Hold just a moment longer, old friend.

ELIZABETH: God, protect your servant and protect me from this nightmare!

<u>SOUND EFFECT: SOUND CONTINUES TO GROW, BECOMING UNNERVING, TERRIFYING</u>

ELIZABETH: Please stop! Whoever you are, please stop! Stop it! Please! In the name of the Almighty I beg you! Stop! Stop!

WATSON: I must help her.

HOLMES: Wait! Not yet!

ELIZABETH: Stop this! We are on holy ground! No demon can hurt me! Oh God, help me! Save me! Save me!

WATSON: Holmes, I insist!

HOLMES: There! The fireplace!

WATSON: The fire is wild . . . .

HOLMES: Not the fire. To the side of the fireplace.

WATSON: I don't . . . wait . . . *The fireplace is moving!*

HOLMES: A hidden entrance.

WATSON: Someone's coming through!

ELIZABETH: Keep away from me! Keep back! Keep away!

WATSON: It's going to kill her!

<u>SOUND EFFECT: DRAPES FLUNG ASIDE</u>

HOLMES: If you make one more move towards this woman, I assure you that Doctor Watson will not miss with his revolver. Doctor, if you would be so kind as to block our guest's escape.

ELIZABETH: Mr. Holmes? What . . . ?

HOLMES: Stay where you are, Mrs. Morris. Do not move.

ELIZABETH: You see, Mr. Holmes? You see it? I'm not mad. What fiend is this?

HOLMES: Nothing spectral, I assure you. There is evil aplenty in this world. No need to borrow from the next. (TO THE FIGURE) Remove the hood. There is no escape for you.

SOUND EFFECT: DOOR OPENS

PATRICK: It's a foul night outside, Elizabeth . . . . What is happening here?

HOLMES: Ah, Reverend, it's good you're here. Mrs. Priddy, the game is up. Kindly remove your hood.

SOUND EFFECT: CLOTH REMOVED

ELIZABETH: Mrs. Priddy? I don't understand.

PATRICK: I am entirely at a loss with this situation.

MRS. PRIDDY: I haven't done anything –

HOLMES: Oh, it won't do, Mrs. Priddy. It really won't. Parish records in a town this small can be quite revealing, even after someone has quite clumsily tried to alter them.

MRS. PRIDDY: I have served this household faithfully –

HOLMES: Faithfully, perhaps, but not honestly.

PATRICK: What are you saying, Holmes?

HOLMES: Will you tell them, Mrs. Priddy? Or shall I?

325

MRS. PRIDDY: There's nothing to tell –

HOLMES: There is no Mr. Priddy, is there? There never was.

MRS. PRIDDY: How can you – I mean, he died in Africa. He was a soldier.

HOLMES: A soldier he may have been, but not your husband. And your poor widowed niece is not your niece at all, is she?

MRS. PRIDDY: I . . . I . . . .

WATSON: Mrs. Priddy, if you have something to tell, it will go better for you if you say it now.

MRS. PRIDDY: No, no, I can't – There's nothing –

HOLMES: She's your daughter. Left alone in the world with a small child to raise. Not widowed, no. Not widowed. *Abandoned.* As you once were.

MRS. PRIDDY: (BREAKING DOWN) Oh, help me. God help me.

PATRICK: Holmes, what is the meaning of this? Mrs. Priddy, is this true?

HOLMES: When was it that you decided to drive your mistress from this house? Perhaps drive her insane? Or, at any rate, make her seem so to her husband to the extent that he would have her committed.

MRS. PRIDDY: I didn't mean – I didn't want to hurt anyone.

HOLMES: Was it when the good reverend here started to show special attention to the two members of his parish who were most important to you? You knew of his desire to have a family, to have children. You saw him give the affection that he hungered to give his own child, to yours.

ELIZABETH: Patrick!

PATRICK: Elizabeth, it wasn't like that. It was pure. It was good. I was only trying to help.

MRS. PRIDDY: (SUDDENLY VICIOUS) They didn't need your help! They didn't need your pity! They needed a home! They needed respect! I won't have them pitied, treated like dirt the way I was. Your wife was no wife to you! She couldn't give you what you wanted. She failed! Failed at the one thing she was supposed to give you. But I could give it to you. You're such a good man. You deserve to have a family and they needed a home. A respectable home!

PATRICK: What are you saying? You thought you could replace my wife with . . . with . . . Get out of this house! Get out!

HOLMES: I'm sorry, but I'm afraid I can't allow that.

WATSON: Yes, Holmes. I'll fetch the constable.

ELIZABETH: Wait, please! I don't understand. This is all your doing, Mrs. Priddy? The moaning, the howling? The candles were gutted in this room with the windows and doors shut. There could have been no breeze, yet I felt one. The baby crying. How?

HOLMES: It is perfectly simple, Mrs. Morris. I deduced the basic facts in your husband's study. When we read of the priest's miraculous escape, it could only have been through a passage between the church and one of the buildings nearby. The parlour here is the oldest part of the house, and the fireplace is at its centre. There is a passage between the fireplace and the church, used in times past by terrified Catholic clergy. You see its entrance beside the fire. When the entrance in the church is open as well, a strong breeze would blow through the passage and into this room. A breeze that could gutter candles and cause the fire in the hearth to blaze up. If we search the passage I am sure we will find the speaking trumpet which Mrs. Priddy used to amplify her voice into an unearthly howl.

ELIZABETH: But why would she do such a thing?

HOLMES: That was the crux of the matter. Why, and more importantly, *who*? It had to be someone who had access to the parish records in your husband's study, who knew the house well enough to know about the secret passage. When the reverend found us in his study, his outdoor boots were wet from the storm outside, yet Mrs. Priddy, who had been visiting her daughter, had completely dry shoes. The only logical answer is that she took a dry path home. But if Mrs. Priddy was the actress in this drama, what would push her to such a bizarre course?

PATRICK: I cannot comprehend.

HOLMES: Two things: Shame at her failings, and a desperate hope to give a better life to her daughter. A daughter who never knew a father, who has never known who her mother was. Forced always to live a lie, in shame – her mother's shame.

MRS. PRIDDY: No one should have to live the way I did. No one.

PATRICK: We have shown you only kindness since we brought you into our home. This is how you repay it?

MRS. PRIDDY: You would have been happy with Irene. She's a good girl, Irene is.

PATRICK: Say no more, or I shall forget that I am a man of God!

MUSIC: BRIDGE

SOUND EFFECT: TRAIN INTERIOR

WATSON: You were able to put together Mrs. Priddy's story from the records at the Hyndford town hall?

HOLMES: There was some conjecture involved, but it was highly likely that my suppositions were true. Mrs. Priddy, then named Alice Sheffield, left Hyndford at the tender age of sixteen under a cloud. She evidently entered into that most disreputable of professions in London –

WATSON: You don't mean –

328

HOLMES: I mean *acting*. She spent several years there, and perhaps other places as well, and then finally returned to Hyndford as Mrs. Priddy with a mysterious niece, Irene, in tow. Mrs. Priddy claimed Irene was a widow, but there was no Certificate of Death for the husband. Mrs. Priddy claimed herself to be the widow of an army Sergeant-Major, but there was no Marriage Certificate and no pension. It was not unwarranted to make the inferences that I did.

WATSON: And the reverend took her in, gave her a position, and gave her niece – that is, her daughter – a house in which to live. Did you never suspect the reverend in all this? With all the trouble he was having with his wife, for a moment I thought he might be having a *liaison* with the niece.

HOLMES: The daughter.

WATSON: Yes.

HOLMES: Perhaps he is.

WATSON: Is? But he told Elizabeth that his attentions were pure.

HOLMES: Yes, that is what he told her.

WATSON: I see.

HOLMES: I have never had a particular understanding of love. It is instructive to me that, after all that had happened, Elizabeth Morris forgave Priddy of her crimes, asked that we set her free. Was it for love of Priddy? For her illegitimate daughter? For humanity at large? What was the emotion that produced Priddy's daughter? Love? What of the love that caused Irene's husband to marry her and then abandon her? And what of Priddy's love for her daughter that caused her to torment Elizabeth Morris to the point of madness? There are times when I think that when we love, we are at our most unkind.

WATSON: Well, I feel very fortunate to have known love. And I hope that I may know it again.

HOLMES: Good old Watson! You always cut to the heart of the matter.

MUSIC: *DANSE MACABRE*

WATSON: This is Dr. John H. Watson. I've had many more adventures with Sherlock Holmes, and I'll tell you another one . . . *when next we meet!*

MUSIC: (FADE OUT)

The Adventure of *The Sleeping Cardinal*

or

The Doctor's Case

by Jeremy B. Holstein and
John Patrick Lowrie

CHARACTERS

- SHERLOCK HOLMES
- DR. JOHN H. WATSON
- INSPECTOR LESTRADE
- MARY WATSON
- LADY MARGARET GROSVENOR-SOMERSET
- BENJAMIN PARDMAN
- BILLY COOPER
- CONSTABLE
- PADDY MAGUIRE

SOUND EFFECT: OPENING SEQUENCE, BIG BEN

ANNOUNCER: *The Further Adventures of Sherlock Holmes*, featuring John Patrick Lowrie as Sherlock Holmes, and Lawrence Albert as Dr. John H. Watson.

MUSIC: *DANSE MACABRE* (UP AND UNDER)

MUSIC: AIMLESS DISTANT VIOLIN

WATSON: (NARRATING) My name is Doctor John H. Watson, and it was my privilege to share the adventures of Sherlock Holmes. The summer of 1896 was one of the hottest on record. The air hung thick and humid, inducing a languid torpor in man and best alike. One would think that under such intolerable conditions, any man would accept a respite from work with gladness, and perhaps entertain the notion of taking a holiday at the seaside. But my friend was not just any man . . . .

HOLMES: Bah! This is interminable, Watson! Interminable!

WATSON: What's that, Holmes?

HOLMES: This inactivity! Has the entire criminal population of London gone on Holiday? Give me a case to solve, a problem to unravel! Anything but this endless boredom!

WATSON: Calm down, Holmes. Something will turn up soon. Have some breakfast.

HOLMES: I don't need food, Watson, I need clients! I am a thinking machine, and a machine without a load will burn itself out!

WATSON: Perhaps there's something in the paper for your mind to chew on. Ah, here's an interesting item. They've found Henry Tuttle alive and in hiding! He'd faked his death to avoid his creditors.

HOLMES: A case to solve. A problem to unravel. Where is the mystery in this news?

WATSON: Umm, right. Well, how about this? Apparently *The Sleeping Cardinal* has been put up for auction.

HOLMES: Ah, yes. The painting you recovered while I was away.

WATSON: Away for far too long!

HOLMES: (MUTTERING) Perhaps not for long enough.

WATSON: Now, Holmes.

HOLMES: Very well. If the criminals of the present cannot challenge my mind, then perhaps the criminals of the past can. Tell me your tale, Watson.

WATSON: You –

HOLMES: About the painting.

WATSON: You want –

HOLMES: The one that you recovered.

WATSON: But you never liked my writing, Holmes.

HOLMES: And if you write this one down, I probably won't like it either. But I'm *in extremis*, Watson. It is either your story or the needle. I leave the decision to you.

WATSON: Yes, of course. Of course. Well. Where to begin? (PAUSE) It was the summer of 1892, as I recall. A summer almost as hot and miserable as this one. It had been a year since your battle with Moriarty at the Reichenbach Falls, and two more before your reappearance in London. I thought you were dead. I focused my time and energies on my medical practice, and the health of my beloved wife, Mary.

HOLMES: God rest her soul.

WATSON: (PAUSE) Yes. (PAUSE) It was a beastly hot summer. I had just finished treating a patient for heat exhaustion when the bell rang again. But it wasn't a patient this time. It was our old friend, Inspector Lestrade.

MUSIC: STING

SOUND EFFECT: DOOR OPENING

WATSON: Inspector?

LESTRADE: Dr. Watson. Sorry to trouble you.

WATSON: Not at all. Come in, come in.

SOUND EFFECT: DOOR CLOSES

WATSON: What can I do for you?

LESTRADE: I never thought I'd say this, but, well, there are times I miss the meddling of our old friend, Mr. Holmes! He could be helpful. Quite helpful at time.

WATSON: Good of you to say so, Inspector. Are you working on a case now?

LESTRADE: Yes. A robbery. Just the sort of case Mr. Holmes would have enjoyed.

WATSON: I see. (PAUSE) I'm not really in the consulting detective business anymore.

LESTRADE: But you know Holmes's methods, probably better than any man in London.

WATSON: I suppose so.

LESTRADE: This is a bit irregular, but are you busy? I could use a fresh set of eyes on this one.

WATSON: I'd be honored. Let me . . . check in on my wife.

LESTRADE: Capital. I'll outline the details of the case *en-route*.

WATSON: Yes. Let me just . . . . (RESIGNED) I'll be right back.

MUSIC: BRIDGE

WATSON: (SOFTLY) Mary? How are you feeling?

MARY: (WEAKLY) Well, I wish it wasn't so hot. (PAUSE) I'm fine, John.

WATSON: Good.

MARY: (STRONGER) What is it? What's worrying you?

WATSON: Inspector Lestrade's downstairs. He, uh . . . he wants my help on a case.

MARY: Ah, how wonderful! (COUGHS) It'll be good for you to get out of the house.

WATSON: I . . . I want to be sure you'll be all right.

MARY: Oh, don't worry. I have my fan, and . . . and my lemonade. Mrs. Pritchard is right next door if I need anything else.

WATSON: Well, I . . . . (RESIGNED) All right. You take care of yourself. I won't be gone long!

MARY: Go. I'll be fine.

SOUND EFFECT: CARRIAGE SOUNDS (UNDER)

LESTRADE: It's like this, Doctor. Last night one Lady Margaret Grosvenor-Somerset checks into the Hotel Metropole, carrying with her a very expensive painting, called . . . .

SOUND EFFECT: FLIPPING PAPER AS HE CHECKS HIS NOTES

LESTRADE: . . . *The Sleeping Cardinal.*

WATSON: I'm not familiar with it.

LESTRADE: Neither was I before now, but they say it's a masterpiece and worth a king's ransom. Lady Margaret had brought the painting into town for an exhibition. Not wanting to leave it in her room, she asks the manager . . . .

SOUND EFFECT: MORE PAPER SHUFFLING

LESTRADE: . . . one Benjamin Pardman if he'll store it in the hotel safe for the night. Pardman agrees, and locks the painting up in his office before heading home. You follow me so far?

WATSON: Perfectly.

LESTRADE: Well, imagine his surprise when he arrives the next morning, goes to open the safe, and finds the painting gone!

WATSON: Stolen?

LESTRADE: One would think so, but there's no evidence of a

336

break-in at all. The safe is stored in Pardman's office, a small room with no windows and only one entrance in or out, a door just behind the main desk of the hotel.

WATSON: And the desk was manned all night?

LESTRADE: They assure me it was. By one . . . .

SOUND EFFECT: EVEN MORE PAPER FLIPPING

LESTRADE: . . . Billy Cooper, I believe.

WATSON: Billy Cooper. I know that name from somewhere.

LESTRADE: Cooper claims no one else entered the office that night.

WATSON: Was the office locked? Could someone have slipped in while Cooper wasn't looking? Or perhaps . . . even Cooper himself?

LESTRADE: Mr. Pardman assures me that he locks the door when he leaves at night, and only unlocks it first thing in the morning.

WATSON: No sign of tampering?

LESTRADE: None.

WATSON: This is a bit of a stretch, but could Pardman himself have taken the painting?

LESTRADE: He was seen that night leaving the hotel by both Cooper and the door-man. He wasn't even carrying a bag, let alone a painting.

WATSON: Mmm. Yes, you're right, Lestrade. This is exactly the sort of case Holmes would have enjoyed.

LESTRADE: Lady Margaret is distraught, and demanding the hotel cover the value in currency. If we can't find the culprit and recover the painting, the hotel will find itself in a financial bind, to say the least. Ah, here we are.

337

WATSON: (NARRATING) We entered into an opulent hotel lobby –

HOLMES: (INTERRUPTING) Yes, I've been to the Metropole.

WATSON: Oh. Of course. (PAUSE) Well, it was empty, save for a constable guarding three people by the main desk. The lone woman, who I took to be –

HOLMES: Lady Margaret.

WATSON: (TRYING TO BE PATIENT) Yes. (PAUSE) She was well dressed and ample, while the two gentlemen could not have looked more different from each other. One, who I soon learned was Benjamin Pardman, was a tall, handsome fellow. The other, Billy Cooper, was short and rat-faced.

MARGARET: At last! What took you so long?

LESTRADE: My apologies, Lady Margaret. Yard business.

MARGARET: I don't understand what could possibly be more important than my compensation.

LESTRADE: (NOT RUFFLED BY THIS IN THE LEAST. HE IS A PROFESSIONAL) This my colleague, Doctor Watson. He'll be assisting me with the investigation. Doctor, this is Lady Margaret, Benjamin Pardman, and Billy Cooper.

PARDMAN: Actually, *I'm* Mr. Pardman.

COOPER: And I'm Mr. Cooper.

LESTRADE: Oh, yes.

PARDMAN: Excuse me, but are you the same Dr. Watson who works with Sherlock Holmes?

WATSON: I am.

PARDMAN: Bless me! It's an honor sir! An honor!

WATSON: You've read my stories?

PARDMAN: Well, not as such, no. But you're quite popular among the hotel guests. They're always chatting about your friend's exploits. Is he here with you now? It would be a privilege to meet him.

WATSON: (PAUSE) I'm afraid not, Mr. Pardman.

LESTRADE: If we can get back to the business at hand, please. Now, Lady Margaret, you checked into the hotel last night around seven, is that right?

MARGARET: That is correct.

LESTRADE: And while checking in, you turned the painting over to Mr. Pardman for safe-keeping.

MARGARET: I couldn't have such a priceless masterpiece lying around my room, now could I? You never know who works at these sorts of places.

PARDMAN: Madam, the Metropole is among the best hotels in London –

MARGARET: The best in thievery, you mean.

PARDMAN: (OUTRAGED GASP)

LESTRADE: If I can continue? Lady Margaret, can you describe the painting in question?

MARGARET: It is a Renee Sovretair, at the height of her powers. A cardinal with flowers –

LESTRADE: (INTERRUPTING) Just the size of the painting will do.

MARGARET: I would say about three feet by five, in a gilded mahogany frame.

LESTRADE: Thank you. Now, Mr. Pardman. You put the painting immediately into your safe, is that correct?

PARDMAN: Immediately, sir. Security is a top priority.

LESTRADE: And you locked the safe thereafter?

PARDMAN: Of course. I even double-checked the lock.

LESTRADE: And at what time did you leave the hotel?

PARDMAN: Just after eight that night. Mr. Cooper had came on to work the desk shortly before Lady Margaret checked in, and I retired to my office to finish some paperwork. When I was done, I locked the office and bid Mr. Cooper good night.

LESTRADE: Mr. Cooper, can you confirm the time?

COOPER: Indeed, sir. Eight o'clock. Mr. Pardman goes home every night at that time.

LESTRADE: And you're absolutely certain no one entered the office between eight that evening and when Mr. Pardman arrived for work the next morning?

COOPER: On my honor, sir. It was a quiet evening, and I never left my post at the desk.

WATSON: Excuse me, Mr. Cooper, but you look very familiar. Have we met before?

COOPER: (OBVIOUSLY LYING) I don't believe so, sir.

LESTRADE: What time did Mr. Pardman return?

COOPER: Mr. Pardman comes in at six.

PARDMAN: Six on the dot, Inspector. Punctuality is my motto.

LESTRADE: And it was then you discovered the painting missing.

PARDMAN: Well, not immediately. It wasn't until Lady Margaret came down and asked to check on her painting that I opened the safe.

LESTRADE: Lady Margaret, what time did you come down?

MARGARET: Just past six-thirty.

WATSON: Mr. Pardman, could we have a look at this safe?

PARDMAN: Of course. Anything I can do to help. This way, gentlemen.

WATSON: (NARRATING) Pardman ushered us into a spartan office, devoid of any charm or character.

HOLMES: (INTERRUPTING) Facts, Watson! Charm and character are undefinable terms.

WATSON: Right. All right. Let me say that no pictures adorned its windowless walls, and the only furniture was a single desk, two chairs, and the large safe pushed into the far corner.

HOLMES: Better.

WATSON: (SIGH) The only luxury the room offered was its fireplace, a prize during the cold London winters, I was sure.

PARDMAN: As you can see, gentlemen, the door is the only way in or out.

LESTRADE: I see no signs of tampering on the safe, do you, Doctor?

WATSON: No. (PAUSE) How many people know the combination?

PARDMAN: Only myself, although I do keep it recorded on my desk-ledger right here.

LESTRADE: Isn't that a security risk?

PARDMAN: Perhaps, but I've got a terrible memory, so it's better to have it written down than not. Besides, the office is locked at

341

all times when I'm not here.

LESTRADE: (ASIDE TO WATSON) Little doubt how the thief got into the safe, is there, Doctor?

WATSON: Indeed, Inspector. But there's still the question of how he got into the office in the first place.

LESTRADE: Who all has the key to your office, Pardman?

PARDMAN: There's only one key, Inspector. I keep it with me at all times.

SOUND EFFECT: CLINKING KEYS

WATSON: That's a rather unusual looking key, Mr. Pardman.

PARDMAN: A Roman design, Doctor. A trick for my memory to know which key fits my office lock.

LESTRADE: How long has Mr. Cooper been with the hotel?

PARDMAN: Less than a year. But he came with references from the Savoy Hotel.

WATSON: And how long have you been with the Metropole, Mr. Pardman?

PARDMAN: It'll be twenty years this January. I'm second only to the hotel's owner, Mr. Saul.

LESTRADE: Zacharias Saul? One of the richest men in London.

WATSON: Mm. This fireplace. Is it possible someone could have entered the office by the chimney?

LESTRADE: They would have left traces in the ashes in the fireplace, Doctor. And as you can see, the ashes are undisturbed.

PARDMAN: Besides, the chimney's only a foot in diameter. Makes it very difficult for Father Christmas, don't you know.

(LAUGHS)

WATSON: (ALERT) I beg your pardon . . . ?

PARDMAN: Father Christmas. He's supposed to, uh, come down the chimney . . . .

WATSON: Dash it! I know where I've seen Billy Cooper before.

LESTRADE: We're all ears, Doctor.

WATSON: It was three years ago Christmas that Holmes and I investigated the theft of the Rothchild Diamond from the Savoy Hotel. Holmes determined the thief to be Billy Cooper. The Rothchilds didn't want a scandal, so it was never brought to the police.

PARDMAN: What? You're saying Mr. Cooper is a criminal?

LESTRADE: Left alone to do his dirty work for nigh on eight hours. Glad I brought you along, Dr. Watson! (CALLING) Constable! Hold Mr. Cooper, please!

CONSTABLE: Yes, sir.

COOPER: (FROM THE OTHER ROOM) What? No, no! It wasn't – I . . . I never –

LESTRADE: Hold him tight while I search his pockets. Where's his coat?

PARDMAN: Hanging from that hook, Inspector.

LESTRADE: Let's see what we can find. Ah! What's this, then?

SOUND EFFECT: CLINKING METAL OF KEYS BRUSHED TOGETHER

WATSON: A duplicate key. Same Roman design.

LESTRADE: Billy Cooper – You're under arrest for the theft of *The Sleeping Cardinal*.

343

COOPER: But that key isn't mine! I've never seen it before in my life!

LESTRADE: Come along.

WATSON: (NARRATING) Despite Coopers's protests, Lestrade led him away, assuring both Pardman and Lady Margaret he would procure the painting's location during the interrogation.

HOLMES: Ah, the good Inspector. Never one to avoid over promising.

WATSON: Yes. And as I watched him escort Cooper down the Strand, I had the nagging suspicion that I had missed something.

HOLMES: Ah!

WATSON: Some detail that would turn this case around – but I couldn't put my finger on it.

HOLMES: You do me proud, Watson. An excellent student is a good reflection on the teacher. Pray, continue!

MUSIC: BRIDGE

WATSON: (NARRATING) That evening I spent in the manner which had become my custom: Reading the evening paper at the hearth, Mary at my side.

SOUND EFFECT: CRACKLING FIRE

MARY: Ah! Did you see this article, John?

WATSON: Which one?

MARY: (READING) *"Inspector Lestrade of Scotland Yard arrested one William Cooper for the theft of* The Sleeping Cardinal *from the Hotel Metropole. Assisting in the investigation was long-time associate of Sherlock Holmes, Doctor John Watson!"* (LAUGHS) My famous husband. (COUGHS)

344

WATSON: Oh, dear. Mary, you should get to bed.

MARY: I'll be all right. I'm so happy for you. There's a sparkle in your eye when you're involved in a mystery. It's just like you used to say about Sherlock Holmes: You're happiest when there's a problem to unravel.

WATSON: Perhaps you're right. I just can't get this case out of my mind. Something doesn't feel right about it.

MARY: You don't think Cooper's your man.

WATSON: He certainly had ample opportunity. Although how he thought he'd get away with it strikes me as incredible.

MARY: I know you'll get to the bottom of it. Just keep your energies focused – (BEGINS PAINFULLY COUGHING)

WATSON: All right, Mary. All right, ret's get you to bed. I'll get you a tincture of cocaine.

HOLMES: (QUIETLY) That must have been difficult for you.

WATSON: The irony was not lost on me, I assure you.

HOLMES: (A BEAT) Are you all right?

WATSON: Yes. (PAUSE) Lestrade was kind enough to keep me informed of his progress, and even though Cooper continued to protest his innocence, Lestrade assured me it was only a matter of time before he gave up the location of the painting. And that likely would have been the end of my involvement in the matter, if not for a message that arrived at our doorstep a week later.

MARY: John? A telegram's arrived for you.

WATSON: Oh? Who's it from?

MARY: It doesn't say. Just initials at the bottom. The letters "*M. H.*".

WATSON: *M.H.*? Let me see that.

SOUND EFFECT: RUSTLING PAPER

WATSON: (READING) *"Where is the painting? Consult Sherlock's contacts. Consider the ashes. – M.H."* (MUSING TO HIMSELF) Consider the ashes . . . ?

MARY: What does it mean, John? Who are Sherlock's contacts?

WATSON: Holmes kept numerous sources among London's underworld. They helped him in his investigations.

MARY: And you know these gentlemen?

WATSON: Gentlemen? Not really. (PAUSE) And . . . yes. A few of them.

MARY: John, It might be dangerous.

WATSON: Yes.

MARY: But . . . there's no stopping you, is there? (LAUGHS) I know that look in your eye. All right, John. Just be careful.

WATSON: (QUIETLY) Thank you. I will, Mary. For your sake. (NARRATING) The telegram had reawakened the case in my mind. What had happened to *The Sleeping Cardinal*? There seemed to be two possibilities: Either it had been hidden prior to Cooper's arrest, or it had been secreted from the hotel to be sold on the black market.

HOLMES: Reasonable.

WATSON: Seeing as the police had conducted a thorough search of the hotel, I decided to pursue the second possibility. To that end, I sought out Paddy Maguire.

HOLMES: Paddy! Always a good resource.

WATSON: I found him drinking –

346

HOLMES: At the Plumber's Arms, no doubt.

WATSON: Yes.

SOUND EFFECT: NOISE OF A CROWDED PUB

WATSON: Paddy Maguire?

MAGUIRE: Who wants to know?

WATSON: My name is Doctor Watson. You might remember from the times you visited . . . .

MAGUIRE: (INTERRUPTING) Not so loud! You want everyone in the pub to know who you are? I remember you. (WHISPERING SO NO ONE ELSE CAN HEAR) Did Mister H. send you? Haven't seen him around lately.

WATSON: No. No, he's . . . not in London at this time.

MAGUIRE: Pity. I could use the work.

WATSON: Well, I was wondering if you could help me.

MAGUIRE: Good help's hard to find.

WATSON: Yes. Umm, how much?

MAGUIRE: Depends on how helpful you want me to be.

WATSON: I'm looking for a painting.

MAGUIRE: Oh! And not just any paintin'! You're lookin' for *The Sleepin' Cardinal* that got lifted out of the Metropole just last week.

WATSON: Why, yes. How did you know that?

MAGUIRE: 'Cause you ain't the only one. Scotland Yard's been down here lookin' for it as well.

347

WATSON: You have it, then?

MAGUIRE: Good lord, no! You think I'm going to touch somethin' that hot?

WATSON: Then this has been a wasted journey.

MAGUIRE: Sit down, sit down. Where you going? I might not be able to help you find the paintin', but I can give you a hint as to who took it. There's this fellow, see? Works at the Hotel Metropole, and he's in for some serious money with the local bookies. Likes the ponies, and isn't the luckiest man in the world.

WATSON: Who is he?

MAGUIRE: Well, I don't know his name. How would I?

WATSON: Can you describe him?

MAGUIRE: 'Course I can.

WATSON: (DISGUSTED) How much?

MAGUIRE: Make me an offer.

WATSON: I'm not sure –

MAGUIRE: Five pounds.

WATSON: Five pounds? That's outrageous!

MAGUIRE: You think it over. I'm not going anywhere. Not with it being so blasted hot outside.

WATSON: It certainly is that. It hasn't been this warm since . . . . Good lord! I have it!

MAGUIRE: Have what?

WATSON: The ashes! *Consider the ashes*! I know who took *The Cardinal*!

348

MAGUIRE: (SNEERS) Do you now?

WATSON: I have to go to Scotland Yard at once! Thank you very much, Mr. Maguire. You've been most helpful. Oh, here's a crown for your trouble.

MAGUIRE: One crown? (LOUDER) Mr. H. would have made it at least two!

WATSON: (NARRATING) My mind was buzzing with excitement. I could see it all now, exactly who had taken the painting and how.

HOLMES: A-ha!

MUSIC: BRIDGE

WATSON: (NARRATING) I rushed to Scotland Yard and sought out Lestrade. Making my case, I convinced him to go with me. We then made our way to Covent Garden and were soon standing before a small set of rooms near the Hotel Metropole.

SOUND EFFECT: KNOCKING. DOOR OPENING

PARDMAN: Yes? Ah, Inspector. And Doctor Watson! What a surprise.

LESTRADE: May we come in?

PARDMAN: Of course, of course.

SOUND EFFECT: SHUFFLING FOOTSTEPS AND DOOR CLOSING

PARDMAN: May I, uh, offer you gentlemen some brandy?

LESTRADE: I'm afraid we're here on business.

PARDMAN: Oh? You have word of *The Sleeping Cardinal* then?

LESTRADE: We do.

PARDMAN: Well, that is welcome news. Lady Margaret is demanding her compensation by no later than noon tomorrow. Mr. Saul is most unhappy with the situation.

WATSON: I can imagine.

PARDMAN: Well, where is it?

WATSON: That's what we've come to ask you, Mr. Pardman.

PARDMAN: I don't understand. You seemed to think that Billy Cooper –

WATSON: That's what you *wanted* us to think. How did you come to know that Cooper had stolen the Rothchild Diamond?

PARDMAN: I, uh . . . How would I –

WATSON: I imagine that if we look at the Metropole register, we'll find that the Rothchilds stayed there at one time or another. No doubt a passing indiscretion on their part brought Cooper's name to your ears.

PARDMAN: Well, I –

LESTRADE: You knew he'd make a perfect mark.

PARDMAN: I say –

WATSON: All you had to do was somehow mention Cooper and Rothchild Diamond theft to the proper authorities and his arrest for any new robbery was almost assured.

PARDMAN: But I . . . I . . . .

WATSON: My appearance at the scene must have seemed an early Christmas present to you. You didn't even have to raise the affair of the diamond. A known associate of Sherlock Holmes did it for you.

LESTRADE: The duplicate key was a nice touch in the frame-up,

350

only you made a small slip up there.

PARDMAN: What do you mean?

WATSON: You said you never let the key of your sight. How then could Cooper have made a copy? Should we check with the locksmiths in the area of the Hotel?

PARDMAN: I . . . I –

WATSON: They'd remember making a copy for *you*, Mr. Pardman, not Cooper.

PARDMAN: I have keys made for the hotel all the time.

WATSON: But the rest of the hotel uses standard keys, while the key to your office is Roman. Something with that unique a design is bound to stick out in a locksmith's mind.

LESTRADE: You slipped the duplicate into Cooper's coat so I could find it, completing your frame up. A very clever touch, but not clever enough for an officer of the Yard.

PARDMAN: And where am I supposed to have secreted the painting?

WATSON: The painting's disappearance is really only a mystery if we assume it was ever in the safe to begin with, and we only have your word for that. If, however, the opposite were true, and the painting were never in the safe, then the solution becomes obvious.

PARDMAN: I . . . I . . . I . . . .

LESTRADE: You walked out of the Hotel Metropole that evening with the painting in hand, determined to sell it on the black market.

PARDMAN: That's ridiculous! How could I walk out with a painting that size and not be seen? The idea's ludicrous!

WATSON: It is ludicrous, until you remember the ashes in your fireplace.

PARDMAN: I beg your pardon?

WATSON: Lestrade noted the ashes in your office as evidence that
no one had snuck down the chimney, but what we should have
been asking is why you were burning a fire at all during the
hottest summer in recent memory?

PARDMAN: Well –

WATSON: The answer is you were burning the frame upon which
the *Cardinal* was mounted!

LESTRADE: With the frame removed, you simply rolled up the
painting and slipped it beneath your coat. You walked out of the
hotel right in front of both Cooper and the door-man, with
neither the wiser.

PARDMAN: But . . . but it's madness! Why should I do such a
thing? I've been loyal to that hotel for twenty years!

WATSON: Yes. I wondered about that, too. Why would you steal
from your own hotel? But then, I am an associate of Sherlock
Holmes, and he has many contacts in the underworld.

PARDMAN: But you can't –

LESTRADE: We know about the bookies. We know about the
gambling, and we know how much you owe them. The game's
up, Pardman. Why don't you give us the canvas and be done
with it?

WATSON: We know you haven't sold it, or you would have paid
off your bookies. We know you *can't* sell it, because it's too hot
to handle, which means you won't be able to pay them off.

PARDMAN: (GRUMBLE)

WATSON: Mr. Pardman, you'll be much safer in jail than on the
street. (NARRATING) Pardman retrieved *The Sleeping
Cardinal* from its hiding place, and Lestrade took him away to

the Yard. That evening, with the painting in hand, Lestrade and I visited Lady Margaret to return her property.

HOLMES: Yes?

WATSON: She seemed oddly cold to the *Cardinal*'s return. She didn't even bother to thank us. But Justice had been served and I felt satisfied. And that, Holmes, is the story of *The Sleeping Cardinal*'s recovery.

HOLMES: An entertaining tale, Doctor. I'm sure the readers of *The Strand* magazine will enjoy it.

WATSON: Oh, I'll never write it up. It's your adventures they want, not mine.

HOLMES: Mm. (PAUSE) Perhaps I had more to do with the case than you realize.

WATSON: How do you figure that, Holmes?

HOLMES: Did you never wonder who sent you the mysterious telegram?

WATSON: Well, I had always assumed the message came from your brother, Mycroft.

HOLMES: You are only partly correct. The telegram was indeed from Mycroft. The message, on the other hand, was from me.

WATSON: You?

HOLMES: My brother was keeping tabs on you during my absence and sending me full reports of your progress. When he sent me Lestrade's police report on your involvement with the robbery of *The Sleeping Cardinal* I couldn't help but smile.

WATSON: At how poorly I did on the investigation?

HOLMES: My dear fellow, you under-estimate yourself! You had the tenacity to question the obvious, while Lestrade rushed toward the easiest conclusion. I knew if I provided you a small push in the right direction, you would find the truth. No, I smiled as, despite my absence, you were still in the game.

WATSON: Ah. (PAUSE) Well, thank you, Holmes.

HOLMES: You did, however, miss one avenue of investigation.

WATSON: Oh? And what's that?

HOLMES: I find it difficult to believe that a woman who has just had her priceless painting stolen would immediately demand compensation rather than the canvas's recovery. I find it very probable that she planned the theft together with Mr. Pardman.

WATSON: Now that really is too much!

HOLMES: Consider that Pardman knew immediately how to smuggle the painting out of the hotel, almost as if he'd had warning. The duplicate key alone is indication of prior planning. Consider that Lady Margaret chose not to store her painting in the gallery where it was to be exhibited, but instead to store it in a hotel safe. And finally, consider that she chose to not to stay in a hotel near the exhibition, but instead in a building owned by one of the richest men in London.

WATSON: Good Lord.

HOLMES: But we shall never know for certain. It was her estate sale you saw in the paper. Lady Margaret died last week. Cheer up, Watson. You did find the thief and recover *The Sleeping Cardinal*. As good an outcome as could be hoped for.

WATSON: (GLUM) Yes.

HOLMES: What is it, old fellow?

WATSON: It just all seems rather unimportant. I lost Mary the next year . . . .

HOLMES: Yes. (PAUSE) One of the finest women that I've ever known. She will always be missed.

MUSIC: *DANSE MACABRE*

WATSON: This is Dr. John H. Watson. I've had many more adventures with Sherlock Holmes, and I'll tell you another one *. . . when next we meet!*

MUSIC: (FADE OUT)

The Case of the
Confounded Chronicler
by Daniel McGachey

CHARACTERS

- SHERLOCK HOLMES – *Who has found himself dangerously bored and in a mood which careens carelessly between playfulness and irritation*
- DR. JOHN H. WATSON – *Who has found his patience tested by Holmes's moods, and is valiantly holding off from thoughts of fetching his old service revolver and giving Holmes a final case to solve, albeit posthumously*
- At certain points, HOLMES and WATSON shall impersonate both INSPECTOR LESTRADE and MRS. HUDSON, and also each other. These impersonations are presented as quotes, with the character being impersonated indicated in brackets as:

  - ➤ (**SH**) – Holmes
  - ➤ (**DW**) – Watson
  - ➤ (**IL**) – Lestrade
  - ➤ (**MH**) – Mrs. Hudson
  - ➤ (**SELF**) – Holmes or Watson speaking as themselves

SOUND EFFECT: OPENING SEQUENCE, BIG BEN

ANNOUNCER: *The Further Adventures of Sherlock Holmes*, starring John Patrick Lowrie as Sherlock Holmes, and Lawrence Albert as Dr. John H. Watson.

MUSIC: *DANSE MACABRE* (UP AND UNDER)

MUSIC: OUT

WATSON: (NARRATING) The name John H. Watson is known not only as that of the friend and associate of the detective, Sherlock Holmes, but also as the chronicler of the adventures both have shared together. In truth, both callings carry their own difficulties, as Holmes was never the most willing subject of biography . . . .

SOUND EFFECT: SITTING ROOM NOISES AND AMBIENCE THROUGHOUT, FIRE CRACKLING AND CLOCK TICKING. DOOR OPENS AND WATSON'S FOOTSTEPS ENTER

HOLMES: Watson, you return looking as wet and chill as the late October night.

WATSON: That's almost exactly what Mrs. Hudson just said. "You look soaked to the skin and frozen to the marrow, Doctor," she said. (CHUCKLES) To which I replied . . . .

HOLMES: "As your other tenant might put it, Mrs. Hudson," you replied, "the two factors are not entirely unconnected."

WATSON: (DEFLATED) Well . . . yes. Yes, something of the sort. Were you listening, Holmes?

HOLMES: As bored as I find myself, I've not yet stooped, literally or otherwise, to listening at keyholes. I do, however, possess an excellent memory, and I've heard those words, or a variation of them, before.

WATSON: Well, your boredom may be at an end, old fellow. Mrs. Hudson asked me to bring up this telegram for you.

HOLMES: On the mantel, Watson . . . .

WATSON: Don't you want to read it? It might be a vital case.

HOLMES: If it was vital, the sender would call in person rather than wait for a delivery and a reply. On the mantel, and under the knife with it, old boy.

SOUND EFFECT: KNIFE PINNING MAIL TO MANTEL

WATSON: And if you're wrong?

358

HOLMES: Then, if the matter remains urgent, they will still call, reply or not.

WATSON: I'm sure there's some logic to that. Very well, I shall just carry on with a few . . . er . . . notes . . . .

SOUND EFFECT: PEN IN INK BOTTLE. THEN ON PAPER

HOLMES: While I cannot stop you in your efforts, my dear fellow, I really must advise against it. Any new readers gained amongst those seeking the sensational and the grotesque would be at the expense of an, until now, enjoyable and fruitful association.

SOUND EFFECT: WRITING STOPS, CHAIR PUSHED BACK

WATSON: (STARTLED) What is this, Holmes?

HOLMES: What it is, Watson, is a promise – reluctantly given but resolute nonetheless – that if you should endeavour to publish a version of the events surrounding the demise of the banker, Crosby, I will have no choice other than to terminate our association and suggest that you seek alternative accommodation.

WATSON: But why on earth would you make such a threat?

HOLMES: Because this agency must remain the last bastion of cold, unemotional, rational thought, casting light where emotion and fear may cloud the view, And were the truth of the circumstances surrounding the death of that esteemed banker to become known . . .

WATSON: . . . And of the repulsive red leech that caused it . . . .

HOLMES: . . . then the reputation I have sought to create would be fatally compromised, and who knows what sort of client would materialise at our door bearing what manner of bizarre or outlandish tale?

WATSON: But you thrive on the outlandish! You abhor the commonplace and seek the weird and the unusual.

HOLMES: Only in such instances as logic may be applied. To the superstitious, logic holds no sway, and these are surely the very types of individual who would come flocking to muddy our carpets, and take up time better devoted to more earthbound matters with stories of witchcraft and vampirism and curses.

WATSON: But did our own investigations not lay to rest the dreadful Baskerville curse, whose fatal effects had been felt for over a century?

HOLMES: Hah! You mean our investigations that led to my shooting to death of a half-starved mongrel in order to settle a squalid family dispute?

WATSON: Really, Holmes, you are a paradox! On the one hand, you display a massive conceit over your methods and their results, while on the other, you dismiss possibly our most terrifying adventure in such a trivial and off-hand manner! I believe this inactivity of the past few days has done much to sour your mood.

HOLMES: I dismiss your claims of any supernatural agency. Such foolish talk from a supposedly scientific man, Doctor, would sour any mood.

WATSON: Well, even though the supposedly spectral hound we encountered on the moors proved mortal, what of that original demonic dog that inspired the legend? Could we be sure that it was also of flesh and blood?

HOLMES: Whatever it was is long dead, thus of no concern to us. Nothing comes back from the dead . . . (SIGH) Nearly nothing . . . Perhaps instead of another chronicle, you might write my epitaph . . .

WATSON: What? Another one? I hope not for a long time to come.

HOLMES: . . . as I fear I rose from my watery grave at Reichenbach – figuratively speaking – only to expire of boredom in my own sitting room.

WATSON: And again this refrain? How can you claim you're bored? It's not as if you lack a case.

HOLMES: What I lack is anything of the slightest interest.

WATSON: But the mystery Lestrade presented you with just yesterday? Jonas Ambrose, the gentleman who vanished from his hotel room in the night . . . .

HOLMES: Curses and vanishing gentlemen? (TUTS) Two valiant attempts at a subject change, Watson, but I'm not to be diverted. No, pain me as it would, were you to seek to publish this chronicle, I would be forced to publicly denounce your work as a piece of lurid fiction.

WATSON: Little change there, then! But be assured I have no plan to publish it. Who would believe it if I did? I'm not even convinced that I do, and I saw . . . Blast it, you know what we *both* saw! That abominable, unnatural thing, gorged on the blood of . . . . (A SHUDDER) No! My sole reason for revisiting the case is to make some sort of sense in my own mind of what I witnessed.

HOLMES: Then I am in error, and I owe you an apology. If I . . . .

WATSON: (SHUSHING HIM) A moment, please, Holmes . . . .

SOUND EFFECT: QUICK BURST OF PEN ON PAPER

HOLMES: Inspiration strikes for some dire turn of phrase?

WATSON: No. Merely recording the momentous occasion when those two statements passed your lips. You? Wrong about something and owing an apology? Well! What you actually owe me is an explanation. How came you to know that I was chronicling that grim business?

HOLMES: Ah. You look as if I had just reached out and produced the Crown Jewels from the coal scuttle. Yet if I explain all, you will declare it perfectly simple. I should remain sphinx-like and silent, as if I had reached my conclusions by some feat of

361

mystical prowess. But I fear this would only add to the aura of the uncanny I have just been at such pains to dispel.

WATSON: Oh, come now! I know you're as eager to expound on your route toward your conclusion as I am to hear it!

HOLMES: Very well. I entered this room some days ago to find you at your desk. You at once became so nonchalant about your activities that it was clear you wished me to pay them no attention, while steadily shifting your chair's position so that I would be unable to even glimpse what you wrote without literally peering over your shoulder. You also took great care to unobtrusively lock the papers in the desk and pocket the key whenever you left the room, no matter how briefly.

WATSON: Could it not be that I was writing something of a personal nature?

HOLMES: Since there have been no callers, nor post, you have gone out only to procure fresh supplies of ink and paper, and the only flowers you purchase are those you lay each week upon the late Mrs. Watson's grave, then I could reasonably conclude that you do not have some secret sweetheart to whom you were writing.

WATSON: (SADDENED) No. That you may conclude.

HOLMES: Watson . . . Again I must apologise, my dear fellow. It was an inappropriate remark.

WATSON: (CLEARS THROAT) It was nothing. Please continue.

HOLMES: What, then, could be your reason for not wishing me to know what you were about? Unless, somehow, it involved me? Nothing uncommon there, as I am by now resigned to your compulsion to transform those incidents in which my theories of deductive technique are put to practical use into melodrama for the masses. So, a matter in which I was involved that I had specifically requested you omit from your records?

WATSON: That would cover a whole list of possibilities, from the nefarious exploits of Baron Maupertuis, to the true identity of the infamous Boulevard Assassin . . . .

362

HOLMES: A-ha! A hellcat, Watson! A positive hellcat! And it really is remarkable that we survived our encounter without the scratches to show for it. Mademoiselle Marianne Huret! I have added her details to my biographical index under her Christian name. She may keep Moriarty and Moran fitting company under "*M*".

WATSON: Alongside your thank you letter from the French President – After whose arrival there was scarcely a word of English past your lips for weeks.

HOLMES: *Me pardonner. Je suis tres désolé* . . . . But really, Watson! A "thank you letter"? You make it sound like a note to the milkman. There was more than a mere "*merci beaucoup*" in His Excellency's communiqué.

WATSON: I know. Your invitation to accept the Legion of Honour. And entirely deserved, as the "Boulevard Assassin" had been sought across the entire Continent, until you clipped her claws. And then the other accounts. Scandalous and horrifying! The truth of the matter of the Second Stain! The Obsidian Chalice! The Limping Waxwork! And, let's not forget the Giant Sumatran Rat . . . .

HOLMES: Rats and hellcats and hounds and leeches? This isn't some morbid menagerie! Let us *please* forget the Rat, Watson. You, of all men, should understand my refusal to allow you to unleash such horror on an unprepared world!

WATSON: Indeed! I can still practically feel that rank breath on the back of my neck, and hear that hideous shrieking as it bore down on us . . . .

HOLMES: (SHARPLY) But, as you were saying . . . ?

WATSON: As I was saying, with all these cases you have insisted I suppress, what is it that leads you to nominate the red leech business as my subject matter.

HOLMES: Throughout your sojourn at the writing desk, you have made frequent use of your diary. The volume's first three quarters have been filled, while the remaining pages sit tight in their binding. Thus, it can only be this year's diary, as yet unfinished. You have repeatedly consulted a point some two-thirds of the way into the book, which tallies exactly with the time of year in which we became enmeshed in that tragedy.

WATSON: I see. And was there anything more to betray me?

HOLMES: Only the way in which you would reread pages with a look of thunderstruck horror on your face. Such an expression is normally followed by a chuckle of delight that you have reached some lurid crescendo, and a fresh assault upon the inkwell. Yet, here, your revulsion suggested the genuine air of dread was not one upon which you could improve. That loathsome parasite would certainly leave such a grim impression. There is your evidence, and rather an abundance of it. It is as well you are a solid, law abiding citizen, old fellow, since you would make an appalling criminal.

WATSON: Well . . . you *do* make it sound perfectly simple. I can take no issue with what you have observed, because, typically, you are correct in every particular. Though it is also typical that you follow so closely on the heels of an apology with another insult. "Resigned to my compulsion"? Then it has been the most vocal and disagreeable resignation I have ever encountered. Yet I publish my accounts of your cases for your benefit.

HOLMES: Indeed? And how precisely does this benefit me?

WATSON: Surely I need not mention that boredom between cases leaves you far from your rational self, and there are dangerous extremes of behavior in warding off such *ennui* that are to be avoided?

HOLMES: Surely. And thank you for not mentioning it.

WATSON: Since I first took up my pen to ensure the general populace became aware of the results of your investigations, they have lined up at our door with all manner of new cases, and you no longer need rely upon the grudging approaches of the official police.

HOLMES: What do the general populace know of crimes of individuality? To them, mere burglary is an event. Let them lose a wallet or purse and it is the crime of the century! And the public inevitably did hear the results of my investigations – the successful ones, at any rate.

WATSON: Yes, but with Scotland Yard taking all the credit and leaving the real hero unknown and unsung. Thanks to my humble efforts, the truth is known!

HOLMES: You talk of "truth" as if it were a valuable commodity. If that were so, what need would society have of corsets and cosmetics, advertising or politics?

WATSON: But our lives are pledged to seeking the truth!

HOLMES: Then you should record it! For while I cannot argue with the humbleness of your efforts, there is much more besides the truth in them.

WATSON: If my accounts are not merely monographs on your methodology, you must admit that the fame they have afforded you has led to the most singular cases being brought to your attention, and thus, in this instance the pen truly may be declared mightier than the sword.

HOLMES: Indeed it might. For depending on who wields them, both may be described as offensive weapons . . . . My dear Watson, are you quite alright? You really have gone the most alarming shade of scarlet!

MUSIC: STING

SOUND EFFECT: VIOLENT RUSTLING OF PAGES

WATSON: Here, then! Read this for yourself, Holmes! My account of "The Crimson Leech Horror" . . . .

HOLMES: (GROANS) Watson, with such a gaudy title you practically make my case for me.

WATSON: Look past the title! Read, and then tell me if there is anything here that doesn't tally with the events!

HOLMES: Calm yourself, my dear friend. I'm not accusing you of lying . . . .

WATSON: I should damn well hope not!

HOLMES: . . . merely of obscuring the facts with touches of melodrama. You know I have no taste for such trifles, which is why I no longer read your work. As for my agreement about your efforts being humble . . . .

WATSON: Yes! That was unworthy of you, Holmes.

HOLMES: You are altogether too humble in your own estimation of your talents and abilities. Were you to move your gaze from my work into writing purely fictional tales of derring-do, I'm sure your career would flourish.

WATSON: The thought had crossed my mind, from time to time.

HOLMES: And at least fictional characters cannot answer their author back in so insolent a fashion.

WATSON: No. But having gone through such adventures as we've shared, anything else I may try to conjure out of fresh air and fantasy simply falls flat on the page.

HOLMES: Would that you could conjure up a client from fresh air . . . .

WATSON: But I remind you again, you have a client! Inspector Lestrade, with his vanished Jonas Ambrose. He disappeared from his hotel room into the night nearly a week ago, and no-one knows where he has gone.

HOLMES: Not so. *You* know where he has gone. I told you, when I told Lestrade where to look.

WATSON: But how? You haven't left these rooms? Lestrade requested you visit the scene of the crime . . . .

HOLMES: If there was a crime!

WATSON: . . . But you waved him off without a sniff of interest.

HOLMES: You think I was too hasty? Very well, Watson. Let us reconstruct. You are Lestrade . . . though I apologise for presenting you with such a demeaning role . . . .

WATSON: Lestrade? Me? I don't think I can . . . .

HOLMES: I know you were taking notes. You always do in case there is the beginning for one of your lurid potboilers. That dispatch case of yours must be bursting at the seams with uneventful chronicles of requests to find missing bicycles and to trail errant spouses.

WATSON: Let's not get back into that again, Holmes!

HOLMES: Quite right. Then returning to our missing gentleman. Yesterday morning. An officious rap at the door . . . .

SOUND EFFECT: HOLMES RAPS TABLE

WATSON: Why are you knocking on . . . ? Oh, I see. The rap at the door. You really mean to re-enact it all?

HOLMES: It may ease the tedium for a few precious moments.

WATSON: Very well, then. If it helps. Again, if you please . . . .

SOUND EFFECT: RAP ON TABLE

HOLMES: A rap on the door. Enter Lestrade of the Yard . . . .

WATSON: Ah . . . . (CLEARS THROAT, TRIES TO MIMIC **IL**) "Good morning, gentlemen. Might I come in? It's a wet day, and I'm chilled to the bone."

HOLMES: Those two factors are not entirely unconnected, Lestrade.

WATSON: Ah, yes . . . It does sound familiar now you remind me, Holmes. (**IL**) "Ah, perhaps I might ask for a medicinal brandy, Dr. Watson?" (**SELF**) To which I said . . . .

HOLMES: (**DW**) "Medicinal, Inspector?"

WATSON: (**IL**) "Well, you are a doctor, aren't you?" (SNORTS)

HOLMES: Excellent, Watson, though you might adjust your voice by half an octave, to really capture Lestrade. And possibly shift several leagues down the mental scale. Now, leaving aside the usual mumbled inanities about "no particular reason for a visit", then . . . (**IL**) "Just one thing, Mr. Holmes . . . ."

WATSON: (**IL**) "Er . . . there is just one thing, Mr. Holmes . . . ."

HOLMES: Aha! There's our intrepid Lestrade!

WATSON: (**IL**) "A trifling thing, I'm sure you'll find. I'm just heading back from the Holbrough Hotel."

HOLMES: And you just happened to be passing Baker Street, a mere five miles off your path?

WATSON: (**IL**) "Hrrmmph! Well, I thought it might divert you. The thing is, he's disappeared. Mr. Jonas Ambrose, that is. Gone and not a trace to be found. The young man draws his savings from his account and books himself into the Holbrough . . . ."

HOLMES: His savings? How much, exactly?

WATSON: (**IL**) "Forty pounds. A tidy amount, and his parents fear that he has been murdered for the sake of the money."

HOLMES: Fears are not fact, Inspector. Kindly stick to the latter.

WATSON: (**IL**) "He had last been heard of stopping at the hotel – " (**SELF**) Then I had a query for the inspector. I said . . . .

HOLMES: (**DW**) "Then he's not from the city, Lestrade?"

WATSON: Yes, that's it . . . . "Then he's not from . . . ." Wait a moment! Was that supposed to be me, just then?

HOLMES: Yes. (**DW**) "For why would he need to stay in a hotel if he lived locally?" (**SELF**) Then Lestrade replied . . .

WATSON: Ah, Lestrade replied . . . (**IL**) "Exactly, Doctor Watson. He'd come from the country that very day."

HOLMES: He'd come alone?

WATSON: (**IL**) "That's right. And checked in alone. In the evening he went to a music hall performance."

HOLMES: And we know this how?

WATSON: (**IL**) "From the hotel clerk, from whom Ambrose asked directions to the theatre, and from the ticket stub later found in his room."

HOLMES: Excellent. Please proceed, Inspector.

WATSON: (**IL**) "He came out of the music hall about ten o'clock, returned to his hotel, where that same clerk chatted to him about the acts on the evening's bill, before he went up to his room, changed his evening clothes . . . ."

HOLMES: (**DW**) "Great Scott, how could you know he'd changed if he was alone and never seen again?"

WATSON: To which you responded . . . .

HOLMES: Evidently his evening suit was found in his hotel room the next day. With the ticket stub in the pocket?

WATSON: (**IL**) "Exactly so, Mr. Holmes. His clothing remained, but the gentleman had disappeared utterly. No-one saw him leave the hotel, but a man occupying a neighbouring room has declared that he had heard him moving during the night. At three a.m., or thereabouts. Yet, come morning and the maid's knock on the door, and only an empty room and an empty suit remained."

HOLMES: (**DW**) '"Gone, like a ghost by dawn? Utterly baffling!"

WATSON: (**IL**) "A week has elapsed, but we've discovered nothing. Where is the man, Mr. Holmes?"

HOLMES: Inspector, why do you plague me with trivialities? The fellow is evidently alive, though you must look beyond the hotel and turn your gaze northwards.

WATSON: (**IL**) "Northwards, Mr. Holmes?"

HOLMES: (**DW**) "Heavens, Holmes. How can you know this?"

WATSON: Yes. How *can* you know it? You never explained.

HOLMES: Nor should I, for as your stories amply demonstrate, a solution explained is a mystery spoiled. However, before I could offer that explanation, an unwarrantable and disruptive intrusion took place . . . .

WATSON: It did? When? I don't recall . . . .

SOUND EFFECT: NOISY RAPPING

HOLMES: There came a sudden pounding on the door! The door was then flung open wide . . . .

SOUND EFFECT: DOOR CRASHES OPEN

HOLMES: . . . and into our sitting room burst the figure of –

WATSON: – Of Mrs. Hudson! Holmes, Mrs. Hudson knocked politely at the door . . . .

SOUND EFFECT: POLITE KNOCK

WATSON: . . . and came in perfectly calmly with a tea-tray. You make it sound like the barbarians at the gates. And you insist *I* overdramatise?

SOUND EFFECT: DOOR CLOSING GENTLY

HOLMES: I do. And you do. And any intrusion, no matter how slight, upon my mental processes may have the same effect as those besieging barbarians. Very well, our landlady enters on dainty feet . . . . If you will, Watson . . . .

WATSON: What? You can't want me to . . . . I can't impersonate –

HOLMES: Mrs. Hudson! I took my breakfast things downstairs half-an-hour ago.

WATSON: (**MH**) "Uneaten. Again! Dr. Watson, I do wish you'd have a word."

HOLMES: (**DW**, DISTRACTED) "But . . . Northwards? Of the Holbrough Hotel? You mean Barnet? Stevenage?"

WATSON: (**MH**) "What was that, Dr. Watson?"

HOLMES: The Good Doctor is frequently reminding me of how badly I treat myself. However, since I cannot imagine you came up merely to lecture me on my diet . . . .

WATSON: (**MH**) "Certainly not! I came with tea for you and your guest." (**SELF**) Holmes, I feel deuced silly doing this!

HOLMES: Oh, come now, Doctor. It's not as if you've been asked to don an apron and shave off your moustache and serve up breakfast. We are merely reconstructing, as accurately as possible, the events of that morning.

WATSON: (GROANS) (**MH**) "Is Doctor Watson all right?"

HOLMES: You'll forgive him, I'm sure. His mind is elsewhere.

WATSON: (**MH**) "I know. It seems to be at the Holbrough Hotel. You're as bad as each other, with your riddles."

HOLMES: And, speaking of elsewhere, Mrs. Hudson, perhaps you'd care to take yourself there.

WATSON: (**MH**) "What? Me? Go to that hotel? I'd not thank you for that! My cousin stayed there overnight when she visited London, and she didn't get a wink of sleep. It was like a madhouse at all hours, she told me . . . ."

HOLMES: Elsewhere, Mrs. Hudson. To the hotel, if you wish, or the theatre, or to visit your cousin. Anywhere as long as it isn't here in the middle of my sitting room.

WATSON: (**MH**) "*My* sitting room, I'll remind you. Madhouses? I could tell her a thing or two about madhouses . . . ."

SOUND EFFECT: DOOR SLAM

WATSON: Admittedly she *did* slam the door that time.

HOLMES: Lestrade, you are still here?

WATSON: What? Oh! (**IL**) "Well, I thought, if you might just accompany me . . . ."

HOLMES: To the hotel? Mere moments of your men's attentions are usually sufficient to see all trace of useful clues obliterated, so what hope is there after a week?

WATSON: (**IL**) "Then you won't help?"

HOLMES: I believe I already have.

WATSON: (**IL**) "Have you? How, exactly?"

SOUND EFFECT: PEN ON PAPER, THEN FOLDING OF PAPER

HOLMES: I have given you a direction. If you seek a more precise location, I offer you a choice of two.

WATSON: (**IL**) "Thank you, Mr. Holmes. Dr. Watson."

HOLMES: And, pocketing the clear instructions I'd given him . . . Into your pocket with them, Watson . . . .

WATSON: Pocketed, Holmes.

SOUND EFFECT: DOOR OPEN AND SHUT AGAIN

HOLMES: . . . he set off again. You remember those instructions?

WATSON: (**IL**) *"Give Ambrose description to forces in Glasgow and Edinburgh.'* (**SELF**) And you arrived at this solution without once setting foot outside this room?

HOLMES: As could you, my boy. You have all the data which was ever given to me. You merely need to indicate the links which make the chain between our vanishing man and those great Scottish cities.

WATSON: Easier said than done. Unless . . . .

HOLMES: "Unless", Watson?

WATSON: Not Watson, my dear fellow. If I am to reconstruct, I will require all the finely honed skills of the expert. The attention to detail, and the precise and analytical faculties before which the most abstruse cryptogram is mere child's play! Therefore John H. Watson must step aside, and I must become the true master of deduction! (**SH**) I must become Sherlock Holmes!

HOLMES: (**DW**) "Great Scott!"

MUSIC: STING

MUSIC: URGENT AND LOW IN BACKGROUND

WATSON: (**SH**) "The first thing we must do is look at the facts and separate what is certain from what is conjecture."

HOLMES: (**DW**) "Incredible!"

WATSON: (**SH**) "It is *all* certain, except for the statement of the person who heard the missing man in the night."

373

HOLMES: (**DW**) "The guest in the adjoining room? Then he lied to Lestrade? Perhaps he is part of some fiendish conspiracy to spirit away Mr. Ambrose in the night!"

WATSON: (**SH**) "For forty pounds? There would be no great reward for fiendish conspirators there, Holmes . . . ."

HOLMES: (DISCREET COUGH) "Watson".

WATSON: So sorry. (**SH**) "There would be no great reward for fiendish conspirators there, *Watson*."

HOLMES: (**DW**) "Quite so, Holmes. Ridiculous suggestion."

WATSON: (**SH**) "I don't know when last you had occasion to stay in a transport hotel, but the effect – as Mrs. Hudson's cousin could clearly attest – can be close to Bedlam, with doors slamming and floorboards creaking throughout the night. I . . . that is, *you*, Watson, will remember that from those unsettled months of hotels and boarding houses on your return from Afghanistan."

HOLMES: (**DW**) "By Jove, yes. When I was drawn to London, that great cesspool into which all the loungers and idlers of the Empire are irresistibly drained."

WATSON: (**SH**) "Well put!" (CHUCKLES, **SELF**) You don't need me to supply all those hotel noises too, do you?

HOLMES: Our reconstruction will survive without. Pray go on. It's fascinating to watch a true master in action.

WATSON: (**SH**) "Add these noises and I think you'll find it is impossible to differentiate between the pacing of the floor in the next room and a million other sounds."

HOLMES: (**DW**) "So, we can safely rule out that testimony, then."

WATSON: (**SH**) "And with the certainty of Ambrose's presence in his room at three a.m. dispelled, our impossible vanishing becomes suddenly all too possible."

HOLMES: (**DW**) "What could cause a man to simply disappear?"

WATSON: (**SH**) "He disappeared because he wished to disappear."

HOLMES: (**DW**) "Amazing, Holmes. Positively amazing!"

WATSON: Now, just see here a moment, Holmes! I don't really go on like that, do I? Constantly exclaiming, and blustering, and gasping in amazement.

HOLMES: The John H. Watson who features in those accounts of our adventures does. And as I'm assured that these are true, accurate, and unembellished reports . . . .

WATSON: Oh, very amusing! So, this whole charade is an excuse to relieve your boredom by making fun of me!

HOLMES: Never, old friend. But if you wish us to stop . . . ?

WATSON: Oh, of course not. We've come this far, and may as well see it through to the finish.

HOLMES: Ha! I thought I knew my Watson.

WATSON: Your *Holmes*, Holmes. (**SH**) "Our man had meant to disappear. Why else should he draw all his money? He then had to get out of the hotel unseen."

HOLMES: (**DW**) "But there's a night-porter in all hotels, and it's impossible to get out without his knowledge when the door is shut and locked, surely?"

WATSON: (**SH**) '"Then he must have left . . . Ah . . . He left . . . ."

HOLMES: (**DW**) "Before the door was shut? Which would be after the theatre-goers return . . . ."

WATSON: (**SH**) "Precisely! Allowing for stragglers – let us say at twelve o'clock. Therefore, our man left the hotel *before* midnight. He had come from the music hall at ten, had changed his clothes, and had departed with his bag."

HOLMES: (**DW**) "And no-one had seen him do so?"

WATSON: (**SH**) "The inference is . . . yes . . . that he made his exit when the lobby was full of returning guests, therefore from eleven till eleven-thirty. With fewer people coming and going, a man with a bag would be easily spotted, but a crowd makes for ideal concealment."

HOLMES: (**DW**) "But why leave his evening clothes behind?"

WATSON: (**SH**) "Fewer clothes mean less baggage, reinforcing the theory that he wished to flee unencumbered."

HOLMES: (**DW**) "But why go to the hotel at all, and not straight to his destination?"

WATSON: (**SH**) "Indeed! Why not? Why not, indeed . . . ?"

HOLMES: (**DW**) "You mean since that destination isn't in London at all? And he needed somewhere to while the hours away until he could catch a train to carry him off?"

WATSON: (**SH**) "Exactly! Which is why I stated that Lestrade would find his man Northwards of London itself!"

HOLMES: (**DW**) "Amazing! But isn't a man deposited in any provincial station during the night likely to be noticed, and when the description of a missing man circulates, he'd realise a guard or porter would remember him?"

WATSON: (**SH**) "Ah. You spotted that flaw? Well done. Yes, his destination would be some large town, distant enough that he would reach it in daytime, not as a nocturnal stranger but as a respectable traveller. A terminus, in fact, where all his fellow passengers would dismount, and yet again he could find concealment in a crowd."

SOUND EFFECT: BOOK OPENS, PAGES TURNING

HOLMES: (**DW**) "And turning to our faithful Bradshaw guide, confirmation that the great Scottish expresses bound for Glasgow and Edinburgh start off about midnight – "

WATSON: **(SH)** " – Just as our gentleman vanishes into the night. And here we have the links that form the chain."

HOLMES: **(DW)** "How perfectly simple!"

WATSON: It is! (SIGH) Or it is with you guiding me every step of the way. I don't know that I could exchange places with you if it were anything more elaborate than a mental exercise to prove a point.

HOLMES: It was more than that, surely. The note, Watson . . . .

WATSON: Lestrade left with it in his pocket . . . Oh, this note?

SOUND EFFECT: PAPER UNFOLDING

WATSON: This mentions nothing about Glasgow or Edinburgh.

HOLMES: No?

WATSON: It just says, *"Read the telegram, Watson."* The telegram! I'd entirely forgotten the blessed thing!

SOUND EFFECT: KNIFE BEING PULLED OUT, PAPER UNFOLDING

WATSON: It's from Lestrade. **(IL)** "Missing man . . . ." **(SELF)** Oh, very clever, Holmes. **(IL)** "Missing man located in Glasgow." **(SELF)** Well, despite my earlier protests, if I may just gasp, and exclaim . . . "Extraordinary!"

HOLMES: Merely ordinary. Very dull and ordinary.

WATSON: Then I trust you'd have no objection to my chronicling *this* affair? No state secrecy, no curses, no noble houses that may topple at the merest breath of scandal!

HOLMES: No pale and shivering yet bravely determined client to throw herself upon our hearthrug and our mercy, pleading for us to recover her lost amour? No hectic chases through the night!

Not even a bloodstained glove in the pocket of that abandoned evening jacket.

WATSON: Well, perhaps it lacks a little . . . something.

HOLMES: A little *every*thing. This is prosaic, not prose. Whether our quarry was fleeing problems at work, or running from the arms of one woman or into those of another, none of this concerned us, and the lack of these details did not deflect our investigations. Yet their lack will affect your account, whose readers will surely bemoan its dearth of drama. Though I'm sure you can invent a plentiful supply of that ingredient.

WATSON: And the conversation turns back to where it began.

HOLMES: Yet you still do not deny it. In your rush to embellish and dramatise, facts will be ignored or altered to suit.

WATSON: While I admit that I occasionally amplify or condense events, my reasons are not merely for dramatic effect. For example, where I am inconsistent in dates – if posterity is to place you in a certain location at a particular time, it serves to obscure your true activities on those assignments whose ramifications would be too colossal to risk by divulging your participation.

HOLMES: I am aware of this, and it is appreciated.

WATSON: And where identities are concealed or altered, it has been with an eye to preserving the anonymity of those innocent parties that are often swept up into our orbit during times of despair and calamity.

HOLMES: Again, I acknowledge and applaud your efforts.

WATSON: And if I sometimes stretch the truth, I am by no means the only one here guilty of such a crime.

HOLMES: And when did I commit such an act?

WATSON: (AS **SH** IMPERSONATING **DW**) "Great Scott, Holmes!" "Oh, extraordinary!" (**SH**) "Just as in your lurid chronicles, Watson." (**SELF**) Yet within the last half-hour, you told me you no longer read my chronicles. How do you explain that, Holmes?

HOLMES: Ah . . . As you yourself have noted, I am clearly not my most rational self, and there are no limits to the dangerous extremes I might go to when I'm bored.

SOUND EFFECT: STAMPING FOOTSTEPS

WATSON: There is the ink. There a pen! I assume you can detect the paper for yourself? As you can evidently do better, write your own damn records, then!

SOUND EFFECT: DOOR SLAMS

HOLMES: (**DW**) "That was unworthy of you, Holmes . . . ."

SOUND EFFECT: FOOTSTEPS CROSS THE ROOM, PAPERS SHUFFLE, PEN DIPS IN INK, THEN WRITES

HOLMES: (AS HE WRITES) *"The name John H. Watson is known not only as that of the friend and associate of the detective, Sherlock Holmes, but also as the chronicler of the adventures both have shared together. In truth, both callings carry their own difficulties, as Holmes was never the most willing subject of biography . . . ."*

SOUND EFFECT: QUIETLY, IN BACKGROUND, DOOR OPENS

HOLMES: *"Yet the fact is, that biography would be far better focussed upon this keen, courageous, and almost . . . supernaturally patient friend and companion. To use his own misapplied phrase in describing one unworthy of the term, 'the best and wisest man . . . .'"*

WATSON: (NOT AS **SH**, BUT LIGHTLY EMPLOYING HIS TONE) While I cannot stop you in your efforts, my dear fellow, I really must advise against it . . . .

SOUND EFFECT: PAPER FOLDED. KEY IN METAL LOCK

HOLMES: Watson? Why . . . ?

WATSON: . . . Because, this agency must remain the last bastion of cold, unemotional, rational thought . . . or the reputation you – and I – have sought to create would be fatally compromised –

SOUND EFFECT: LID OF TIN BOX CREAKING OPEN

WATSON: So, this can join the others – the giant rat, the hellcat, the waxwork, and the chalice, and, yes, the repulsive red leech, in that dispatch case bursting at the seams with all those other suppressed chronicles that might, with all possible danger passed, serve as a diversion for further generations of adventure seekers.

SOUND EFFECT: LID CLOSES, KEY TURNS

HOLMES: Watson, if I might just say . . . .

SOUND EFFECT: RACING FOOTSTEPS ON STAIRS OUTSIDE

WATSON: (SHUSHING HIM) One moment, Holmes! Listen . . . Footsteps on the stairs. Racing . . . .

SOUND EFFECT: FRANTIC DOOR KNOCKING

HOLMES: . . . and frantic pounding on our door? Which invariably means a client, and judging by their urgency, one with a case which may yet prove vital.

WATSON: Then, while it may be a little premature before we know the full facts, just this once, might I say it?

HOLMES: Say what, precisely?

WATSON: *Quick, my dear Holmes! The game is afoot!*

HOLMES: *Great Scott, Watson! Astonishing!*

BOTH: (WRY, WARM LAUGHTER)

MUSIC: *DANSE MACABRE*

Appendix

The Further Adventures of *Sherlock Holmes*: Radio Logs

*T*he *Further Adventures of Sherlock Holmes* ran on *Imagination Theatre* as part of its rotating line-up of shows from March 3rd, 1998 to August 6th, 2017. Initially, all of the episodes were written by founder Jim French. However, beginning with episode 037, "The Strange Case of Lord Halworth's Kitchen", Mr. French welcomed other authors into the stable by co-writing a script with Gareth Tilley. Episode 041, "The Amateur Mendicant Society", featured the first non-French solo script by Matthew J. Elliott, who would go on to become the primary script writer for the show.

Additionally, from November 20th, 2005 to January 24th, 2016, Matthew would write the scripts for *Imagination Theatre*'s presentation of the entire Sherlock Holmes Canon, *The Classic Adventures of Sherlock Holmes*. This accomplished several firsts, including being the first time that these adaptations had all been done by the same writer, the first time that they had been performed by the same two American actors, John Patrick Lowrie and Lawrence Albert as Holmes and Watson, respectively, and the first time that the entire Canon had been performed in this way in its entirety on American Radio.

Additionally, these episodes, when combined with those making up the entire run of *The Further Adventures of Sherlock Holmes*, have made John and Larry the longest running Holmes and Watson in American Radio, and have given Larry the distinct honor of portraying Dr. Watson the longest in any format.

For such a large body of work, the number of writers involved was actually quite small:

- Jim French
- Matthew J. Elliott
- Larry Albert
- John Patrick Lowrie
- Gareth Tilley
- Matthew Booth
- J.R. Campbell

- Jeremy B. Holstein
- Roger Silverwood
- Teresa Collard
- John Hall
- Steven Phillip Jones
- Daniel McGachey
- Iain McLaughlin and Claire Bartlett
- David Marcum

After *Imagination Theatre* closed its doors in early 2017, fans were bereft. But then, without warning, a "lost" broadcast, No. 129, "The Strange Case", appeared. It was written by Iain McLaughlin, and considered too good to waste. It was recorded in mid-2017, and broadcast on *Imagination Theatre*'s *YouTube* website in August.

And even that isn't the end. In September 2017, the cast reassembled to record a new Holmes adventure, one of several that are planned during 2017 and 2018.

The Further Adventures of Sherlock Holmes

No.   Episode Title – Date (Month/Day/Year) – Author(s)

001   The Poet of Death – 03/08/1998 – Jim French
002   The Sealed Room – 06/21/1998 – Jim French
003   The Adventure of the Blind Man – 07/12/1998 – Jim French
004   The Woman from Virginia – 08/02/1998 – Jim French
005   The Adventure of the Seven Shares – 09/20/1998 – Jim French
006   The Adventure of the Painted Leaf – 10/25/1998 – Jim French
007   The Secret of the Fives – 11/29/1998 – Jim French
008   The Quartermaine Curse – 02/14/1999 – Jim French
009   The Adventure of the Bishop's Ring – 04/18/1999 – Jim French
010   The Adventure of the Samovar – 08/08/1999 – Jim French
011   The Adventure of the Red Death – 09/26/1999 – Jim French
012   The Adventure of the Silver Siphon – 10/31/1999 – Jim French
013   The Dark Chamber – 02/27/2000 – Jim French
014   The Ragwort Puzzle – 03/26/2000 – Jim French
015   The Adventure of the Mind Reader – 04/23/2000 – Jim French
016   The Gambrinus Cure – 07/02/2000 – Jim French
017   The Billingsgate Horror – 10/29/2000 – Jim French
018   The Adventure of the Missing Link – 11/26/2000 – Jim French
019   The Adventure of the Edison Sender – 03/25/2001 – Jim French
020   The Estonian Countess – 05/27/2001 – Jim French
021   School for Scoundrels – 07/15/2001 – Jim French
022   The Adventure of the Dover Maiden – 08/19/200 – Jim French

The Further Adventures of Sherlock Holmes
will continue . . . .

The MX Book of New Sherlock Holmes Stories

"This is the finest volume of Sherlockian fiction I have
ever read, and I have read, literally, thousands."
– Philip K. Jones

"Beyond Impressive . . . This is a
splendid venture for a great cause!
– Roger Johnson, Editor, *The Sherlock Holmes Journal,*
The Sherlock Holmes Society of London

The MX Book of New Sherlock Holmes Stories
Edited by David Marcum
(MX Publishing, 2015-   )

Part I: 1881-1889
Part II: 1890-1895
Part III: 1896-1929
Part IV: 2016 Annual
Part V: Christmas Adventures
Part VI: 2017 Annual
Part VII: Eliminate the Impossible – 1880-1891
Part VIII: Eliminate the Impossible – 1892-1905

<u>In Preparation</u>
Part IX: 2018 Annual
Part X: Some Untold Cases

. . . and more to come!

MX Publishing

MX Publishing is the world's largest specialist Sherlock Holmes publisher, with several hundred titles and over a hundred authors creating the latest in Sherlock Holmes fiction and non-fiction.

From traditional short stories and novels to travel guides and quiz books, MX Publishing caters to all Holmes fans.

The collection includes leading titles such as *Benedict Cumberbatch In Transition* and *The Norwood Author*, which won the 2011 *Tony Howlett Award* (Sherlock Holmes Book of the Year).

MX Publishing also has one of the largest communities of Holmes fans on *Facebook*, with regular contributions from dozens of authors.

www.mxpublishing.co.uk (UK) and *www.mxpublishing.com* (USA)

Lightning Source UK Ltd.
Milton Keynes UK
UKOW04f2309291117
313578UK00001B/40/P